2nd Timothy 4:7-8

"I have fought the good fight, I have finished the race, I have kept the faith. Now there is in store for me the crown of righteousness, which the Lord, the righteous Judge, will award to me on that day—and not only to me, but also to all who have longed for his appearing."

The Blesser and the Charred Medallion

The Blesser, Volume 1

A.L. Schank

Published by A.L. Schank, 2024.

Table of Contents

Dedicated to my Lord and Savior, and sweet baby niece

Nations of Lykos

Vaska:

Population 2.mil

Dire Saulder- platinum blond hair, silver eyes
Dire of Vaska.
Son of Zastar and Lore
Alias: The Dreaded Dire Saulder
Zastar- black hair, silver eyes
Ex-dire of Vaska
Husband of Lore. Father of Saulder and Sova
Lore- white hair, blue eyes
Ex-queen of Vaska. Seavallian
Wife to Zastar. Mother of Saulder and Sova
Sova- platinum blond hair, silver eyes
Prince of Vaska
Son of Zastar and Lore
Alias: The Royal Traitor
Casavore- brown hair, blue eyes
Blesser of Vaska. Eradusk Mind Melder
Husband to Fala. Father of Feran
Fala- brown hair, brown eyes
Mosharick maiden.
Wife of Casavore. Mother of Feran
Feran- brown hair, brown eyes
Mind Melder
Alias: The Dire's Damsel

The Mosharick Plains:

Population 500.k

Oland- bald, hazel eyes
Leader of the Blind Seers. Dormant Hyde Howler
Husband of Saphelle. Father of Roeseph
Alias: The Blind Hound
Roeseph- light brown hair, blue eyes

Blind Seer
Son of Oland
Alias: The Last Soldier
Chemon- black hair, green eyes
Chief of Mosharick Village
Husband of Sulia. Father of Elling and Kandon
Sulia- black hair, black eyes
Mosharick Villager
Wife of Chemon. Mother of Elling and Kandon
Elling- black hair, green eyes
Shepherdess
Daughter of Chemon and Sulia
Alias: The Feral Shepherd
Kandon- black hair, black eyes
Son of Chemon and Sulia

Seavale

Population 100.k

Kyce- dark brown hair, amber eyes
Mysterious tavern fighter
Alias: The Eradite Exile

Eradawn:

Population 40.k

Lanton: silver hair, brown eyes
Elderly chief of Eradawn
Uncle of Vohwe
Vohwe: red haired, yellow eyes
Standing Eradawn Chief

Eradusk:

Population 35.k

Willowreed- dark brown hair, yellow eyes
Chief of Eradusk
Mother of Kometis. Sister of Jerah
Jerah- dark brown hair, amber eyes

Eradusk Royal
Brother of Willowreed
Kometis- black hair, brown eyes
General of Eradusk
Son of Willowreed

Prologue

"*Saulder?*" *Prince Sova croaked*, clutching his brother's arm as they stared at the carnage ahead. "Saulder, is he... is he dead?"

Prince Saulder was silent, his face white with terror.

Pale light shone past torn curtains, waving somberly like white flags, on a hall littered with corpses, some encased in armor, others in rags. Quiet sobs filled the palace. A woman with dark skin, and amethyst eyes knelt at the end of the hall, cradling a man to her breastplate.

Blood gushed from a hidden wound under the man's dark hair, streaming down the side of his still face.

"Zastar," the woman wept, her tears chiming through the palace when they hit the black armor. "Dire Zastar, please..."

Sova stared at the general and his father in disbelief. He asked himself, *How could this happen?*

Not three hours ago, he, his brother, and Feran were playing in the garden. They had all been so happy. Well, not happy. Feran had threatened to use hypnosis on Sova multiple times before her mother, Fala, overheard, and swept her away for a scolding.

"You know better, Feran," he'd overheard Fala say. "Your father would be mortified if he saw you using your gift in such a way."

Feran had gripped her medallion and said, "I think he would've found it funny."

Fala and Feran hadn't been gone for more than five minutes when Sova and Saulder heard the cries of battle, and ran into the palace. Inside, men in blue-rags, with hard, stubbled faces, swarmed the halls like a plague of locusts, cutting down every Vaskan guard in their path.

Sova had heard Saulder gasp and whisper under his breath, "Venom Tongues..." Seavale's most brutal gang, and Vaska's longest enemy.

One of the Venom Tongues looked up at the princes after plunging his sword through the stomach of a Vaskan. His eyes flickering with bloodlust, he charged toward them. Saulder stepped in front of his brother as both stumbled back into the wall.

Just as the Venom Tongue raised his sword, a man in black armor lunged in front of the Princes and lashed his sword through the Venom Tongue's throat. The Venom Tongue fell to the floor, clutching his neck as he gurgled and gasped.

Sova stared at the pirate in horror as the life shrunk out of his eyes. In his eleven years, he'd never seen a man die before.

A gloved hand grabbed he and Saulder by their shoulders and jerked them around to meet their savior. The sides of the helmet curved up like two horns. The eye holes were slanted in a permanent glare. And the grate over the mouth was jagged, like the jaws of a monster.

To Sova's relief, the man ripped off the ghastly helmet, reveling fierce, silver eyes and a dark, scowling face.

"What in the name of Lykos is the matter with you!" the man roared. "Are you brainless? What are you doing out here?"

Before Sova or Saulder could open their mouths to speak, a voice called out from the back of the battle.

"Dire Zastar!"

Zastar looked back. A woman met his gaze over the battle; the very same who would later hold his dying body.

"Where is the Blesser?" she yelled over the chaos.

"I told him to guard Lore!"

"You did what?"

"I told him—Hylan, look out!"

Hylan lashed around, catching a Venom Tongue's sword against her own, just an inch from her brow and kicked him to the ground. Placing her boot on his chest she gritted her teeth and plunged her blade deep into his heart before spinning around to face the dire.

"Casavore is a mind melder!" she yelled as she fought. "A hypnotist warrior delivered to you straight from the Cliffs of Era, and you send him to babysit your queen?"

"She needs protecting!"

"*We* need protecting!"

Zastar groaned through clenched teeth and dragged Saulder and Sova down the hall adjacent to the fight. When they were far enough away so that the cries of battle sounded like distant thunder, Dire Zastar pulled the boys into his chamber and to his wardrobe, where he shoved them in like discarded robes.

"Stay here until I come for you," Zastar ordered sternly.

Saulder's eyes went big. "Wait—Wait!" he stammered as he tried to struggle past. "Feran! I need to get Feran!"

Zastar shoved Saulder back into the wardrobe, his fist knotted in the young prince's silk, purple shirt.

"You will stay here with your brother, or I will skin you alive, you hear me?"

"Let me go!" Saulder pled, accidentally shoving a curtain of clothes into Sova and smushing him against the wall. "Let me go! She needs me!"

"She's a mind melder, she's better off in this fight then you are!"

"Let me through!"

Zastar pushed Saulder violently into the wall and scraped him to the floor. Sova pressed himself into the corner, his heart beating frantically in his chest. Never in his life had he seen his father so furious.

"You listen to me!" Zastar roared, his silver eyes burning like hellfire. "I told you to stay in here and you're going to stay here. I'm your father—I am your dire! You do as I say!"

Saulder stared up at his father, his silver eyes sparkling with tears behind a tuff of fallen white hair. Zastar's scowl softened with guilt. Unbaling his fist from Saulder's shirt, he placed his hand on his sons' shoulders.

"Listen here, both of you," he said at the end of a gulp. "I know that you want to help—"

He was wrong. Sova was perfectly content with sacrificing Feran to the wolves. He had no problem with it at all.

"—But this isn't your fight. And as long as I'm Dire, I'm going to make sure it never will be. You boys are the things I care about most in this world, I couldn't survive if something happened to you."

"What about you?" Sova croaked. "What if you get hurt?"

Zastar chuckled. "Are you kidding? General Hylan has been watching my back since we were kids. They won't get past her." Zastar gripped the white hair on the back of Saulder and Sova's necks, drawing them in. "Everything's going to be ok. I promise. Keep each other safe. I'll be back as soon as I can."

Zastar closed the wardrobe, separating his sons by a line of light bleeding through the gap, and fled out the chamber.

Saulder and Sova sat in the dark, forced to listen to the other's slow, quiet breathing. The sounds of battle swelled outside, making Sova crunch into a ball.

"I hate this," he whimpered.

Saulder grabbed Sova's shoulder.

"You're fine," he said, not looking away from the gap in the doors. "You're fine, Sova. We're fine. We're going to be fine."

Sova sniffled. "How'd they even get into the palace?"

Saulder swallowed hard, his voice shaking when he went to speak again. "I don't know. But it's going to be ok. I'm not going to let anything happen to you..." Saulder looked down at his brother, his lips trembling as they spread into a grin. "Are you seriously crying? You're hardly a kid anymore, Sova, you can't cry. Baby." He gave Sova a gentle shake and looked back to the gap. "You're ok. Pop is gonna come back. He's going to come back for us. We're going to be ok..."

HOURS PASSED, AND STILL, Dire Zastar never came. Only when the palace fell silent did the two princes leave their hiding place.

Now they stood at the end of the hall where the battle had taken place, watching as their general sobbed over their father's limp, bleeding body.

Sova stood behind Saulder, his brother's silk sleeve balled in his hand. "Saulder?" he croaked. "Saulder, tell me he isn't dead."

Saulder stayed quiet.

Suddenly, a sharp cry rose through the hall, "Zastar!"

Saulder looked back and jerked his little brother out of the way as their mother charged by in a blur of platinum hair and violet garments. She hadn't even noticed they were there. Then again, she hardly ever noticed them at all.

Queen Lore collapsed at Zastar's side, tears streaming down her copper cheeks as she wept. "What happened to him?" she cried, her blue eyes turning dark when they reached General Hylan. "What have you done?"

"He was right behind me," Hylan sobbed, not looking away from Zastar. "He was right behind me. He heard you scream, and he tried to get to you—"

"You were supposed to protect him!" Lore yelled. "I'll have you exiled for your incompetence!"

"I'm sorry," Hylan sobbed as she cradled Zastar's head to her neck. "I'm so sorry, Zastar."

Saulder stepped forward, his voice coming out in broken fragments. "F—Feran." Hylan and Lore looked up. "Where—Where is Feran?"

Lore scoffed and shook her head. "Probably in that dreadful shack with her mother. Blesser Casavore left me to look for them there. He'll be punished too. I'll make sure of it."

Saulder shot out of the palace, Sova following like a shadow sewn to his heels.

They crossed the gardens and came to a modest shack wedged between two rose bushes near the palace wall. The door was slanted against its frame, ripped from its hinges. Inside, a bearded man in a modest cloak with a gold medallion around his neck sat on the floor, cradling a beautiful corpse in his arms.

His name was Blesser Casavore.

Like all Blessers, Casavore was a mind melder born to the Mountains of Era, kidnapped by his rival tribe, and given to the dire as a slave. But unlike most Blessers, Casavore grew fond of his master, and he and Zastar loved each other like brothers.

The only thing to ever come between them, was a Mosharick maiden by the name Fala, the woman the previous dire had selected Zastar to marry. Casavore fell for Fala. And though Zastar didn't love her, he wouldn't break his father's command.

But on the day they were to marry, the Kingdom of Vaska awoke to the news Zastar had not taken Fala as his queen, but rather a Seavallian palace maid named Lore.

The fools of Lykos believe Zastar had a change of heart, but the wise knew the truth. Casavore had hypnotized Zastar to fall for Lore so he could have Fala all to himself. And so he had her.

He had her dead in his arms.

"Cas?" Saulder whispered, his shadow seeping across the Blesser's trembling back. "Cas, where's Feran?"

The Blesser didn't look up. "She's gone," he wept. "The Venom Tongues took her. They took Feran. My little girl is gone..."

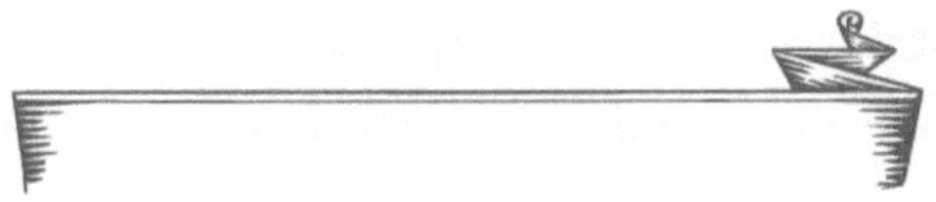

Chapter One: Ten Years Later

The Mosharick Plains...

Sharick Fawns were a peculiar beast—born with the slender body of a deer, the long flowing beard of a goat, the curved horn of a fisherman's hook, and the round black eyes of a seal. They grazed in the rolling hills of the Mosharick Plains, a land stretching to all four horizons like the rolling waves of a green ocean.

As they grazed, their shepherdess, Elling, watched from a knoll. Her eyes were an emerald-green, like the very plains she grew from, and her hair was as black as raven feathers. She smiled on the herd, her head resting against her rod as she lounged in the warmth of the autumn day. Suddenly, a doe's cry shot up from the shallow hills. Her smile ceased.

What on Lykos was that? She thought.

Crossing the pastures, Elling stopped at the river between the Mosharick Plains and the Vaskan forests. She looked up, catching a glimpse of the walls of Vaska peeking over the treetops. As a child, Elling wondered what the streets of Vaska looked like, and if they were really as splendid as the passing merchants said. Now the thought of the kingdom sickened her. She'd never want to go near the awful place. Not after what happened five years ago.

She didn't remember much. Only that she wandered into the forest to retrieve a lost fawn and fell asleep in the shade of a tree. When she returned home, her village greeted her with relief. She had been gone for three days.

A chill rolled down Elling's spine. *What a ghastly place.*

She looked down. As if Moses had taken his staff to the water, a long streak of blood drifted with the tide.

Taking a step back, she gasped, "What in Lykos' name?"

She looked upstream to a bend in the river where the red tint was thickest and ran to investigate. When she turned the corner, she found the corpse of a headless sharick-doe laying in the shallows, its intestines spilling out its open gut and cursing the water red. Elling had never seen a massacre so cruel.

"What could've done this?"

Pawprints the size of Elling's head circled the fawn and disappeared into the river. She didn't know a beast in the Valley of Lykos that could possibly compare to the size. Maybe a bear, but even so it had to be the largest bear she'd ever seen.

Is it still here? Elling gulped and looked to the forest beyond the river.

Just then, a voice called in the wind, "Elling!"

Elling lashed around, her heart lurching with fear.

"Kandon?"

"Elling, where are you?"

"Just stay where you are," Elling ordered. "I'm coming."

Thankful to leave the poor fawn behind, Elling ran back to the herd where she found a little boy in oversized garments chasing the fawns like a wolf in boy's clothing.

"Kandon!" she scolded through a laugh. "Will you stop tormenting the fawns?"

"Elling!" Kandon shouted, his dark black eyes twinkling, as he fled into his sister's embrace and snuggled into her soft cloak.

"What are you doing all the way out here?" Elling laughed as she stroked his hair.

"Papa sent me to get you. He wants you home to help with the Harvest Feast."

"Oh, well, then we better get going."

Elling gathered the fawns with haste, eager to leave the unknown beast in her wake.

"Where were you anyway?" Kandon asked as he and Elling started home.

"Just—" she looked nervously over her shoulder, "trying to save a lost fawn..."

As Elling and her brother disappeared over the hills, a dark figure watched from the shadows of the Vaskan forest. A monster standing at ten feet, with fur white as snow, blood-stained jaws sharp as ice picks, and wings like an angel's roamed in the darkness. Its amber eyes burned into Elling as she drifted away with the herd, growling hungrily. Before the monster could give chase, a lonely whistle called from afar. The monster's ears perked and looked back. Reluctantly, the white beast turned from its prey and bounded after its master, leaving bloody paw prints in its wake.

A DAYS WALK AWAY, IN the northern territory of the Mosharick Plains where wild sharick fawns grazed, a storm ambushed the bliss of day, and darkness befell the land. As the fawns fled, a large man with a hefty gut and wide, bald head, marched toward the center of the storm. Under his hood, white gauze wrapped his skull and ears. 'The Blind Hound,' the people called him; the leader of the Blind Seers, and Vaska's most notorious enemy since the fall of the Venom Tongues.

He stopped. A short walk ahead, a lonely man stood on a knoll before a secluded grave.

The Blind Hound withdrew his hood and sighed. "My dear friend," he shook his head. "Why do you torture yourself so?"

The man before the grave was none other than the Blesser of Vaska himself. Blesser Casavore. Silver streaked his tangled beard, and sorrow dulled his once lively blue eyes. His muscular physique had faded to frail, and his shoulders hunched forward as if he carried a tremendous burden. Hanging from his neck was a gold medallion, the only treasure left of his homeland.

Casavore sighed, tears falling to his wife beneath the grave.

"I'm sorry, Fala," he whispered. "I failed you."

"Casavore," called a strong voice through the pounding rain. Casavore turned to find his on old friend march up the muddy mound. The Blind Hound unwound the gauze from his head. As long as the storm reigned, there was no threat of a Siren's Call. No threat of being turned into a *Hyde Howler*.

"Oland, my old friend," The Blesser grinned. "What brings you here?"

"One of my informants said a man wearing a gold medallion was wandering the Mosharick Plains," Oland stated. "I had to come out and see for myself if the Blesser of Vaska was truly in our midst."

Casavore's smile faded, and he looked to his wife's grave.

Oland dipped his chin. "Casavore?"

"Ten years," the Blesser sighed. "Ten years ago, those monsters came and took them from me. Feran would be twenty-two today. She'd be a woman... And a great mind melder no doubt. She was already showing great promise as a little girl. She would've brought every mind-melder of Eradawn and Eradusk to shame."

"Why do you do this to yourself, Casavore? Why do you continue to come here?"

"She wouldn't want to be alone. Fala never liked to be alone. I know better than to think she's sleeping in the ground, but I—" the Blesser choked and looked away, lest his tears be seen.

Oland laid his hand on the Blesser's shoulder.

"I know, Casavore," he said. "I know."

"She wanted to be buried in her homeland. That much I could give her," Casavore wiped his sleeve under his eye and looked to the storm-covered heavens. "Once a year, Dire Saulder allows me to leave the palace to visit her. And every year I ask him to come with me. He refuses each time."

"Probably for the best," Oland grunted. "If that monster ever stepped foot in my Mosharick Plains, he'd be dead in a second."

"I know how you feel about the dire, Oland," Casavore began softly. "But he's still dear to me. He's the son of my brother after all."

"Zastar is not your kin. He's a bloody monster, just like his hell-spawn. I take that back. Saulder is worse."

Casavore surrendered. He wouldn't argue in his wife's presence.

"I'm sorry, Casavore," Oland apologized. "I let my temper get away from me again."

"It's alright, Oland," Casavore nodded as he clutched his medallion. "Though, if you hate the dire, then you must hate me as well. I'm the one that put that curse on you after all."

"Come now. You know that you're not at fault for the Hyde Howler in me."

"But I was the one who—"

"You were under the dire's orders. You might as well have had a knife to your throat."

Casavore went silent. Of all the sins the Dire forced him to commit, creating Hyde Howlers was the cruelest.

Oland sighed. "Look, I won't disturb you much longer." Reaching into his cloak, he drew a folded letter tied in brown string. "I just wanted to give you this."

"What is it?" Casavore asked. "A love letter, perhaps?"

"I want you to read it come the next time that dire tests your patience. It includes the location of where the Blind Seers and I will be staying until the first snow."

"Oland—"

"Please. Keep it. Just in case."

Casavore looked from the letter to Oland. Sighing, he tucked the letter into his pocket. "I will."

"Good," Oland nodded and looked to the rumbling sky where a serpent of light dove in and out of its cloudy burrow. "I should get home before the storm gets worse or Roeseph will have the entirety of the Blind Seers after me."

Casavore snorted. "You mustn't be too hard on him, Oland. Sons fear for their fathers."

"He has nothing to fear," Oland laughed, his eyes twinkling with youthful trouble. "I've taken care of myself for this long."

"Get home safe, Oland," Casavore called as his friend descended the mound.

"You as well, Blesser," Oland waved as the heavy rain devoured him. "Remember my offer."

Chapter Two: The Dreaded Dire

The Kingdom of Vaska...

Beyond the river and in the middle of the Vaskan Forest stood a stone wall so tall it scathed the clouds. Within this stone fortress stood a massive kingdom. The taverns, cottages, and mills nestled on shallow mounds leading like stairsteps up to the palace of Vaska.

In the highest tower, behind the curtains of a canopy bed, lay a tarnished soul in a broken body. Labored breath lifted heavy purple sheets, the only indication the corpse-guised man lived.

The man was Zastar, the once great Dire of Vaska. His portrait hung throughout the palace in elegant copper frames, portraying him as young and strong, with dark skin, cloudy silver eyes, wavy ebony hair, and a thin beard along his strong jaw.

The Zastar of the portraits was now a memory. His muscular frame had withered to bones dressed in skin. His hair had greyed. And his once brilliant silver eyes were strangers to the decade. Dire Zastar was but an artifact—a living soul trapped in a dead man's body.

At Zastar's side, on a wooden chair sat his son, Dire Saulder, wearing his father's midnight-black armor.

His helmet at his feet, Dire Saulder watched his father with a heavy heart as he slept. Saulder wished the pain in his chest would go away. He often asked Blesser Casavore to make him not feel anything at all. But each time the Blesser said:

"My dire, a mind melder is only so strong. I can't withdraw emotions like hate, love, or sorrow. I can only take away what I have placed in you. If I had hypnotized you to suffer like this, then I could take it away easily. But this pain is

your own. I can only mend the wound, but I lack the power of God to completely erase it."

Excuses, Dire Saulder thought.

The door creaked open behind him, and his mother walked into the room.

"Good morning, my dire," Lore said as she leaned against the door, shutting it behind her. "I thought I'd find you here."

"I didn't call you here," Saulder said, not looking back. "Leave me."

"Come now, my dire," Lore said, "is that a way to speak to your mother?"

Dire Saulder glared over his shoulder. "What do you want, Lore?" Saulder never called her mother.

Lore exhaled, annoyed. "I heard that you let the Blesser out of the palace without an escort. I wanted to ask why."

"Because ten years ago the man lost his wife and daughter. He spends all his hours in this palace. He deserves a day to mourn."

"Is this weakness I sense in you, my dire?" Lore said, spinning her web of paranoia. "You forget, the Blesser is loyal only to your father. His tolerance of you is simply out of duty to protect the son his master left behind."

"That's enough," Saulder stood abruptly, causing the stool to crash to the floor.

Lore stepped back in alarm.

"I'm just trying to look out for you, my dire," she said. "You've already lost so much. I'd hate for you to hurt again."

"The greatest pain a wench like you can give me is disobedience," Saulder replied.

Lore stumbled back as he approached.

"You are not the dire," he spoke softly. "Don't forget that."

The door opened and a man stepped into the room wearing the plain silver armor of a Vaskan soldier. He resembled Saulder all the way from his helmet to his boots, except his hair was short and wild and Saulder's was long and braided.

"Ah," the man said, "there you are. The soldiers are ready to depart to the Mosharick Plains. They're growing impatient, and my jokes aren't getting anywhere with them. I fear an uprising is imminent."

Saulder glared at the walking reflection of himself then looked back to Lore. His fists coiled at his side, he grabbed his helmet from the floor.

"Let's go," he said, his voice masked by the helmet's metal ring. "Don't keep me waiting, Sova."

Saulder slammed his shoulder into his brother and walked out the door.

Sova chuckled and rubbed a forming bruise. "Moody today, aren't we?"

Sova looked at his mother who pouted on the other side of the room. He smirked, satisfied the palace witch had failed to manipulate his brother.

"What's wrong, Lore?" he asked. "Did the dire not roll over and show you his belly like you asked?"

"Don't mock me, boy," Lore growled. "If you cared for your brother like you say you do, you'd watch out for him as well."

"I am watching out for him. I'm watching out for him by making sure you don't try and execute his Blesser."

"Casavore is a liability."

"He's been like a father to us for the past ten years, which is more than you can say," Sova said, the playfulness in his eyes fading. "And if you try to get Casavore in trouble again like you did General Hylan, you'll not only fear the wrath of the dire, but mine as well."

Sova left the room, his mother's glare following him.

DIRE SAULDER STOOD at the end of a great hall before a window overlooking his kingdom. He eyed a vicious storm in the west. He wondered if his Blesser had come across it.

It better not prevent him from getting back...

"Saulder," Sova's cheerful voice echoed through the halls.

Dire Saulder glared through the holes of his helmet at his younger brother running to meet him.

Sova stopped, hands resting on his knees. "Wow, you're fast. I can't believe you can move so swiftly in that armor. I think I threw out my back once just trying to lift one of the legs—"

"Are the soldiers prepared to depart?"

"Yeah." Sova nodded as he straightened. "All ready."

"Good." The Dire glared out the window. "My informants tell me a Mosharick village just across the river has been aiding an unknown rogue for the past month now."

"You think it's the Blind Hound?"

"Perhaps. We need to make haste if we are to catch him." The Dire turned to walk down the hall.

"Why didn't you go with Casavore?" Sova asked as he followed. His words sliced through Saulder like an arrow making him halt. "I mean, he asks you to go with him every year. And yet, you continue to refuse his offer."

"I have nothing to mourn," Saulder said impatiently.

"Come on, Saulder. Fala was like a mother to us. More so than Lore ever was. You need to mourn," Sova paused then scoffed. "Not to mention you haven't exactly recovered from loss of your Blesser's feral spawn, that blasted F—"

Saulder grabbed Sova's shoulder. "Watch yourself," he warned through gritted teeth.

"Sorry," Sova said, holding his hands up in surrender. "I meant to say you haven't recovered from the loss of Casavore's daughter, your betrothed—the girl who made my life a living nightmare—Feran."

The two continued walking.

"Honestly," Sova said, "I never understood what you saw in her. Remember the time when I was eight, and she hypnotized me to wet myself every time I heard a rooster crow? I couldn't bring myself to go anywhere near a farm for like five years—"

"It's pointless," Saulder said. "Feran was lost a long time ago. There's no grave, no memorial, no tomb I can mourn over. So it would be pointless to let her death weigh on me."

"And yet it still does."

Saulder glared at his brother, his patience tested.

"Make haste," he ordered as he turned from the prince. "I want to be in the Mosharick Plains before sundown."

"You're not going to wait for Casavore?" Sova asked. "Won't you need the Blesser if things get ugly?"

"No need," Saulder said, his heavy footsteps echoing through the palace halls. "I have a weapon hidden among our enemies."

THE MOSHARICK PLAINS...

The joyful noise of Harvest Day rang across Elling's village under the eye of a clear, night sky. Elling and the other villagers danced around the fire, painted orange by the flames as she balanced her little brother on her toes.

The chief, Chemon, and his wife, Sulia, stood outside the celebration, leaning against a sharick fawn pen as they watched their children and people dance.

Chemon's eyes were like Elling's, green as the Mosharick Plains, and his hair a curly grey. His wife, Sulia, possessed a beauty so unmatched even the flowers of the plains wept with jealousy. Only her daughter, Elling, could compare to such grace.

"Alright, everyone," Chemon called over the lyre. "Let us take a break from embarrassing ourselves and eat."

The villagers gathered around a low-platformed table where a bountiful feast waited in the gentle light of a candle's flame. Chemon settled at the head of the table, his wife, daughter, and son at his side.

"Now," he said, "let us say grace."

All heads bowed, and all eyes closed.

"Father," Chemon prayed, "we thank you for this bountiful meal and for blessing our village with an abundant year that has filled this table with a beautiful Harvest Feast. Thank you for all these people who celebrate with me tonight and for the family you have blessed me with to keep me company in my older years. We pray that this food nourish our bodies and that you will lead us through the approaching winter. And all of God's people said..."

"Amen," the people chanted in unison.

Upon the prayer's end the people lunged at the food, desperate to fill their bellies.

"Kandon," scolded Sulia. Her son had stolen a sip of her wine. "You know better than to drink that."

She pulled her goblet away as Kandon wiped the bitter liquor from his lips.

"It tastes disgusting," he griped.

Chemon chuckled, amused, and turned to his daughter.

"So. How were the pastures, Elling? I heard there was a storm up north. I was worried you might've gotten caught in the middle of it."

"I was fine," Elling smiled. "It was nowhere near me. Though, I did have to chase a lost sharick-fawn to the river."

"The river?" Sulia gasped with alarm. "Elling, you should know better than to go near the Vaskan Forest after what happened the last time. I couldn't take it if you disappeared like that again."

"I didn't go anywhere near the forest, Mama," Elling assured. "One of the sharick fawns was killed by an animal."

"What kind of animal?" Sulia asked.

"I don't know," Elling shrugged. "But it was massive. I never actually saw it, but its paw prints were huge. Bigger than a bear's even."

Chemon took a sip of his wine. "Perhaps you should start taking someone with you into the pastures from now on," he said. "Just to be safe."

"Papa. You know I'm perfectly capable of taking care of myself."

"Be quiet, Elling."

"No, really, Father. I'm fine—"

"I said be quiet," Chemon ordered as he rose from the table, looking to the darkness beyond the village.

"Is everything ok, dear?" Sulia whispered, grabbing her husband's hand.

"No," Chemon replied. The villagers looked to their chief, silenced. "Something's out there."

Kandon clung to Elling's arm, his little heart bruising her skin.

"Is it the monster?" he whimpered.

"No," Chemon answered. "Not the one Elling witnessed at least. The Dire of Vaska is in our midst."

The shadows of Vaskan soldiers seeped from the darkness and into the light of the village. They circled the people like wolves, their horses' misty breath filling the air. Atop a black stallion was their leader—the nightmare in human flesh. The dreaded Dire Saulder, dressed in ghastly black armor. At his side, atop a silver mare, was Prince Sova, in silver armor.

Elling looked to the Vaskan tyrant, her stomach twisting.

What is he doing here? She thought. *We've done nothing wrong, what is the Dire of Vaska doing in the Mosharick Plains?*

Dire Saulder glared at the villagers as they huddled close to one another. The gossip of the crickets died, and the sun fled from sight; neither could bear to witness to what was sure to come.

Sova cleared his throat.

"Good evening. I am Prince Sova of Vaska. My brother and I come in search of your chief, Chemon."

"I am Chemon," the chief replied as he stepped away from his people. "Why does the dire seek me?"

Sova looked to Saulder. Still, the dire did not speak. Sova cleared his throat again.

"Our informants tell us that you have been aiding a drifter whom we believe to be the Blind Hound."

"I have no allegiance to the Hyde Howler. Or any Blind Seer for that matter," Chemon replied. "Now, I'm afraid I must ask you and your men to leave."

Sova looked nervously at his brother as the dire glared at Chemon.

"Sova," Saulder growled lowly.

Sova leaned as close to his brother as he could without falling from his horse. "Yes, my dire?"

"Bring me the girl. The one with the green eyes."

Elling gasped as her mother embraced her.

Sova paused and he looked hesitantly from his brother to the frightened shepherdess. "Surely we can come to some other agreement, Dire Saul—"

"Don't make me repeat myself again, brother," Saulder warned.

Sova hesitated. Drawing a deep breath, the prince descended his steed and approached the villagers, his sword hissing as he unsheathed it.

"You leave her be!" Chemon snarled, and rushed the prince.

Sova rammed his iron shoulder into Chemon, sending the old chief to the ground.

"Papa!" Elling screamed and tore toward her father.

Sulia reached after her daughter, screaming, "Elling, no!"

Just as Elling fell to her father's side, Sova grabbed her by the arm and jerked her away.

"Let me go!" she pled as the prince dragged her away, beating at his hand locked around her wrist. "Let me go!"

"No—" Chemon grunted and struggled to his hands and knees. "No, leave her be!"

Sova looked away to hide the guilt in his eyes.

"Let me go!" Elling screamed again.

Finally, Sova tossed her to the ground. Elling coughed, her chest smarting from the fall as she rose onto shaking elbows. A heavy hoof stomped the grass in front of her and she froze, following the length of the horse's leg all the way up to the dire that sat on top of it, glaring down at her.

Elling looked back to the ground, afraid to look the Vaskan beast in the eye.

Dire Saulder slid off his horse and stopped before Elling, his black shadow crushing the shepherd girl to the ground.

"You'll do," he muttered.

"Saulder," Sova whispered to his brother. "This is wrong. We're not even sure if the Blind Hound or his Blind Seers are associated with these people. We're threatening to destroy this village under the pretense of a rumor." Sova touched his shoulder. "Let's just go home before any more damage is done."

Saulder looked to his brother, his eyes blazing like silver fire

"Remove your hand, soldier," Saulder warned.

Sova stepped back in surrender as Dire Saulder looked to Elling.

"Come now, Shepherd Girl," he said, his voice softening. "Why do you, a being so powerful, cower in my presence?"

Elling didn't answer. All she could do was shake and pray—pray to wake up from this horrible nightmare.

Chemon struggled to his feet, his knees buckling beneath him. "Leave her be!" he shouted. "She's innocent!"

"Is she?" the dire challenged. "It seems you don't know your daughter as well as you thought, Chemon."

Chemon's brows furrowed.

"Your daughter and I have met before, actually," Saulder shrugged, his voice careless and calm.

Elling looked up, her emerald eyes glistening with tears.

"That—That's not true," she sniffled. "I've never even been to Vaska. I've never met you, my Dire."

"Haven't you?" Saulder chuckled. "I remember not five years ago, my patrol brought a little Mosharick girl to my palace. She looked just like you. Same hair. Same pretty face. She even had the same fear in her eyes that you do now. Of course, we treated her hospitably and kept her for two nights. And when the day came for her to return home, I sent her away with a gift. A gift rare to many. My soldiers left her unharmed in the shade of a tree. But, you don't remember this, do you?"

Elling's jaw trembled open as a gasp got lodged halfway-up her throat.

Chemon's eyes widened. "No..." he whispered. "L—Let her go! Don't hurt her!"

"On the contrary, Chief Chemon," Saulder said as he reached in the back of his cape. "She's going to hurt you."

Elling flinched as the dire drew something from under his violet cape. She expected a sword, or a blade. Instead, he drew a small bugle-horn. The instrument reminded her of Chemon's wooden pipe he smoked in his younger years.

Saulder brought the bugle horn to the grate over his lips.

"Saulder, no!" the prince shouted as Dire Saulder breathed into the instrument. A sorrowful melody pirouetted through the air.

Elling sat up at the peculiar sound as a strange numbness rippled through her body. Her face, once strained with fear, softened to blank. Her pupils shrunk to the heads of pins. And a red mist fell over her gaze. She stood still. Emotionless. Barely living. She was a zombified soldier. A Hyde Howler.

Chapter Three: The Feral Shepherd

S aulder... Sova thought, his heart sinking at the wretched creation summoned from the gentle vessel. *What have you done?*

"El—Elling?" Kandon's timid voice rose from the huddled village. "What's wrong?"

Elling said nothing.

Dire Saulder chuckled, pleased with his new monster.

"Rise, shepherd girl," he ordered, and Elling stood. Whatever timid nature overwhelmed her before, the Hyde Howler devoured.

"God, please," Sova prayed beneath his breath. "Stop this."

Cupping Elling's cheek, Dire Saulder forced her zombified gaze to meet his.

"Beautiful," he whispered and looked to Chemon. "Last chance, Chief. Tell me who you aid and where I can find them. Or else..."

Chemon glared at the dire. His face wrinkled into a sneer. "Go throw yourself from the Cliffs of Era."

Dire Saulder smirked. In one swift movement, he grabbed Sova's sword from his sheath and held it out for Elling.

"Shepherd Girl," he ordered. "Slaughter every last man, woman, and child in your village. But leave the chief alive. I want him to witness what his daughter's done."

"Saulder—" Sova snapped.

Elling took the sword from her master and turned toward the village, her eyes void of soul. Her people begged and pleaded for mercy, but it was no use. To try and reason with a Hyde Howler was for a man to try and stop a tsunami with his bare hands. Pointless. Sova turned away, unable to gaze upon the cruelty, while Dire Saulder watched with dark anticipation.

One by one, Elling struck down her people like a woodsman among trees, as blood-soaked screams echoed through the plains. Not even Samson with his jawbone could've killed so effortlessly.

Sova cringed as the cry of a mother and babe haunted his ears.

"I'm so sorry," he uttered through clenched teeth. "I am so—so sorry."

Dire Saulder and his soldiers watched as an ocean of red flooded the village. Like an artist with a sword, Elling created a masterpiece within death. Without so much as a day of combat training, the meek shepherd girl slaughtered like a warlord.

As she sliced a man's final wail from his throat, a cry like that of a frightened lamb rose from all the rest.

"Elling!" Kandon screamed.

Elling slowly looked over her shoulder. Her emotionless gaze narrowed on her little brother, the one she loved most, now a stranger in her eyes. Like a shark stalking a seal, she turned and advanced her newfound prey. Kandon stumbled back, his heel snagging the ground. He crawled away from his sister, his back colliding into the support of a sharick-skin hut.

Before Elling could descend her blade on her beloved brother, Sulia dove at her son and took him into her arms.

"Elling, wake up!" Sulia begged her daughter as she hid Kandon's eyes in her chest. "Elling, wake up now! Please!"

Elling stared at her mother, not an ounce of sympathy in her gaze. Just as Sova dared to look over his shoulder, Elling thrust her blade through her mother and brother like an ax through timber. Their screams barely fled their throats by the time Heaven stole their souls.

Sova's stomach rolled, and his throat flexed. Racing his gut, he tilted his helmet above his brow and vomited.

Saulder rolled his eyes at his brother's weakness to war. When his sickness ended, Sova turned to face the massacre. His stomach twirled with uncertainty. In all his years of tolerating the cruelty of his brother, he had never seen the dire commit such a blasphemous crime.

"That's enough," the dire called. Elling looked up. All around her, people she loved and cared for laid in a sea of their own blood. And yet, she held not an ounce of sympathy for any one of them. "Bring me the old man," Saulder ordered.

Elling found the Chief Chemon curled up in a ball, painted in the blood of his people and mumbling tongues of desolation. She grabbed him by the hair, making him wince as she dragged him away and threw him at the dire's boots.

"Look at this mess, Chief Chemon," Saulder sighed and looked around. "All this death, all this sorrow. And you could've stopped it." Saulder knelt to be eye-level with the chief, his silver eyes burning through his helmet. "Now, tell me the name of the man you aid. Or I'll lose my patience."

"Go to Hell, you monster," Chemon cursed.

Saulder sighed, and clicked his tongue.

"Very well. But I might as well bring someone with me," Saulder looked to the Hyde Howler. "Shepherd Girl—turn the sword on yourself." Elling did as she was told and placed the blade to her gut. "Very good," Saulder praised. "Now, when I count to three, I want you to plunge the sword as deep as it will go."

Chemon looked up, his eyes wide and raining.

"No—No," he wailed. "Leave her be!"

"One," Saulder began.

"This is madness. Let her go, you monster!"

"Two."

"You tyrant! You son of Hell!"

"Thru—"

"Alright, I'll tell you! I'll tell you!" Chemon sobbed and clutched the Dire's cape. "Just leave her be! Leave her be."

"Lower your sword Shepherd Girl."

Elling lowered the blade. She was mere seconds from death, and she didn't even care. Her soul was on pause—absent under the Blesser's curse.

Saulder looked to Chemon, his patience on the verge of extinction. "Speak."

Chemon sniffled. "I have been aiding someone, but it isn't the Blind Hound. Nor is he a Blind Seer—or—or any enemy of Vaska."

"Then who is he?"

"I don't know. I've never seen his face. I—I came across him one night about a year ago when I was tending the sharick-fawns. His dog—or—or something like a dog...his beast, killed one of my fawns. The man offered to pay for it, but I turned him down. I simply asked that the next time he pass through, he keep watch over my fawns. I promised I'd pay him with furs and meat. I've only seen him twice since then. But that's it. He's a rogue. A stranger to every kingdom and all peoples."

Saulder's head tilted, and he growled, "That's it? I came all this way because you've been babysitting a man and his mutt? Great. Just great. I'll make those informants pay for wasting my time."

"I've told you everything I know," Chemon gulped. "Now, please, let my daughter go."

Saulder scoffed and looked from the blood-soaked girl to the pleading chief. "You would still have her? Even after everything she's done?"

"A father never loses the love he has for his children," Chemon trembled. "I just want her home."

Dire Saulder grunted, slightly amused by the chief's desperation.

"You may want her home. But believe me," he drew his sword, "she's not going to want to wake up from this."

Saulder wheeled back his sword to strike Elling. Without thinking, Chemon dove in front of his daughter and caught the dire's blade between his ribs. Blood sputtered from the chief's lips, and he fell to the ground. He gasped, choked by his own breath.

"Saulder!" Sova shouted and fell to the chief's side, clutching the wound. "What have you done?"

Saulder, without an ounce of sympathy in his silver eyes, drew the sword from Chemon's rib. The chief screamed as blood rushed from the wound. The dire wiped the scarlet essence from his sword and looked to Chemon.

"Best not to let him suffer," said the dire. "Step away, Sova."

Sova glared at the dire. For the first time since Saulder took the throne, Sova saw something other than the brother he wished so dearly would return. He saw a monster. Nothing more. He remained at the injured man's side.

"I said step away," Saulder warned.

Sova didn't move.

The dire looked to Elling. "Shepherd Girl," he ordered. "Remove him."

Before Sova could protest, Elling had him by the back of his armor and dragged him away.

"Let go of me!" Sova raged, hating his brother more with each breath he drew. "Let go of me! You don't know what you're doing! Let go!"

Saulder raised his sword, his silver eyes blazing through his helmet. "Goodbye, Chief Chemon."

Before the dire could claim another life, a ghastly roar fell from the sky like thunder, and he froze. Every eye darted to the stars where the shadow of a monster eclipsed the moon. It was massive, about ten feet tall, with the body of a wolf and wings of a bat. Amber eyes blazing, the beast snarled and shot toward its prey. Toward the dire.

The monster hurtled into the dire, taking him to the ground. Saulder's sword grazed the beast's brow before fleeing his hand. The soldiers gasped in alarm as the white monster towered over its victim. Blood dripped from a slit through the beast's brow and cheek, contrasting the moon-white hide constricted around its snarl. It was like a white angel, sent down from Heaven to punish Saulder for his sins.

The beast's dagger-like teeth came down on the dire's shoulder, tearing through his armor as if it were made of cotton instead of steel. Saulder screamed, his wail of agony echoing through the sin-stained night. The monster pulled away, lips framed with the dire's blood.

"Shepherd girl!" Saulder shouted. "Kill that thing!"

Elling dropped Sova and charged the beast just as the white monster leaped into the stars and disappeared in the hills over the horizon. Unable to give up her mission, Elling stole the dire's horse and pursued the beast.

"Stop!" Sova called, though his protests were pointless. Only the dire could command a Hyde Howler.

"Leave her," Saulder snapped as he sat, blood weeping from his shoulder. "Get me to Casavore, now!"

Sova slung his brother's arm over his shoulders and helped him onto his horse. If God was good, maybe the tyrant would bleed out before they reached the Blesser.

Chapter Four: The White Angel

Elling rode over the green plains in pursuit of the *White Angel*. In the distance, the monster descend into a shallow ditch, where it sat with its wings folded against its side and its ears to the wind. It remained there—quietly. Patiently.

Elling drove the black stallion toward the winged wolf, her sword tight in hand. The white angel's ears pricked at her coming, and turned. Amber eyes bursting into flames, it snarled and lunged into the sky. Like a hawk, the beast dove at Elling, and threw her from the stallion. She hit the ground, her sword lost to the green stalks a couple feet away as her steed whinnied and ran into the night.

The white angel charged the defenseless Hyde Howler, fangs shining in the moonlight. But before death could embrace Elling, a stranger in a black cloak dove in front of her and lifted their hands to the feral beast. The white angel froze, and its snarl softened.

With the beast distracted, Elling reached for her sword. The stranger's boot came down on her wrist, pinning her just short of the handle. The cloaked stranger stood against the stars, wearing a gold medallion, charred a smoky brass color along the rim.

Before Elling could bring herself to fight, the cloaked master drew their medallion and swung the gold trinket like the tongue of a great grandfather clock. A frost struck Elling's body, and she froze, at the mercy of the stranger's spell.

"Shepherd girl of the Mosharick Plains," the medallion wielder began with a warm and captivating voice. *"Awake from your rage. Remember your innocence taken from you by the Siren's Call. Become the good soul that you once bore. Awake from this curse and remember no more."*

Elling's body rippled with a warmth so severe she fell from consciousness. Wavered between lucidness and dreams, she heard the cloaked medallion wielder say to the beast. "We were too late, Saber. There's nothing we can do for Chemon now. We need to get out of here before whoever summoned the Siren's Call sends more Hyde Howlers after us."

The medallion wielder sprung onto the white angels' back and launched into the sky. Elling stared at them as they soared, darkness clouding her vision until everything became black.

WHEN ELLING CAME TO, she awoke alone, with thick red paint on her hands and a sword at her side.

"My head," she groaned and gingerly touched her temple.

She didn't remember anything between when the dire arrived and waking up in the plains, but it was night, so she couldn't have been asleep long. Taking the strange sword, she hurried east toward home.

When she came to her village, she stopped in her tracks and gasped with horror. Bodies littered the ground, resting in what appeared to be remnants of a red flood.

Who could've done this? Elling thought as tears streamed down her face. Despite her fears, Elling ran into the village and checked each body. Not one bore breath. Elling dropped to her knees as grief like a spear pierced her heart.

"M—Mama?" she cried. "Mama? Papa? Kandon?"

A voice like a creaking branch answered her sobs. "El—Elling?"

Elling looked up to see her father laying on the permitter of camp, his bloody hand raised in the still air.

"Papa," Elling gasped as she crawled to her father's side. She lifted his shoulders to rest in her lap.. "Who's done this to you?"

"Elling, you need to run," Chemon rasped. "You need to get as far from here as you can."

"Where's Mama?" Elling questioned. "She—She can help. I'm going to go find her."

"No, Elling. Don't look for your mother," Chemon flinched through the pain, his eyes glittering like glass. "Or your brother. You need to run."

"W—Why? Where's Mama and Kandon?"

"I'm so sorry, Elling," Chemon whimpered. "This is all my fault. What happened to you is all my fault. I should've known. I should've known what you were."

"What are you talking about? What happened to me?"

"The dire…" Chemon sniffled. "He cursed you."

"I don't understand?"

"It wasn't your fault. It—It wasn't your fault, Elling."

"What are you saying?" Elling froze and looked to the blood on her hands and the surrounding bodies. A shaken breath fell from her lungs, and her soul went cold with terror. "Who did this, Papa?"

"Please, Elling. Just go—"

"Who did this, Chief Chemon!" Elling yelled. Her father flinched and looked away from his gentle daughter. His reaction was all Elling needed to know what had become of her people. What became of her. "No…"

"I don't blame you, Elling. You didn't mean it," Chemon shuddered and laid his quivering bloody hand on her cheek. "You didn't mean…"

Chemon's soul slipped from his eyes, and his face softened to nothing. Like a leaf succumbing to autumn's will, his hand fell from his daughter's face.

"Papa?" Elling whimpered. He didn't answer. "Papa?…"

Chapter Five: The Rogue

The Kingdom of Vaska...
　　The autumn sun rose from the eastern cliffs of Era and shined on the frost-traced royal gardens. Brilliant white roses, soft and rich in fragrance, fenced in a broad, green yard beneath the dire's balcony. In the center stood a marble fountain singing an aquatic lullaby as glittering water fell from a series of plates to the pool bellow.

Casavore stood before the fountain dressed in a humble brown robe. He closed his eyes and breathed in the sweetness of the garden, the floral scents tickling his lungs. He exhaled, his spirit soothed by the cold morning. Nothing could ruin such a blissful moment.

"Good morning, Casavore," came a voice that burned his ear like venom.

Casavore's eyes opened in a glare. He sighed.

"I'm busy, Lore."

"Is that any way to talk to an old friend?" the white-haired vixen chuckled. She sat on the rim of the marble fountain and stroked the shallow waters. She wore a strapless magenta dress that pressed her bronzed breasts to her chin and her lips were stained with an alluring pomegranate paint. It amazed Casavore how a soul so ugly could reside in a creature so captivating.

"You aren't my friend, Lore," Casavore exhaled. "What do you want?"

"Nothing really. I just thought it would be interesting to hear the final words of a dead man."

Casavore sighed, annoyed. "What are you talking about, Lore?"

"I was in your shack earlier today. And I found this."

Lore whipped out a folded-up piece of paper tied in brown string. Oland's letter. Casavore didn't so much as bat an eye. This wasn't the first time Lore had caught him. But she didn't know that.

Lore smugly untied the string and opened the letter, a poet's tone on her tongue.

"*Dear Casavore,*" she began. "*I know that my attempts to persuade you to the good fight have gone in vain. Still, I can't help but feel led to ask you again to join my ranks. I know your answer will be no, but still, I ask you. If you do come to your senses, please join us in the southern Mosharick villages, where we'll be staying till the winter. I do hope you will join us, Casavore. God Bless. Your friend, Oland...*"

Lore clicked her tongue and folded the letter. Casavore was silent, his eyes blank as a winter sky.

"What exactly do you plan to do with that, Lore?" he asked.

"Turn it over to the dire, of course. Then we'll send our troops to arrest Oland and then execute you both," Lore waved the letter on her face like a fan. "I just wanted to hear you beg first. Go ahead, try to persuade me."

Casavore sighed and shook his head, exhausted.

"I truly do regret making you queen, Lore," the Blesser griped. "Zastar and his boys deserved better."

"That's your own fault for falling in love with Zastar's betrothed. Now, obey me, Casavore. Beg."

"You really expect me to give in to your commands?" Casavore looked at the feral woman. "I only serve my dire and my God. No one else."

"Then you will die, Casavore," Lore laughed.

"That's your problem, Lore," Casavore reached into his robe. "You can't help but taunt."

Before Lore could realize what was happening, Casavore revealed his gold medallion and froze Lore in a trance. With no eye to witness his mutiny, Casavore began his hypnosis.

"*Lore, daughter of Seavale, and thorn in my side. Forget all your allegations against me. Forget the letter by which you've seen. Forget my alliance with the Blind Hound. Forget it all. In your mind, I place a memory. You've come to scold me for venturing beyond the palace. That is all...*"

In one swift motion, Casavore stole the letter out of Lore's hand and hid it in his cloak. Placing his medallion around his neck, he snapped his fingers. Lore flinched and blinked away her daze.

"What—what just happened?" she groaned.

"You were going on about how I shouldn't have left the palace despite being granted permission from the dire," Casavore griped.

"Ah yes," Lore smiled, having forgotten the letter completely. "And furthermore—"

"Blesser Casavore!" a voice called. Lore and Casavore looked up from their dispute to a Vaskan guard charging into the garden. "Come quick. The dire's been injured."

CASAVORE AND LORE RACED through the palace toward the dire's chambers, the pounding of their feet echoing the halls like a thunderstorm.

"This is impossible," Lore snapped. "Dire Saulder is the most skilled warrior in all of Lykos. How could he have been injured in battle?"

"It doesn't matter how," Casavore gulped. "Right now we just have to pray that he's ok."

Please, God, Casavore begged, *be with Zastar's son.*

Casavore and Lore charged through the dire's chamber door to find Dire Saulder in his canopy bed under violet sheets with Sova standing at his bedside. White gauze wrapped the dire's shoulder, stained red by the weeping gash underneath.

"Casavore," Sova exhaled, a sort of disappointment in his voice.

"It's about time!" Saulder snapped. "What took you so long?"

Casavore rushed to the bed, his eyes alive with fear.

"What happened?" he asked.

"He got what was coming to him," Sova growled. "That's what happened."

Saulder glared up at his brother as Casavore unwound the gauze.

"I swear, Sova," Saulder snarled. "When I get my hands on you, I'll—"

"You'll what?" Sova spat. "Turn me into a Hyde Howler like you did that girl? Make me slaughter an entire village?"

"Chemon deserved it! He must've known we were coming, and sent that monster to attack me!"

"It should've killed you!"

"That's enough!" Casavore shouted and pointed across the room. "Sova, go stand over there and let me do my job." Glaring at his brother, Sova stepped away. "And you," Casavore turned to Saulder. "Hold still."

Dire Saulder reclined against his pillow and stared angrily at the ceiling while Casavore unwound his gauze. The Blesser paused, horrified to find shallow gashes aligning the front and back of the dire's shoulder in the shape of an upside-down triangle. The rest of the wounds would heal fine, except for a long, jagged gash shaped like a crescent moon along the dire's pectoral.

Filled with questions but unable to ask, Casavore withdrew his medallion to entrance the dire.

"*Dire Saulder*," he began. "*Your pain is great, and your panic greater. But I tell you, let me cast out your pain. Remember it no more so that you may be soothed..*"

Casavore snapped his fingers in front of Saulder. Saulder exhaled with relief, his head sinking deeper into his pillow.

"Better?" Casavore asked. Saulder nodded. With the dire soothed, Casavore stitched and cleaned his wounds with a dampened cloth. "You're lucky, Saulder," Casavore said softly, his heart tendered by the state of his master's son. "Much longer, and the wound might've become infected. You should heal fine, but I'm worried about that scar on your chest. Best to not overwork yourself."

Saulder grumbled in irritation and looked away. Casavore puzzled at the dire. He could've sworn Saulder had a look of disappointment to him. Almost as if he hadn't wanted to survive.

"What attacked you anyway?" Casavore asked. "This is not the mark of a sword. A bear, maybe?"

"A monster," Sova answered from the back of the room and walked up to stand by Casavore. "It attacked us at the end of the massacre. Saulder had just released a Hyde Howler on her own village. She killed everyone."

Poor girl, Casavore thought. He looked to Saulder, who bore not so much as an ounce of guilt in his face. It troubled Casavore. This was not the boy his daughter cared for, nor was he the kind son of his dear friend, Zastar.

"A monster, you say?" Casavore arched an eyebrow. "What did it look like?"

"I've never seen anything like it," Sova shook his head. "It was as big as a horse. Bigger actually. With the body of a wolf, but these wings that stretched 'this' long," Sova reached out his arms. "Longer, actually. It was white as snow and had these yellow-orangish eyes that seemed to glow—"

"You're certain?" Casavore snapped and turned to Sova. "You're certain this is the beast you saw?"

"Y—Yeah," Sova stammered. "Wait, do you know what it is?"

"I should. I had one."

Saulder sat up. "You what?"

"They're called Soaring Wolves," Casavore stated. "Savage beasts native to the Cliffs of Era. They're normally untamable, but using mind melding they can be turned into fiercely loyal companions. Every young Eradite is bonded to one when they turn eighteen. I had one myself. But he was killed by the Eradawns when they traded me to Dire Zastar as his Blesser..."

"So, wait," Sova interrupted, "why haven't we ever seen one before?"

"Because they're intensely territorial. They never leave the Cliffs of Era. Maybe to hunt something just beneath the cliffs, but that's as far as they'll go. The only reason I could think for a soaring wolf venturing this far is if—"

"If it was following its master," Saulder finished.

Casavore nodded as a wave of silence struck the chamber.

"By the Soul of Seavale," Lore whispered. "After all these years... There's an Eradite in the Valley of Lykos."

Saulder gripped his blanket, his eyes tinted red with fury.

"What is one doing here?" Sova wondered aloud. "The Eradites are far too self-righteous to step foot in Lykos. Why now?"

"Isn't it obvious?" Lore intervened. "To overthrow the dire, of course. This rogue must be an assassin."

Casavore turned on the Vaskan Queen, his face drawn in a sneer.

"The Eradites would never do something so cowardly," he defended.

"Oh, they wouldn't?" Lore challenged. "Wasn't it the Eradawns who killed your flying dog, beat you half to death, and handed you over to Zastar?"

"Soaring. Wolf," Casavore corrected through a hiss. "And whether an Eradawn or Eradusk, the Eradites are a holy people. They aren't fighters, let alone instigators of war."

"Holy people are sinners as well, Casavore," Lore seethed through a glare. "I mean, look at you. You consider yourself to be a man of God... Also a liar. And a cheater."

Sova took an aggressive step toward his mother, only for Casavore to grab him by the arm and haul him back. Lore raised her chin to the Blesser and prince, a smirk drawing in her lips. Casavore's heart sunk. He knew the look. It was the same one Lore always had when she was about to spin a web of manipulation.

"Dire," she turned to her son, her eyes twinkling with false concern. "Attacks like these can't be tolerated. If you are to keep the three nations in check, you should rid yourself of all threats."

"We don't even know if this Eradite was working under the influence of either Eradite tribes," Casavore protested. "We need to act rationally."

"Rationally?" Sova scoffed down at Saulder. "The man killed an entire village last night because of a rumor. There isn't a rational bone in his body."

"That's enough, Sova," Casavore cautioned.

Saulder glared at his brother, his teeth gritted in a snarl as he sneered, "If you think I acted so out of turn, then what do you have to say about the Chief Chemon harboring that beast?"

"He said he encountered the monster and its master over a year ago," Sova snapped. "If Chemon or the Eradite in question intended to wage war on Vaska, don't you think it would've happened a long time ago?"

"They were waiting for an opportunity to attack!"

"The blasted thing has wings!" Sova lunged, only for Casavore to take him under the arms and drag him back. "Every moment is the right moment to attack. It could very well fly through your balcony and eat you in your sleep if it wanted to!"

"I've had it with you questioning my orders!" Saulder snarled. "Speak out of turn again, and you'll be punished!"

"Maybe I wouldn't question you if you weren't such a tyrant!"

Saulder leaped from his bed and stood an inch away from his brother's face. "Get out of my sight before I lose my temper."

"You killed all those people!" Sova snapped. "You're a monster, Saulder!"

"Watch yourself, Sova!" Saulder threatened.

"You're more of a beast than that soaring wolf! If Feran still lived, she'd curse you. She'd wish you were dead!"

Saulder's anvil-like hand fist collided with Sova's cheek, and the prince hit the floor.

"Saulder!" Casavore shouted.

Sova wiped his wrist under a bloodied nose and looked up. Saulder stood over him, his long, Samson-like hair falling over his face and lashing at his breath.

Quick to diffuse the imminent battle, Casavore ushered Sova to his feet and dragged him toward the doors.

"Move it," he uttered. "Don't say anything to upset him further."

"Step out of line again, Sova, and I'll kill your!" Saulder threatened as Sova and the Blesser fled. "And Casavore..."

The Blesser stopped in his tracks.

"Send word to the soldiers to invade the Mosharick Plains. Have them bring me the Eradite alive. I'll kill him myself."

Chapter Six: Man of Tarsus

Casavore helped Sova into his shack and sat him on his bed.

"Keep your head back, Sova," Casavore instructed and scooped Sova's chin so his skull tilted back. "Let me get something for your nose."

Casavore threw his cloak onto the bed next to Sova and sauntered to his medicine collection stacked along the shelves. As he rummaged, Sova's eyes fell to Casavore's cloak. A letter tied with brown twine peeked out from beneath its fold. Like coals in a fire, Sova's curiosity burned.

"This brings back some good memories, huh?" Casavore sighed as he hunted the shelves. "Remember how you'd always be in here because Feran beat you up?"

"Oh yeah, good times," Sova growled through a nasally voice.

"Ha. Remember the time she hypnotized you to wet your—"

"How's that gauze coming along, Cas?"

Casavore sighed. "Looks like I'm out of gauze. I'm going to see if there's any left in the servant's quarters. Stay here, would you?"

"Sure."

The Blesser whisked out of the shack and slammed the door behind him. When Sova was sure he was alone, he withdrew the letter from Casavore's cloak and opened it. With each tar-printed word of the letter he scanned, his eyes widened.

No way... he thought.

CASAVORE RETURNED NOT five minutes later to find Sova on his bed, a Bible in his lap.

"Why the sudden urge to study the Gospel?" Casavore smirked and closed the door behind him. "Did Saulder slap you into the next life?"

"Ha. Ha," Sova replied. "Very funny."

The Blesser chuckled and tossed a wad of gauze into Sova's lap.

"What book are you reading?" Casavore asked as he sat down next to the red-nosed prince.

"Where you left off," Sova replied, holding the now red gauze over his nose. "Acts. Boy, this Saul guy seems like a real scum bag."

"He's not really," Casavore shook his head. "His story was actually one of Feran's favorite Bible stories. She would have Fala, and I read it about a thousand times."

"Shocker," Sova scoffed. "That sick little savage favored a monster."

"He's not a monster. At first, maybe. But not in the long run."

"What happened?" Sova asked, curious.

"Well," Casavore began. "Saul of Tarsus spent a great deal of his time persecuting the followers of Christ. Imprisoning them. Executing them. All the horrible things you can think of. And to make it worse, he was doing so in the name of God."

"Yeah, Casavore, he sounds like a real sweetheart."

"But then he met Jesus. And I mean, *actually* met Jesus. He was on the road to Damascus when he encountered a blinding light. The light spoke to him, saying, 'Saul. Saul, why do you persecute me?' When Saul asked who was speaking to him, Christ replied, 'I am Jesus, whom you are persecuting. It is hard for you to kick against the goads.'"

"What's a goad?"

"I don't know, shut up and pay attention. Jesus then replied with 'Rise up and go into the city, and you will be told what you must do.' When the light disappeared, Saul was blinded. He was taken to Damascus, where he didn't eat or drink for three days. On the brink of death, God called upon a man named Ananias to go and heal him. And so, Ananias went and blessed Saul. Saul was then baptized and devoted his life to Christ. He even preached amongst the gentiles. During his missionary, he changed his name to Paul. Nearing the days of his execution in Rome, he wrote, '*I have fought the good fight. I have finished the race, I have kept the faith.*'"

Sova looked up at Casavore, surprised to find tears in the Blesser's eyes. Sova closed the Bible, his heart like a lead weight in his chest.

"You seem to think a lot of this man."

"He gives me hope," Casavore smiled. "I can only do so much. I can plant seeds, but I can't force them to grow. But God shows up to people. He makes them something new. Just as he can make life from sand he can make a man out of a monster."

"Well, I'm not so sure even God can make a man out of *our* monster."

"Saulder didn't mean it, Sova," Casavore sighed. "Your brother's just—"

"That's not what I mean, Cas," Sova interrupted. "I mean, I got off easy getting hit. You didn't see what he did to that poor girl and her village. And even after forcing the shepherdess to slaughter her family, he sent her on a suicide mission to kill that stupid soaring wolf. I mean—what God would want to use someone like him?"

"You'd be surprised, Sova," the Blesser sighed and laid his hand on the prince's shoulder. "We just have to have patience. Be merciful, kind, slow to anger—"

"No," Sova shook his head. "No, we should've been quicker to anger. The massacre that happened last night was just one of many. Only difference is I can't stomach it anymore."

"What are you saying, Sova?"

"I mean, I can't do this anymore," Sova lashed up from the bed and started pacing. "Saulder needs to be taken down. I can't let him hurt people anymore. And I'm tired of hanging onto this false hope that the brother I knew might miraculously show up one day."

"Sova—"

"No, Casavore. I'm tired of it. And you should be tired of it too. Why haven't you given up on him? Why don't you make him good again? You have the power."

"You know I can't do that, Sova," Casavore sighed. "As a mind melder, I can only manipulate emotions like hate, love, and fear that *I* put there. *Fake* emotions if you will. My powers can help your brother along the way to healing, but if he's unwilling to budge, then there's nothing I can do."

"Well, then why haven't you used your powers to overthrow him? Why haven't you risen against him? You've had countless opportunities. You have the resources. You haven't even tried to escape. Why haven't you tried to go home? Zastar is more dead than alive, and your wife and daughter are gone. What's keeping you here?"

Casavore paused, his sorrow-filled eyes weighing on Sova like two boulders. "You are, Sova," the Blesser said. "Yes, I lost a lot the day the Venom Tongues attacked, just as you did. But I still have Zastar's children to watch out for. I could never just leave you and your brother."

"And that's why you won't revolt against, Saulder? Because of some sort of messed up loyalty to my father?"

"Because I consider you my sons just as much as you are his," Casavore exhaled and rose. "I understand your frustration, Sova. And I don't condone the acts of your brother. But I won't betray my dire."

"So, you won't do anything?" Sova gulped, his jaw clenching with anger. "You're just going to let him ruin people's lives?"

"I won't betray him, Sova."

Sova nodded. "Fine. I'll find someone that will," he shoved past the Blesser.

"Where are you going, Sova?"

"Out. I need to get away from this place for a night. If my brother asks, tell him I left with the evening patrol."

"Sova," Casavore called, making Sova stop halfway out the door. "Forgive him. Maybe not now. But one day, forgive him."

"Why, because the *Bible tells me so*?"

"The Apostle Peter once asked his master how many times he should forgive his brother. Christ said that he should forgive his brother as many as seventy times seven."

Sova scoffed and shook his head. "And you don't think Saulder has killed four hundred and ninety people?"

Sova closed the door behind him and rushed across the gardens. Hidden in the shadow of a palace wall, he looked from left to right to see if any witnesses were about him. When he knew he was alone, he withdrew the Blesser's stolen letter from his pocket.

"*Dear Casavore,*" he read under his breath. "*I know that my attempts to persuade you to the good fight have gone in vain. Still, I can't help but feel led to ask you again to join my ranks. I know your answer will be no, but still, I ask you. If you do come to your senses, please join us in the southern Mosharick villages, where we'll be staying till the winter. I do hope you will join us, Casavore. God Bless. Your friend, Oland...*"

Sova folded the letter back into his pocket then ran to the stables where he acquired a horse and cloak. Armed with steed and letter, he left for the Mosharick Plains. He finally found someone willing to join the good fight.

Chapter Seven: The Rebel's Letter

The Mosharick Plains...
   On the southern border of the Mosharick Plains, where the salty musk of Seavale's waves carried into the fresh Mosharick air, a tiny village stood in the center of a flat grove of dandelions. In the center of the village, red coals hissed into the ember dusk and lit the humble camp in amber light.

Five Blind Seers, followers of the Blind Hound, surrounded the flames. Among the rebels was a tall, handsome soldier, with sword-calloused hands he used to strike a stone against his sword. Sparks jumped off his blade, looking like tiny little spirts of lightning. The soldier's skin was light, and his tawny-brown hair, cropped. His eyes were captivating, like that of a dark blue sky just turning to dusk.

As he worked, a swarm of young, pretty, girls watched him from across the village, their cheeks pink with obsession as they giggled.

One of the soldiers leaned toward the handsome sword-brandisher, a jealous glint in his eye.

"Roeseph, my friend, how I envy you," he growled and looked to the girls.

The soldier, Roeseph, smirked as he sharpened his blade. "Don't be too hard on yourself, friend," he sighed. "One of these days, you'll trick a woman into falling for you."

Another soldier, a woman with chestnut brown hair, scoffed, "Not even the Blesser of Vaska could find that mongrel a woman."

Hardy laughter filled the quiet air, but Roeseph was silent. He wished he were somewhere else.

"Why the long face, Roeseph?" a soldier jeered.

Roeseph looked up from his sword. "Hmm, what?"

"Your face," the soldier chuckled. "You look like a pup left out in the cold. What's eating you?"

"Nothing," Roeseph shrugged. "I'm fine."

"What, are we boring you?"

"Yes," Roeseph taunted and struck the stone extra hard against his blade.

"Aww, are you upset because you weren't allowed to go to *Daddy's* war meeting?" another soldier pouted his lip. "Get over it. Only the generals were permitted to go anyway. We all had to miss it."

"Come on, Roeseph, enjoy yourself," another solder cut in. "It's a beautiful night. Go talk to one of those girls if you want. Have a good time."

Roeseph laughed and shook his head. "Not tonight. Maybe some other time."

As the young Blind Seers talked, a shadow rose from the dandelion grove beyond the light of the village. The fawns that grazed from the white plains fled at the shadow, provoking a snowfall of dandelion seeds in their wake.

Roeseph looked up from his sword, his dusk blue eyes narrowing on the shadow in the distance. A man in a black cloak approached from beyond the village's light, riding a magnificent chestnut stallion bred from the royal stables of Vaska. Roeseph stood, freshly sharpened sword in hand as his comrades silenced.

"Is Oland expecting anyone else?" one of them asked.

"No. He isn't," Roeseph growled. "Guard the village. I'll be right back."

SOVA HUNCHED FORWARD on his stolen steed. His back ached from the journey, and his stomach gnawed savagely at his organs.

Great Lykos, when does it end? He looked up from his horse, relieved to see the outline of a village in the distance. *Finally*, he exhaled and drove his steed forward. He was eager to reach the village and whatever comforting embrace awaited him. Maybe they'd even feed him.

"Casavore," Sova growled to himself. "The Blind Hound better be here, or I'll—"

Before Sova could finish his thought, his stallion reared back and whinnied into the autumn wind, launching him off his back before it galloped away.

Stupid horse, Sova groaned as he struggled to sit up in a dandelion blizzard.

Before he could wonder what could've frightened his horse, the sound of a blade sliced through air, and the winter-cold touch of a sword settled just beneath the bulge of his throat. The Vaskan prince froze and looked up the length of a sword to meet its wielder.

Roeseph glared down at the cloaked intruder, his deep blue eyes alive with sapphire flames.

"Nice sword you got there," Sova squeaked. "Vaskan steel or Seavallian iron?"

"Who are you?" Roeseph growled. "And why have you come here?"

"Well—" Sova gulped. "I—I'm a friend. I'm looking for the Blind Hound. You might know him as Oland?"

Roeseph glared at Sova. He pressed his sword deeper into the Vaskan intruder's neck, making him flinch.

"If you've come to hurt my father," Roeseph sneered, "then you've only asked for death."

"No—No," Sova stammered. "I didn't ask for that at all. I've actually come to seek your father's help."

"Why would my father ever help the likes of Vaskan scum like you?"

"Good question," Sova's eyes widened as he suddenly realized he had no plan. "Why would he help me?" *Why would he help me?* "Oh! I know."

Sova pulled Oland's letter from his cloak and handed it to the man holding him at knifepoint. Roeseph, with a cautious hand, unfolded the paper and scanned the letter.

"This is my father's hand," he mumbled as he withdrew his sword. He looked from the letter to the cloaked stranger, in awe of the pathetic man lying in the dandelion patch.

"You're the Blesser Casavore?" he whispered.

"Pardon?" Sova paused. *He thinks I'm Casavore?... Hmmm. He thinks I'm Casavore.*

Rubbing his throat, Sova thought to himself. There were consequences to pretending to be the Blesser. Almost every single one of them ended in death. Only a fool would act so thoughtlessly to give his life for such a pitiful lie.

"Yes," Sova replied with an ecstatic finger-gun.

Beyond the Mosharick village in the heart of a hill, laid a bunker composed of dirt walls and floors. Inside, Generals and high-ranking officials of the Blind Seers bickered around a wooden table where a single candle burned.

Oland sat at the end of the table, his brow flexed in a furrow, with his hands folded against pierced lips. Even with his ears bound in white gauze, his people's voices impaled the wraps like blades. For two hours, the war meeting waged. In that time, not a single soul offered a solution to winning the war.

One of the Blind Seers, a general from the western villages, stood from his seat.

"The dire was in the Mosharick Lands no more than two days ago," he cried. "He's onto us. Our best course of action is to retreat to Seavale and hide there until his wrath subsides."

Shouts of agreement and protest rose from the crowd. Oland's eyes closed and drew in a deep breath, his patience slowly reaching its climax.

A decorated warrior rose to protest her colleague. "We can't just turn around and run every time we think the dire is near," she spat. "We need to face this tyrant once and for all! Destroy his army and free all of Lykos!"

"How?" another voice rose. "The man faced a monster just a few days ago. A flying monster! Some even say a soldier of Heaven. And you expect us to fight him? You'd sooner see the Eradites come down from their high pedestal to join the fight!"

The crowd pressed closer around the table, barking in each other's faces like rabid, slobbering dogs.

I've had enough of this. Oland sneered and pounded his meaty fist down on the table, making the entire bunker shake. The Blind Seers fell to their chairs like a bunch of well-trained dogs—silent at the command of the Blind Hound.

"Are you all done bickering like children?" Oland asked sternly. None answered. "Very well then," Oland sighed and reclined in his chair. "While I don't agree with running away with our tails between our legs, we need to have an effective plan for attack rather than just wishing ourselves into the heart of Vaska. So, if anyone has an *actual* plan as to how we get near the dire, please, do speak up."

The bunker door opened, and frantic boots descended the stairs. All turned to the staircase to find Oland's only son, Roeseph.

"Father," he huffed.

"Roeseph," Oland began sternly. "I told you that you weren't permitted to attend this meeting."

"I know, Father," Roeseph swallowed and fell to his knee. "And I'd never deliberately disobey your orders if there wasn't something of great importance. An ally has come to join the fight. He seeks your council."

"And what ally do you speak of, Roeseph?"

"The Blesser of Vaska, sir. Casavore."

Muted gasps rose from the crowd like embers. After all those years, the Blesser had finally come to join their ranks. Oland was silent, his face blank. Gripping his sword, he rose from his chair.

"Take me to him."

SOVA LAID BENEATH THE shade of a lonesome tree, tormented by the emerald grass poking through his cloak. Staring at the night sky, he plucked at the dandelions and brought the fuzzy white domes to his lips to make yet another pointless wish born out of boredom.

"...Oh sure. Take your time," Sova grumbled as he blew into the fluffy weed. "Not like I traveled an entire day to get here... Wouldn't kill them to bring me something to eat either."

"Blesser Casavore!" Roeseph's voice rose from the hills.

Cas is here? Sova thought with a furrowed brow. *Oh, wait, that's me.*

Sova's head tilted against the grass to see two men approach from the black and green horizon. The man who held him at knifepoint, Roeseph, walked toward him with a massive, bald headed man whose ears were bound with white gauze.

Sova held his breath. *It's him. It's the Blind Hound. Look alive, Sova!* Sova leaped to his feet and drew his hood to hide his face. *What are the chances I can trick him too?*

Roeseph led his father to the imposter, eyes bright and cheery.

"See?" he smiled and looked back at his father. "I told you. I told you he was here."

Oland's gaze fell to Sova. His face was blank, and his eyes empty.

I'm going to die, Sova smiled.

"Roeseph. Would you please leave me and our guest to speak in private?" Oland asked with a gentle voice that bore a secret power, like a tsunami concealed in a still ocean.

Roeseph looked from the cloaked stranger to his father, a disappointed look on his face. "Are you sure? I would truly be honored to—"

"Thank you, Roeseph," Oland looked to his son. "That'll be all."

Roeseph stood there for a moment and looked from his father to Sova. Giving into his father's commands, he disappeared toward the village.

Take me with you, Sova begged.

"So," Sova clapped, feeling as small as a flea beside an elephant. "Long time no see, Oland. How's the wife?"

Oland's blank expression snapped into a sneer, and he grabbed Sova by the throat. Before Sova could gasp or pray, the Blind Hound had him pinned to the tree, rough bark stabbing through his cloak. Breathless, Sova kicked at the grass.

"Before you even think of reaching for that blasted bugle of yours,," Oland seethed, his head tilting to the side, "I'll snap your neck like a twig."

"I—I believe you," Sova rasped and motioned to the gauze around Oland's ears. "Can you hear me through those things by chance?" Oland thrust him harder against the tree. "I'll take that as a yes."

"In my lifetime, many Vaskan men have come to kill me," Oland growled. "But none have been so stupid as to approach my son."

"I wasn't going to hurt him. In fact," Sova paused to draw breath past Oland's hand. "I was the only one in serious danger. Man's a little too eager with a sword."

"Give me one good reason why I shouldn't kill you right now."

"I'm going to be honest. I'm drawing a blank here."

"Very well then—"

"I'm the dire's brother!" Sova spat.

Oland's brow furrowed. "That doesn't really help your situation, son," he growled and drew his sword. He pressed the cold steel to Sova's throat, making his captive flinch. "It just makes me want to kill you more."

"The dire thinks that I'm out on patrol. If I don't return in one piece, he'll come for this land—for this village."

"So, you came here just to deceive my son and threaten me with war?"

"No, I came here because I need help taking down my brother. And as far as I'm concerned, you're the only one willing to help."

Oland's eyes widened and he released the prince's throat. Sova fell to his knee, gasping over the grass.

"Quite a grip you have there, sir," he coughed as he rubbed his neck. "I think I saw my life flash before my eyes." Oland grabbed Sova by the back of his cloak and jerked him upright. "Oh," Sova gulped. "There it goes again."

"Why should I believe a thing you say? For all I know, this is a trap."

"I have the location of the Blind Hound and the Blind Seers," Sova defended. "Don't you think if I wanted to destroy you, I would've come with an army instead of by myself?"

"You could be a spy."

"And what a spy I would be, giving up my identity to the enemy."

"I should gut you right here. Vaskan filth like yourself can't be trusted."

"Cas trusts me," Sova reached into his cloak and drew Oland's letter. "And from what I've read, you trust him a great deal. I mean, asking the dire's most loyal follower to join your army. Very bold."

Oland snatched the letter from Sova's hand and threw him to the side.

"How did you get this?" Oland shook the paper in Sova's face.

"Cas gave it to me," Sova lied.

"He gave it to you?"

"Gave—stole, same thing," Sova shrugged and ripped the paper out of Oland's hand. "Look," he tucked the letter into his cloak. "I needed to find a way to overthrow the dire. Cas wasn't going to budge, so I took it upon myself to find allies. Allies being you."

"Why are you doing this? Why overthrow your brother? Is this a way for you to take the throne so an equally destructive dire can terrify Lykos?"

"Yeah, right," Sova chuckled. "I'd sooner jump from the Cliffs of Era than become dire after watching what it did to Saulder. I admit, dethroning the dire with no willing heir is a little risky, but it's better than letting him reign another day."

"Then why?" Oland challenged. "Why now? After all these years of watching your brother terrorize this entire Valley, what pushed you to betray your dire?"

Sova drew back his hood, revealing his guilt-ridden silver eyes to the moonlight.

"Did you hear about the Mosharick Village that got attacked several nights ago?" Sova sighed.

"Everyone has, but it's just a story."

"What do you know about it?"

"The dire came into the Mosharick Plains in search of the Blind Seers and happened upon a village that had been slaughtered by some large, mythical, flying white beast. He slayed the monster and left it to rot. But it's just more Vaskan propaganda to glorify their dire—"

"The white angel didn't kill those people," Sova interrupted. "Their chief, Chemon, his daughter was a Hyde Howler."

Oland's face softened with pity.

"Oh no..." he whispered beneath his breath.

"Saulder released her on her people. She killed everyone. Including her mother, father, brother."

"So, then what of this white beast?"

"It's real. Cas called it a soaring wolf—a beast of Era. It attacked Saulder after the girl slaughtered her people and disappeared."

"So that means there's an Eradite in Lykos?"

"Yeah—Yeah, we were all very shocked too. Now focus. Fact of the matter is, Saulder is injured and vulnerable. If the Blind Seers attack now, we might have a shot at defeating him."

"And how would you suppose I do that?"

"Call on every Blind Seer and ally willing to fight. Bring them to the sewer pipes that empty into the Vaskan forest. Follow upriver as far as it'll go. You'll come to a grate that leads beneath the palace. Not any sword or blade can cut through those bars, but if you have a guy on the inside—" Sova pointed his thumbs at himself, "—me—that has the keys to open the grate, you can walk straight into the palace where we'll ambush the dire and slay him in his bed."

"You would be willing to betray your kingdom?"

"I'd be saving my kingdom," Sova said. He stuck out his hand to the Blind Hound. "So, do we have a deal or not?"

Oland hesitated, and then throwing caution to the unpredictable wind, took the Vaskan prince's hand.

"If you're just leading my people into a trap—"

"I'm not," Sova shook his head. "I promise."

"Very well then," Oland stepped back. "I'll send word to our allies. We'll depart to Vaska in three days."

Oland turned and started back to his bunker, only for the Vaskan prince to stop him.

"I do have one condition if you and I are to go to war."

"And what's that?" Oland asked over his shoulder.

"Saulder is mine to kill."

Chapter Eight: A Son's Lament

The Kingdom of Vaska...

Three suns and three moons surrendered since the white angel's attack. While bedridden, Dire Saulder ordered Casavore to multiply the Hyde Howlers and send them out in search of the Rogue Eradite and its winged beast. Not one returned victorious.

The morning sun streamed in through the dire's balcony, throwing a golden blanket over the canopy bed where Saulder laid. He sat against a pillow with book in hand—the great histories of Vaska and all her dires.

Peace abandoned Saulder. Not even Casavore's powers could calm his soul. How could he be calm? There was an enemy out there. Not just an ordinary enemy, but an Eradite. If he didn't strike first, then there was no guarantee he'd live to see the next sunrise.

Saulder put his book in his lap, unable to focus. He exhaled and looked around. He was utterly alone, with only the dire's armor on a stand across the room to keep him company.

The dire hated being bedridden. He hated feeling vulnerable. He hated the image of himself lying, useless, and injured in bed, like his father. He would never become like that. He would sooner die than become that.

He glanced his long, ivory hair falling over his shoulders. He never cut his hair, for to cut his hair would be to cut a memory. Running his hand through his locks, he remembered a tender time before he held the dire's burden.

"Why do you let your hair get so long" a little girl's voice called from the depths of his memories.

"Because," a young Saulder replied, *"I want to be strong like Samson. Samson is strong because of his hair."*

"Samson wasn't strong because of his hair!"

"Yes, he was!"

"Nuh—uh!" The little girl argued back.

Saulder smirked, engrossed in the sweet memory.

"My daddy said Samson was strong because of God," the ghostly voice continued. *"Remember? Samson lost all his strength when his wife cut all his hair off. God gave him back his strength so he could defeat everyone!"*

"Then what happened?"

"Oh. He died."

Saulder chuckled and shook his head.

"You—You wouldn't—" the young Saulder gulped, *"you wouldn't try to cut my hair, would you, Feran?"*

"Hmmm. No, I wouldn't. Sova might, though."

"Yeah."

"Let's go chop off his hair instead!"

"Feran!"

"What? We won't get in trouble this time."

Saulder's fond smile sunk as he gripped his hair with white knuckles. Once upon a time, when he and his betrothed were children, Feran made a promise never to cut his hair, so he'd never lose his strength. But she broke her promise. She had taken his strength. For his strength died with her.

Before Saulder could linger in his isolated grief, Lore pushed open the doors and walked into the chamber with a triangular object wrapped in brown paper under her arm.

"Good morning, my dire," she smiled and shut the door. "You're looking much better."

Saulder exhaled, annoyed. "I ordered only Casavore could visit me. What are you doing here, Lore?"

"I had the carpenters make a gift for you. A weapon to take down the Rogue Eradite and his soaring wolf."

"I didn't ask you to do that."

"I know," Lore laid the object on the bed next to Saulder. "But let's face it. Swords and spears might not bode well against a flying monster. So, I had them make something special."

"What kind of special?" Saulder asked cautiously as he pulled the weapon into his lap.

"Oh, just a sort of bow and arrow. The carpenter told me it could fire as high as the Cliffs of Era. I thought you might want to equip the soldiers with them."

Saulder looked at his mother, not an ounce of gratitude in his eyes. "Leave me," he ordered.

Her face tensed in irritation, Lore started toward the door. "You know, dire," she began, halfway out. "While I was queen, I also served as wise council to your father. Perhaps I could be of help in—"

"You were queen because Casavore hypnotized Zastar to fall in love with you."

Lore went pale, and her Seavallian-blue eyes widened. "Oh come now, dire," she laughed. "You don't really believe those stories, do you? Your father and I were madly in love."

"Legends or not, I know my father. He would've never married you. A queen that manipulates her way onto the throne is only fit for treason. Now leave me before I lose my temper."

Lore took a nervous step back before disappearing out the door. Alone, Dire Saulder tore away the wrapping paper on the strange weapon. Brow raised, he lifted the object, examining the fine carpentry and slender arrow. He had never seen a finer crossbow.

BENEATH VASKA, A REBEL force marched through a dark labyrinth of sewage tunnels toward the dire's fortress, their torches casting their shadows to the walls. The Blind Hound led the pack toward their destination, Roeseph at his side, while the entirety of the Blind Seers followed.

They came to a rusty grate at the end of the tunnel where brown water flossed through the bottom bars. Oland huffed, his sweat sparkling in the torch's light

Roeseph looked up and down, perplexed by the roadblock. "Is this the place?" he asked, his voice rippling through the tunnel.

"This is the place," Oland sighed. "And now, the moment of truth." The Blind Hound placed his hands in the holes of the grate and gave it a light jiggle. The iron bars creaked then slowly opened. Oland smirked, his eyes flickering with delight. "Boys, we're in."

Roars of war-lust on their tongues, the Blind Seers tore by Oland and down the tunnel. Roeseph laid his hand on his sword, ready to launch himself into battle, only for Oland to grab him by the arm.

"Not you," he dismissed. "You're going to stand guard."

"S—Stand what?" Roeseph repeated. "You can't be serious."

"I am serious. If this goes south, I need you to secure our exit."

"Is this because of what happened with the Vaskan prince? Father, I said I was sorry. I know it was foolish to believe his words, but he had Casavore's letter. I would never intentionally endanger the Blind Seers. I never even saw the man's face—"

"I'm not punishing you, Roeseph," Oland silenced. "I'm ordering you to stand guard."

Roeseph's jaw clenched, and he looked away. Oland exhaled and laid his hand on his son's shoulder. "You're a very capable soldier, Roeseph. But I won't throw you into this battle. You've fought plenty for me."

"I'll fight again. I'll lay down my life for you, Father."

"I know you will," Oland grinned. "Now stand guard."

Before Roeseph could argue, Oland disappeared down the tunnel after his army, the slushing of his boots in the sewage growing fainter until he was swallowed by the darkness. Roeseph sighed and leaned back against the open grate.

"Great Lykos, it stinks in here."

IN THE HIGHEST TOWER of the Vaskan palace, Casavore sat at Zastar's bedside, the Holy Book open in his lap.

"*But Elymas the sorcerer opposed them and tried to turn the proconsul from the faith,*" Casavore recited from the book of Acts. "*Then Saul, who was also called Paul, filled with the Holy Spirit, looked straight at Elymas and said, 'You are a child of the devil and an enemy of everything that is right! You are full of all kinds of deceit and trickery. Will you never stop perverting the right ways of the Lord? Now the hand of the Lord is against you. You are going to be blind for a time, not even able to see the light of the sun.'..."*

Casavore looked to Zastar. He'd been reading to the old dire since sunrise, and still, Zastar remained motionless. Casavore sighed.

"Why don't we take a break, Zastar?" Casavore closed the Bible in his lap as he looked around. "Beautiful morning, huh?" A long moment of silence passed before the Blesser spoke again. "Saulder was doing better this morning. I checked his wounds yesterday. Everything looks like it's going to heal except for a scar right here," he said and traced a crescent-shaped scar in the center of his pectoral. "But it'll be a good story to tell the children one day."

Zastar coughed. His fit of sickness cut into Casavore's heart like a blade. He hated when his brother suffered. The storm inside Zastar's throat subsided, and he became motionless again.

"Sova got back yesterday morning," Casavore said, trying to smother the quake in his voice. "Ate everything in sight. You'd think he hadn't eaten in decades." At the end of a hollow chuckle, Casavore gulped and drew a ragged breath, "I'm worried for him, Zastar. For Saulder too. Those boys lost so much when you left... I—I lost so much when you left." Casavore gripped his medallion and rubbed his thumb back and forth across the sleek gold surface. "Sova's finally lost hope in his brother. And I'm going to be honest. It seems like with each passing day I feel my prayers are said in vain. I don't know what to do for him. I've asked to read to him or pray with him, but he turns me away every time..."

As Casavore lingered in his dread, a fond memory entered his mind.

"You know who could've gotten to him? Feran," he smiled, his eyes glittering like ice. "Man, she... She would've gotten through to him. Do you remember how those two would run around as babies? Feran was smaller and slower, but Saulder always waited for her to catch up. He was such a kind child. I can't say the same for my daughter," Casavore sniffled and shook his head. "Do—Do you remember how she used to torment, Sova?"

Zastar was silent.

"That poor boy couldn't catch a break. They were always fighting for Saulder's attention. Saulder did a pretty good job of including them both.

But man, those two fought like cats and dogs." Casavore ran his sleeve under his eye to intercept a tear. "I remember, when Feran was nine, I gave her a medallion like mine. What I didn't expect was for her to hypnotize Sova to pee his pants every time a rooster crowed."

Casavore hunched over as soft laughter rippled through his chest. "She called it, 'Peter's Punishment,'" he shook his head. "I was able to undo everything, but Sova was horrified of hypnotism after that. I've never seen my Fala so livid. But you have to admit. It was clever. Feran was very clever."

Zastar didn't so much as sigh with contentment. Casavore's smile sunk away, and grief consumed his eyes like a returning storm.

"Why do you stay this way?" he asked. "You've been like this for ten years. Ten years... Your wounds have healed, and yet you refuse to wake up. Your sons need you. I need you. I already lost my wife and daughter. You could do me the courtesy of giving me back my brother."

Silence filled the room like floodwaters. Casavore shook his head, hurt by Zastar's stillness. "What is keeping you like this?"

The chamber door opened. Casavore looked over his shoulder to find the Vaskan prince dressed in silver mesh with his helmet rested against his hip and a sword hanging from his belt.

"Sova," Casavore said, surprised, and wiped away his tears. "What brings you here?"

Sova swallowed hard. "I was looking for you, actually. I wanted to talk to you before I head out."

"Head out? You're going on another patrol?"

"Yeah," Sova lied through a nod. "Something like that."

Sova sat at Casavore's side and looked on his father's living corpse.

"I was just reading to him," Casavore sniffled as he opened his Bible. "You're welcome to sit with us if you'd like."

Sova looked from his father to the door. "I think I have time."

Casavore smiled and opened the Bible to where he left off. Before he could begin, he looked up from the scriptures to see pain dimming Prince Sova's once lively eyes.

"Sova?" he asked, his heart sinking. "Is everything ok?"

Sova exhaled. "I wanted to tell my father something, but..." he shook his head, "It feels kind of pointless if he can't hear me."

"You never know," Casavore shrugged. "Why don't you try?"

Sova sighed. Resting his elbows on his knees, he leaned forward.

"Hey, Pops," he said, uncertain. "So, um... I just wanted to say that I love you. And uh. Well, I miss you..." He looked to Casavore to see how well he was doing.

"Go on," Casavore encouraged.

"And well, I um—" Sova cleared his voice. "I didn't do a lot of things right. I let Saulder get worse. I watched a lot of people get hurt. And, well, I gave up on my brother. I really let you down..."

Casavore shook his head. "You didn't let anyone down, Sova."

"No, I did. I wasn't enough. If Feran would've survived the Venom Tongue attack, she could've done something different. But me—" Sova shook his head, his jaw clenched. "I can't save him."

"Sova," Casavore said. "that's not your burden to carry—"

"But I can save everyone else."

Casavore's brow furrowed as a coldness set into the room.

"What do you mean, Sova?" the Blesser asked nervously. "How are you going to save everyone?"

Sova looked at Casavore, his usual playful, silver eyes hollow, and his face, blank. For a moment, Sova looked exactly like Saulder—lost and consumed by hatred. It horrified the Blesser.

Before Casavore could interrogate the Vaskan prince, a soft roar grew within the palace. Casavore sat up. His chin turned over his shoulder and he stared out the chamber door. The walls trembled as the roar grew into a storm of war-bleeding cries.

Casavore snapped from where he sat. "What is that?"

"Don't know," Sova uttered as he rose from his father's bedside. "I'm sure it's nothing. Why don't you stay here with my father, and I'll check it out?"

"I think the palace is under attack," Casavore exhaled and gripped his medallion. "We need to warn, Saulder."

Before the Blesser could rush to defend the dire, Sova grabbed his arm. "Stay here, Casavore. I told you, I'm sure it's nothing."

Casavore looked back at Sova, horrified by the darkness in the prince's once pure eyes. "Sova..." Casavore whispered, "what have you done?"

Sova paused. Then, reaching into his cloak, withdrew a folded piece of paper tied in brown twine.

Casavore grabbed the letter from the prince's hand. "Where did you get this?"

Sova swallowed and looked to his father sleeping beneath the tomb-like covers of his bed.

"I'm sorry, Father," Sova whispered. "So that the innocent can live, your son must die."

Before Casavore could protest, Sova marched out of the chamber and drew his sword. Casavore ran after him, only for Sova to slam the door in his face and lock it.

"Sova!" Casavore pounded on the door. "Sova, open this door now!"

"I'm sorry, Cas," Sova called. "I told you. Saulder needs to be stopped."

"Sova, this is madness! Open the door right now!"

Casavore could hear Sova's steps grow fainter as he disappeared down the stairwell.

"Sova!" Casavore yelled. As he beat at the door, Zastar lay on his bed behind him, still as a corpse. A single tear fell from the old dire's eye—proof he heard Sova's promise. One of his sons was to die.

Chapter Nine: The Garden

The Blind Seers fled the sewage tunnels beneath the palace, and like a deadly plague, swept through the royal fortress. Each Vaskan soldier they met, they struck down, their cries of war like a thunder's roar. Oland led his troops through the palace and into the gardens to where a battalion of Vaskan guards waited, and met them head-on.

Blood doused the once white roses, and a shadow of death passed over the gentle Vaskan morning like a storm cloud. Blind Seer and Vaskan souls alike departed to the heavens, lost to an enemy's blade as their screams echoed through the kingdom.

Sword in hand and face dappled with scarlet rain, Oland butchered every Vaskan enemy within reach, tearing through battle like a sweeping wind. He was standing over the corpse of a Vaskan guard when a dark presence plunged a chill down his spine. Drawing his sword from his victim, Oland looked to the balcony overlooking the gardens to see the dire dressed in his night-black armor looking down on them.

"Dire Saulder..." the Blind Hound growled.

"*Hound*!" the dire shouted, the blood-lust in his stormy silver eyes shining in his helmet. "Surrender, or you and your Blind Seers will be slaughtered!"

"Come down here and face me, you coward!" Oland threatened. "Or do you fear I might have a worse bite than that flying white dog who bested you?"

Saulder's black gloves clasped the railing, and his glare intensified into silver flames as he looked to a Vaskan soldier fighting on the garden's edge.

"Lieutenant Arison!" Saulder shouted. The soldier stopped and he looked to his dire with the same amethyst eyes as his mother. "Release the prisoners from the dungeon and send them to the gardens."

"But, sir!" the lieutenant protested.

"Do it, or I'll have your head!"

Upon hearing the dire's threat, the lieutenant fled. Saulder then reached into his belt and drew a curved bugle horn. Oland's eyes widened, and his brave expression sunk. As the dire raised the bugle to his lips, Oland dropped to his knee and covered his hands over his gauze-wrapped ears.

"This can't happen," he whispered. "Not today."

A song like a wolf's howl trapped in a thunderstorm oozed from the bugle and swept through the sky like a winter's wind. Oland held his hands tightly to his ears so only soundless bells rang in his head as the lonesome howl of the Siren's Call faded into an echo. Slowly, Oland peeled his shaking hands from his ears and looked around. He was still himself. The Hyde Howler's curse had failed.

Oland cackled and looked to the dire on his balcony.

"Is that the best you can do?" he taunted.

The marching of heavy boots pulsed through the ground, trembling the blood-splattered roses. Oland's smirk sunk and he turned to see skeleton-like men and women march toward the battle in perfect sync, the song of their broken shackles chiming in their wake. The zombified prisoners stopped at the edge of the blood splattered garden, awaiting their call to kill.

"No," Oland whispered. Before him stood an entire dungeon's worth of Hyde Howlers.

"Hyde Howlers!" the dire roared. Every Hyde Howler's gaze snapped to the balcony. "I, your dire, order you to slay every Blind Seer in sight, as well as any man or woman who tries to stop you. Those who surrender, throw in the dungeon. Otherwise, slaughter them all."

The Hyde Howlers rushed the battle like a tidal wave.

AS THE DIRE WATCHED from his balcony, a sick smirk on his lips, his chamber door creaked open, and a shadow crept across the floor. Dire

Saulder turned from the balcony to see his brother in the doorway, sword in hand and dressed in silver armor.

"Sova!" Saulder snapped. "What are you doing here? Your brothers are dying out there. Go and fight for your kingdom!"

"Oh," Sova seethed, a sort of malice in his usual mischievous tone. "I intend to." He locked the door behind him.

Saulder glared at his brother. "Sova, I've been patient with you despite your constant refusal to follow orders. But I won't ask again. Go down there and defend your kingdom."

Sova looked to the ceiling as if he were lost in thought, his jaw swinging to the side. "Hmmm," he hummed. "Nah."

"It isn't your decision to make, Sova," Saulder warned. "Go down there, or you'll spend the night in the dungeon."

"Seems like a fitting punishment," Sova shrugged as he paced. "You know, since I'm the one who let the Blind Seers in."

Saulder's eyes darkened, the blade of betrayal twisting in his heart. "Why?" he growled lowly, his voice like distant thunder.

"Why?" Sova scoffed. "Wouldn't you rather know how? I really wanted to believe Casavore, Saulder. I really did. But he was wrong to think that there was much of a man left inside that armor of yours. My notion was confirmed when you ordered that poor Mosharick girl to annihilate her village. So, I sought to find Oland. Turns out our dear Blesser and the Blind Hound are pen pals," Sova chuckled. "I guess Casavore isn't as loyal as you thought."

Saulder's teeth gritted in a snarl.

Sova smirked at his brother and continued, "Don't worry, Saulder. Casavore never intended to betray you. I asked him myself if he would help take you down, but he refused. It seems the man is still sworn to his delusions. So, pretending to be the Blesser, I was able to track down Oland and the Blind Seers. Met Oland's son, by the way. Roeseph. Nice guy—a bit of a golden boy, though—you know the type. His father, on the other hand—a bit intense. But, anyway. I helped devise a plan to break into the palace, and in turn, Oland would see the dire fall, and I—" Sova shook his head, smirking. "I would get to make sure you get all that was coming to you."

"Why would you do this?" Saulder snarled. "Why?"

"Because," Sova began, his voice no longer taunting. "My brother is gone. Has been for ten years. I'm done playing pretend like Casavore. I won't stand idly by saying my prayers and hoping for the best while you destroy innocent people's lives."

"So," Saulder grumbled as he drew in a sharp breath through his helmet. "You and the Blesser have been conspiring against me all along? Who knew Lore's suspicions of Casavore were true?"

"Cas had nothing to do with this. He turned me away when I suggested rising against you," Sova drew his sword. "This was all me."

Saulder eyed his brother's blade. "Surrender, Sova," he warned. "I will not tolerate mutiny."

Sova chuckled. "Good. I wouldn't expect you to."

The dire drew his sword, the sun reflecting in the blade panning across Sova's smirk. Like a pair of lions, the brothers lunged at each other.

IN THE TALLEST TOWER in the Vaskan palace the Blesser worked to free himself from his prison. With the strength of a bull, Casavore threw a stool at the chamber door. The wooden seat shattered on impact and crumbled into a pile of timber. Casavore screamed in frustration and threw himself shoulder-first into the door repeatedly until his shoulder blackened with bruises.

"I'm in here!" he roared into the emptiness beyond the door. "I'm the Blesser! Let me out!"

Casavore slammed his fists against the door like a toddler mid-tantrum before pressing his back to the wood and sliding to the floor.

"You know," he huffed at Zastar. "I could use a little help here!"

Zastar laid motionless in his bed, silent.

As Casavore contemplated attacking a man in a coma, the chamber door flung open, and he tumbled back. Just as soon as the door opened, it slammed shut right into his head, making him curse and rub his skull. Lore locked the door and backed away, her sea-blue eyes wide with fear. Her violet dress was wrinkled from a sweaty run. Her neat, ivory hair frizzed into a tumbleweed. And her ruby-red lips were smudged across its copper canvas.

"Lore," Casavore said, for the first time in his life, relieved to see the twisted queen. "What's happening out there?"

"They're—They're killing each other," Lore gasped as she stumbled toward Zastar's bed and slumped down beside him. "The Blind Seers are here. The dire released the Hyde Howlers on them, but I'm not sure we'll be able to withstand them much longer."

Sova, what have you done? "Where is Saulder? Did he join his troops?"

"No," Lore gulped. "Saulder's still locked up in his room. I passed Sova in the halls. He was on his way to protect him."

Casavore's heart stooped to the depths of the earth, and a mortified breath shattered over his lips.

"My Lykos, he's going to kill him," he whispered, clutching his medallion. "Sova's going to kill Saulder."

Lore's eyes narrowed. "What did you say?... Is—Is Sova to blame for all of this?"

"Stay here," Casavore ordered and charged the door.

"Casavore, don't be stupid! If you go out there, you'll be killed!"

"I won't be killed."

"How do you know?"

"Oland is my friend. He won't let the Blind Seers hurt me. And I need to get to Saulder before it's too late."

Lore's jaw dropped to the floor, shocked, as Casavore fled out of the chamber and rushed down the twisting staircase.

INSIDE THE DIRE'S CHAMBERS, a battle waged between blood. Sova and Saulder circled one another, bruises and cuts coating their skin while silver fire flickered in their death-yearning eyes. Both lost their helmets in the fight, leaving their throats vulnerable to the other's blade.

"You were a prince of Vaska," Saulder growled. "A respected and trusted royal to this kingdom. And you just threw it all away."

"Because I care for my kingdom," Sova fired back. "I won't let you hold my people hostage any longer."

Sova lashed his sword at his brother, only for the dire to catch it against his own.

"I'm the one holding them hostage?" Saulder hissed, his breath fogging the blade between them. "You brought Vaska's greatest enemies into the palace. You're a traitor to your nation!"

"No," Sova shook his head. "I'm its savior!"

Sova punched Saulder in his injured shoulder, making the dire roar and stumble back. Cradling his shoulder, Saulder looked up to see Sova dive at him with the ferocity of a lion. Saulder caught his brother by the wrist, causing the prince to drop his sword, and slammed his fist into Sova's stomach.

Sova gasped airlessly and curled into a ball next to his sword. Jaws bared, Saulder grabbed Sova by the ankle and dragged him to the far side of the room. Sova clawed at the stone floor, desperate to reach his sword growing further away.

Saulder dropped his brother's leg and kicked him in the stomach, making Sova cough and gasp with each brutal attack.

"How could you turn your back on Vaska?" Saulder shouted between kicks, his long ivory locks lashing wildly.

Sova gasped in pain. Unable to answer.

"How could you turn on your dire?" Saulder roared. "How could you betray our father? How could you betray me, your brother?"

"How could *you*?" Sova managed to yell. "Since Feran died, you've become a completely different person. You're a tyrant. And you've only gotten worse. Becoming the dire changed you. You used to be so kind, so merciful. I wanted to be just like you. Everyone was so proud of you and eagerly awaited the day you'd surpass our father. Instead, you've become a monster. What would Feran say if she saw you like this?"

Saulder roared out in rage-masked agony and kicked Sova square in his jaw, sending Sova flying across the floor and into the wall. He laid motionless.

"Feran isn't here," Saulder exhaled through heavy breaths as he turned from his brother and marched to his bed.

Sova groaned and looked through the bulge of his black eye to see Saulder grab a crossbow from his bed—the wolf-killer Lore gifted him.

"Enough is enough," Saulder growled and loaded an arrow into the crossbow. "The Blind Hound dies today."

"N—No," Sova sputtered past his busted lip. As he shakily rose to his hands and knees, Saulder stomped his heel down on Sova's back, pinning him to the floor. His grimace cold against the floor Sova glared up at his brother with eyes of loathing.

"I hate you," he hissed.

"Stay down," Saulder ordered and started toward the balcony. Standing against the railing, he stared into his battle-plagued garden. Oland stood in the center, chopping down Vaskan guards and Hyde Howlers alike with each swing of his sword, unaware of Dire Saulder raising his crossbow to his gauze-wrapped head.

Sova shakily rose to unstable feet and looked up to see his brother take aim. Eyes wide, he picked up his sword and lunged. "Leave them alone!"

Dire Saulder looked back, his eyes wide with alarm as Casavore burst the chamber doors.

"No!" the Blesser screamed.

In that moment, an arrow was fired, a sword drew blood, and everything went black.

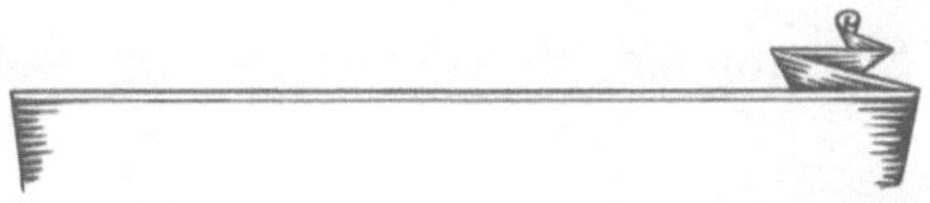

Chapter Ten: The Royal Traitor

"*Sova! Sova, can you hear me? Sova? Sova?*" Casavore's voice faded in the wind like a distant drum, almost unheard. Sova grew cold as an unearthly chill coiled his body.

Where am I? he asked himself as he opened his eyes. The world around him was black. There was no horizon, no shadows of life—just blackness—and yet, despite there being no sun nor candle, the abyss was unusually bright.

Is this Hell? Sova thought. *Nah. Nah I'm too likeable for Hell.*

"Hello?" Sova called, his voice carrying on for eternity. "Casavore? Are you there?"

From the eerie silence of the bright darkness, the sound of a sword being drawn from its sheath lashed through the void. The Vaskan prince turned around to find the dire dressed in his black armor a distance away, sword in hand.

Sova exhaled with relief, for once, happy to see his tyrannical brother. He wasn't alone.

"Saulder. Thank Lykos. Do you know where we are?"

The dire's eyes scorched his brother through the holes of his helmet like silver coals.

"Saulder?" Sova said, unsettled by his silence.

"Who are you?" the dire asked in a voice that wasn't Saulder's. It was dark, layered, in a word, demonic.

Sova's head cocked back, confused by what his brother had said. "What do you mean? It's me. Sova."

"Who are you?" the dire asked again. Louder. Fiercer.

"Your brother," Sova replied, his stomach sinking. "Saulder, what's wrong with you?"

"Who are you?"

Before Sova could repeat himself, the dark armored dire charged him like a rabid bull. Sova fell to the ground, his eyes widening as the dire pounced.

SOVA WOKE WITH A GASP, the stole floor cold against his back as he stared at the Dire Saulder's ceiling. Warm blood flowed down his face from a notch in his brow, cut by the dire's blade. He blinked, unsure where he was.

What's going on? He thought. *What happened?*

"Sova?" The Blesser's voice rang. "Sova, can you hear me?"

Sova winced at Casavore's gentle voice, his head aching as if someone had taken a mallet to his skull.

"Yeah," he croaked. "I can hear you. Could you lower your voice, please?"

"Do you remember what happened?" Casavore asked, a sense of urgency in his voice.

"Not really," Sova grumbled and lightly touched the cut in his eyebrow. "Actually, everything's kind of scattered. When's my birthday again?"

Casavore gulped, a fear like no other blazing in his eyes. "You—You hit your head when you were fighting S—" he paused to swallow. "S—Saulder. You might've forgotten a few things, but it should all come back."

"Saulder..." Sova's stomach rolled as he remembered his fight with the dire. He sat up fast and became dizzy. "Where—Where is he? Where's the dire?"

"Gone," Casavore eased, and supported his hand against Sova's back. "After—After you went down, he left. He ordered me to keep an eye on you."

Sova groaned with pain. He looked to his shoulder, surprised to find it wrapped in fresh, white gauze. "What happened there?"

"Saulder shot you," Casavore answered.

"He what?" Sova squeaked. "Why—Why don't I feel anything?"

"I hypnotized you, so the pain wasn't too unbearable."

"Well, thanks," Sova said as he struggled to his feet. Casavore stood up with him, holding him by the arm to keep him steady.

"Try not to push yourself, son."

"I—I need to find, Saulder. I need to end this."

"Sova, you can't. You can't beat him."

"I can. Now we're both injured. I've evened the playing field."

"Sova."

"This was my intention all along—"

"Sova," Casavore stepped in front of the prince. "Saulder is probably in the protection of his guards by now. You won't get near him."

"So now the dire hides from a fight," Sova scoffed and shook his head. "Coward."

Casavore swallowed hard, his eyes twinkling with tears. "Sova..." he gulped, unable to bring himself to speak. "I hereby banish you from the Kingdom of Vaska."

"Pardon?" Sova arched an eyebrow.

"You attacked the dire," Casavore shuddered. "Mutiny won't be tolerated in Vaska."

Sova shook his head, his jaw swinging to the side. "Playing favorites, are we, Cas? Still upset I read your private letters?"

"I'm trying to help you, Sova," Casavore said. "Saulder may be your brother, but he won't forgive what you've done. You'd be lucky to live the rest of your days in the dungeon, but—"

"He's going to have me executed, isn't he?"

Casavore's bearded chin trembled, and a single tear fell down his cheek.

"He told me himself," the Blesser sniffled. "'*I want to watch the Royal Traitor bleed.*'"

"Royal Traitor," Sova smirked, trying to hide the sorrow in his eyes. "Has a nice ring to it."

"You need to run, Sova. I can't save you this time."

"I'm not going to run from him—"

"You will, or I'll make you," Casavore hissed and clutched his medallion. Sova took a nervous step back, frightened by the viciousness in the Blesser's tone.

"C—Cas," Sova whispered, the fear of his voice splitting the heart within the Blesser's eyes in two.

"Please, Sova. I've lost..." Casavore paused. "I've lost *everyone*. Let me save you."

"I—" Sova paused and looked from the Blesser to the door. "Where will I go?"

"Go to the forest and stay there. I'll come for you when all is safe."

"C—Can't you just come with me?"

"I can't."

Sova took a step back, his heart aching. "After all he's done," Sova shook his head in disbelief, "you still remain at that monster's side. After all the people's he's killed—after he tried to kill me!"

Casavore grabbed Sova by his head, forcing him to meet his eyes.

"I'm doing this to save you, Sova!" the Blesser sneered as tears like hail tumbled down his face. "There's something I need to take care of. Otherwise, you'll never be safe. Now please... go."

Sova swallowed hard, his eyes stinging with threat of tears. Casavore snapped Sova into his arms and hugged him tightly.

"Why would you do it?..." he sobbed through gritted teeth. "How could you?"

Sova's heart sunk as guilt like an anvil crushed his spirit. He didn't regret challenging the dire. But he hated hurting the Blesser—a man who was as much a father to him as Zastar.

Pulling away, Casavore took his medallion from his neck and handed it to Sova. "Take this," he ordered. "I'll come back for you when all is safe."

"Cas, I can't take this."

"Please. It isn't safe here with the dire."

Sova looked from the gold medallion to the Blesser. Casavore suddenly looked like a lion without a mane. Incomplete.

"You have to promise you'll come back for it," Sova pushed.

"I will," Casavore nodded and wrapped his cloak around the Royal Traitor. "Now go."

Sova charged past the Blesser and toward the chamber door.

"Sova, wait!" Casavore called. Sova stopped midway out the door and looked back. "The scar on your shoulder..." Casavore continued. "Never show it to anyone. Lest they figure out who you are. You'll be an enemy to Vaska come morning."

Sova looked at his shoulder, fearing the scar beneath the gauze. "I won't, Cas."

Placing the medallion around his neck, Sova ran out of the chamber and shot through the Palace.

Casavore was left alone in the dire's chamber with only his grief to comfort him. He looked at the floor, where a bloodstain streaked across the floor toward the dire's bed. Underneath the bed laid a secret wrapped in a blood-soaked comforter, a secret that would destroy Vaska.

"What have I done?" Casavore trembled as he dropped to his knees. "What have I done?..."

ROESEPH WAITED IN THE darkness of the sewage tunnels with his back against the slime-covered walls. He sighed, the shrill sound of his breath echoing through the tunnel.

He looked left, then right, anxious for the return of his father and troops.

What's taking them so long? He wondered. *Why haven't they come back?*

The sound of feet sloshing through the sewage blared through the tunnel. Roeseph leaned away from the wall and looked down the murky labyrinth. Before he could draw his sword, a cloaked, medallion-wearing man charged toward.

"Look out!" the man shouted. Barreling into Roeseph, the two fell to the gruesome sludge.

Roeseph and the medallion wearer coughed, disgusted by the oozing sewage on their skin.

"It got in my mouth," the medallion wearer gagged. "Oh, great Lykos, it got in my mouth."

Roeseph grabbed the man by the back of his cloak and threw him against the sewage tunnel. The stranger's hood fell, revealing the silver eyes, and white hair of the Vaskan prince.

"You..." Roeseph growled.

"You," Sova replied in an awkward, chipper voice. "I'm going to be honest... I have no idea who you are."

"You tricked me into thinking you were the Blesser and manipulated me into bringing you to my father."

"Uh huh," Sova nodded. "Look, I just really hurt my head trying to kill my brother in a sword fight. You know how brothers do. And I'm having trouble remembering some things. But it was nice seeing you again."

Sova tried to push past, only for Roeseph to shove him back.

"Or I can stay here," Sova surrendered with a straight-lined grin.

"Where do you think you're going?" Roeseph growled. "You can't abandon the fight you brought my father and my brothers into."

"Well, that's what I'm doing."

"You coward," Roeseph reached for his sword.

"Wait—Wait—Wait, I have to!" Sova screeched and held up the Blesser's medallion for Roeseph to see. "Casavore told me to get this thing as far away from Vaska as I can."

"Why would the Blesser give up his medallion to the likes of you?"

"Because we're losing. The dire's wrath has only been provoked further, and he's going to do everything in his power to get a hold of this. If he gets it, not the Mosharick Plains, nor Seavale, nor Vaska will know peace."

Roeseph's heart sunk and the rage in his dusk-blue eyes subsided. "We—We're losing?" he gulped.

"Yes. Badly."

Roeseph looked down the tunnel to where his father and the troops had disappeared, a fear as cold as a winter sun rapturing his heart. "I have to help him," he gasped and lunged forward.

Sova grabbed Roeseph by the wrist. "Not a good idea, fella."

"Let me go," Roeseph hissed.

"The dire released his entire guard and Hyde Howlers on the Blind Seers. There's no way they're coming out of this. Going in there is suicide."

"Then I'll die saving them," Roeseph argued.

"If you want to save them, help me get this medallion as far away from Vaska as possible."

Roeseph gulped and looked down the tunnel. "I—I can't abandon him."

"If you leave with me, Casavore can help us. He can free them, but only if his medallion is kept as far away from the dire as we can get it."

Roeseph looked at Sova. "If we go, you have to promise we'll come back for them."

"Of course, we're coming back," Sova smirked. "My brother shot me in the shoulder. I'm not going to stop until I have his head on a stick. But we have to go now before the guards come for us."

Roeseph's heart wailed. He wished his father would return.

"Fine," he grumbled through gritted teeth. "Fine. Let's go."

Roeseph and Sova shot down the tunnel, the splash of their boots filling the echo-prone labyrinth of sewage. From that moment forward, they would be known as the *Last Soldier* and the *Royal Traitor*.

OLAND STOOD IN THE center of the blood-soaked gardens, sword and arm drenched in red. One by one, his soldiers either surrendered to the dungeons or to death. Oland's heart broke for them. Had he not allowed his pride and ambition to cloud his judgment, he would've realized they'd fought a battle destined to be lost.

The stench of smoke suddenly clogged Oland's nostrils and he looked to the dire's balcony where pillars of black clouds rose from within the chamber.

What is going on? he thought as the smoke eclipsed the sun.

Knowing fully well the battle was lost, Oland fled the gardens and rushed into the palace toward the dire's chamber. Successfully evading the guards, he threw himself through the dire's chamber door. He froze, alarmed by what he saw.

Casavore knelt before a rolled-up blanket set ablaze and burning in the center of the room. Crystal tears rolled down the Blesser's blank expression, leaving clean lines through the ash of his cheeks.

"Cas—Casavore?" Oland stammered. "What are you doing?"

Casavore looked away from the fire. "Oland..." the Blesser whispered. "I've done something awful."

"What—What did you do?"

Casavore's throat flexed, and his tongue knotted. He could barely bring himself to speak. "...I—"

Before the Blesser could answer, a hoard of Vaskan soldiers invaded the chamber like a stampede of wild bulls. They brought Oland to his knees and shackled his wrists behind his back. They bound the Blesser next, and threw him to the floor beside the Blind Hound.

"What are you idiots doing?" Oland spat. "How dare you disrespect the Blesser of Vaska like that? He outranks you!"

"Not anymore, he doesn't," a voice like smooth acid oozed into the room. Oland and Casavore looked up. Lore strode into the chamber, accompanied by a Vaskan soldier. She grinned, amused by Oland and Casavore's powerlessness.

"What is the meaning of this, Lore?" Casavore growled.

"You are under arrest for mutiny and conspiracy against Vaska."

Oland lunged, only for a Vaskan soldier to force him down. "The Blesser is innocent," he seethed. "He had nothing to do with this!"

"Oh, he didn't?" Lore smirked as she drew the Blind Hound's letter from her breast and waved it before the crowd. "Evidence proving the Blesser has been scheming with the Blind Seers."

Casavore glared at Lore, his face wrenched in a scowl.

"Do you have anything to say for yourself, dear Blesser?" Lore taunted with a smile.

"You won't win, Lore," Casavore said. "He's gone with the medallion. And he'll be back to take what is his."

Lore shook her head and clicked her tongue, unamused.

"We'll see what the dire has to say about that." She looked to the soldiers. "Place them both in the dungeon and keep them there until the dire calls upon them."

The soldiers forced Oland and Casavore up from where they knelt and led them out the door. The Blesser looked over his shoulder at the fire burning the blanket and the secret it held to ash. All evidence was gone, lost to the flames. At last, the Royal Traitor was safe.

"Zastar," Casavore whispered. "Forgive me..."

Chapter Eleven: The Town of Sinners

The Vaskan Forest...

A month had passed since the Blind Seer attack. Legend of the Royal Traitor and the Last Soldier's escape spread through the Great Valley of Lykos like a winter frost. In their refuge, the dire decreed the two runaways enemies of the crown. Besides the Rogue Eradite, Roeseph and Sova were the most wanted individuals in the Valley of Lykos.

Roeseph and Sova made camp beside a gentle stream locked in ice. While Roeseph sat beside the frozen stream, Sova curled up in his igloo, asleep. Sova shivered, both because of the cold and because a familiar enemy had returned to visit his dreams.

An unearthly cold overcame Sova and he and opened his eyes to find himself in the same colorless abyss.

Not this again, he groaned.

"Who are you?" came the dire's demonic voice, making Sova lash around to face him.

"You again?" Sova snapped, taking a nervous step back. "What do you want?"

"Who are you?" the dire snarled once more, his blade scraping the floor.

"Let me out of here! I don't want anything to do with you!"

"Who are you?" the dire charged and raised his sword.

Just as the blade descended the Royal Traitor, Sova woke. He gasped, lashed upright, and slammed his head into the icy ceiling. He cursed and fell back, rubbing his bruising forehead.

"You're having a nightmare again," Roeseph called from outside, unphased.

Sova glared into the golden light beyond the igloo's exit.

"Thanks for waking me up," he grumbled as he crawled out of the igloo, the Blesser's medallion around his neck shining in the light of the snow-covered forest. "I appreciate it." Sova drew in a deep breath, his lungs swelling with the mint-chilled air of a newborn winter. "Good morning, Roe."

Roeseph sat beside the frozen brook, his elbows rested on his knees as he stared out into nothing. He sighed, annoyed by Sova's presence.

"My name's not *Roe*, Sova. It's Roeseph."

"For sure, Roe." Sova looked around the peaceful winter forest, content with the alliance between the chilly breeze and the warm sun. He glanced down to see the gauze on his shoulder had scuffed and fell off his skin in coils.

Great, Sova growled. "Hey, Roe—"

"Name's not *Roe*."

"Well anyway, Roe. Can you help me re-do my bandages again?"

"Can't you do them yourself?" Roeseph exhaled and looked over his shoulder. "You're a grown man."

"But no one does them like you," Sova pouted, batting his lashes.

Roeseph grimaced, "You disgust me."

"Aww, thanks, bud," Sova smiled and sat beside Roeseph.

Giving a sigh, the Last Soldier began to unwind the gauze from the Royal Traitor's shoulder. Sova looked to the sky, unable to stomach the sight of his wound. After a month of being on the run, and word of his infamous scar reaching all four corners of Lykos, Sova had yet to see his scar.

Roeseph looked at his partner in exile. "Why don't you learn how to do it yourself?"

"Hmm?" Sova looked down, careful not to glance at the wound.

"Why don't you learn how to dress your bandages yourself?" Roeseph asked as he readjusted the gauze.

"Because what else would we bond over?"

"I'm being serious, Sova."

The Royal Traitor's mischievous defense faltered, and he looked back to the sky.

"I don't want to remember what my brother did to me," he admitted. "I don't remember a whole lot of the fight between Saulder and I, and I'd prefer to keep it that way. I already have the nightmares going for me. I don't need anything else to remind me how much of a monster the dire is."

Roeseph looked up from his work, his dusk-blue eyes filled with sympathy.

"Besides," Sova continued. "People don't really have the kindest of feelings toward the *Royal Traitor* of Vaska, and the scar might give me away. Casavore said it was safer if no one saw it. I might as well not see it either."

"Fair enough," Roeseph shrugged.

"So, what does it look like?" Sova asked giddily. "Robust? Tough?"

"Ugly. Really ugly. It doesn't even look you got shot with an arrow."

"Aw, you've hurt my feelings," Sova pouted. "You should be grateful. You're the only man in Lykos to have seen the legendary scar of the Royal Traitor."

"Believe me, it's no honor," Roeseph rolled his eyes and fixed the last of Sova's gauze. "But those old wraps won't hold long. We'll have to go back into town to get some new ones."

Sova fell against the snow, sending up a wave of white powder, and stared at the crisp blue sky. "So, what's got you down? You look more depressing than usual."

Roeseph glared at Sova.

"I mean that in the nicest way, of course," Sova winked.

"Of all the people I had to be exiled with... Why you?"

"God wanted to bless you I guess," Sova smiled. "But seriously, what's got you down?"

Roeseph sighed and looked across the ice-coated brook, his face sinking slightly. "I'm worried for my father. I don't know what's happening to him or if he even survived the battle."

"Oland's fine," Sova said as he played with the Blesser's medallion hanging from his neck. "Casavore wouldn't let anything bad happen to him."

"Casavore is just as much a prisoner as my father, Sova."

"That's not true—"

"Isn't it? Your Blesser was receiving letters from the Blind Hound. He helped the Royal Traitor escape. And he gave away his medallion to repress the dire's authority. What do you think happened to him?"

Sova sat up, a heavy stone plopping into his gut. He hated to admit it, but Roeseph was right.

"Face it, Sova," Roeseph grumbled and looked back to the frozen stream. "The Blesser isn't coming for us. And my father's been abandoned again."

Sova straightened and raised an eyebrow. "Again?" he asked. "What do you mean, again?"

"It's private."

"Private? Private! I trusted you with my secret scar, Roe. I'm hurt."

"My name's not R—"

"It is now, so shut up and tell me things." Sova scooted as close to Roeseph as he could get, his eyes wide and provoking.

Roeseph shook his head and looked up to the sky as if to glare down God for the curse he'd set upon him in the form of Sova.

"When my father—" Roeseph paused to swallow a lump in his throat. "When my father left for Vaska to free Fala, the Blesser's wife, he left my mother expecting their first child."

Sova gasped. "Was it you?" Roeseph glared at him, annoyed. "Sorry. Continue."

"After Casavore helped my father escape from his imprisonment, my father returned home as a dormant Hyde Howler. My mother left us both when I was just a few days old. She couldn't take being married to a Hyde Howler. No one has seen her since."

"She abandoned you?" Sova asked, his voice no longer taunting.

"No. I wasn't abandoned. She's no more my mother than you are. I care nothing of her. But she was my father's love, and when she left, she hurt him. Every now and then, I catch my father lost in his own world thinking about her. Sometimes, he'll tell me how much I remind him of her. He means it as a compliment, but it infuriates me more than anything else. I'm nothing like her. I would never abandon him—and yet..."

Roeseph's voice faded, clotted by the threat of tears.

"You didn't abandon him, Roe," Sova assured. "You were saving Lykos."

"Didn't I?" Roeseph scoffed. "Casavore and Oland are probably sharing a cell in the dire's dungeon. There's no hope for my father and my troops. No hope to destroy the dire."

"No hope, huh?" Sova sighed. "What a little ray of sunshine you are."

"What made your brother like this?" Roeseph asked. "How could a man become such a horrible, disgusting, evil—" Roeseph stopped in his rant and turned to find Sova staring at the clouds, a forlorn glint in his silver eyes. "Sorry, I didn't mean—"

"No, it's alright," Sova smirked sadly. "I'm aware of what my brother is. He's a monster, you can say it. I say it," he drew a deep breath. "Funny thing was he didn't use to be that way. Once upon a time, before he was the dire, he was just Saulder. My older brother. Man, he was probably the most noble kid I ever knew. Funny as the Cliffs of Era are tall too. He was my hero. I couldn't wait for the day he finally became the dire."

"What happened?"

Sova paused and his jaw cocked to the side. "Feran happened. You probably know her from the legends as the Dire's Damsel. Man, people really like to romanticize her death and make her seem like a little angel. And she was an angel, in the same way Satan was an angel."

Roeseph snorted. "I take it you two didn't get along?"

"Didn't get along?" Sova looked at Roeseph, offended. "She terrorized me. When I was eight years old, she hypnotized me to wet myself every time I heard a rooster crow."

Roeseph barreled over, laughing so hard his throat nearly broke open.

Sova glared at him, annoyed. "It's not funny, Roe."

"It's a little funny," Roeseph snickered.

"I was traumatized!"

Roeseph sat up and wiped his sleeve under his eye. "I'm sorry," he sighed through a laugh. "Continue."

Sova's eyes narrowed, and he straightened to continue his tale.

"Well anyway, while the little brat was the bane of my existence, she was Saulder's entire universe. I know how crazy it sounds, but I'm positive the man has been in love with her since he was seven years old. And, I mean, Feran and I had our differences, but Saulder always made sure we felt we were getting enough of his attention. Life was good... until the Venom Tongues invaded the palace. They hurt my father so badly he still hasn't woken after ten years. They killed Casavore's wife, Fala. They took Feran..."

"But she could still be alive, right?" Roeseph shrugged. "I mean, they never found a body."

"We did find something, though. One of Saulder's first decrees as dire was to send out a search party for her. After a month of searching, they found a campsite right beneath the western cliffs of Era. There were signs of human remains, probably got eaten away by the buzzards. But..."

"No Feran."

"Venom Tongues aren't known to keep hostages... I think that's what broke Saulder—what happened to the girl who was supposed to be his wife," Sova inhaled deeply, exhausted by the emotional turmoil. "But that doesn't give him an excuse to do what he's done. I lost plenty too, and I'm fine."

"Yeah," Roeseph arched an eyebrow. "*Fine.*"

"...And he's going to keep hurting people until he's stopped."

"What do you want us to do?"

"Well, waiting isn't going to get us anywhere," Sova exhaled and stood on the icy brook. "And we can't keep waiting for Casavore to come to our rescue. Not to mention if we stay out here any longer, you're probably going to end up killing me."

"I would never—"

"Roe."

"I admit I have thought about it once or twice."

"We're going to get your father out of Vaska," Sova promised. "Casavore too. Everyone. But we need troops. Are there any Blind Seers that weren't in the fight?"

"I doubt it," Roeseph shook his head. "Even if there are any left, none are going to join the rebellion as long as the Blind Hound is behind bars."

Sova clicked his jaw. "So, I guess that just means we'll have to build our own army," he concluded and crossed his arms.

Roeseph arched an eyebrow. "A new Blind Seers?"

"Sure. But I'm thinking more like, '*The Royal Traitor's Troop.*'"

"I'm not calling us that."

"*And friends.*"

"Sova."

"So, are you in, or not?" Sova extended his hand.

Roeseph drew a deep breath. "What the heck. If I'm dying out here, I might as well die trying to put my sword through the dire's heart."

Roeseph stood from the snowy riverbank and took Sova's hand. Sova smiled, giddy. "The Royal Traitor's Troop is happening."

"Stop," Roeseph begged, exhausted.

"Sorry. *And Friends.*"

Roeseph sighed and looked up and down the frozen stream. "So, where do we look first?"

"Seavale," Sova nodded south.

"Seavale?" Roeseph tilted his head. "Is that a good idea? The town is crawling with bounty hunters. If someone recognizes us—"

"Then they'll fall in love with my winning personality and let us go. I'm very likeable, Roe."

Roeseph looked to the blue-glazed heavens. "Yep. We're going to die."

"Ah, you'll be fine," Sova swung his arm around Roeseph's neck. "Stick with me, Roe. They won't even notice you."

Leaving their camp to melt in the winter sun, the two set off toward Seavale—The Town of Sinners.

SEAVALE...

In the southern tip of the Valley of Lykos, where the Cliffs of Era end and the great ocean begins, a sanctuary for even the most corrupt of sinners laid carved in the side of one of the cliffs. Seavale it was called, made from driftwood, stolen roof shingles, rust, and blood. The sun only shone on the dark town at dusk, when the sun fell to the ocean. The only light to brighten the sin-stained town were the torches lining the taverns and inns. Drunken melodies filled the bitter air, and shattered glass broke across the town like a rooster's crow.

Among the pirates, thugs, and criminals stood an outlier—a sheep in wolf's clothing. Her name was Elling, the daughter of a Mosharick Chief, a girl living in the skin of her worst enemy.

Elling sat outside a tavern, wrapped in a tattered brown cloak, with her callused feet dipped in a damp puddle along the cobblestone street. Her stomach growled, hunger gnawing her mind like a dog on a bone. She curved inward and drew a low but agonized breath. She never knew hunger back in the village, lest her mother die of a heart attack. The mother whom she killed.

Two burly men dressed in black ink stomped out of the tavern she camped outside, overflowing mugs in hand. They laughed and cackled against the other's shoulder, singing drunken sea shanties for the whole town to hear. Elling curled tighter into a ball, trying to hide between the chipped cracks in the sidewalk.

Despite her attempts, she'd caught the attention of the largest of the two men, a thug named Pyne.

"Hungry, are we, Shepherd Girl?" he growled, his eyes flickering with trouble.

Elling looked away.

"I can help you, ya know," the thug, Pyne, said as he lowered to the frightened young woman. "All it'll cost you is a night and a morning."

Elling turned away to hide the bubbling in her lips.

"Hey!" Pyne snapped, and grabbed hold of Elling's cloak. "I'm talking to you—"

A silver sword pressed to Pyne's throat, and he froze. Elling gasped with alarm, her gaze trailing up the length of the blade to see two handsome men, their eyes dark with warning.

"Leave the lady be," Roeseph ordered.

Glaring at Roeseph, Pyne rose from Elling. Roeseph drew back his sword.

"How dare you threaten me, boy?" Pyne snarled.

Sova stepped forward, a conman's smile on his lips. "Sorry for my friend's outburst," he chuckled. "He's just cranky because we've been walking aimlessly for three days trying to get here."

"Your *friend* needs to be taught some respect," the thug, Vae, growled in defense of his comrade.

"Oh, and respect will be taught," Sova said and rested his elbow on Roeseph's shoulder. "But we're the teachers. You see, for three days, we've been traveling, living off rabbits and whatever food this frost-bitten winter has to offer. Not to mention, we've been getting on each other's nerves for quite some time now, and both of us are at our breaking point. We're in desperate need to blow off some steam. So, please. Make our day."

Sova leaned against Roeseph, his eyes glistened with a lust for trouble. Pyne took a step toward the two strangers, only for Vae to pull him back and whisper something in his ear as he nodded to the medallion hanging from Sova's neck.

Pyne's eyes widened and he chuckled. "You boys enjoy Seavale." Smirking he and Vae disappeared into the sludge-covered streets of Seavale.

Sova puffed out his chest. "Yeah, you better run."

Roeseph lowered himself to meet Elling's eyes. She looked away, hidden in the darkness of her cloak.

"Are you alright, ma'am?" Roeseph said in a soft voice that reminded Elling of the pastures of the Mosharick Plains. Roeseph withdrew two silver coins from his pocket. "I don't know how much this'll get you in Seavale," he whispered and laid the two coins next to Elling. "But please, do try to find something to eat."

Elling's eyes widened with disbelief. Charity was extinct in the likes of Seavale, and yet, it found her. She scooped the coins into her lap, hiding them from the eyes of the sinner's town.

"So," Sova looked around, "where to begin?"

Elling flinched at his voice. She had heard it before. Straining her emerald eyes to peek out the top of her cloak, she spied the Royal Traitor.

His eyes... she thought to herself. *Those silver eyes...* She'd seen them before indeed.

"How do you suppose we find fighters?" Roeseph asked as he rose and looked around the saltwater-drowned town.

A man hurtled through the glass window of the tavern next to them and rolled into the center of the street. He groaned, bleeding from nearly every hole in his face. Eyes wide, Roeseph and Sova looked back to the vicious drinking house.

"There," Sova pointed.

Roeseph shut his eyes. "How did I get myself into this?"

"Fate, Roe. Fate," Sova smiled and dragged Roeseph through the tavern doors. Elling stared after them, her frightened, emerald eyes darkening with rage.

You were there... she whispered to herself.

Chapter Twelve: The Tavern Fighter

Sova and Roeseph stood in the tavern, overcome by the stench of sweat, booze, and the slight hint of feces. The entirety of the tavern crowded in a circle in the center of the tavern, shouting with their fists raised to the ceiling. In the middle of the ring, two men brawled like savage dogs over the last scrap of meat. To the far side of the tavern, far from the fight, a bartender, with a grease-stained goat's beard and tired eyes stood behind an oakwood bar, cleaning a mug.

"Roe," Sova whispered as he drew in the essence of the tavern, his eyes glittering. "This. This is where I belong. These... These are my people."

Roeseph arched an eyebrow. "One of your people is beating up a bar stool."

"He's just confused." The two strode to the bar and sat.

"What can I get you boys?" the bartender grumbled and spat in the mug he cleaned.

Roeseph grimaced. "I'm good, sir," he said, "Thank you."

"Says you," Sova exclaimed. Laying his entire body across the bar, Sova waved two silver coins in the bartender's face, his face shining like a candle. "Give me the strongest thing you got!"

The bartender smirked darkly and set down his mug. "One Odin Slayer, coming up."

The bartender turned to the shelf of booze to concoct the infamous Odin Slayer. As Sova hovered over the bar, Roeseph looked down to see the Blesser's medallion hanging out. He grabbed Sova by the back of his shirt and threw him back on the stool.

"Are you insane?" he growled in the Royal Traitor's ear.

"What?" Sova squeaked.

Roeseph grabbed the Blesser's medallion and shoved it down Sova's shirt. "You're wearing the Blesser's medallion for all of Seavale to see."

"It brings out my eyes."

"If anyone sees that, they'll—"

"They won't. There's a reason Casavore trusted me with his medallion, Roe. I'm a very reliable person."

The bartender returned with a mug filled with olive-green liquid and emerald foam smelling of burnt oil and sailor sweat. Roeseph's eyes widened at the monstrosity while Sova licked his lips.

"One Odin Slayer," the bartender chuckled and placed the horrid drink before his customer.

"Try to relax, Roe," Sova said, grabbing the mug. "I have everything under control."

THREE EMPTY MUGS OF Odin Slayer laid across the bar top. Among them, the Royal Traitor, collapsed over the sticky surface with his cheek in a pool of his own drool.

"Roe?" he whimpered, his stomach churned like ocean waves as he blinked at the swirling world.

Roeseph sighed and crossed his arms over the bar. "Yes, Sova?"

"You're my best friend. You know that, right?"

"Yes, Sova. You've said that a couple times now."

"Am—Am—" Sova paused to swallow rising vomit and leaned against his unwilling partner in exile. "Am I your best friend too?"

"No, Sova," Roeseph said. "I've told you. I can't stand you."

The blade of Roeseph's statement pierced Sova's liquor-corrupt heart like a blade. Sova grabbed hold of his chest, the cold touch of the medallion frosting the bare skin beneath his shirt. "Why—Why would you say that?"

The bartender set another serving of Odin Slayer before Sova. "Here you go, stranger. Drink up."

Sova reached for the liquid mind-corroder, only for Roeseph to slide it across the length of the bar, outside of Sova's reach.

"Why?" the Royal Traitor whimpered. "Why would you do that?"

Roeseph rolled his eyes and looked to the bartender as he cleaned another glass. "Sir, a moment please?" Roeseph asked politely.

"How can I help you, sailor?" the bartender smirked.

"My friend and I are looking to find fighters. People willing to lay down their life for a noble cause. Know where we can find gentlemen such as that?"

The bartender laughed. "Sorry, son. Men are only noble here if you pay them to be. You don't have any coin on ya, do you?"

"Well, we did," Roeseph exhaled and looked to Sova who was rolling an empty mug back and forth across the counter like a kitten with a ball of yarn. "But someone spent it all."

"Odin Slayer..." Sova hiccupped and giggled drunkenly.

Roeseph shook his head and turned back to the bartender. "Regardless of money, where would I find fighters?"

The bartender scoffed and nodded to the crowd gathered in the center of the tavern. "If it's a fighter you're looking for, *he* might be your best bet. Comes in every other day, placing bets that no one can best him in a fight. He's undefeated to this day."

Roeseph turned in his stool. His eyes craned over the crowd to see a silhouette of a man weave in the circle, beating whatever sorry sap wandered into his territory. Roeseph cringed as a scream of pain throttled the air.

"You're not worried he'll start scaring away customers?" he frowned.

"Scare 'em away?" the bartender cackled. "The lad brings in more paying customers than this place ever had. After he beats up one or two guys, they come to me for drinks. I've become a wealthy man because of the brute."

"Where does he hail from? Vaska? the Mosharick Plains?"

"No one knows. Showed up in Seavale eight years ago. He lives in between whore houses and taverns. Has nothing of his own but the horse he rode in on. Peculiar beast that one is..."

"What do you mean?"

"The fighter is a very private man and lives on his lonesome with just his steed to keep him company. But he's very protective of the beast. 'Covers it in a sheet whenever he rides into town. Once a drunk tried to take a peek under the cloak, and the fighter beat him half to death. No one has messed with the horse or him since... well, except for when they're paying to. You'd have to be a fool to challenge him."

Roeseph nodded. "Well, maybe we can try to talk to him next time he's on break. What do you think, Sova?" he looked to the side, surprised to find the Royal Traitor had disappeared. "Sova?"

Sova wobbled through the crowd, falling against strangers, and taking their curses like an arrow to a shield. He stumbled into the circle, straightening as high as the weight of drunkenness would allow.

"Hello?" he called, trying to locate a face through the blurry haze. "I would like to fight someone," he burped. "Please."

Gut bursting laughter fired from the Seavallian men, shaking the entire tavern. Sova smiled and looked around. He wondered what they were laughing at.

"You sure about that, stranger?" a daunting voice craned over the laughter. "I'm no ordinary fighter."

Sova stared across the fighting circle to see a man on the other end, his back turned as he wiped a red-stained towel over his face. He turned to face Sova. Crystal beads of sweat dappled tawny skin. Damp, mahogany hair fell over amber eyes glowing like embers born from the strongest flame. On both shoulders he bore tattoos of the sun, one resembling the sunset and the other, the sunrise. The fighter threw his towel to the crowd.

Sova gulped down a bourbon-flavored swallow. "Hello sir," he wobbled. "My name is drunk, and I am a little Sova. What's yours?"

The fighter smirked and shook his head out of pity for the pathetic wanderer. "Kyce."

"Well, Kyce," Sova stumbled. "I'm going to win this fight. And if I do... I want the nice bartender to name a drink after me in my honor."

"Do you?"

Roeseph sprung from the crowd and took Sova by the arm.

"Sorry—I am so sorry," he smiled nervously at the fighter. "He's just confused. He doesn't want to fight."

"Yes, I do," Sova growled, offended.

"No, you don't."

"Yes, I do."

"You're drunk, Sova."

"The Odin Slayer has given me strength."

Kyce took a step toward Roeseph and Sova. "If your friend wants to fight, let him fight."

Roeseph glared at Kyce, disgusted. "You would fight a man in his state?"

"I'd fight anyone for gold," Kyce warned and nodded to the crowd. "Now stand back, or I'll fight you too."

Roeseph looked from Kyce to Sova. "I hope you know what you're doing, Sova."

"I do," Sova nodded as Roeseph sunk into the crowd. "What am I doing again?"

Kyce charged the Royal Traitor, his bleached knuckles unsheathed, and his teeth gritted in a snarl. Sova's eyes widened as the haze of his drunkenness fled—cured by threat of death. He barreled to the side, avoiding the incoming fist. Kyce lashed around, his amber ember eyes burning into Sova like a welding iron.

Sova roared forward and pulled his fist back. As if Kyce could read the future, he ducked to the side and locked Sova's extended arm in his elbow, then flipped him over his back. Sova whipped against the splintered ground, a ragged breath lurching from his flattened lungs and stinging his throat.

Roeseph hissed sympathetically through clenched teeth. "Ouch..."

"Roeseph," Sova gasped through locked lungs. "The Odin Slayer has deceived me."

Kyce lifted Sova by his shirt and reared his fist back. Before he could deliver the devastating blow, Sova hooked his leg around the back of Kyce's knee and pulled him to the ground. The tavern roared in support of the underdog. As Kyce rose, his glare fell to a gold medallion slipping out of Sova's collar.

The embers in his gaze doused, and his eyes widened. "Where did you get that?" Kyce whispered.

Sova looked down, his heart sinking rapidly at the sight of the Blesser's medallion. "Uh—" he shoved the pendant violently back down his shirt. "A friend gave it to me."

His scowl returning, Kyce clenched his fists. "That doesn't belong to you."

Sova took a nervous step back. "Look, I don't want any trouble."

Kyce lunged at Sova and lifted him by the collar of his shirt. Before Sova could protest, Kyce ripped the medallion from his neck.

Roeseph sprung from the crowd. "That's not yours to take!"

Like a gladiator armed with spear, Kyce threw Sova into Roeseph. Like a wild stallion let loose, Kyce sprinted through the crowd and out the door.

"He's got the medallion!" Roeseph shouted as he and Sova rose from the floor and hurtled out the tavern doors and into the damp cobblestone street. They looked up and down the drunk-littered roads, desperate to locate the Blesser's stolen medallion.

Sova looked to the left, spotting Kyce running toward the mouth of the Seavallian cave where the stalactites formed a monstrous jaw.

"There!" Sova shouted. The two exiles sprinted after Kyce, unaware of the emerald-eyed Hyde Howler tailing them from the shadows.

Nearing the cave's exit, Kyce looked over his shoulder to see Sova and Roeseph gaining on him. He stopped at the edge of Seavale, a fence of stalagmites severing his path, and turned to face his enemies.

"Give it up, Kyce," Sova panted. "We've got you cornered. Nowhere to go. Nowhere to hide."

Kyce's grip tightened on the medallion and his teeth clenched in fury. "Eradite treasures don't belong to the likes of Lykos."

"It doesn't belong to the likes of you either," Sova growled. "Now surrender the medallion. You're outnumbered."

"Am I?" Kyce chuckled.

A massive beast lunged out from behind the stalagmites and leaped in front of Kyce.

"Woah!" Sova shouted in alarm as he and Roeseph fell to the floor and crawled away from the monster. The beast had the body of a wolf, stood about nine feet, and had dark, oakwood fur and burning chestnut eyes. The monster resembled the white angel Sova saw back in the Mosharick Plains, except it was slightly smaller and had stumpy, branch-like limbs sticking from its shoulder blades where its wings should've been.

The wingless soaring wolf snarled at her master's attackers, flashing her pearl-like fangs as Kyce leaped on her back and grinned on his foes.

Giving a sly wink, he rode his wingless soaring wolf out of Seavale's cave, across the beach, and into the Vaskan Forest.

"What in Lykos was that?" Roeseph shouted as he and Sova stood.

"I suppose it was Kyce's *'horse'* the bartender told us about," Sova grumbled. "Welp, now we know why Kyce was so secretive about it. It's a soaring wolf."

"Is it—" Roeseph gulped. "Is it the White Angel from the legends? The one that attacked the dire?"

"No," Sova shook his head. "The soaring wolf that attacked the dire was bigger, and it was white. Not to mention that one lacks wings."

"Well, what do we do?"

"We get back the Blesser's medallion and beat that man so senseless he sees the face of God."

"How? He's got a soaring wolf."

Sova looked around. "There has to be something here we could use to incapacitate him."

Just then, Sova spied a small anchor and robe covered in scum and barnacles tucked between the stalagmites, probably abandoned by a drunken sailor.

Sova smirked deviously. "I have an idea."

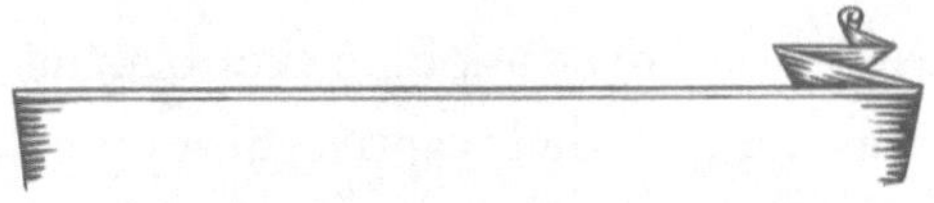

Chapter Thirteen: Rescue

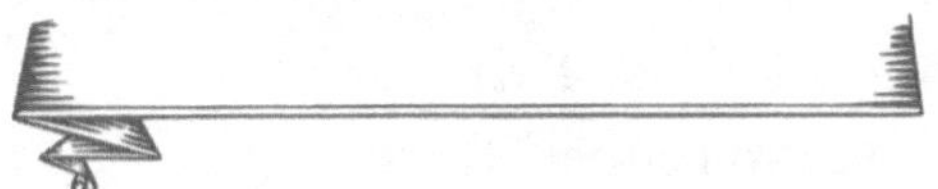

Kyce and his wingless soaring wolf, Whisp, rushed through the snow-covered forest, the frigid winter wind lashing their faces like icicle whips as the falling sun turned the trees black against a cloudless magenta sky. The little branch-like stumps jutting from Whisp's side flapped excitedly in the wind. It was the perfect day for a flight.

Kyce stared at the Blesser's medallion in his hand, a stone settling in his stomach as emotions long repressed resurrected. He hadn't seen a mind melder's medallion in over eight years.

Kyce looked over his shoulder where Seavale laid and wondered, *How did those two idiots manage to steal an Eradite medallion?*

Out from the shadows of the snow-covered wood, a rust-coated anchor and rope shot across Whisp's path and slung around her four paws like a grappling hook. She yelped and flipped over the snowy path, sending Kyce flying to the cold ground. Kyce grunted and rolled into the trunk of a massive pine tree. He laid on his stomach, waiting for the swaying world to still.

"Whisp?" he groaned and pressed his palm to a weeping gash in the side of his head. "Whisp, are you ok?"

Whisp laid in a pile of snow a short distance away, her paws bound with an anchor and rope as she whined for her master. Just as Kyce rose to his hands, a heel drove between his shoulder blades and forced him back to the frost-coated grass.

Whisp snarled as two strange men surrounded her master, helpless to stop them.

"Long time no see," came Sova's provoking voice.

Kyce growled in frustration and strained his eyes to see the two wanderers he mugged back in Seavale loom over him. Roeseph pressed his heel harder into Kyce's back, his dusk-blue eyes blazing while Sova crossed his arms and smirked smugly at their captive. Stooping down, he ripped the medallion from Kyce's hand.

"I'll take that, thank you," he taunted and wiped the snow from the medallion.

"That doesn't belong to you," Kyce snarled.

"It doesn't belong to you either," Roeseph glared.

"That belongs to the Cliffs of Era, you thieves."

Sova twirled the medallion around his finger as he mocked. "What are you going to do? You're outnumbered, pal." The cold touch of a ragged blade pressed to Sova's throat, trapping his pride before he could swallow it. "I stand corrected."

Roeseph's gaze lashed to the side to see the cloaked girl he defended back in Seavale holding Sova at knife point from behind.

"You were there," Elling hissed through a tear-damp voice. "You were there."

"You're going to have to be more specific, sweetheart," Sova said.

"You were there," Elling whimpered, her knife trembling against Sova's throat. "You were there when the dire came."

Sova's smug expression sunk, and a sort of forlornness eclipsed his arrogance.

Kyce tried to force himself up only for Roeseph to press him back into the snow.

"Don't even think about it," Roeseph warned.

"You were there," Elling gasped between wails, her cheeks charred by hot tears. "You were there when he made me a monster!"

Sova paused. "You're the Shepherdess... Chemon's daughter."

Elling pressed the blade harder against Sova's throat, making him flinch. "You were there..." she sniveled. "I remember your voice. You were there."

"I am so sorry," Sova whispered. "I can't begin to—"

"I don't want your apology!" Elling screamed. "I want my father back! I want them all back! I don't want to be a monster!"

Mistaking Elling's screams for aggression, Whisp lunged, barely moving a yard from where she lay. Elling yelped and stumbled back, compromising her grip on Sova. Seeing an opening, Roeseph abandoned Kyce and shoved

Elling away. Kyce leaped to his feet and slugged Sova in the face. In perfect sync, the four drew their blades on one another.

Elling, Roeseph, Sova, and Kyce glared from one person to the next, unsure who would strike first.

Kyce bared his teeth at Sova. "I'll kill you, you incompetent thief."

Sova arched his brow, "You'll have to get in line, pal."

"We didn't steal the medallion," Roeseph assured. "It belongs to the Blesser of Vaska. He gave it to us so the dire couldn't use it to terrorize Lykos."

"You're lying," Kyce growled.

Elling shook her head. "He's not lying," she whimpered, a stream of tears collecting at her chin. "I've seen it in dreams... nightmares. It's the medallion that turned me into a monster... A Hyde Howler. That medallion made me kill my—" she covered her mouth to stop the sobs racking from her chest. "It made me a killer..." Dropping the knife, she fell to her knees.

Roeseph gulped, his eyes filling with sympathy. "You're not a killer," he assured and lowered his blade.

Sova looked frantically from Roeseph to Kyce. "Roe. Roe! Pick your sword back up, man."

Roeseph stepped away from the circle of death and knelt before Elling.

"You're not a killer," Roeseph repeated.

"You didn't see what I did," she shook her head, sobbing. "You don't know what it's like."

"I do. My Father is Oland, of the Blind Seers."

Elling froze, her emerald eyes widening beneath her hood.

"You're the Blind Hound's son?" Kyce uttered, equally shocked. "You're the Last Soldier—the only Blind Seer to escape the attack on the Vaskan palace. The one that the dire's been after."

Ignoring Kyce's narration, Roeseph asked the shepherd girl, "What's your name, miss?"

Elling paused, unsure whether to speak. When she grew bold, she drew her emerald eyes from her hood and revealed her soft face to the light of the magenta dusk.

"Elling," she answered.

Roeseph stilled, his eyes swelling with awe. "Hello, Elling," he offered his hand. "My name's Roeseph."

Sova poked his head just above Roeseph's shoulder. "His friends call him Roe."

"No," Roeseph spat and shook his head. "No, they don't."

"He's lying. He loves to be called that."

Kyce tucked his blade into his sheath. "If he's the Last Soldier, does that make you the Royal Traitor?" he asked, eyes still fiery.

"In the flesh." Sova smiled and surrendered his sword to his belt.

"So that medallion," Kyce nodded to the gold trinket in Sova's hand, "it really is the Blesser's?"

"Yep," Sova nodded as he placed the gold chain around his neck. "And it's mine to protect. So don't touch my stuff."

"Why would the Blesser entrust a traitor like you with the greatest weapon known to Lykos?"

"Because I'm reliable," Sova replied and puffed his chest. All eyes turned to the Royal Traitor, their brows drawn in an arch. Sova looked about them, offended. "What's with the faces?"

Roeseph rolled his eyes then looked to Kyce. "What about you? Not every Seavallian man has a soaring wolf or knowledge of Eradite treasures. Who are you exactly?"

Kyce paused and raised his chin. "An exile, like you," he answered. "Just not an exile of Lykos."

"Ah, another, Eradite," Sova smiled. "That's two in one month. So, do you know the Eradite that attacked the dire by chance? I'm a big fan of his work."

"Not all Eradites know each other, you imbecile," Kyce growled.

"Do you know why another Eradite would be down here?" Roeseph asked as he stood. "Could he be another exile?"

"No," Kyce shook his head. "The Eradites would never send one of their own down here unless it was to offer one of their enemies' mind melders to the dire. The worst punishment you can receive in Era is a life in prison. To be sent down to Lykos is unheard of."

Sova shrugged. "Well, you're down here. What did you do to earn such a *drastic* punishment?"

Kyce clenched his jaw. "That's none of your business."

"Well, obviously, you were hated enough for them never to let you come back home again," Sova mocked and nodded to Whisp tied on the ground.

"That soaring wolf's wings have been cut. I'd assume, so you can't fly back to Era. So, what did you do that was worthy of exile? I'd love to hear why such a *righteous* and *holy* bunch of stiffs could damn one of their own to a *hell* such as Lykos."

Kyce shook his head, steam practically radiating off his skin as he reached for a knife. "You son of a—"

A twig snapped in the darkness.

"What was that?" Elling asked as she gripped her cloak. Roeseph stepped closer to the dormant Hyde Howler and drew his blade. Sova, and Kyce followed his lead. Whisp writhed on the ground, her claws drawing lines in the dirt as she snarled at the darkness.

Kyce looked to his wingless soaring wolf, concerned by her aggression. "There's something out there."

Roeseph pressed closer to Elling. "What is it? A wolf? A bear?"

"No," Kyce shook his head. "Whisp wouldn't be freaking out like this if it were a mere animal."

Sova shrugged. "Well, I mean, we have a Hyde Howler. We could try releasing her."

Elling flinched and pulled her knees close to her chest.

"Sova!" Roeseph bellowed.

"I'm just saying," Sova shrugged, "wouldn't be much of a fight if we got her involved."

"Sova, shut up!"

Another stick snapped in the darkness.

"Look out!" Elling shouted.

Seven Seavallian thugs lunged from the shadows like a pride of lions, roaring their bourbon-soaked battle cries as they swung their swords. Whisp snarled as they tied her muzzle shut, her jaws prying against the ropes as lassoes strung around her snout, neck, and legs.

Kyce looked to his beast, his eyes blistering with rage.

"Whisp!" he shouted and tore toward his wingless wolf. A large Seavallian man barreled into his side, knocking him to the ground.

Sova, Roeseph, and Elling were forced to kneel in the middle of the trail, their hands bound behind their backs while several thugs crowded Kyce and kicked him until his skin swarmed with bruises, and blood sputtered from his lips. Whisp yelped for her master as he laid motionless, his chest rising and falling with labored breath.

The two thugs Roeseph and Sova encountered in Seavale, Pyne, and Vae, stalked toward the beaten Kyce, their lips drawn back in a sickening smirk.

"Well—Well—Well," Pyne chuckled. "Not so tough anymore, are you, son?"

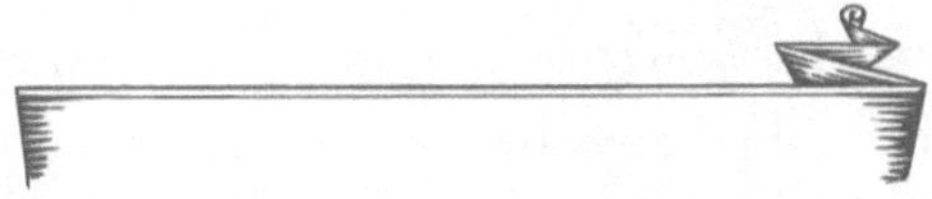

Chapter Fourteen: The Ghost

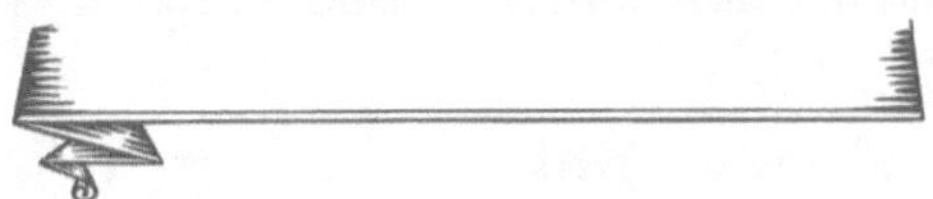

Kyce *vomited at the thugs' feet.* Sova and Roeseph watched from the sidelines, pitying the beaten exile, while Elling trembled with fright.

"Get 'em up," Pyne ordered. Two thugs grabbed Kyce under the arms and threw him against Sova. His eye was blackened shut, and a long gash cut down the middle of his lip. He didn't look like the vicious fighter from before. If anything, he looked like Sova's father, Dire Zastar; more dead than alive.

The Seavallian thugs circled the four, swords sparking at their side.

"Well, what do we have here?" Pyne taunted with malicious, serpent-like eyes.

Sova gulped and smirked nervously. "Look, I think there's been a mistake here. We don't have any money."

"I'm not interested in money, boy."

Sova's head fell forward with a sigh. "Look, sir," he began. "I'm flattered, but you're really not my type."

Pyne lurched his heel into Sova's jaw, sending him whipping against Roeseph.

"Not too fond of rejection, I see," Sova coughed as he rotated his throbbing jaw.

"If I were you, I'd keep my trap shut," Pyne snarled.

"Yes, sir."

Roeseph glared at Pyne, his dusk-blue eyes shining with foolish bravery. "Let us go. We've done nothing to deserve this."

"Brave one, aren't you?" Pyne chuckled. "You truly are the son of the Blind Hound."

Roeseph's boldness sunk, and his brave eyes grew fearful.

"You don't know what you're talking about," Sova snapped.

"Don't I?" Pyne grabbed Sova by the face, his iron grip nearly shattering Sova's bruised jaw to dust. "You know, I've heard many stories about the two of you. The Royal Traitor—the silver eyed beauty left scarred by his brother. You and the *Last Soldier* have a massive bounty hanging over your head for taking the Blesser's medallion."

"You're mistaken," Sova snarled. "We aren't who you think us to be."

"We heard everything," Pyne said as he dropped Sova. "There's no denying it, you Vaskan brat."

Pyne stood from Sova and knelt before Elling. She looked away.

"You surprised me, though. Sweet Elling," The Seavallian thug chuckled and tucked a strand of raven hair behind her ear. Elling shuddered at his touch. "I never expected you to be a Hyde Howler. Venom Tongues pay top dollar for such beasts. I'm sure they'd have a field day with you."

"You leave her alone!" Roeseph bellowed and lunged to Elling's defense. "She has nothing to do with this!"

Pyne grabbed hold of Roeseph's throat, making him croak. "You watch your tone, boy."

Roeseph wheezed, his eyes red with a scarlet haze. Pyne's head tilted to the side, a sinner's smirk spreading his lips. "But you are right. She is the most innocent out of you fools. However," he looked to Kyce, a string of red spittle dangling from the tavern fighter's lip. "*He* is not."

The Seavallian thug threw Roeseph to the ground.

"Take a deep breath," Sova ordered as he shuffled toward his near-suffocated comrade. "You're alright."

Roeseph coughed, his breath like wind through busted bagpipes, as he turned to Elling and huffed, "Are you ok?"

"Yeah," Elling whispered with a nod.

Kyce glared at Pyne through a swollen black eye as his foe knelt before him, his amber eyes burning like magma.

"I've heard stories of the rogue Eradite who tried to assassinate the dire," Pyne smiled. "I never dreamed it would be the likes of you, tavern fighter."

"I didn't attack the Dire of Vaska," Kyce growled.

"That beast over there says otherwise," Pyne motioned to Whisp laying bound on the forest floor.

"That wasn't my soaring wolf or me," Kyce snapped. "The monster the rogue sent was white and flew. Whisp lost her wings a long time ago."

"You could've cut her wings," Pyne shrugged. "And the dire was attacked in the night. It was dark. The monster could've very well been brown instead of white."

"You know that's ludicrous," Kyce snarled an inch away from Pyne's face.

The thug shoved him back by his throat. "It doesn't matter," Pyne said. "As long as I give the dire an Eradite and a soaring wolf, I'll get paid."

Sova scooted to Kyce and helped him upright. "I'll tell the dire you lied," The Royal Traitor threatened the Venom Tongue. "You'll be executed for deceiving him."

Pyne drew his sword, pressing the blade to Sova's throat. "I'm willing to bring you to the dire *dead*."

"Then again," Sova laughed. "It was dark. How could I know?"

Kyce glared at Sova. "You have the backbone of a river reed."

"Sticks and stones," Sova hissed through the gaps in his forced smile.

The Seavallian thug, Vae walked up to Pyne, a concerned look on his face. "Pyne. We have a problem."

"What is it this time?" Pyne exhaled.

"It's the monster. We've immobilized it, but we can't get it to move. The men are scared to get close."

"Well, the only ones the dire wanted alive were the Royal Traitor, the Last Soldier, and the Eradite," Pyne smirked. "Just lob off its head. That should be enough to satisfy that Vaskan tyrant."

Kyce lunged in defense of his beast. "You leave her alone!"

Pyne struck him across the face, sending him whipping into the other three hostages so they fell like dominos. With the wind knocked out of his hostages, Pyne turned to Vae and whispered under his breath. "Get it over with. We have to move now if we want to be in Vaska by sundown tomorrow."

Vae nodded and drew his sword. Stalking like a lion in the night, the Seavallian thug approached the snarling soaring wolf. Groaning in agony, Kyce sat up from his fellow hostages. When he saw Vae was nearly upon Whisp, he shouted, "Stop!"

He lunged in Whisp's defense, only for Pyne to kick him down and pin him under his boot.

"Leave her alone!" the Eradite Exile shouted as he struggled.

Whisp snarled as Vae's shadow crept across her fur. Like a woodsmen lining his ax to a tree, Vae laid his sword on her neck. Elling, Roeseph, and Sova watched from the sidelines, their hearts trembling at the sound of Kyce's helpless cries.

Vae raised his sword. "So, you're the beast that attacked the dreaded dire?" he chuckled.

Whisp growled in response and flapped her stumpy wings.

"I was expecting more," the Seavallian thug snickered.

Before Vae could bring down his blade, a bright flash of white dove across the path like a bolt of lightning and Vae vanished, leaving only a cry of peril to fill his absence. The Seavallian thugs drew their swords.

"Forsake the Valley!" Pyne cursed and looked from left to right. "Where did he go?"

Jaws hung in shock, the four hostages looked around.

"What in Lykos was that?" Roeseph whispered.

Sova gulped, his soul frigid with fear. "It's back..." he whispered. "My Lykos, the monster is back."

Dragging the tip of his sword through the snow, Pyne paced. "Vae! Vae, come out right now, or I'll have you flogged!"

When Vae didn't show himself, Pyne lashed around to meet his thugs. "You," he pointed to a small, stocky man with an eyepatch. "Go get Vae."

The small thug gulped. "S—Sir, what about the monster—"

"Don't make me ask again, boy," Pyne snapped, and the eyepatch-wearing thug disappeared into the forest.

Kyce swallowed, his gaze latched on Whisp across the trail.

"You ok, girl?" he called.

Whisp yipped in reassurance and fluttered her stumpy wings.

Elling shivered. "We're going to die here," she whimpered.

Roeseph edged closer to the dormant Hyde Howler, his voice soft and reassuring. "No, we're going to be fine. We're going to get out of here. All of us."

A body hurtled through the branches like a comet and fell before the hostages.

"Well, maybe not him," Sova corrected.

Vae laid before them, his jaw ripped from one hinge. His eyes bulged with fright, and his entrails bubbled from his stomach through a gaping wound running from his throat to his naval.

Pyne approached the corpse, eyes wide and mortified.

"Vae?" he whispered in shock. "How did—" Pyne looked to the hole in the tree line his comrade had made. "How did he get up there?"

Sova scoffed in his throat, "Flew perhaps?"

Pyne turned from Vae's corpse and stalked toward Sova. "Why, you little—"

A stick cracked in the darkness, and a shadow creeped out. Pyne turned from Sova. The eyepatch-wearing thug sent to find Vae stood behind him—his eye big as a moon. His jaw hung open as if he were frozen mid-scream, and he walked choppily, like a zombie.

"Laurven," Pyne shouted to the eyepatch wearer. "What is the matter with you?"

The eyepatch wearer, Laurven, looked frantically around the trail.

"The snakes," he trembled. "The snakes are everywhere. Everywhere."

"What's wrong with him?" Roeseph wondered aloud.

"I don't know," Sova replied. "But there's something familiar about his face. I've seen that look before."

"Snakes, everywhere," Laurven screeched. "They're everywhere."

His eyes twinkling like lashing fire, he scratched at his arm until he bled. The Seavallian thugs closed around him, baffled by his behavior.

"Calm down, Laurven," Pyne ordered.

"The snakes are everywhere!" Laurven drew his sword. Without warning, he slashed one of his comrades across the throat. The once controlled hostage situation turned to chaos as Laurven slayed his comrades like a woodsmen through trees.

"Get down!" Roeseph shouted as the battle drew close, and threw himself over the other three.

Blood painted Laurven's face like a canvas as he trembled.

"The snakes are everywhere," he shouted again, unaware of Pyne creeping behind. "Everywhere!"

Pyne slashed Laurven across the throat and he fell, dead. Pyne glared at his surviving troops, his face wrenched in a scowl.

"I've had enough of this!" he shouted. "I've lost too many men to this fight. Now one of you kill that blasted soaring wolf," he snarled and pointed to Whisp, "so we can get on with our lives!"

Before any of the thugs could act upon their master's command, their eyes raised to the tree line and their faces turned a ghostly white.

"What now?" Pyne sneered.

One of the thugs pointed behind him. Pyne turned. Standing behind him was a white, wolf-like beast, standing as tall as ten feet, with open wings stretching as far as oak branches. It glared down at Pyne, its glowing amber eyes scorching the man's soul.

"My Lykos," Pyne whispered. "The Angel..."

Snarling, the soaring wolf bit into Pyne's shoulder and flung him into the trees where the man's back snapped against a sturdy trunk. The Seavallian thugs lunged to attack the beast. The white wolf reared back, its wings eclipsing the light of the moon, and charged, its roar filling the night.

Sova gulped as he and the others huddled close, his heart beating so loudly his ears deafened.

The White Angel pinned a Seavallian thug to the ground and tore into his stomach, ripping out his entrails as he screamed, unaware of the thug creeping from behind. Before the gangster could do away with the massive wolf, a cloaked figure shot from the darkness and grabbed the man by his wrist, making him drop his sword.

The shade of their hood hid the stranger's face. Tan gauze wrapped their right hand. And around their neck, they wore a gold medallion with a distinct charred crescent-shaped mark on the side. No doubt about it. This stranger was the Rogue Eradite—the one whose beast attacked the dire.

"*Wicked thug, Seavallian brute,*" the cloaked stranger began as they swung the charred medallion before their victim. "*My patience has been spent, and my mercy long gone. So, your mind I will capture, and your body I'll control. Your flesh, it turns, and scales take place. Across your visage forms a monster's face. Human, you are no more. Be gone as the beast endures.*"

The man's eyes widened under the influence of the trance, and he looked down at his fleshy human hands, horrified by what he saw.

"What—What's happening to me?" he wailed and ran into the forest. Witnessing the madness of their comrade, the surviving Seavallians screamed toward Seavale, eager to leave the White Angel and its master behind.

The white soaring wolf sprung after them, only for its master to call it back. "Saber," the cloaked stranger called. "Leave them be."

Snarl softening, the beast called Saber returned to his master and nuzzled his blood-stained snout under their hood.

"Yes," the cloaked mind melder sputtered and shoved Saber's face away. "You did a good job. You did a very good job."

Elling, Kyce, and Roeseph's jaws hung, in awe of the mind melder's control over the feral beast.

"We're saved!" Sova shouted, making the White Angel look up. "Praise the Lord, we're saved!"

The beast lunged at Sova, pinning him beneath a massive paw as Elling, Roeseph, and Kyce stumbled back in terror. Saber snarled down at his victim, warm blood dripping from his fangs onto Sova's cheek.

"I was wrong," Sova coughed. "I was very wrong."

The cloaked mind melder walked out from behind Saber, fiddling with their charred medallion as she stared down at the Royal Traitor.

"Miss," Sova began desperately, "would you please get control of your dog? He's crushing my lungs."

The mind melder tilted her head, puzzling. Sova grew irritated by her silence, his frustration building in his chest like a dormant geyser about to break through the earth.

"Listen, lady! I am a prince of Vaska. Now you do as I say and get this fleabag off me!"

The mind melder's eyes widened with shock. "No. Way," she breathed, her head falling back when throat tearing laughter ripped open her throat. The hostages and Sova puzzled at the woman, confused by her sudden hysteria.

"I'm sorry," the mind melder shook her head as her laughter faded. "I just didn't think I'd ever see the likes of you again. Let alone save you from a gang of Seavallians."

Sova glared at the woman, his eyes narrowing into slits, "You know who I am?"

"How could I not? White hair and silver eyes are hard to come by in Lykos," the mind melder shrugged. "Though I have to admit, I mistook you for your brother. Congratulations. You're not as ugly as you used to be."

"*Ugly?*" Sova gasped. "Who do you think you are?"

"Haven't you guessed?" The mind melder chuckled. She peeled back her hood, revealing long, waving chestnut locks, mahogany eyes, and a beautiful, tan face.

Sova's jaw dropped, as did his heart. "No," he shook his head, whining. "No. No. No. This can't be happening!"

"Still fussy as ever I see?" the mind melder arched her eyebrow.

"God, what have I done to deserve such torture?" Sova shouted at the sky.

"That's a little excessive."

Roeseph looked from the mind melder to Sova. "Sova," he whispered in the Royal Traitor's ear, "what's going on? Who is she?"

"The devil," Sova growled.

The mind melder rolled her eyes. "You might know me from the legends as the Dire's Damsel or the lost daughter of the Blesser Casavore," she corrected. "But you can call me Feran."

All eyes widened.

"What's the matter?" Feran taunted as she scratched Saber behind the ear. "You all look like you've seen a ghost."

Sova slammed his head back on the ground. "My Lykos, why does God hate me so?"

"Don't worry," Feran assured. "It'll be over soon. For all of you."

Sova's brow furrowed as Feran stooped beside his head and wove her charred medallion in front of his face. His mind went numb, and all focus transferred to the charred trinket rocking back and forth like the tongue of a grandfather clock.

"Goodnight, Sova," she said with a smirk as all went dark.

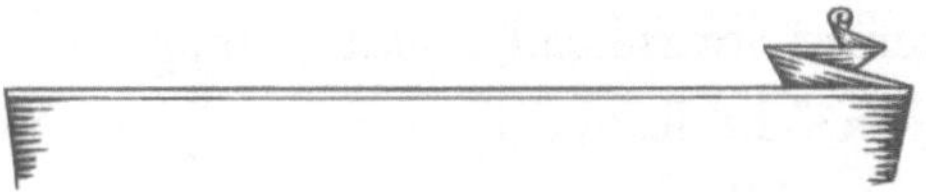

Chapter Fifteen: The Cave of Legends

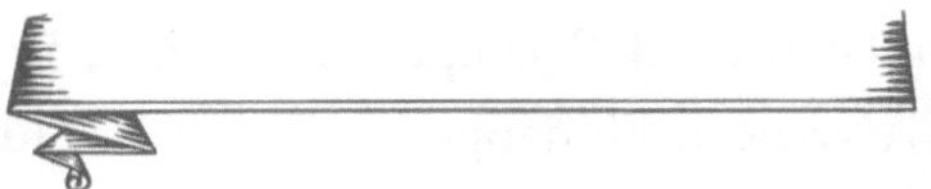

Sova gasped and opened his eyes to cold, endless darkness. He glanced left to right, his heart sinking like a pebble thrown to the waves. *Not this again...*

"Roe?" he called nervously, his voice immortalized in an echo. "Miss Hyde Howler? Angry man? Where are you?"

Like clockwork, the demonic voice of the dire called to him. "Who are you?"

Sova's head hung back, and he exhaled. "Great..."

He turned to see the black armor of the dire across the abyss, hand rested on a holstered sword. "Who are you?" the dire asked again.

"Ah, there you are, Saulder," Sova smiled tightly. "Hey, you're never going to guess who I saw earlier."

"Who are you?" the dire snarled and drew his sword.

Sova shrugged. "I guess I can tell you later. Meet back same time tomorrow?"

Roaring, the dire lunged into the black sky and brought down his sword on his enemy.

SOVA WOKE UPRIGHT WITH a gasp, his heart thumping like fast little rabbit feet in his chest.

What happened? He wondered as he looked around. *All I can remember is the medallion...*

Sova sat in the mouth of a small, warm cave, surrounded by stalactites and stalagmites reaching to another like separated lovers. A fire flickered in the center of the cave, casting twitching shadows on the walls.

A sharp ring pierced Sova's head, making him groan.

"What's going on?" he leaned forward, only to find his hands bound behind a tall stalagmite. "What?"

He looked around. Roeseph, Elling, and Kyce sat tied to the stalagmites next to him, fast asleep.

"*Psst*," Sova leaned toward Roeseph. "Roe. Roe. Roe, wake up. We've been kidnapped. We've been kidnapped by my worst nightmare." Roeseph groaned in sleep and shifted away. Sova exhaled, annoyed. "Great help you are."

A low growl filled the cave, making Sova snap upright. At the mouth of the cave, where a grey wall of blistering snow blew by, the White Angel, Saber, laid stretched out on the warm cave floor. Kyce's soaring wolf, Whisp, stood tied to a stalagmite a couple yards away, standing on her two back legs as she tried to reach Saber for a game of play. Saber growled and tucked his face into his tail, hiding from the energetic beast.

The Dire's Damsel, Feran, sat before the fire in the center of the cave, her medallion glowing in the flames as she wrapped her hand in white gauze. Sova gazed at her, both repulsed and in awe. She looked the way she did when she was little, and yet she had matured into a surprisingly beautiful, young woman. Her chestnut hair fell in curled clumps, like ocean waves in the aging dusk, and her magnificent brown eyes glowed in the light of the embers like pieces of copper. She pulled tight on the gauze around her hand and reclined from the fire's warmth, her eyes shutting. Careful to not disturb her, Sova tried twisting out of his binds; unsuccessful.

"So, the rumors are true," Feran sighed. "You're a traitor of Vaska." Laughing, she turned onto her side to face Sova. "You must've done something absolutely atrocious to make Saulder cast you out."

Sova's jaw cocked to the side. "It wasn't all that hard. He's got a bit of a temper."

Smirk sinking, Feran nodded. "So I've heard," she rose and pulled a bushel of green weeds out of her pocket.

"What are those?" Sova asked as Feran approached.

"Mivander Blossom," Feran replied and shoved the plant under his nose. The overwhelming stench of mint and lavender ambushed Sova's nostrils, fizzing his brain and sparking his blood.

"Forsake Lykos!" he coughed, struggling as far away as his restraints would allow him. "What was that?"

"It's to wake you up," Feran said as she walked to Roeseph. "You guys have been asleep for two days."

"Two days?"

"That's what I said, didn't I?"

"Well, that explains the gnawing feeling in my stomach," Sova said over the howl of his hollow gut. Feran rolled her eyes and knelt before Roeseph to place the Mivander Blossom under his nose. Flinching upright, Roeseph coughed away the suffocating stench in his lungs as Feran did the same to Elling and Kyce.

"What's happening?" Roeseph looked around. "What's going on?"

Pulling at his binds, Kyce glared at Feran. "How dare you take us hostage!"

Feran shrugged. "Well, for starters, it was really easy."

"Don't mock me, wench," Kyce threatened. "My soaring wolf would have your head in a second."

"Your *soaring* wolf is a bit busy," Feran nodded to Whisp at the mouth of the cave. Balancing on her hind legs, Whisp pulled against her rope and yipped at Saber, pleading for play while Saber growled and scooted away.

Kyce scowled.

Feran smirked, "*Horrifying*, isn't she?"

"Why did you bring us here?" Elling whispered. "We have no money. Nothing to offer."

"Relax, missy," Feran said. "I don't plan on robbing any of you. I brought you here for your own safety. Once word got out that I was in the Vaskan Forest, you all would've been tracked down and tortured for information."

Roeseph sat up. "Then why wouldn't you just tell us that? We would've complied."

Feran scoffed and looked at Sova, catching him with his tongue out and pointed at her. He looked away quickly with a guilty whistle.

"Is that so?" Feran arched a brow.

"*Most* of us would've complied," Roeseph corrected.

"Well then, if *all of you* promise to behave—that means you, Sova."

Sova grunted and looked away.

"Then I'll cut you all free," Feran drew a blade. "Deal?"

The four refuges surrounded the fire, blessed by the warmth while Whisp remained tied up at the mouth of the cave, having proven herself too much of a nuisance for Saber to bear.

Roeseph sat across the fire from Elling, watching as she shivered and rubbed her hands up and down her arms.

"Excuse me, miss," Roeseph said to Feran, so she looked up from kindling the fire. "Do you have a blanket or a cloak or something?"

"Yeah," Feran nodded and started toward the mouth of the cave where her cloak dried on a stalagmite.

She returned and tossed her cloak to Roeseph. Kneeling behind Elling, he laid the warm cloak around her shoulders.

"Thank you," Elling whispered. Roeseph nodded and sat beside her.

"I'm cold too, Roe," Sova pouted and batted his eyelashes.

Roeseph glared at him. "How about I put your face in the fire? Would that help?"

Smiling, Sova scooted away from the flames.

Whisps's whimpers filled the cave as she struggled against her rope, begging to be near Saber as he laid curled around Feran, his snout perched on her thigh.

Kyce stared at Whisp as she cried, his scowl deepening with each heart-breaking whine. "I've had enough of this," he growled as he snapped to his feet and hovered over Feran. "Give me the knife. I'm cutting her free."

Feran glanced up at Kyce, unthreatened. "Go for it," she tossed him the blade.

Stomping across the cave, Kyce cut Whisp free. Like a wild horse released from the stables, the wingless soaring wolf frolicked about the cave, yipping happily, and chasing the shadows the fire cast. Saber growled, annoyed.

"So, you're an Eradite?" Feran looked to Kyce as he settled by the fire. "I didn't take you for one."

Kyce glared at her, "What's that supposed to mean?"

"You just don't give off that holier-than-thou vibe those stuck-up hypocrites in the mountains have."

Roeseph, Elling, and Sova stared at Feran, their eyes wide with fear.

"Well, I can't say I disagree with you," Kyce grumbled and reclined to stare at the jagged stalactites. "Leaving Era was the best decision I ever made."

Sova sat up, "I thought they exiled you."

"Keep talking, and I'll feed you to Whisp," Kyce threatened.

"Oh sure," Sova griped sarcastically. "*She* insults your entire people, and I nearly get my head bitten off for correcting your story."

"An Eradite exile, huh?" Feran smirked and raised her chin. "To be sent down to Lykos is a fate worse than death in Era. What did you do to make your tribe cast you out?"

"Nothing," Kyce spat. "I was wrongly exiled."

"Uh huh. So, what tribe do you hail from? Eradusk or Eradawn?"

"None of your business," Kyce growled.

Feran smirked, unphased by the Eradite Exile's temper, and looked to Sova. "What happened there?" she asked and pointed to his gauze-wrapped shoulder

Sova looked from his wound to Feran, his gaze turning dark like Kyce's. "Nosey one, aren't you?"

"Yeesh," Feran shrugged. "Everything's a sensitive subject with you guys."

Roeseph leaned toward Feran and whispered, "Saulder shot him with a crossbow."

"Roe!" Sova snapped.

Feran's jaw dropped open. "Saulder shot you?" she laughed, her head falling back against Saber. "Oh, that's hilarious. Good for him."

Sova rolled his eyes, his gaze then falling to Feran's gauze-wrapped hand. "Well, what happened there?"

"Sensitive subject," Feran diverted. "I don't feel like talking about it with you. You should learn to respect people's privacy."

Sova raised his hands and let them smack against the floor. After all those years, Feran could still irritate him like no other. Roeseph snorted and smirked behind his hand.

"What?" Sova growled at him.

"Nothing," Roeseph coughed and stretched away his smile. "Nothing at all."

"Mhmm."

Feran looked to Elling across the fire wrapped tightly in her cocoon as she stared at the flames.

"What about you?" Feran asked. "What's your story?"

Elling looked at Feran with timid eyes. "Sorry?"

"What brought you to Seavale. You hail from the Mosharick Plains, don't you? What made you run away from home?"

Roeseph, Sova, and Kyce froze and looked to Elling as the Mosharick shepherd girl tightened the cloak around her trembling body.

Roeseph looked from Elling to Feran. "She doesn't need to talk if she doesn't—"

"I'm a Hyde Howler," Elling interrupted, her statement echoing through the cave.

Feran didn't so much as flinch. "I remember you now," she said coolly. "You're Chemon's daughter."

Elling straightened. "You knew my father?"

Feran nodded. "A little over a year ago, Saber and I were passing through Chemon's territory when Saber killed one of his fawns. I tried to pay him for the life of the fawn he lost, but he turned me away and asked that I simply tend his flock from time to time. He sent us away with food and furs. Chemon was a very kind man..." Feran's voice drifted, and her eyes fell to the flame. "... Saber and I were passing through when we heard the Vaskan soldiers were marching on your village. I sent Saber to defend Chemon's people, but it was too late. When I found you, you were in the middle of your Hyde Howler trance. I was able to awaken you, but should you hear a Siren's Call again, I'm afraid the Hyde Howler will be activated. I'm sorry I couldn't do more."

Biting her tongue, Elling buried her face in her knees. The four looked away from the shepherd girl's grief, hearts heavy with sympathy.

"My father, Oland, is a Hyde Howler," Roeseph said. "He was able to prevent the curse by binding his ears with gauze. Is there anything that you can do as a mind melder to help them?"

"I can release Elling from her trance if she ever becomes a Hyde Howler again," Feran stated. "But as for completely eradicating the hypnosis, I don't know. If you're looking for answers, your best bet would be the tribes of Era. They know more about hypnotism than I do."

Sova scoffed and clicked his jaw to the side. "I don't know," he said. "You knew enough to make my childhood a living nightmare."

Feran rolled her eyes. "Forsake Lykos. Are you still not over that?"

"You traumatized me!"

"That was over thirteen years ago."

"I wasn't able to go near chickens for over five years!"

Kyce and Elling looked at each other, confused.

"Don't ask," Roeseph exhaled. "It'll just make it worse."

"Whatever, Sova," Feran sighed at the ceiling as she reclined against Saber. "Complain and be a baby about it. I don't care."

"I care! It took Casavore hours to undo your hypnosis!"

"My father thought it was hilarious," Feran smirked. "That's your problem, Sova. You don't have a sense of humor."

Sova snapped to his feet, all the wrath of Hell shining in his eyes. "You take that back."

Kyce looked to Feran, his brow drawn up in an arch. "So, if you're not an Eradite, how did you come across that soaring wolf of yours?"

"A story for another time, my hot-headed friend," Feran smiled as she stroked the fur behind Saber's ears.

"Well, I mean," Kyce scoffed through a smirk and looked to the others, "I think we all want to know the story behind the beast that took a chunk out of the dire."

Feran's grin faded and she sat up. "What are you talking about?"

"You know," Kyce shrugged. "Your wolf, he attacked the dire in the Mosharick Plains."

"I don't know where you heard that, but it's a lie."

Sova snickered and crossed his arms. "It aint no lie. I was there. Your overgrown canine bit straight through the dire's armor. Why else do you think the dire's after you?"

"Wait, what?" Feran sat up straighter. "Is he ok?"

"Depends what you mean by, *ok*."

"Sova!"

"He's fine," Sova groaned. "He's gonna have a scar for the rest of his life, but the tyrant deserves it."

"I just assumed the dire sent his troops after me because I intervened," Feran muttered. "I didn't know he was at Chemon's camp, let alone that Saber attacked him."

Elling glared at Feran. "Why do you care?" she asked coldly. "Dire Saulder is a monster."

"He's not a monster," Feran snapped.

Sova puzzled at Feran, surprised by her quick defense. "Feran," he began, "you didn't see what I saw. Saulder isn't the boy you and I knew as children. He's a killer. A tyrant. What he did to Chemon's village is just one of the hundreds of massacres he's led."

"And so you tried to kill him?" Feran glared. "You were that quick to give up on your brother?"

"*That quick*?" Sova stood, his eyes dark. "Feran, you haven't seen Saulder in over ten years. I had to deal with him every single day. I should've been *quicker* to act."

Feran cocked her jaw to the side. "Still a coward, just as you always were."

Sova took an aggressive step toward Feran, making Saber's head snap upright as a growl filled his throat.

"I'm the coward?" Sova hissed. "You never came back. You were alive this whole time, and you never came back. Saulder got *sick* the moment you were taken. How could you have been so selfish to let Saulder—to let Casavore suffer like that?"

"Because I would've been killed if I had gone back!" Feran shouted as she rose to her feet. Her echo filled the cave like floodwaters, followed by an eon of silence.

"What are you talking about?" Sova asked. "There's no place safer in Lykos than Vaska."

Feran swallowed hard, her lips parting slightly as she stared at Sova. "You don't know, do you?"

"Know what?"

Feran sighed as she massaged her temple. "Sova, how was it the Blind Seers attacked the palace?"

"Because I let them in," Sova shrugged.

"And could they have gotten in without you?"

"No," Sova shook his head. "It's impossible to infiltrate the palace without someone on the inside."

"Exactly," Feran nodded as she stroked her medallion, her eyes falling to the floor. "Someone on the inside..."

"What are you getting at, Feran?" Sova challenged.

Feran met his eyes. "Ten years ago, when the Venom Tongues attacked... It was Lore who let them in."

Sova froze, his eyes widening at the realization. It didn't shock him that his power-hungry mother had ties with the Venom Tongues. Still, he never thought she'd be behind the attack that killed Casavore's wife and crippled Dire Zastar.

"How?" Sova questioned. "How do you know?"

Feran played with her medallion, her tortured gaze falling to the floor. "When the Venom Tongues took me, they would talk about how Lore was going to do right by them. That once the dire and his heirs were dead, she'd take the throne, and she'd give the Venom Tongues unlimited power."

"But then Saulder took the throne," Sova whispered. "And he sought to destroy the Venom Tongues... But what I don't understand was why my mother supported his cause—"

"Because the Venom Tongues knew she was a traitor. She never intended to reward them. The more of them Saulder killed, the less likely the attack would get back to her."

"She tried to kill us..." Sova's hands coiled into fists at his side. "She's why my father—" He bit his lip as hot tears rose in his throat, burning him. "She needs to pay. She and Saulder both need to pay." He looked to Roeseph. "We need to make her pay."

"And we will," Roeseph stood. "But we need a plan. We can't go into Vaska, just the two of us. We need an army."

Sova paused as a brilliant idea blossomed in his mind. "...Or maybe just one extra person," he looked to Feran.

She drew a sharp breath and stiffened, as if she knew what he was going to say before he even said it. "No," she shook her head and stepped back.

"You are the only one who can reason with Saulder," Sova said. "He won't listen to Casavore or I. Feran, you could have Lore thrown in prison and bring Saulder back to how he was before. You can fix everything."

"No, that won't work."

"Why not? Feran, he's still in love with you. If he learned you were alive, then—"

"No, I won't go back," Feran spat, clinging to herself as if she might fall apart. "Lore... Lore won't let me come back."

Only the sound of the crackling fire filled the cave. Heart heavy, Sova withdrew the Blesser's medallion from under his shirt for Feran to see.

"Is that..." Feran whispered, her eyes widening.

"The Blesser's medallion," Sova confirmed. "Casavore knew Saulder would use it for evil, so he gave it to me. He's in the dungeon now for his betrayal. You could save him and everyone else."

Roeseph stepped forward, his dusk-blue eyes big and pleading. "Please, Feran. My father was taken prisoner for the attack on the palace. I need to get him out."

"I—" Feran choked. "I'm sorry. I can't. I just can't."

Sova's jaw clenched, and his eyes burned with anger, as if a stray ember had found its way in. "All your power, and you won't use it. And you say I'm the coward."

Feran swallowed and she looked to the ground. Sova couldn't have been sure, but he could've sworn he saw shame in her eyes—something he thought the Blesser's brat was incapable of feeling. When Feran looked back up, her face was fixed in a scowl, and she ripped the Blesser's medallion from Sova's hand. To the group and his own surprise, Sova didn't fight her.

"You all can stay here until the blizzard lets up," Feran said and shoved the Blesser's medallion into her pocket. "Come morning, I want you gone."

Followed by Saber, Feran marched to the far mouth of the cave and laid before the blizzard, protected from the cold behind the wall of fur that was her soaring wolf.

She was who you loved, Saulder? Sova thought, baffled. *She's the one who destroyed you? Her?*

"Come on," Roeseph laid his hand on Sova's shoulder. "Let's get some rest. We'll figure everything out in the morning."

Rest? Sova Thought. *We've literally been asleep for two days.*

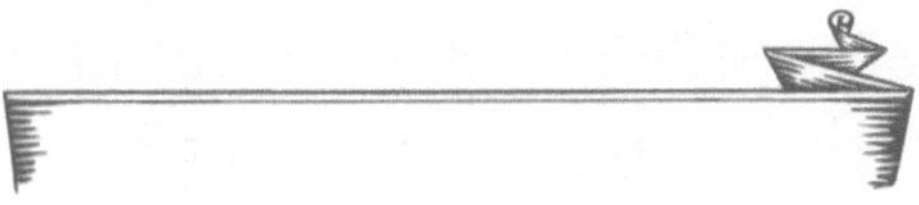

Chapter Sixteen: The Attempt

The Kingdom of Vaska...

Renaissance-inspired art curved across the dome ceiling of the Vaskan throne room; depictions of the past dires and all their bloody victories. A long, violet carpet rolled down the cobblestone to a platform where a great, silver throne stood. Sitting in it was the Dire of Vaska in his dreadful, black armor with the bladed shoulder plates.

The doors burst open and two Vaskan guards dragged in a prisoner by his withered arms, throwing him before the dire's throne.

The dire glowered at his prisoner, pleased by the deep, red lacerations in his back. "Casavore," he began in a voice masked by the metallic ring of his helmet. "You're looking well. How is prisoner life treating you?"

Casavore glared at the dire, not an ounce of love nor sympathy in his eyes as he launched blood-tinted spit on the tyrant's boot. The Vaskan Guard reared his boot back and kicked Casavore in the ribs. The old Blesser gasped and collapsed to the floor.

"You've been testing my patience, Casavore," the dire sighed. "Despite betraying me and Vaska, I have offered numerous times to make you my Blesser once more, and still you refuse. I have crafted many dazzling medallions to replace your own, and still, you turn me away. You're being an ungrateful guest."

"I would sooner die than be your, Blesser," Casavore hissed through a dry and ragged voice. "You have never been, and never will be my dire."

The dire glared at Casavore, annoyed. Since the Blesser's strike, Hyde Howler creation had stalled completely. The dire's army grew weaker by the day. He needed the Blesser's loyalty back; immediately.

"Get him out of my sight," the dire ordered. The Vaskan guards took Casavore by the arms and dragged him out of the throne room. Casavore glared at the dire as he went, his once holy and righteous eyes darkened by hate.

Left to his solitude, the dire sighed, exhausted. Casavore used to be so loyal to the dire, but ever since the Blind Seer attack, he loathed the Vaskan lord more than any man in Lykos. Then again, the old Blesser knew things of the dire others did not—secrets capable of destroying Vaska.

The tall doors swung open again, revealing two guards and a pair of shackled Seavallian thugs.

"What is the meaning of this?" the dire hissed and sat up in his throne. "I didn't summon you."

One of the guards stepped forward, his head bowed in submission. "My dire. These men come from Seavale. They claim to have seen the Rogue Eradite and his White Angel."

The guards forced the Seavallians to kneel as they trembled in the gaze of the dreaded dire.

"Speak," the dire ordered. "I don't have all day."

"My dire," one of the Seavallian thugs stammered as he dared to meet the dire's gaze. "Two days ago, our leader Pyne led us into the Vaskan Forest to capture your enemies—the Royal Traitor, and the Last Soldier."

The dire leaned forward in his throne.

"We—We—" the thug stammered and cleared his throat. "We were able to apprehend them, but were attacked by the White Angel. The beast killed our leader and his second in command, as well as over half our forces."

"And the Rogue Eradite?" the dire said. "Was he there?"

"*She*, my dire. The one who wields the White Angel is a woman. And—She—She wasn't no normal Eradite."

"How so?"

"She was a mind melder, sir. She made two of our men go insane with her medallion. We've never seen anything like it. She's a monster."

The dire clenched his fists. "And did you see this mind melder's face?"

"No, sir. But I can tell you, she's no ordinary mind melder. Her powers border on that of supernatural. Why, she might be even better than the Blesser of Vaska, sir."

The dire's heart plunged into the floor. If what the Seavallians said about the Rogue Eradite was true, then she could very well bring him and all of Vaska to their knees.

She needs to be taken care of.

"Pardon me, my dire," the thug whimpered. "But we've come a long way and were wondering when we might see our reward."

The dire looked up from his thoughts. "Reward?"

"Yes. For passing along this information."

"A reward, you say?" the dire rose from his throne and descended the platform. "Yes," the dire agreed sinisterly as he stopped before the ruffians. "You will indeed be rewarded."

The dire drew his sword and slashed both their throats. The guards stepped away, alarmed, while the Seavallians fell to the floor, clutching their throats as they choked on their own blood. Finally, the panic in their eyes softened, and they fell still.

The dire huffed and looked to the guards. "Send out a hunting party," he ordered as his sword hissed back into its sheath. "I want the mind melder dead."

THE VASKAN FOREST...

Like an army after a raid, the blizzard moved on, leaving a blanket of silver snow outside the cave to twinkle in the moonlight. Inside, Sova slept near the fire pit now expired to dimming coals. A wet nose pressed to his cheek, making him flinch and turn away. Not a moment later, a ragged tongue raked across his face.

"What? What?" he sputtered. Whisp sat before Sova, her tongue bounced out her jaws as she panted.

"*Shhh*," came Kyce's voice. "Be quiet. Do you want to wake the mind melder?" he pointed to Feran dozing at the mouth of the cave, snuggled in the center of Saber's curled up body.

Sova blinked tiredly and looked up at Kyce. "Why?" he groaned. "Why did you do this? What have I done to you?"

"What do you mean? What did I do to you?"

"Wake me up," Sova pouted. Kyce rolled his eyes and turned to Roeseph sleeping against a stalagmite just a short distance from Elling.

"Roeseph," Kyce whispered as he shook him. "Roeseph, wake up."

Roeseph blinked and yawned.

"Oh sure," Sova spat enviously. "He gets a gentle wake up call, while I have *Stumpy* sicked on me." Whisp sat at Sova's side, her stump-like wings flapping giddily.

Roeseph stretched through a yawn, "What's going on?"

"I know how you can defeat the dire," Kyce whispered. Sova and Roeseph traded a hopeful glance and huddled close to the Seavallian tavern fighter.

"How?" Sova whispered.

"The Eradites," Kyce replied.

"Uh huh..." Sova said and clicked his jaw to the side. "I'm going back to bed." He started toward his spot by the fire.

"Wait," Roeseph urged and pulled Sova back by his shirt. "Let's hear him out."

"Look," Kyce began, checking over his shoulder to see if Feran was still asleep, "I know that the Eradites have never intervened before in matters of Lykos, but if we go up there ourselves, maybe we can convince them to join your army and fight the dire."

"How would we get there?" Roeseph asked.

Kyce pointed to the sleeping, white soaring wolf. "The White Angel."

Sova's jaw dropped open. "Oh, that is a terrible idea."

Roeseph furrowed his brow at Kyce. "Why?" he asked. "Why help us?"

"Because," Kyce hissed, "I need that soaring wolf to get to Era and I'm not going to be able to steal it on my own."

"Why do you want to go back? I thought you were exiled."

"*Wrongly* exiled. Era is my home, and I was unjustly cast out. I'm not giving up without a fight."

Sova shrugged, "Fair enough."

Roeseph rubbed a tense muscle in his neck. "Fine," he sighed. "Ok—Fine. You guys get the wolf. I'll get Elling."

"What do we need Elling for?" Sova asked. "What's she going to do? Get nervous?"

"Just do it," Roeseph exhaled. As Kyce, Sova, and Whisp stalked toward Feran and Saber, Roeseph stooped beside the sleeping shepherdess. "Elling," he whispered and shook her lightly. "Elling, wake up."

Elling moaned and blinked away her daze. "Roeseph?" she whispered, sitting up slowly. "What is it?"

"We're going to the Cliffs of Era."

"Hmm?" Elling yawned as she rubbed her eyes.

"We're going to recruit the Eradites to help us fight the dire."

"You're leaving?" Elling said sadly.

"Yes," Roeseph whispered. "And you're coming with me."

Elling's eyes snapped wide. "I—I am?"

"Remember what Feran said? The people in Era might be able to help you. They might be able to lift the Hyde Howler hypnosis."

"Can they really?"

"Maybe," Roeseph shrugged and looked at Kyce and Sova across the cave. "That's if those two can figure *that* out."

Kyce and Sova stood around Feran and Saber. The first order of business was to separate the Dire's Damsel from her soaring wolf. Problem was, they had absolutely no clue how to do so.

"Any ideas?" Sova whispered.

"Shut up," Kyce scolded. "I'm thinking."

"I'll take that as a no."

Kyce rolled his eyes. His gaze then fell to the ropes Feran had tied them with collected in a pile across the cave. "I have an idea," he whispered and stalked off.

Sova stooped before Feran, watching as she snuggled close to Saber, her father's medallion clutched in hand. "I'll take that," he said smugly and stole the Blesser's treasure, "thank you."

"Ok," Kyce touched Sova's shoulder. "Move the girl. I'll handle the dog."

Sova nodded and lifted Feran into his arms. She sank against his chest, her head snuggling the gauze of his shoulder as he swiftly carried her to the far side of the cave. He laid her by the fire, covering her with her cloak to keep warm. Sova stared at Feran as she slept. In sleep, where she wasn't abusing her mind melding power like a psychopath, she actually looked quite peaceful.

Beautiful even. She looked exactly like the maiden Fala, but the big, round shape of her eyes came from Casavore.

As he stared, a strange, unfamiliar feeling awakened in his chest. It was warm, and slightly painful, yet satisfying.

Perhaps... he thought to himself. *Perhaps this is what Saulder saw in her...* Sova grimaced and shook away the crawling in his skin. *Yep. I'm losing my mind.*

Elling and Roeseph stood around Kyce as he wound Saber's muzzle and neck in rope.

"Is this a good idea, Kyce?" Roeseph asked as he stepped in front of Elling, acting as a burier between her and the monster.

"Of course," Kyce shrugged as he twisted the rope in hand. "Now, who wants to be the one to poke it?"

"*Poke it?*" Elling repeated.

"Well yeah," Kyce hissed. "We have to wake it up somehow. So who's poking it?"

Sova marched up to join the three. "I think I hallucinated just now," he said, rubbing his temples. "So, what are we talking about?"

"Him," Roeseph pointed at Sova. "He'll do it."

Sova shrugged. "Sure. What am I doing?"

"I FEEL AS IF I'M BEING taken advantage of," Sova grumbled.

Kyce and Roeseph stood a short distance away from Saber holding the ropes, while Sova stood near the monster's jaws with only a long stick to defend himself.

"Shut up and poke it," Kyce growled.

Roeseph added, "Oh, and don't die."

Sova glared at Roeseph. "You are a great help." Sova drew in a deep breath and raised the stick ever so slightly. "Roe, Ky, El, remember me when I go."

Elling and Kyce traded a confused glance.

"El?" Elling repeated.

"Ky?" Kyce grimaced.

Roeseph sighed. "He's afraid of syllables. Just go with it."

Holding his breath, Sova edged the stick toward the snoring beast. *How did I get here? He wondered. I was bloody royalty. A prince of Vaska. How in the name of the Great Valley of Lykos did I end up in this situation?*

"God," Sova prayed, the stick now an inch from the monster's face. "It's me, Sova. Remember how I got baptized when I was ten? That has to count for something, right?"

"Just poke the stupid wolf, Sova!" Kyce snapped.

Saber's amber eyes flashed open, revealing Sova's frightened expression in his pupil. The beast snarled, enraged.

Sova gulped. "Hey there, buddy?" he smirked. "Sleep well?"

Saber lunged to his paws, sending Roeseph and Kyce flying across the cave floor by the ropes they held.

Holding his stick like a sword, Sova yelled, "Stay back! I'm warning you!"

Saber chomped down on the stick, just short of Sova's hands. Sova gazed at his broken weapon. "Oh," he laughed timidly. "That's unfortunate."

Elling peaked out from behind a stalagmite, trembling. "Sova?"

"Yeah, El?" Sova replied calmly.

"You—You should run."

"Yeah. Yeah, I agree."

Chucking the last of his stick at Saber, Sova darted out the mouth of the cave and sprinted through the snow. Saber chased after him, his snarl rumbling out his jaws like hot thunder, as he dragged Roeseph and Kyce by the ropes.

Elling fled out of the cave, pleading for the soaring wolf to stop while Whisp joined the chase, her tail wagging rapidly.

"He's going to eat me!" Sova wailed.

"Sova!" Roeseph shouted as waves of snow splashed his face. "Sova, stop running!"

Kyce raised his chin and yelled, "No! We're weighing him down! Just keep running!"

"*You* keep running!" Sova snapped.

"What—What do I do?" Elling called from the sidelines as she watched Saber chase Sova back and forth across the snow.

"Nothing!" Roeseph called. "Nothing. We got this covered. Thank you."

"I'm going to die!" Sova shrieked into the night.

Saber made a tight turn, sending Roeseph and Kyce rolling into a tree.

"Roeseph?" Elling shrieked as she ran to his side. "Roeseph? Are you ok?"

Roeseph groaned and blinked away his daze. "Yeah," he grumbled. "I think I hit a tree."

Whisp bounded up to them, sending up a wave of snow as she nestled next to Kyce to lick the frost from his face.

Kyce shoved her away, sputtering. "What happened?" he asked as he looked around. "Did we win?"

Sova screamed.

"Apparently not," Kyce concluded.

Saber roared and swiped his paw at Sova's legs. The Royal Traitor fell to the snow, his face stinging from the frost. Sova turned onto his back to find Saber snarling down at him.

"Good doggy," he said nervously. Saber snarled again.

"Sova, no!" Roeseph shouted as he, Kyce, and Elling sprung to their feet.

Saber's jaws opened wide, his canines strung together by threads of saliva. Sova pressed himself to the ground and looked away.

Someone snapped their fingers. The White Angel looked up, his amber eyes shifting from murderous to gentle. Sova dared to open his eyes. Feran stood at the mouth of the cave, her cloak thrown over her shoulder, with her jaw flexed to the side.

Sova smiled guiltily and waved. "Hey, Feran. Why you up? Bad dream?"

Feran crossed her arms and marched out into the snow to stand by Saber.

"We have to stop meeting like this," she said down at Sova.

"It's not ideal," Sova agreed. Saber snarled at the Royal Traitor. "What's his problem? Why am I the only one he attacks?"

"I don't know," Feran shrugged. "He does seem to have a distinct aversion to you. But then again, you have that effect on people."

"It's a gift."

Feran stooped to Sova and plucked her father's medallion from his neck.

"I was—uh," Sova hesitated. "I was keeping that warm for you."

"I appreciate it," Feran arched her brow as she stood. "And as for trying to steal, Saber?"

"*Kyce* was trying to keep him warm for you," Sova pointed at his partner in crime.

"Was he?" Feran looked to the Eradite Exile. He hadn't a speck of remorse in his eyes.

Roeseph approached the medallion-wielding hermit. "I apologize for taking advantage of your hospitality," he groveled. "But it's crucial we get to the Cliffs of Era, and your soaring wolf is our only way to get there. I am sorry to have deceived you, but for the sake of Lykos and all its nations, please, we need to—"

"Fine," Feran sighed.

"Pardon me?"

"I can take you as far as Era, but I won't go further than there. Whatever business you have with the tribes, you're on your own."

"You'll—You'll take us there?"

"Sure," Feran shrugged. "After all, I can't imagine a greater pleasure than leaving Sova stranded on a mountain for dead."

Sova glared at her from beneath Saber. "You are a very, very bitter woman."

Feran winked.

Elling stepped out from behind Roeseph. "Will you really take us to Era?" she asked, her eyes shining with hope.

"I don't have anything better to do," Feran said. "And I owe it to Chemon to make sure you get there in one piece."

"So," Sova smiled nervously at Feran. "No hard feelings, right, Feran? Everything that happened between you and I, water under the bridge?"

Feran smirked as she fiddled with her charred medallion, "Oh, the floodwaters have totaled the bridge. And I need to make up for the ten years of torturing you that I missed out on."

Sova gulped.

"Oh, I like her," Roeseph scoffed.

"Everyone, on Saber," Feran ordered and pulled herself onto the tall beast. Roeseph helped Elling onto Saber, then pulled himself up to sit behind her.

"Woah," Elling trembled.

"You ok, ma'am?" Roeseph asked.

"Yeah," Elling gulped. "It's just a lot higher than I expected."

Kyce pulled himself onto Whisp and rode beside Saber.

Feran eyed the wingless soaring wolf up and down. "You're gonna want to leave that thing here," she advised. "She won't be able to keep up with us when we fly."

"She goes, or none of us go," Kyce growled, his amber eyes flaming.

Feran sighed. "Alright, fine. I guess we can walk... Just added an extra three days to our journey. No big woop."

Sova stood from the snow, wiping the white powder from his shoulder as he stalked toward Saber. The white soaring wolf snarled at his closeness, causing Sova to stumble and fall into the snow again. His comrades cackled from above.

"Sorry, Sova," Feran snickered. "What Saber says goes. You can ride with Kyce."

"He gets his winning personality from you," Sova grumbled and pulled himself onto Whisp's back to sit behind Kyce.

Leaning forward, Feran drove Saber north, followed by Whisp.

"So," Sova began, "this is pretty exciting, huh? I mean, people could be talking about this journey for centuries."

"Why do I have the feeling *you'll* be talking for centuries, Sova?" Roeseph exhaled.

"You complain now, but journeys can get boring without interesting conversation, Roe."

Feran snorted and looked back. "*Roe*?" she taunted. "You let him call you that?"

Elling exhaled. "We all have nicknames, actually."

Feran laughed. "That's hilarious. What's mine, Sova?"

"You don't get one," Sova growled.

Kyce glared enviously at the mind melder. "Lucky."

"You'll all see," Sova continued, "they'll be talking about us for years and years to come. Me, Sova, the Royal Traitor. Roeseph, the Last Soldier. Kyce, the Eradite Exile. Elling, the uh... the Feral Shepherd?"

Elling grimaced and shuddered. "I don't—I don't like that name."

"You get what you get," Sova grumbled.

Feran smirked at her old foe, "And what about me?"

"You're already a legend," Sova spat. "We won't tell them about you."

Feran rolled her eyes and faced forward.

"Hey Sova," she called, making the Royal Traitor look up. "Catch."

She tossed him Casavore's medallion. Sova looked from the powerful pendant in his hand and back at Feran, confused by her kindness.

"If my father gave you his medallion, he gave it to you for a reason," she admitted. "But if you lose it, I'll feed you to Saber."

"He already lost it once," Kyce added eagerly.

"You stole it from me!"

Chapter Seventeen: The Trail of Traitors

The Vaskan Forest...

The sun rose from the Eradawn cliffs, shining through the gaps in the trees as the forest floor glittered like shaved gold. Large paw prints tarnished the snow, left by the soaring wolves, Whisp and Saber. The five exiles they carried hunched forward, their backs sore from the perilous ride.

Sova reclined on Whisp, watching as the treetops drifted overhead. "Are we there yet?" he whined.

Feran, Roeseph, Kyce, and Elling groaned in annoyance.

"Just like I said five minutes ago..." Feran seethed. "...No."

"I'm so bored," Sova sighed and sat upright. "How about a game?"

"*No!*" all shouted in sync.

"Ok, I spy..." Sova looked around, "something... blue!"

Elling sighed dreadfully, "The sky."

"Yes!"

Feran glared back at Elling. "You're enabling him."

"I spy something white," Sova continued.

"The snow," Elling rubbed her temple.

"Nope."

"The clouds."

"Right again."

Roeseph snapped upright, his eyes wide with sleep-deprived madness. "Ok!" he shouted. "How about instead we play a different game."

"I don't like your games," Sova said. "You made us play the quiet game last time."

Kyce sighed with a nod, "That was a fun game..."

"Sova," Feran glared back at the Royal Traitor. "Stop complaining or else."

"Or else what?" Sova laughed.

Feran lifted her charred medallion and arched a brow. Sova eyed her half-burnt trinket—a weapon capable of turning even the sanest of men into blubbering fools.

"Ha!" Sova mocked. "Jokes on you," he held up Casavore's medallion, "I have one too!"

Feran pulled on the scruff of Saber's neck, making him stop and snarl at Sova. Sova scrambled behind Kyce, his human shield, clinging to him like a squirrel on a branch. Smirking at his cowardice, Feran drove Saber forward.

Kyce let out a hot breath through clenched teeth, his bulging muscles trembling with fury. "You have three seconds to get your hands off me before I feed them to Whisp," he growled, his amber eyes glowing with rage. "One. Two. Three—"

Sova scooted to Whisp's rump and held his hands up in surrender. "My bad."

Roeseph looked to Feran. "Thank you."

"It's my pleasure," she grinned.

Sova glared at Feran. "It's scary that people like you get to have the power of a mind melder."

"Keep talking Sova, and I'll make you soil yourself around farm animals again."

"Of all the enchantments," Sova turned away, shaking his head. "Why that one?"

Feran chuckled to herself,

"Speaking of mind melders," Roeseph began, "how long do you suppose till we reach the Cliffs of Era? Or at least start climbing?"

"Well," Feran drew a long, frosty breath. "If we'd flown, we would be there by morning, but walking is another story. It's still about four days away, but first, we need to find the Pera River—"

"Hey," Sova sat up, his eyes bright. "That's the river my great-grandmother Pera named after herself."

All glared at Sova. "Still not allowed to talk," Sova said and gave a thumbs up. "Ok, good. Proceed, *Witch*."

Feran rolled her eyes and returned her focus to the path. "About ten miles north, we'll come to a merge between the Pera River and the river that flows from the Falls of Era. From there, we'll follow against the current to the Falls of Era, where Saber and I can take you guys up."

The group continued in silence for several strides as the sound of snow crunching under heavy paws sang through the forest, loud as thunder.

Kyce looked to his comrades in exile, his jaw clenched in disdain. "They won't listen to you, you know," he said bitterly. "The Eradites, they don't listen to anyone but their God. And they don't even do too good a job at that."

"You don't know that for sure," Roeseph defended. "Yahweh can move mountains from one spot to the next. He can do the same with the hearts of the Eradites."

"You're being naive," Kyce spat back. "The moment they find out you're on their land, they'll cast you from the Cliffs of Era. You're pursuing a lost cause."

Elling looked down, her eyes dim with hopelessness. If they did make it to Era, would the people even bother to help her? Was she to be stuck a Hyde Howler forever?

Roeseph looked at Elling then glared at Kyce, his eyes dark with defense. "If you think going to the Eradites is hopeless, why are you coming?"

"I'm not seeking the Eradites' help," Kyce fired back. "My journey is purely out of spite." He looked ahead, teeth grinding into dust, "They need to acknowledge that they've wrongly banished me."

Silence once again vanquished the forest as tension brewed between the exiles.

Feran sighed, annoyed by the ear-piercing quiet. "So," she said, "let's say the Eradites do help you. What's the plan after that?"

Sova laughed sharply. "I'll tell you what we're going to do. First, we're going to storm Vaska. Then raid the dungeons and release all the Blind Seers who have been wrongly imprisoned. Casavore too. Then, with the Blind Seers and the Eradites at our side, we'll invade the palace and take Vaska."

"And what of Saulder?" Feran asked. "What will happen to him?"

"I'll kill him. And this time," Sova slapped his gauze wrapped shoulder, "he'll be the one who gets shot."

Feran froze, her heart sinking rapidly. "You'd do that to Saulder?" she challenged. "You'd actually kill your own brother?"

"He didn't have a problem trying to kill *me*," Sova growled. "Do you know what Casavore told me he said? '*I want to watch the Royal Traitor bleed.*' The only reason I'm here right now is because Casavore spared me."

"It doesn't matter," Feran argued. "He's the dire of Vaska and the son of Zastar. He's entitled to his life."

"A crown unearned doesn't entitle him to anything, Feran," Sova growled. "He's a monster. The sooner you let go of this silly delusion that he's anything else, the better."

"Did my father let go of this *silly delusion*? Don't you think that if Saulder is really as bad as you say, Casavore would've stopped him?"

"Your father is blinded by the brotherhood he and Zastar shared. The Blesser can't bring himself to kill Zastar's son, so he tolerates the dire's monstrosities and calls it Godly mercy."

"And who are you to say God can't show mercy to those like Saulder? You forget, your sins don't outweigh that of his."

"Oh, I beg to differ," Sova spat. "The worst thing I've done is charm a chambermaid or two. He's destroyed more families than some people have had meals. And don't give me that '*I can't change him, but God can*' spiel. I get that enough from Casavore."

"If God says He can change Saulder's heart, then He can."

"Yeah, God also says '*But let justice roll down like waters, and righteousness like an ever-flowing stream.*' That's what we're doing. Saulder hasn't built a stream in his life. He builds dams."

Roeseph cleared his throat. "If I may speak, Feran," he intervened. "Sova's right. You've been in hiding for a long time. You haven't seen what he's done to people. What he's done to us."

Feran ignored Roeseph, and dug her spear-like glare into Sova. "Nonetheless, Saulder is still your brother and my friend. We both have a duty to defend him."

"*We?*" Sova scoffed. "No, Feran, there is no *we*. You gave up that duty when you abandoned him ten years ago."

Feran lost her voice. Her lips pierced in a sneer turned forward. Sova clicked his tongue, annoyed by her ignorance and stubbornness.

"You do me one thing," Feran grumbled. "Whatever happens, you make sure Lore pays for what she took from me."

Sova reclined on Whisp and crossed his arms behind his head. "With pleasure," he said resentfully.

Sova stared up at the sky, watching as the kaleidoscopes of winter leaves ruffled and swayed overhead. He sighed, the fire in his chest soothed by the serenity.

As he listened to the sweet song of winter, the sound of heavy hooves cutting through the snow rose into the air. Sova's brow crinkled, and he craned his head back. In the distance, noble stallions dressed in purple ribbons carried armed Vaskan soldiers, trampling the pawprints they left in their wake.

Sova sprung uptight, terror ravaging his heart. *They found us.* "Run," he said in a steady voice.

Kyce looked back. "What are you babbling about, now?" he growled.

"Run," Sova repeated, his voice escalating from steady to panicked. "Run. Run. Run!"

Kyce looked up. "Forsake Lykos!" he cursed and kicked Whisp sharply in the side. The two soaring wolves plunged into a sprint.

"How did they find us?" Elling cried as she clung to Saber's fur.

Feran glanced back at their enemies, her face knotted in a scowl. "It doesn't matter how they found us. What matters is that we lose them."

Sova glanced at their enemies to see they wielded crossbows, the very same the dire used to shoot him in the shoulder.

"Scatter!" Sova shouted and ducked against Whisp's chestnut fur. Like a needle in a quilt, Saber and Whisp wove through the trees. As they ran, a crossbow's silver tongue fired and rushed up to join the race. It grazed Kyce's cheek, making him shout in pain and clamp the shallow wound.

"Are you hit?" Roeseph called from Saber.

Kyce lowered his hand to find blood painted his palm. "I'm fine. How do we lose these guys?"

Feran sat upright, her eyes shining with a brilliant idea. "Everyone, off Saber!" she ordered.

"Why?" Sova snarled. "Are you trying to ditch us?"

"Kind of," Feran shrugged and looked back at Roeseph and Elling. "Now get off my wolf, or I'll have him throw you off."

Hastily, Roeseph and Elling leaped onto Whisp, making the wingless soaring wolf yelp at the added weight. Without so much as a 'goodbye,' Feran launched Saber through the treetops and disappeared into the winter sky, leaving just a spotlight in the leaves to remember her by.

"See what I mean?" Sova pointed. "*The worst.*"

Before his comrades could agree, a storm of arrows surrounded them on each side. The exiles lowered themselves to Whisp's back, desperate to escape the piercing kiss of death.

Growing closer, the Vaskans aimed their crossbows and prepared to fire. Before they could, a ghastly roar shook the forest and the soldiers looked to the trees. Saber dropped through the leaves and slammed his wings into the back of the Vaskan's helmets. The soldiers fell to the snow, trampled by their own horses. Running alongside their enemies, Saber snapped at a neighboring horse, so the stallion shrieked and threw its rider. As a Vaskan raised his crossbow to slay the beast, Feran grabbed the weapon and forced the soldier's aim to the sky then wove her charred medallion before his eyes.

"*Your heart betrays you,*" she entranced. "*Your heart condemns you. As I say to you, you will believe that each of your comrades has been with your wife. You must make them pay, for their sins are due.*"

Winking, Feran rode up to join the others.

The soldier blinked with alarm as the hypnosis purged his sanity. He turned on his comrades, firing at them frantically so many dropped dead or fell back.

Feran chuckled to herself as she rode beside Whisp, a look of victory on her face as the four gawked at her with admiration.

"You're wrong, Sova," Elling shook her head. "She's the best."

Sova glared into nothing, annoyed with Feran's valiance. "Show off."

Behind them, the Vaskans struck down their enchanted comrade and advanced the exiles.

Roeseph looked back, eyes widening. "They're gaining on us!" he warned.

"Can we take them?" Kyce asked.

"No," Feran shook her head. "But we can lose them if we cross the river."

She pointed ahead to a bubbling white river beyond the tree line. The river was wide. Too wide to jump.

"Whisp's not going to make that!" Kyce shouted.

"Do you have a better idea?" Feran challenged.

Unable to argue, Kyce drove Whisp toward the river. Feran rode Saber ahead and launched into the air. As they soared over the rapids, a Vaskan soldier drew their crossbow and fired. The arrow scathed Saber's wing, making him yelp as his wings coiled against his body. Feran gasped in alarm as she and Saber went hurtling toward the water.

"Feran!" Sova shouted as the white-capped waves swallowed both Feran and the White Angel whole. Before the group could mourn, Whisp hurtled toward the river, her stump-like wings flapping perilously as she prepared to jump.

"Whisp, no!" Kyce pleaded.

Whisp leaped into the sky. Gravity found her not a second later, and jerked her toward the water. Lost to the waves and fighting for breath, the river pushed the exiles further downstream, where violent tides beat them against the rocky floor.

The Vaskan soldiers halted where the exiles disappeared.

"Do you think they survived?" a soldier asked.

"It's unlikely," the commander growled. "But we shouldn't consider them dead. Not yet. I'd rather be safe than risk the wrath of the dire should they live."

"Why are they traveling this far north? There's nothing here. No tribes or towns—just, nothing."

"Because they're not looking for something in Lykos... We need to get back to Vaska and speak with Dire Saulder. The Royal Traitor and the Rogue Eradite are headed to Era."

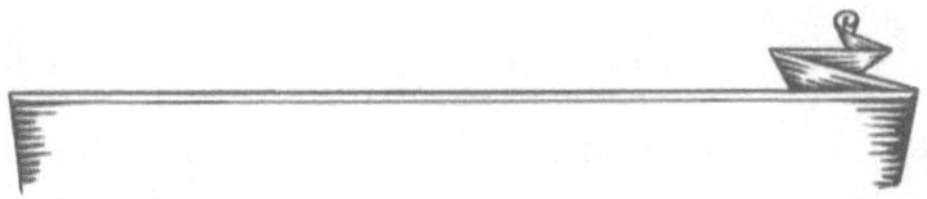

Chapter Eighteen: The River

Sova gasped breathlessly and opened his eyes to a dark void. His lips parted to welcome air, only to find he couldn't breathe, his lungs writhing like a worm speared by a hook. Falling to his knees, he grabbed his throat.

"Help," he wheezed. "Someone, help me."

"Who are you?" came the dire's demonic voice. Sova turned on his hands and knees to see the monster of his dreams a short distance away.

"Saulder," he gasped and reached forward. "Help me."

"Who are you?" the dire growled.

"Please, Saulder," Sova choked. "I can't... breathe..."

"Who are you!" the dire drew his sword.

"I can't—" Sova gasped and fell to the floor, curling into a ball.

Both death and the dire raced toward Sova, their swords sparkling in hand. Struggling under the weight of breathlessness, Sova looked up to find a blade hurtle his way.

SOVA AWOKE, HIS THROAT scorched by frigid liquid lurching from his lips. Feran dragged him out of the river and onto the rough, pebble shore, his back grating against the terrain before she dropped him. She loomed overhead, cold water droplets falling from her hair and onto his face.

"Sova?" she called, tapping him lightly on the cheek. "Sova, can you hear me?"

Sova coughed up at the cloudless sky. "I can hear you," he rasped.

Feran exhaled with relief. They laid beside a river bend where the rapids tamed to gentle ripples. Winter pines stood guard around the pebble shore, their snowcapped tips skimming the crisp, blue sky.

"I'll be right back," Feran exhaled, trembling with cold, "keep breathing."

"I'll try my best," Sova groaned as Feran disappeared toward the river. He looked to the side. Roeseph and Elling laid beside him, unconscious.

Where's Kyce? Sova wondered.

Saber and Whisp herded around Feran as she dragged a man out of the river, their wet fur clinging to their muscular frames.

Kyce kicked and fought in Feran's grasp, his face twisting in a scowl. "Let me go!" he roared. "I said let me go!"

Feran dropped him beside Sova. "You're welcome."

Kyce winced and looked at his ankle, the flesh swollen and black.

"Forsake Lykos," he cursed through gritted teeth as he grabbed his foot.

Feran knelt beside him and reached to examine the injury.

"Don't!" Kyce threatened. "Don't touch me."

"I'm trying to help you," Feran said calmly.

"I don't need your help. I don't want your help—"

"You know what. I don't have time for this." Feran swung her charred medallion before Kyce. He froze, his scowl softening. "*Eradite Exile,*" Feran began. "*Your temper is short, but my patience shorter. You are injured, and wrath is no sedative. Be calm when I offer you help and take it generously. Do as I say or remain here miserably.*"

Kyce blinked away his daze, and a resentful glare brimmed his eyes. Reluctantly, he stretched his leg before Feran for her to examine, wincing every time she grazed a tender spot.

"It may be sprained, but I'm not certain," Feran said as she stood. "I'll make a splint just in case."

Accompanied by Saber, She sprinted into the pine trees to gather branches. Kyce and Sova remained on the shore, aching from the river's torment.

As they waited, Whisp marched up to Kyce and rubbed her nose along his face.

"Whisp—Whisp, I'm fine," Kyce sputtered and tried to shove her away. Whisp shook her wet fur, dousing Kyce, Sova, Roeseph, and Elling in her rainfall.

Roeseph and Elling woke up gasping, alarmed by the frigid water.

"Where are we?" Roeseph gasped. "What happened?"

"I'm not sure," Sova shrugged.

Feran jogged out of the woods and up to Kyce with two branches and a long sturdy reed and began making a splint.

"What happened to Kyce?" Elling asked worriedly.

"He twisted his ankle," Feran stated as she stood upright. "Should be fine in a day or two."

"Is he ok to travel?" Roeseph asked.

Kyce glared at him. "Yes. I am."

"I don't know," Feran said. "I mean, Whisp can carry you the rest of the way, but the journey to Era will be extremely strenuous. Maybe you should consider staying in Lykos. There are some small Mosharick Villages south of here we can take you to—"

"No!" Kyce snapped. "You aren't ditching me. You can't just cast me out. I can't help what happened to me. I deserve to be in Era more than anyone else! You have no right to take me away from my home! You can't just leave me down here! Not again!"

Kyce panted heavily into the wind, his rage filled eyes tinted with tears. The others stared at him, recognizing the anguish in his gaze even when he looked away.

"Ok," Roeseph nodded. "If it's that important to you, we'll get you there."

Kyce looked at Roeseph, his glare softening. "You will?"

"Of course," Sova smirked, laying his hand on Kyce's shoulder. "We'll take turns carrying you if we need to."

Kyce leaned away. "Don't touch me, Sova."

Feran snorted and crossed her arms. "Well," she sighed and looked around the rocky beach, "this is as good a place as any to set up camp. I'll get a fire going..."

THE SUN FELL BEHIND the horizon, hauling a ceiling of stars in its wake. The light bubbling of the gentle river harmonized with the howling wind. And the rustle of the pine needles sounded of the lyre.

The five exiles huddled around the coals of a fire, their faces coated in amber warmth. Elling sighed contently and stretched her palms to the flames. Roeseph sat beside her, smirking at the gentle smile blooming in her lips. Kyce reclined from the flames, his back against Whisp as she gazed wistfully at the sky—the place she so longed to be. Feran prodded a stick at the fire, moving the foundations to secure the flame. She looked to Kyce, who winced as another surge of pain struck his ankle.

"Does it still hurt?" she asked.

Kyce sighed. "A little."

"You know, I can hypnotize the pain away," she held up her charred medallion.

Sova snapped upright, his eyes alive with warning. "Don't do it!"

"Sova," Feran said, "calm down."

"It's a trap."

Kyce chuckled and shook his head. "Thank you, Feran. But I can handle it."

Feran shrugged and resumed poking the fire.

"So, Kyce," Sova began, leaning forward to rest against his knees. "Tell us about Era. What's it like?"

Kyce exhaled, his eyes craning to the sky. "Well... It's a great deal colder in the winter and scorching hot in the summer. Mountains cover the horizons on all sides, and there's pine trees everywhere. The water is always crystal clear, and howls of soaring wolves fill the sky. It's a very peaceful place as long as the people keep to their tribes."

Elling wrapped her knees to her chest and looked hopefully at the Eradite Exile. "And the Eradites?" she mumbled, "Do they all have power like Feran?"

"No," Kyce shook his head. "Only the chief's immediate family and the high priest are trained as mind melders."

"That's what my father was," Feran said, failing to hide the bitterness in her voice. "He was an apprentice to the priest, training to lead Eradusk in the ways of God. He would've been good at it too. If the Eradawns hadn't..." she paused, her jaw clenching. "But they're a skilled people. If there's anyone who could rid you of the Hyde Howler curse, Elling, it's them."

"What if they can't?" Elling whispered. "What if—What if I'm stuck like this?"

Roeseph touched her shoulder. "We'll figure it out," he promised. "We will."

Feran sighed and reclined against Saber, snuggling into the feather-like softness of his fur.

As Feran stroked her soaring wolf's snout, Sova's gaze fell to the gauze wrapping her hand. "So. You really not going to tell us what happened there?" he pointed.

"You really can't mind your own business can you?" Feran said and looked at her childhood foe. She expected his eyes to be prying and invasive like they always were. But instead, they were soft. Concerned even. She'd never witnessed this in Sova before—almost as if he were a different man.

Feran sighed, unwound the gauze, and revealed her palm to the flames. A bubbling red imprint of her medallion scorched her flesh, contorted by raised edges of callused skin.

Sova gulped, and looked up to meet Feran's eyes, "What happened?"

Feran laid her hand in her lap and looked down, her jaw clenching at the horrid sight.

"It happened ten years ago," she gulped. "On the day the Venom Tongues attacked the palace, my mother and I had taken shelter in our shack. But we were found by a group of Venom Tongue pirates. When they saw I had a mind melder's medallion, they decided to sell me for a higher profit. My mother tried to save me, but she..." Feran paused to allow the lump in her throat to pass.

"...Well," She sniffled and choked down her tears. "She paid for it. I was bound at the hands and forced to walk behind the Venom Tongue thugs for four days until we came to the Falls of Era, where they made camp. In those four days, Saulder was made dire in place of Zastar and sent out hundreds of troops to search for me. The Venom Tongues grew restless. In the night, I heard them talking. 'The money isn't worth it,' one said, 'we'll be executed for taking the dire's betrothed.' Another had said, 'Maybe Lore can vouch for us. She let us in. She'll let us out.' Their leader said that because the Venom Tongues had failed to kill the dire and his sons, she'd give them nothing in return. And so, they came to the conclusion that I should die..."

Ear-ringing silence struck the group, so only the song of the river and cackling fire was heard.

"When they came for me," Feran continued, "they threw my medallion in the fire so I couldn't entrance them. Just before they could slit my throat, we heard a roar coming from the Falls of Era. A massive white wolf with the wings of an angel came down and slaughtered every last one of the Venom Tongues, saving me for last... My father once told me that the mind melders of Era would entrance soaring wolves to become devout and loyal followers. I never tried it before, but it was my only shot at survival. So I reached for my medallion in the flames," Feran looked at the burn mark in her palm, recalling every moment of the scorching agony.

She rubbed away the ghostly pain in her hand. "Needless to say, I got burned. When the soaring wolf was upon me, I was able to hypnotize him, and... well, Saber's been at my side ever since."

Saber's tail thumped with glee as he nestled his head against Feran's sternum, begging for pets.

"You could've come home," Sova whispered, his silver eyes dense with sorrow. "Saulder and Casavore would've protected you."

Feran grinned sadly and shook her head. "No. They couldn't have. Believe it or not, Sova, I was the one protecting them. If I ever came back, Lore might've..." her voice trailed off and she cleared her throat. "How about we all get some rest? We have a long journey ahead of us."

Feran turned on her side to hide from her fellow travelers' pity.

"Did you know I've never seen my scar?" Sova said out of the blue.

Feran lifted her head from Saber's side and looked back at him.

He patted the gauze around his shoulder. "I can't bring myself to look at it. Even when I change the gauze, I have to look away. I don't know, I just... Casavore told me I should never let anyone see it, lest they figure out who I am. But, honestly, I don't want to see it either. I don't want to know that my brother would *actually* try to hurt me..."

Sova stretched his arms overhead, groaning tiredly into the night. "Scars really suck, don't they," he smiled at Feran, "Things are hard enough to forget even when we don't wear them in our skin."

Feran looked to the fire, unable to meet Sova's eyes. She knew Saulder as her good-hearted, noble best friend and eventual husband. It seemed impossible for him to do something so feral, especially to his little brother whom he loved.

Kyce crossed his arms and sat up against Whisp.

"I was kicked out for not being loyal to my tribe," he added, unprompted.

"Man, everyone's making confessions now, huh?" Sova snickered.

"Shut up, Sova," Roeseph warned.

"Look, I can't go into detail," Kyce continued. "But long story short, they needed me to devote myself to them and... I had allegiances elsewhere. I shouldn't have been cast out of my home for turning my back on my people's prejudices."

Feran drew a deep breath.

"Well, I hope you all get what you desire," she said briskly. "Elling, I hope you're freed from your curse. Kyce, I hope you get the justice you deserve. And Roeseph... I hope Sova doesn't drive you insane."

"Hey," Sova snapped. "I am a pleasure."

"No," Roeseph shook his head. "No, you are not."

Hardy laughter berated the fire, forcing the flames to shrink then expand. Their quiet teasing filled the night, rising with the embers to join the star-claimed sky.

THE KINGDOM OF VASKA...

News of the exiles' plot to seek Era soon reached the dire, and so a plan was made to intercept them. Below the dire's dwelling laid the dungeons, where freedom laid slaughtered and buried.

Darkness and the snickering of rats festered the prison, with only the dull light of a single torch to fend off the void. The Blind Seers sat alone in their cells, singing hymns of desperation, and praying for the return of Christ—the only man capable of liberating them from their Hell.

At the far end of the dungeon stood two cells, one belonging to Oland, and the other, to Casavore. Oland sat with his back against the wall he and the Blesser shared, his bald head gleaming with sweat. The gauze he wore around his ears laid on the other side of the chamber—there was no point wearing them if there was no hope of freedom.

"Casavore?" he wheezed, his voice dry and crisp from lack of water. "Casavore, are you awake?"

Casavore laid on the other side of the wall, face down in a pool of his own sweat. Long red lashes marked his back—punishment for his mutiny.

"Casavore?" Oland said again. Casavore groaned in response to his friend—proof he lived.

"You'll never guess what I overheard the guards talking about," Oland cackled. "Prince Sova and my boy... they've found the Rogue Eradite. They've made themselves a small army and are headed to Era to gather reinforcements. Isn't that great? Roeseph, my boy. He's coming back for his old man. That's Roeseph," Oland chuckled tiredly. "That's my boy."

Casavore flattened against the floor, exhausted by the weight of guilt crushing his bones to dust.

"God, forgive me," he whispered. "I didn't know what else to do... I didn't know what else to do. Be with *him*, please, for I have sinned against Zastar's son."

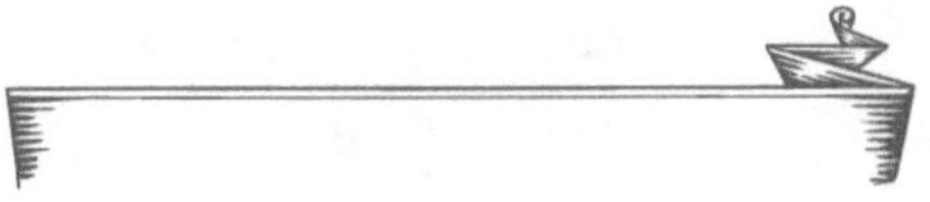

Chapter Nineteen: Mutt

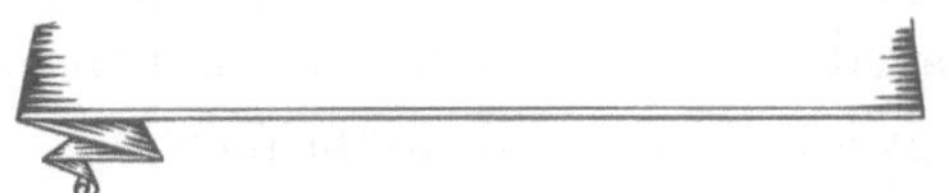

The Vaskan Forest...

The morning sun clawed out of the eastern horizon, casting creamy, orange light over the earth. The outcasts laid around the firepit, lulled to sleep by the river's song.

Sova grumbled in sleep, his lips smacking tiredly.

"I'm telling you, Casavore..." he snored, "it happens every time the rooster crows..."

Sova opened his eyes to stare at a pleasant iridescent sky. He smiled, content with his peaceful night of sleep—not once did he dream of the nightmarish dire. He turned on his side, wincing at the hardness of his pebble bed. Roeseph and Elling laid a short distance away, facing one another and sleeping as close as they could possibly get without touching the other. Sova cringed.

"Get a chamber," he grumbled and sat up. He looked to Kyce, surprised to find the Eradite Exile slept alone.

"Stumpy?" Sova said, eyes dancing around the shore. "Whisp?"

Whisp had vanished, leaving only her paw prints in the damp pebbles to remember her by. Groaning, Sova's head fell back in frustration.

"Great," he growled and marched to Feran, who snoozed softly against Saber's side. Sova stopped and eyed her up and down, pouting his lip the way one does when observing a sleeping babe. Then, without a second thought, he kicked her in the leg.

"Ouch," Feran snapped.

"Oh, good, you're awake."

Feran scowled at Sova, "You are just... the scum of the earth."

"We have a problem."

"What?" Feran yawned through a stretch. Sova nodded to Kyce and the absence of his wingless soaring wolf. "Oh no."

"Yup."

"It's too early for this," Feran whined and fell against Saber.

"Do we tell him?"

"No," Feran forced herself to stand. "He'll just throw a tantrum, and I don't have the energy for that this early in the morning."

"Feran, are you telling me that Kyce has a temper?" Sova said sarcastically. "I never would've guessed."

"Come on. Let's try to find her before *sleeping beauty* wakes up."

Stooping down, she grabbed her gauze drying by the fire and led Sova toward the winter-framed forest.

"WHISP?" FERAN CALLED through a yawn as she and Sova trudged through the snow. "Whisp? Come here, girl."

Sova grinned at the ice traced atmosphere, enamored by the crystal art dripping from the pine branches. Feran glanced at him, eyes narrowing.

"You could help, you know," she grumbled.

"I am helping," Sova shrugged. "I'm looking around, and you're yelling."

Feran exhaled, her jaw swinging to the side. As they walked, she wound her hand in gauze to hide the grotesque scar on her palm.

"Feran, you should know," Sova began abruptly. "I never liked you when we were kids."

"Shocker," Feran rolled her eyes. "Well, if it's any consolation, I couldn't stand you much either."

"Why?" Sova shrugged. "Looking back, you and I were actually very compatible kids. I think we could've been good friends. So why were you so unbearable to be around?"

Feran scoffed through a smirk. "Oh, I was the unbearable one? You followed Saulder and me around every second of every day. We couldn't shake you."

"I was being personable."

"You were being a pain in the—"

"You weren't very pleasant either, I might add," Sova smiled at his old foe. "Shall I bring up your attempts to hypnotize me?"

"Nothing's stopped you before."

Sova laughed to himself, surprised to find Feran laughing with him.

"I have to admit," Sova sighed. "As much as I hated you, I... well, I enjoyed our little war. I mean, not a lot of the time. Not even most of the time. But there were key moments when I actually enjoyed our rivalry."

"Oh, I *really* enjoyed it," Feran smiled. "I always beat you."

"It wasn't ever a competition."

"Oh, yes, it was. Everything was a competition," Feran looked to her childhood-foe. "Sova, why do you think I couldn't stand you? It was because I was—"

A low whimper whisked through the winter wind, causing a chill to race up Sova and Feran's spines. They froze, ankle-deep in the white powder.

"Did you hear that?" Sova said lowly, his eyes shifting among the trees.

"I did."

Stalking low, the two made their way toward the whimper. Whisp laid beneath a pine tree, covered in a thick net held down by heavy cannonball-like weights. Her little stump-like wings fluttered frantically as her pleading whine pierced the air.

"Whisp," Feran gasped in alarm and rushed toward the wingless beast. She fell to her knees, pulling at the net while Sova reached into his back pocket and drew a blade. He sliced at the net.

"Did the Vaskans do this?" Feran asked.

"No," Sova grunted as he cut through the last of the netting. "This net isn't Vaskan. I don't think this was made anywhere in Lykos."

"Well, then who made it?"

The sound of the wind being sliced opened pierced Feran and Sova's ears and a lone arrow flew between their noses and jammed into the tree Whisp laid beneath. Feran and Sova stumbled back in surprise.

"I would assume whoever fired that," Sova said as he plucked the arrow out of the bark. Whisp sprung from the hole in the net and shook her pelt. Hopping onto her back, Sova and Feran raced toward camp. As they fled, several large shadows flashed across the snow.

ROESEPH, ELLING, AND Kyce woke up to the sound of Sova screaming, "Get up! Get up! Get up!"

The three rushed to their feet as Whisp leaped from the forest, carrying both Sova and Feran on her back. The two leaped off the wingless soaring wolf mid-run and tumbled to the pebble shore before rolling upright.

"What's going on?" Roeseph shouted. "What happened?"

"We're under attack," Feran spat.

"By whom?" Elling asked as everyone drew their weapons. Backs turned to one another, the exiles waited for their unknown enemy to emerge.

"I don't know," Sova shrugged and drew the arrow he and Feran found. "But it's not the Vaskans."

"By Lykos, Sova," Roeseph spat. "How many people want to kill you?"

"How much time you got?"

Kyce stole the arrow out of Sova's hand, his eyes wide with fear.

"No," he whispered. "They found us."

"Who found us?" Sova challenged.

Before the Eradite Exile could answer, a dark shadow darted overhead, and a figure shifted in the forest.

"How many are there?" Roeseph snapped.

"I'm not sure," Feran grumbled and sprinted to Saber. "I'm going to get a better view."

She and Saber launched into the sky. Clinging to her medallion, Feran scanned the forest.

"Do you see anything?" Roeseph called from below.

"No," Feran shook her head. "Maybe it was just a hunter or something."

Just then, a black shadow darted through the sky toward Feran.

"Feran, look out!" Kyce screamed.

The black figure rammed into Feran, knocking her clean off Saber's back. Saber roared in anger and bit down on the scruff of the beast's neck as both hurtled toward the river.

Feran splashed into the cold waters, lost from sight.

"Feran!" Sova shouted and sprinted toward the water. Saber and the black comet crashed in front of him, roaring like vicious tumbleweeds about the shallows.

Sova fell back in terror, eyes wide with shock. Before him fought a massive black soaring wolf, just a little shorter than Saber, with glowing brown eyes.

"What is going on?" Sova shouted.

A multitude of men and women dressed in husky ox furs and yellow garments darted from the forest, riding soaring wolves with spears in hand.

While Roeseph, Elling, and Kyce dealt with the wolf riders, Sova ran around Saber and the black soaring wolf and dove into the river. The frigid waves biting his skin, he breached in and out of the ripples to steal breath from the surface before he plunged back in.

Where are you? He thought helplessly. *Where are you?*

Sova emerged, his silver eyes alive with fear as he yelled, "Feran, where are you?"

He turned around, horrified to find a hoard of wolf riders surround and lasso the White Angel. Saber snarled and leaped into the sky, nearly taking his captors with him. They pulled him back to earth then did the same to Whisp.

Sova fought his way out of the water and rushed to save the White Angel. The black soaring wolf lunged in front of Sova and shoved him to the shallows. Sova gazed at the black soaring wolf, breath paralyzed in his lungs.

Backs pressed to one another, Kyce, Elling, and Roeseph stood with their weapons pointed at their enclosing enemies.

"What do we do?" Elling cried.

"Hold your ground," Roeseph ordered.

The circling wolf riders pointed their spears at the exiles, fencing them in by their blades.

"Any ideas now, *captain*?" Kyce challenged.

Two warriors pushed their way into the circle, holding Sova under the arms and cast him at the exiles' feet.

"Sova!" Elling gasped as she helped her comrade to stand.

Sova coughed, his body aching from the fall. "Feran," he wheezed. "I lost Feran."

"I think we all lost," Kyce grumbled, looking at the menacing faces of the wolf riders.

The black soaring wolf strutted into the center of the circle and stopped before the exiles, their reflections sparkling in his gleaming fangs.

Sova sighed. "I'm about to become wolf-meat, aren't I?"

A warrior with long black hair shaved on one side stepped out from the ranks of the wolf riders and stood beside the black soaring wolf. The neck lining of his ox hide was fluffier than the rest, and he wore the gold medallion of a mind melder.

He laid his hand on the black soaring wolf, smirking smugly. "Well—Well—Well, what do we have here?" he tutted.

Roeseph gulped and took a courageous step forward. "I'm sorry if we're intruding on your land, sir," he said calmly. "We're just passing through."

"Passing through to where?" the warrior challenged. "Because our informants tell us you are on your way to Era. You should know that no one of Lykos is allowed there."

"I'm aware of the challenges," Roeseph assured, "but it's crucial that we speak with one of the Eradite tribes."

"You are speaking to one," the warrior chuckled coldly. He turned his right shoulder, revealing a tattoo of the sunset—the mark of the tribe to the western cliffs. "I am Kometis. Son to the chief of Eradusk, and commander of her armies. And I have come down into Lykos to tell you that your journey must end in vain. Return to which you came."

"We can't do that, sir," Roeseph shook his head. "We've come here because our people are in danger—"

"I've heard all about your cause, Roeseph. 'The Last Soldier.' Son to the Blind Hound. And I've heard of you, Sova," Kometis looked at the Vaskan prince, lip shifting in a sneer. "The Royal Traitor. Brother to the dire. Betrayer of his nation."

Sova blushed. "Do you hear that, Roe? We're famous."

"I won't allow the filth of Lykos to invade our lands," Kometis threatened. "Now leave before I lose my temper."

Roeseph drew a deep breath. "I'm afraid I can't do that. My father is in prison, and I intend to get him out by any means necessary. Now I demand to speak with your chief."

"No one sees the chief," Kometis warned. "Be gone, boy. Before I lose my patience."

Before Roeseph could argue back, Kyce sprung forward, his amber eyes burning so violently his gaze left scorch marks in Kometis' skin.

"I nearly got my throat slashed out by a bunch of Seavallian thugs," Kyce ranted with a sneer. "Got attacked by Vaskan troops. Nearly drowned. And have had to spend an insufferable amount of time with that one—" he pointed at Sova, making him frown, "—all in a matter of two days. We are seeing the chief whether we have to climb the Cliffs of Era ourselves."

The wolf riders froze, paralyzed by the sight of the Eradite Exile.

"Kyce?" the Eradusk commander gawked as he eyed the exile up and down. "By Era, you're alive?"

The Eradusk commander scoffed lightly, his disbelief morphing into throat tearing laughter. His troops joined in.

Kometis wiped a tear from his eyes and sighed. "Leave it to the *Mutt* to survive this hell hole."

Kyce's fist clenched at his side, steam practically radiating off his body.

"Kyce," Elling began nervously, "what's he talking about?"

"Oh, did your friend not tell you?" Kometis taunted.

Sova stepped up to stand beside Kyce. "Ky, who is this guy?"

"Yes, *Ky*," Kometis chuckled. "Who am I?"

Kyce exhaled, his jaw swinging to the side as he muttered through clenched teeth, "He's my cousin."

"Your *cousin*?" Elling repeated.

"Kyce is the son of Jerah, the chief's older brother," Kometis smiled. "Also my mentor and uncle."

"I am no more that man's son than you are," Kyce growled, getting nearly an inch away from Kometis' face. "He lost that title when he cast me out of my home."

"You committed treason," Kometis glared. "And your crime forced your father to give up his right to the throne."

"I did nothing!" Kyce snapped. "I was innocent, and your people threw me out for Jerah's sins!"

"You were the illegitimate son to a royal of Eradusk. We couldn't allow a *mutt* like you living amongst our people. Especially not one born from that Eradawn wench."

Kyce lunged forward, only for Roeseph and Sova to drag him away.

"Let me go!" Kyce snarled, practically foaming at the mouth.

"Get a hold of yourself, Kyce," Roeseph warned as he and Sova threw him back. "We're already in enough trouble as is."

Kyce trembled, his eyes red with rage.

"Ky," Sova began, bewildered, "You're an Eradusk *and* an Eradawn?"

"I'm neither," Kyce snapped. "Both disowned me, so I disowned them." The Eradite Exile glared at Kometis. "I have the right to look Jerah in the eye and make him tell me why I wasn't worth protecting. Why I had to pay for *his* mistake."

"Don't you see, Kyce," Kometis sighed. "Jerah didn't withhold his protection to cover up his mistake. He didn't protect you because you *were* the mistake. You're the son of an Eradusk and an Eradawn. A living blasphemy. A *mutt*."

Kyce's rapid breath slowed, and a look of hidden hurt braced his fierce eyes.

Roeseph lashed around, taking the Eradusk commander by surprise. "He is not a mistake," Roeseph challenged. "Born of Eradawn or Eradusk, he is a soldier of my army, and you'll show him your respect."

Kometis glared at Roeseph, no longer amused. "I gave you a chance to run," the commander growled as he reached for his medallion. "My patience has run out."

Sova laid his hands on Roeseph and Kometis' shoulders, acting as if they were chums in a Seavallian bar. "*Fellas*. Why fight? We're all friends here. Why don't we just kick back and chat for a little bit? Anyone got any Odin Slayer? It's a Seavallian drink. Burns like hellfire, but I do recommend."

Kometis looked at the Eradusk medallion hanging from Sova's neck, his eyes blistering with anger.

"Where did you get that?" he growled.

"Hmm?" Sova looked at the Blesser's medallion. *Great...* he muttered and looked back at the Eradusk commander. "Would you believe me if I said it was a gift?"

"That's an Eradusk medallion," Kometis snarled. "You thief."

Sova stepped away and shielded the Blesser's medallion.

"This was given to me by the Blesser Casavore to keep safe from the dire," he stated. "I can't part with it. It's important he gets it back."

"The Blesser is a traitor for serving the dire," Kometis snarled. "A rat has more honor than him."

"He was kidnapped from his home," Sova challenged, blood boiling. "If he's such a traitor, then what does that make you? Your people never even tried to save him. Is this the makings of Eradusk? People that dismiss men like Casavore who relied on your protection? People that cast out the innocent just because one of your royals couldn't control himself with the likes of an Eradawn?"

"I've had enough of this," Kometis snarled and grabbed hold of the Blesser's medallion, initiating a tug of war between him and the exiles, Sova being the rope.

Before the situation could escalate, a figure darted through the crowd and shoved between Sova and the enraged commander. Kometis' eyes widened in alarm, and he whipped out his medallion to entrance the threat. Like a mirror mimicking its host, the figure pulled out a charred medallion and held it before her opponent.

Feran stood before the Eradusks, soaking wet. Chestnut locks framed her soft face, and her mahogany eyes burned like embers born from fire.

"I don't think we've met," she huffed. "I'm Feran. The daughter of that *traitor* you were mentioning."

"That's impossible," Kometis grumbled, medallion shaking in hand. "The dires have never allowed their Blessers to breed before."

"And yet here I am," Feran said. "Bred and everything. And who are you?"

Sova stepped forward and rested his chin on Feran's shoulder.

"Feran, meet Kometis," he introduced. "He's Kyce's cousin from his father's side. An Eradusk general, and a real dirt worth of a person. Oh, did I mention that Kyce is both Eradawn and Eradusk? You missed a lot. It was all quite shocking."

"Yes, Sova, thank you," Feran sighed. "Now get your head off my shoulder before you lose it."

"Yes, ma'am," Sova retreated.

Kometis glared at Feran, enraged by her defiance.

"I am Kometis, the general of Eradusk. And I will not tolerate such disrespect from the spawn of that blasted Blesser."

"Well, I'm not too fond of you or the Eradites either, buddy," Feran smirked. "However, I'm willing to make a deal. Let me and my comrades speak with your chief, and no harm will come to you."

"You are foolish to threaten me."

"No, you're a fool not to take my offer," Feran sneered. "I am the daughter of Casavore, perhaps the greatest mind melder to ever come out of Era, and I might just take that title from him one of these days. At twelve years old, I entranced a soaring wolf to bond to me with no prior training—a skill that takes mind melders years to conquer. And I am losing my patience, so you're going to want to hear me out."

Kometis shifted uncertainly in the intimidating young woman's threatening gaze.

"The dire has abused your people for centuries," Feran continued. "He split your tribe down the middle, and he turns your own children into his puppets. And because my father has fallen out of favor with the dire, it won't be long until he seeks a new Blesser. And since you're a mind melder, I'd say you're in greater danger than you realize. And if it's not you who is made into the dire's servant, it'll be your family or the children you bear."

Kometis gulped, his hand starting to shake.

"Or..." Feran smirked, "you can let my friends speak with your chief to discuss ending Vaska's tyranny. That, or I can just hypnotize you to do it all anyway."

"You're bluffing," Kometis growled through a sneer as a droplet of sweat fell from his temple.

"Am I?" Feran smiled, swaying her medallion ever so slightly. "Shall we find out and see?"

Kometis looked frantically between Feran and her medallion. Her smirk grew deeper, more provoking.

Surrendering his medallion to his neck, Kometis stepped back. "Fine."

Feran lowered her medallion, her chin raised in victory.

"Thank you, Commander," she bowed. "I look forward to our journey."

Kometis growled through clenched teeth and parted from the crowd, followed by his black soaring wolf. "Cut their beasts free," he ordered.

Upon his command, the Eradusks cut the ropes binding Saber and Whisp to the earth. Feran opened her arms as Saber sprinted into her embrace. She clung to his neck, scratching him behind the ear as he whined and nuzzled.

"Good boy," she said, relieved. "You were so brave."

Whisp stalked up to Kyce, whining. "I'm ok, girl. I'm ok," he smiled weakly and looked at Feran. "I have to say, I'm impressed."

"Don't be," Feran shrugged. "There was no real threat."

"Really? How so?"

"Well, first off, he was holding his medallion backward."

Kyce sputtered and looked away to hide his laugh.

"And second," Feran continued. "I'm not afraid of cowards."

"So, this is it?" Roeseph shrugged. "We're going to Era."

Elling sighed with relief and looked to Feran. "Feran," she said. "I know you said you'd only take us as far as the mountains, but... Would you come with us?"

Feran drew a deep breath and looked to the west where the Eradusk tribe hid behind the horizon's cloak; the nation that abandoned her father—the nation she loathed.

"Well..." she huffed. "Might as well. Who knows what *Commander Curt* might do if I'm not around to breathe down his neck? Sova, is that ok with you?"

"I mean," Sova shrugged. "I'll survive."

"What about Whisp?" Kyce looked to his wingless soaring wolf as she fluttered her stumps. "How will we get her to Era?

Feran turned and pointed to a scrawny, young warrior boarding his soaring wolf. "Hey, you!"

The warrior looked up, a bit intimidated by the likes of the Lykos mind melder. "Yes, ma'am?"

"You'll be carrying the wingless soaring wolf with you," she crossed her arms.

The warrior scoffed, "A—Are you serious?"

Kyce stepped forward, eyes fiery once again. "Oh, she's dead serious."

Chapter Twenty: Dusk

Like a fleet of geese, the Eradusks and their soaring wolves dove through the air in a perfect V shape. The veil of mist covering the valley below reached on for an eternity, looking as if they soared over a white ocean. In the back of the pack, Saber carried the five exiles, while next to them flew the young Eradusk warrior Feran had bullied into carrying Whisp.

Feran opened her arms to the wind, smiling as the clouds slammed into her face. Elling clung to Roeseph's back, looking around at the misty majesty.

"It's beautiful," she whispered, trailing her fingertips through the clouds.

Kyce stretched his arms behind his head, grinning as the wind combed his hair.

"Oh, I missed this," he sighed and looked to Whisp laying over the back of the soaring wolf flying next to them. "Don't you love this, girl?"

Whisp yipped in agreement.

"You guys doing ok back there?" Feran called over her shoulder. "Sova?"

"I hate this!" the Royal Traitor cried as he clung to Saber's rump the way a squirrel clings to a branch in a tornado. "This is worse than the rooster!"

Feran laughed so hard her throat nearly bled, making Sova glare.

"Just be glad Saber's letting you ride him," she said.

Roeseph leaned to the side to see something breach from the mist covered horizon.

"Wow," he breathed with awe.

All followed his gaze to what looked like an island poking out from the sea of clouds. The tops of a mountain range impaled the sky, crowned with a halo of ivory fog.

Kyce gulped and scooted back, accidentally pressing into Roeseph.

"Woah there. You ok, Kyce?" Roeseph asked.

"I'm fine," Kyce uttered, his eyes latched on the mountains ahead.

"That's it?" Sova rebuked, unimpressed. "That's what I nearly drowned for? Very disappointing."

Kometis rose his fist at the front of the pack and swung down. Upon his command, the soaring wolves dove beneath the clouds toward the mountain.

"Hold on guys!" Feran smiled as Saber followed them toward the earth.

Screaming perilously, Sova clung to the flying steed. Saber leveled beneath the sky's silver veil. Below them, beyond the sheer cliffs overlooking the Valley of Lykos stood a great civilization carved in the breast of the mountain. Hundreds of elegant buildings stacked up the side of the slope, leading to the top where a beautiful, limestone palace stood with a river flowing out of the front wall and down the mountain.

The group marveled at the scenery, their mouths gawking open.

"I take it back," Sova said. "Well worth the trip."

Feran's jaw clenched and her stomach churned. Eradusk was beautiful, just as her father had said—but it was an Eradite tribe, nonetheless. And despite the stories her father told, nothing could change the fact this nation—these people—were the ones who abandoned him. Eradusk was just as responsible for her father becoming the Blesser as Eradawn.

The warriors and their soaring wolves broke from their flying formation and dove toward Eradusk where their families awaited them.

Kometis led the exiles toward the Eradusk palace and descended the center where a massive garden grew in the middle of four limestone walls. Saber landed gently and collapsed in the green grass, exhausted, while Sova leaped off his back and embraced the ground like an old friend.

"Oh, how I missed you," he whispered as his comrades descended off the soaring wolf's back.

Emerald vines grew up the walls like jade spiderwebs and thick fruit bearing trees stood in each corner. A geyser sprouted near the western wall through a cluster of boulders, cascading down the rock formation before seeping into the river and out an arch in the eastern wall. Despite being the middle of winter, the garden was green, as if it were the last remaining patch of spring.

Whisp yipped and jumped into the brook—the Eradusk's drinking water. Kometis scowled at the flightless soaring wolf then looked to the exiles.

"I'll inform Chief Willowreed of your presence," he said. "You are to wait here until I return. Try not to touch anything."

Kometis marched out of the garden and into the palace. The exiles stood in a circle, silent and in awe of the garden's beauty.

"Meh," Sova shrugged. "My garden's bigger."

"There's peaches," Feran pointed. "It's winter, and they have peaches. How do they have peaches?"

"You're drooling, Feran."

THE EXILES REMAINED in the garden all afternoon—the bright cyan sky mellowing to a soft blue. Saber snoozed in the shade of a peach tree, while Whisp used him as a hurdle for a game of play. Feran sat by the river with Roeseph, Elling, and Sova, waiting for Kometis to return. Kyce, however, hadn't taken a solid breath since arriving. Jaw wrenched shut, he paced the garden, fists coiled at his side.

"Hey, Kyce. Want to sit with us?" Roeseph called.

Kyce didn't stop to look at the Last Soldier. "I'm fine."

"I didn't ask you if you were *fine*. I asked you to sit with us."

Kyce paused, sighed defeatedly, and sat among the outcasts. He looked to the garden's exit where Kometis disappeared, his fist batting in and out of his hand.

"Would you stop?" Sova griped.

Kyce looked to the Royal Traitor. "Stop what?"

"Looking so panicked. You're stressing me out."

"Kometis should've come back by now," Kyce grumbled, his knee bouncing.

Roeseph laid his hand on Kyce's shoulder. "He's just trying to make us sweat. He'll come when the chief asks for us."

Feran, who had gathered all the peaches from the garden into a pile at her side, extended one to Kyce.

"Here, have a peach," she mumbled, her lips leaking nectar from the juicy pods lodged in her cheeks.

Sova grimaced, disgusted. "By Lykos, Feran," he gagged. "At least swallow your food before you speak."

"Don't tell me what to do," Feran tossed the peach to Kyce.

Elling gazed at the Eradite Exile, her kind emerald eyes reading his soul like a scroll. "Are you nervous?" she asked.

"I said I'm fine," Kyce growled frustratedly as he crushed the peach in his hand. Feran died a little inside, broken-hearted to see a perfectly good piece of fruit go to waste.

Elling drew a deep breath and looked at the endless evening sky.

"I'm nervous," she admitted. "Either these people can help me, or they can't. And even if they do have the knowledge to lift the Hyde Howler's curse, they could very well turn me away."

Roeseph looked at Elling, his eyes suddenly very serious. "We won't let them do that."

"We have no control over what they do, Roeseph," Elling smiled.

Kyce glared at Elling. "You don't look nervous," he grumbled jealously.

"Well," Elling shrugged. "I guess that's because if it doesn't work with them, I have hope elsewhere."

"*Hope*?" Kyce chuckled. "And what good has hope done you?"

"Not a whole lot recently. But I've tried the whole hopeless thing. I've found there are better things to believe in."

Kyce's jaw clenched and he looked away.

"Don't be nervous, Ky," Sova said, stealing a peach from Feran's pile. "I'll protect you," he winked and took a bite of the fruit.

"I said I'm fine," Kyce growled irritably.

"Sure you are," Sova pouted his lip. "You're so brave."

Kyce lunged, grabbed Sova around the neck, and dragged him to the brook. Just as Roeseph jumped up to diffuse the fight, Feran grabbed him by the wrist.

"Stop," she said, biting into another peach. "He needs to learn."

Roeseph hesitantly sat beside Elling, watching as Kyce mercilessly dunked Sova in and out of the water. Sova gasped, his head locked in Kyce's death grip.

"Violence won't make the pain go away, Ky," he coughed.

"I beg to differ," Kyce grunted, his grip tightening around the Royal Traitor's neck.

"Come on, buddy, let's just hug it out."

Kyce shoved Sova back into the water, nearly splashing the bystanders.

"Hey!" Feran scolded as she pulled her peaches into her lap. "Watch where you're splashing! You'll get Sova water all over my fruit."

"I'm drowning!" Sova cried.

Feran snapped back, "Do so quietly!"

Elling laughed behind her hand. As Kyce and Sova battled in the Eradusk drinking water, Kometis stalked out from the garden's entrance, his eyes narrow with displeasure.

"Do you mind?" Kometis snapped. "We drink from that you know."

"No. It's ok," Sova coughed and unwound himself from Kyce's grip. "This is therapeutic for, Ky. Next we're going to talk about his childhood—" Kyce punched the Royal Traitor in his gauze-wrapped shoulder. Gasping, Sova grasped his covered wound and arched forward, "—It's a work in progress."

Kometis rolled his eyes. "Chief Willowreed will see you all now. Dry off and follow me. Leave your flea bags here."

"No can do," Feran said as she stood, peaches swaddled in arms. "It's non-negotiable. Sova comes with us."

"*Wench*," Sova grumbled.

"*Rooster Boy*," Feran said back.

KOMETIS LED THE FIVE exiles out of the garden and through the great halls, passing by grand windows overlooking the tribe on the mountain side. Gold medallions mounted the walls—weapons of past chiefs, priests, and royal mind melders.

Sova smirked and elbowed Feran in the arm. "Hey," he motioned to her ancestors' histories displayed across the wall. "Casavore did a pretty good job making your medallion. They look just like yours."

Feran puzzled at her reflection as it swept the gold faces of the mind melder weapons, her heart stinging as she ran her finger over the rough, rusted burn covering half of her medallion.

"No," she mumbled, mourning the once smooth surface. "They don't."

The exiles came to two massive doors looming over them like a two wooden Goliaths. Kometis slipped through and looked back at the five outcasts, his face wrenched in a scowl.

"Wait here until I come for you," he grumbled and slammed the doors shut, making the exiles flinch.

"Like we haven't been waiting all day," Roeseph grumbled.

"Cheer up, Roeseph," Feran sighed as she juggled a peach from the garden. "We'll see the chief Reedwillow soon enough."

"*Willowreed*," Roeseph corrected.

"That's what I said," Feran smiled as she handed him the fruit. "Peach?"

"I'm good, thanks," Roeseph declined as he pushed the half-eaten peach away.

The doors to the throne room creaked open. Kyce froze, his heart beating so loudly the others mistook the sound for muffled thunder.

"Maybe this was a bad idea," he gulped and took a nervous step back. Elling laid her hand on his shoulder.

"We're both going to get what we came for, Kyce," she said.

The doors opened wide to reveal the throne room. Vines seeped through cracks in the tile and climbed the limestone walls, collecting in the center of the ceiling in the form of a jade chandelier. At the far end of the room drifted a massive daffodil-colored veil sparkling like the sun in the dusk.

Behind the veil stood a high limestone platform, and on it, a wooden throne with twisting roots jutting out from the backrest like a thornbush. A woman with tawny skin, bright amber eyes, and wavy dark, nearly black, hair, sat on the Eradusk throne. She wore a formfitting yellow gown with sleeves sloping off her shoulders.

Kometis stood to the right of the throne, a subtle smirk on his lips, and to the left, a stranger. A man with the same tawny skin and dark hair as the woman. His amber eyes burned like magma, and yet they were flameless—doused with a deep mourning.

Kyce glared at the man through the gold curtain, his jaw clenching as he led his comrades toward the throne. The stranger walked down from the platform and pushed through the daffodil veil to meet the Eradite Exile.

"Kyce," he greeted solemnly.

Kyce's jaw clenched. "Jerah."

Sova gasped, silver eyes wide as disks. "*This* is Jerah? This is your father? I mean, I see the resemblance, same face, same hair, but your dad's face is a little thinner, and—" Kyce and Jerah glared at Sova, striking the Royal Traitor silent. Laughing awkwardly, Sova took a timid step back. "And you both look at me with the same homicidal eyes," he cleared his throat. "Proceed."

Jerah looked back to his son, his eyes narrowed. "Kyce, what are you doing back here?" he whispered beneath his breath. "You know the terms of your punishment—"

"And I'll get to that. But first, my fellow *exiles*," Kyce said rather bitterly, "have something to ask your *chief*."

Chief Willowreed gazed at Kyce through the golden veil without a speck of emotion.

"My son says you seek my council," she said coldly. "What is it you want?"

Roeseph stepped forward and bowed. "Chief of Eradusk," he said as he stood upright. "I am sorry to have trespassed onto your lands, but I wouldn't have sought you out if it wasn't urgent. I am Roe—"

"I know who you are," Chief Willowreed interrupted as she stroked the gold medallion hanging from her neck. "You are the son of Oland. Even we of Eradusk know the Legend of the Blind Hound. From what Kometis has told me, you have made quite a name for yourself. They call you *The Last Soldier*—the only Blind Seer to make it out of the Vaskan Palace. *The Last Soldier*—the man who abandoned his father and comrades."

Roeseph returned the chief's gaze, his throat flexing around a hard swallow.

"I hear you travel with *other* Lykos Legends," Willowreed continued and looked to the exiles. "Prince Sova—*The Royal Traitor*. You betrayed your kingdom and brother in conspiring with Vaska's worst enemy. Not only that, but you hold his Blesser's medallion hostage."

Sova chuckled nervously and slid Casavore's medallion beneath his shirt. "Rumors."

"And you," Willowreed looked to Feran. "The *Dire's Damsel*—back from the dead. You were to be wed to the most notorious ruler in Lykos. I honestly don't blame you for abandoning him and that traitorous father of yours."

Feran glared at the Eradusk Chief, steam practically radiating off her skin.

"Ah, and you," Willowreed looked to a cowering Elling. "Elling. Daughter of the chief Chemon of the Mosharick Plains. Such a kind girl... and yet, such a revolting beast."

Kyce stomped in front of Elling. "That's enough," he growled. "She came here to ask for help. They all came here to ask for help, and all you can do is insult them?"

"And what brings you back, nephew?" Willowreed questioned. "You—the illegitimate son of an Eradusk royal, my brother, and an Eradawn woman, an enemy of our tribe. You, dear Kyce, are a walking blasphemy."

Kyce lunged, only for Jerah to step in front of him, clutching his medallion. The Eradite Exile looked past his father to the chief, face wrenched in a scowl. "None of us came here to be judged by the likes of you. They came here for your help—"

"Oh, I'm well aware of why you've come here," Willowreed seethed and looked to Roeseph and Sova. "You come seeking aid against Dire Saulder." She turned to Elling next, making the poor girl shudder. "And you have come to me searching for a cure for the curse the Blesser of Vaska cast on you. And you..." she looked at Feran, who had started gorging herself on another peach. "I'm not sure why the spawn of Blesser Casavore would accompany such a band of miscreants, wanting nothing in return."

Feran shrugged, her mouth full. "I kind of got dragged into it."

Willowreed rolled her eyes, her gaze falling to Kyce lastly, "And you... Kyce. Son of Jerah. You have not come here to beg your way back into my tribe's good graces. So, why have you come?"

Kyce froze, his painful silence taking the exiles by surprise. He then looked to Jerah, who stared back with an emotionless expression.

"Ah," Willowreed grinned. "It is my brother who you seek. Well then, do what you must, Kyce. Strike him. Confess your adoration to him. Beg for forgiveness. Do what you came here to do."

Kyce glared into his father's eyes as Jerah and the other waited for his brutal reprimand. But it never came.

"Kyce?" Sova whispered. "Say what you wanted to say."

Kyce drew a deep breath, his fists coiling at his side. Instead of exploding, his hands fell limp and he looked to the floor.

"Is that all?" Jerah said.

When Kyce didn't speak, Jerah dismissed himself and parted the curtain to stand beside his sister's throne. Willowreed shook her head, her sharpened nails drumming.

"Now that that's over, I'll give you each my answer," she said. "Eradusk will never step foot in Lykos, let alone stand against the dire."

Roeseph's eyes widened with alarm, and he took a nervous step forward. "Chief Willowreed, please—"

"Your feral mind melder there may have deceived my son with her empty threats, but you will not manipulate me. Eradusk will never serve the sinners of Lykos—those souls who reject Christ's teachings." She glanced at Elling. "Nor will our mind melders sully our talents for the likes of a monster."

Elling gasped beneath her breath and took a timid step back.

"That's not fair," Feran spat in defense of the Hyde Howler. "If you can fix her, then you're obligated to!"

"I am not *obligated* to do anything," Willowreed dismissed. "Now get out of my sight. You've wasted enough of my time."

"No!" Feran snapped as she tore through the yellow veil and leaped onto the platform, provoking both Jerah and Kometis to draw their medallions. Feran grappled her medallion around Jerah's, and ripped it out of his hand. Next came, Kometis, who she slugged in the face. He fell from the platform, knocked out cold.

Willowreed snapped from her throne, her amber eyes blazing as she reached for her medallion, "How dare you!"

"Sit down!" Feran ordered and waved her medallion before the chief. Willowreed froze, paralyzed by the threat the Blesser's daughter imposed.

"Willowreed," Jerah urged, "do as she says."

Willowreed lowered to her throne and drew her hand from her medallion, her eyes drawn into slits as she sneered, "Your father was Eradusk. That makes me your chief, you infidel."

"No, that makes you my *nothing*," Feran spat, a strand of hair riding her breath. "You know, for years, my father would tell me all about the tribe of Eradusk—the tribe that raised him. Before I even set foot on your land, I already had a distinct picture of what it looked like in my head, and sure enough, it's just as I imagined. My father described this place perfectly..."

Feran paused. Her eyes became glossy.

"And yet... he was so wrong about his people. He told me how you were a holy tribe who valued Christ and all his teachings. And yet, you all so *righteous* people turned your back on my father. You left him to be traded into slavery by your enemies. I should hate the Eradawns for what they did, and I do. But I loathe you just as much."

"Lykos is a place of sinners," Willowreed growled. "Casavore became just like them when he accepted the Blesser's title. We must keep the sanctity of our tribe pure."

Feran chuckled and shook her head.

"*Pure?*" she snickered. "You people are just as dirty and unworthy of Christ as the rest of us. In fact, I can list several sins you've committed in the last ten minutes, including the disregard of *John thirteen thirty-four*, when you rebuked your own nephew. The neglect of *Hebrews thirteen sixteen*, in doing good, when you refused to help Elling. And lastly, you completely ignore *Matthew twenty-eight nineteen through twenty* in sharing the light of God... Your people haven't sought to teach to the supposed *scum* of Lykos in centuries. All these scriptures I learned from the Blesser Casavore... a *pure* Eradusk like yourself, who went and lived amongst the sinners. And yet in all his wrongs, he has done more right than you in your entire self-righteous life."

Feran hung her medallion around her neck and let out a frustrated breath. Willowreed drummed her fingers, her eyes piercing the disrespectful outsider.

"I want all of you out of Eradusk by sundown," she sneered.

Smirking, Feran shook her head in disbelief. "*Proverbs fifteen thirty-two...* 'Whoever ignores instruction despises himself, but he who listens to reproof gains intelligence...' Good day, Chief Willowreed."

Sova leaned toward Kyce and whispered, "I think Feran just called your aunt stupid in Bible."

Feran stalked down the platform, through the veil, and retreated with her fellow exiles toward the doors.

Willowreed sighed with exhaustion, while Kometis pulled himself from the ground.

"What a bunch of miscreants," he scowled.

Jerah watched from behind the veil as his only son disappeared out the door, surely never to be seen again. Kyce looked back at his father as his comrades made their exit. The doors slammed shut, sending a cold echo chiming through the Eradusk palace.

The five exiles stomped into the palace garden where Saber and Whisp waited. The two soaring wolves looked up from the river, water dripping from their chins before Whisp charged and nuzzled her master.

"Stop, Whisp," Kyce grumbled as he pulled himself onto his soaring wolf.

Sova watched the Eradite Exile, his heart heavy with sorrow, for he knew the pain of being betrayed by one's own blood. "Ky," he began softly, "are you ok?"

"I'm *great*, Sova," Kyce snarled, his strong shoulders trembling. "Can we please just get out of here?"

Elling clung to herself, crystal tears lining her lashes. "They won't help me," she muttered. "I—I'm going to be stuck like this... I'm going to be a monster forever."

"No, you're not," Roeseph argued and placed his hands on her shoulders. "And you're not a monster, Elling. The Eradusks are just a bunch of self-righteous hypocrites too proud to lend their help. But we still have the Eradawns."

Kyce chuckled madly, his amber eyes blazing with hurt. "And you think they'll help you? They're the same as everyone else here. They'll turn you away the moment you step foot on their land."

"You don't know that, Kyce," Roeseph challenged.

"Oh yes, I do. I told you what would happen when you sought their help, and you didn't listen. They don't care about you or any of Lykos' children. Everything they do, they do for themselves. Well, I'm done. I'm done with all of them. Exile was the best thing that could've happened to me. I'm going back to Seavale."

The exiles held their gaze, cautious to not glance the tear rolling down Kyce's scowl.

Feran drew a deep breath and, grabbing a peach from one of the trees, walked up to Whisp's side and offered Kyce the fruit.

"What do you want?" he snapped.

"Eat something, please," Feran said. "You're shaking."

"I'm fine," Kyce looked away.

"Well then be fine and eat something."

Kyce huffed in irritation. Upon meeting her eyes he saw under pane of brown glass a glint of compassion—a treasure lost to him in his eight years of exile. Sighing, he took the peach.

"Look," Feran began, "If you really want to go back, I'll grant you and Whisp passage to Lykos. You have my word. But first, I need to make sure these imbeciles don't get themselves killed crossing the Cliffs of Era."

Kyce stared intensely at the peach. "You're wasting your time. The Eradawns won't listen to you."

"Then we'll fail again," Feran shrugged. "And at the end of it, I'll see you all back to Lykos, and we'll go our separate ways."

Kyce looked at the others. Each one looked on him with hope and pity. Hope for their future, and pity for his past. Taking a vicious bite out of the peach, Kyce tossed the fruit over his shoulder and into the brook.

"Let's get this over with," he growled.

"Thank you," Feran nodded. "But first, there's something I must do. Sova," she turned to address her childhood foe.

"What?" the Royal Traitor replied.

Without warning, Feran grabbed him by his wrist, and hurtled toward the fruit bearing trees..

"We're taking all their peaches!" she cried. "Go—Go—Go."

With lightning movement, Sova and Feran stripped the branches clean, harboring the contraband in the dip of their shirts, and hustled to the soaring wolves. With Whisp carrying Kyce, Roeseph, and Elling, and Saber carrying the *Peach Thieves*, the exiles hurried out of the garden and down the mountain.

As the exiles descended the village carved into the mountainside, Jerah watched from a high balcony within the Eradusk palace as his only son grew further and further from sight. Shutting his eyes, he let out a sigh.

"Quite an evening," came the voice of the Eradusk chief.

Jerah opened his eyes and fixed his sorrowed expression. "Indeed," he said plainly.

Willowreed stepped onto the balcony to stand beside her brother. She looked up, catching a glimpse of sorrow buried in his gaze.

"This is for the best, Brother," she assured.

"I know," Jerah lied with a nod. "I just... He's been alone out there for over eight years."

"To pay the price of his sins."

Jerah scoffed. "*His* sins?"

"Now stop it, Jerah. You're hard enough on yourself already. He had his chance to rebuke his mother's bloodline and swear himself to Eradusk. But he didn't. That's his own fault."

Jerah's jaw cocked to the side. "He was a sixteen-year-old boy. He shouldn't have had to choose between his father and his mother's heritage."

"If he was truly your son, he wouldn't have hesitated. He is no Eradusk. He's a *mutt*."

Jerah stopped himself from saying something he'd regret and swallowed.

"Try not to worry yourself," Willowreed said, laying her hand on her brother's shoulder as she held up her medallion. "If you want, I can make your guilt more tolerable."

"No," Jerah turned away. Mind melding couldn't get rid of emotions—at least not those outside what the mind melder put in a person themselves. The best they could do was dull them for a short time, but whatever demons they cast out always returned. "No thank you. It won't fix anything. Not permanently at least."

"Still, it's better than nothing."

Jerah shook his head. "No. No, not always."

"Very well," Willowreed withdrew her medallion. "Don't let *him* get to you, Jerah. I'm going to the garden, you're welcome to accompany me. I have a severe hankering for peaches."

MANY MILES FROM ERADUSK, where the pine forest ended before a steep, rocky drop, a darkness stirred beneath the cliffs overlooking the Valley of Lykos. Like a murder of crows taking flight, black grappling hooks sprung from the valley and impaled the edge. Once sturdied, five thousand Vaskan soldiers scaled the ropes and pulled themselves onto the sacred Cliffs of Era. Lastly came a man wearing night-black armor and a helmet with horn-like spikes curving out the crown.

Immediately, the Vaskan soldiers fell to their knees and bowed as the Dire marched past his subjects, his violet cape skimming their hands. He stopped and looked west, where the tribe of Eradusk awaited.

"There you are," he smirked and turned to his bowing soldiers. "Rise and draw your swords," he ordered, his voice masked by the steel ring of his helmet.

The Vaskans rose and drew their swords.

"Enemies of Vaska have taken sanctuary in these cliffs," the dire stated. "It won't be long until they've sought out the Eradite tribes. We'll head to Eradusk first."

"Sire," a soldier asked timidly. "What shall we do when we get there. I mean, what would you have us do should the Eradusks attack?"

"Kill them and anyone who stands in your way," The dire growled. "And when you happen upon the Rogue Eradite, destroy *it,* and bring its corpse to me. As for the Royal Traitor... I wish to kill him myself."

Chapter Twenty-One: The Dire Wolves

Saber and Whisp carried the exiles east as the sun fell to Eradusk, turning the sky a drowsy gold. To the left, a pine forest covered a mountain range, and to the right, a blanket of mist covered the Valley of Lykos.

Feran yawned and stretched on Saber. As she stretched, Sova fell forward on her back, his soft snores brushing her ear. She jammed her elbow into his stomach, making him cough and cower back.

"Wake up, Snores," she growled.

"*Merciless*," Sova sneered as he rubbed the searing pain in his stomach. "Merciless, witch."

Roeseph groaned at the sky. "I swear, if you two don't stop bickering—"

"You'll what?" Feran challenged.

Roeseph exhaled and looked away. "Forget it."

"That's what I thought, *Roe–Roe*," Feran mocked.

Sova cackled in approval, "Nice."

"God help me," Roeseph sighed as Feran and Sova high-fived.

Kyce glared at the two Vaskans, his eye twitching with sleep deprivation. "If you two don't shut up, I'm throwing you both over the cliff."

"Ha! Do it, Ky! I dare you," Sova said and began pelting Kyce with the peaches he and Feran stole from the Eradusk garden.

"Not the peaches!" Feran cried.

Kyce flinched as the soft fruit splashed against his skin, coating him in sticky nectar.

"That's it!" he shouted and lunged upright.

"That's enough!" Roeseph ordered and forced Kyce back onto Whisp. "Look, if we keep at this, we're going to kill each other.

"She started it," Sova pointed at Feran. She snapped at his finger like a piranha.

"It doesn't matter who—" Roeseph stopped himself and drew a long breath. "We're all tired, and have had a long day. Let's make camp somewhere and settle down for the night."

"I concur," Feran stretched.

Elling looked ahead, her emerald eyes widening. "Look," she exclaimed.

Beyond a veil of pine trees stood the ruins of a great kingdom carved from limestone. Vines covered the crumbling structures like thick, green robes while a thundering river slithered through the middle of the kingdom and fell over the cliff's edge. The five exiles rode into the center of the ancient ruins, looking around with eyes big with awe..

"What is this place?" Elling whispered.

"The Falls of Era," Kyce answered, looking sentimentally around the skeletons of a past paradise. "This is where the original Eradite tribe once stood before they separated."

Feran looked around with a heavy heart. To her comrades, the ruins were a treasure—a place of immortalized history. To her, the dead civilization was the place where the Eradawns stole her father and made him the dire's Blesser—Vaska's most revered slave.

The group stopped before the river where a grand limestone gazebo stood in the shallows. Just the pillars and part of the railing remained, strangled in dead vines, while the ceiling had crumbled to ash, creating a beautiful skylight.

"Boy," Sova huffed, "they've really let the place go."

Roeseph snorted. "Well, considering no one has lived here for well over a thousand years, I won't hold it against them. We'll camp here for the night."

NIGHT SMOTHERED THE sky's flame as the white embers of twilight filled the black atmosphere. In the heart of the corroded riverside gazebo, the five exiles sat around a flickering fire. Kyce, Sova, and Roeseph reclined against Whisp while Elling and Feran sat across from them against Saber.

Sova shuddered, watching for every slight shift in the abandoned darkness. "Historic lost civilization or not, this place is creepier than a Seavale outhouse."

"Aww," Feran pouted. "Is *Sova–wova* scared?"

"Yes, *Sova–wova* is scared. *Sova–wova* has all the reason to be. Now hand me a peach."

"Eating your feelings won't help, Sova."

"Eating feelings good. Peach now."

Feran smirked and tossed him a peach over the fire's lashing hands. Just as the fruit descended Sova's grasp, Whisp snapped the peach right out of the air and swallowed. Sova stilled, his jaw cocking to the side as his comrades cackled.

"I don't get it," he shook his head. "Why do soaring wolves hate me?"

"Hey now," Roeseph chuckled. "Whisp and Saber don't hate you. Saber let you ride him today."

"He tried to buck me off while flying thousands of miles above the ground."

"Well—I mean, Whisp likes you alright."

"She ate my peach."

"She was probably just hungry."

"She's a carnivore."

"Just be happy she's not eating *you*," Roeseph sighed as he prodded a stick at the fire.

Sova sighed in surrender and reclined against Whisp. "What a day," he said as he stared at the black tapestry waving across the atmosphere.

"You said it," Elling agreed through a stretch. "Those Eradites were perhaps the most unbearable folks I've ever met." Elling flinched as her gaze met Kyce's through the fire. "N—No offense."

"None taken," Kyce chuckled softly. "You haven't said anything untruthful."

Feran glared into the flame, stroking her charred medallion. "You know... I've heard stories about this place. Stories of how the princess of Era betrayed her brother to the Dire, and how he became the first Blesser ever. Most people think of that story when they see this place," Feran paused and squeezed her medallion. "But I think of my father's. He used to be an

Eradusk priest in training, you know. No one ever remembers that though. They just remember him as the dire's Blesser. He came to these ruins to pray. It was here that the Eradawns attacked him and traded him into slavery." Feran gulped and looked at the remarkable civilization she loathed. "This place... it's cursed with betrayal."

"See," Sova interjected, his peaceless silver eyes wide with fear. "I told you this place was creepy."

Kyce smirked. "*Cursed...*" he repeated forlornly. "Cursed is a good word for this place."

"Why do you say that, Kyce?" Elling asked.

"It just breeds betrayal," Kyce continued. "First, the princess of Era betrays her brother, making him the first-ever Blesser of Vaska. It's where the Blesser Casavore was taken and stripped of his freedom by the Eradawns. And it also is the birthplace of, well, me."

Silence filled the ruins so not even the wind dared serenade the winter night.

Kyce drew a deep, reluctant breath. "My mother and father met here patrolling their borders. To make a long story short they fell for each other and would meet here every night to explore the Eradite ruins. It was here that they married in secret, and eventually, it was here that I was born. Both my parents were royals of their tribes, so neither could take me back, lest their superiors question my parentage. So I was raised here. My mother would watch over me during the day and my father during the night. I loved it here. I loved the little family we had. And through all that time, I never once realized that I was a walking sin. A breathing betrayal."

"Kyce," Elling interrupted. "Don't say that. You're not any of those things."

Kyce grinned sadly and shook his head. "I appreciate that, Elling. But it's what I am. I am the son born of a secret union between an Eradawn and an Eradusk—the greatest violation of loyalty my people can fathom. And, it wasn't long till my parents' betrayal was discovered. I um..." Kyce gulped and stared into the flames. "My father gave me Whisp when I was eight years old. Eradites aren't supposed to receive them until they're eighteen, but my father feared I'd grow lonely. Whisp and I were playing in the ruins when she came across the scent of another soaring wolf. It wasn't her fault. She didn't know any better, she just wanted to play, so... she ran. I chased after her, and—well, we ran straight into an Eradawn patrol. I was brought to the chief, my mother's uncle, and she was forced to tell them who I was. Originally, the chief was going to have me killed for my '*impure blood*,' but my mother bargained for my life, saying I should be banished instead...."

Kyce stopped to vanquish the lump building in his throat. "She um—" Kyce gulped. "My mother...."

"It's ok, Kyce," Elling whispered. "You don't have to—"

"I'm fine," Kyce assured. "My mother wanted to go with me. She was going to abandon everyone and go to Lykos to raise her son. But my uncle wouldn't let her. He lost his brother to sickness, his sister-in-law to an Eradusk soldier, and his wife and son to childbirth. My mother was all he had left. So, he had me dragged away, and my mother locked in her room. I remember her screaming to find my father, that he would help me." Kyce chuckled and shook his head. "I love my mother... but she was naïve to think Jerah would choose his *Mutt*-of-a-son over the respect of his tribe. I went to Eradusk with Whisp and was brought before my grandfather, the chief before Willowreed. Like my mother, my father was forced to tell them who I was, and I was met with the same *kindness* of Eradawn. I was to be banished to Lykos unless I rebuked my mother's heritage and vowed myself a full-fledged Eradusk. But I couldn't do it. I couldn't abandon my mother like that, nor my father. So, the chief had Jerah hold me down while the others subdued Whisp and cut her wings. I remember her yelps were so loud—so horrified. It was my father who delivered me to Lykos. He flew Whisp and me to the bottom of the Falls of Era, and... he just left us there. Couldn't even look me in the eyes, even as I begged him...."

Kyce paused, his jaw wrenching as he fought his tears.

"You know," he sniffled through a forced smile, "I always knew I was going to see him again someday. And I was going to look him in the eyes and tell him, and all the Eradites who turned their backs on me, what I needed to say. But—" Kyce shook his head, his lips piercing, "when I finally got the chance, I froze. All those eight years I spent barely getting by in Seavale, I thought of only that... and when the opportunity finally presented itself, I couldn't do it... So yeah," he looked to Feran, the tears in his eyes making her stiffen. "Feran, this place is cursed with betrayal. Only the worst comes out of these ruins. Including me..."

Kyce leaned against Whisp to stare at the stars overhead.

"What were you going to tell him?" Roeseph asked from the cricket singing silence.

Kyce looked up, brow drawn in an arch. "Are you serious?"

"I mean," Roeseph shrugged, "you said you've thought of nothing but, for eight years. There's no pressure anymore. Why not get it out?"

Kyce looked around to find everyone staring at him. Sighing bitterly, he sat up. "When Willowreed asked me why I came back, I was going to walk right up to Jerah and say that 'I came here to speak with my father. I came here to look him in the eye and tell him what I've thought of telling him every single day for the last eight years. But...the man before me is not my father. A father wouldn't damn his child to Lykos and leave him to fend for himself. He wouldn't cut the wings of the very beast he gifted his child–just so he could never return. A father would defend his son, whether innocent or guilty. But my father never did this for me. So, a father I never had'...."

A low, slow applause bloomed from the silence, and all looked to Feran as she clapped in a gradual, eerie rhythm.

"Well done, Kyce," she grinned and tossed him a peach. "Well done."

Kyce scoffed through a smirk and looked down to hide the bashfulness in his eyes.

"I would've loved to see the look on Jerah's face had he heard it," Feran jeered.

"I concur," Sova exclaimed as he raised an invisible goblet to the sky.

"Here—Here," Elling cheered and clinked her own invisible chalice against Sova's. Feran joined, chinking her half-eaten peach against their glasses as they cheered.

"You know what," Feran began as she finished off the last of her peach and tossed the pit into the fire. "Eradawn and Eradusk aren't anything more than a band of self-righteous idiots pretending to be prophets."

"Self-righteous idiots or not," Kyce sighed. "they were my tribe."

"Well then we'll be your tribe."

"Pardon?"

Sova lunged upright and raised his hand to the sky, "I call being chief!"

Roeseph narrowed his eyes. "Not in Heaven nor Hell would you ever be chief, Sova."

"You're just jealous... *Peasant.*"

Feran laughed and crossed her arms. "Guys, I'm serious. Why not be a tribe? We're all exiles anyway, might as well give ourselves a name."

Kyce chuckled. "I would sooner throw myself from the Cliffs of Era than join this ridiculous tribe."

"Here—Here," Roeseph agreed and clinked an imaginary goblet against Kyce's the way the other three had done.

"Fine, I don't need you," Feran hissed back playfully. "Who wants to join my tribe?"

"I do," Sova shot up.

"Not you."

"Aww."

Elling smiled and shook her head as she raised her hand.

"Ok, we got, Elling," Feran exclaimed as she pulled Elling to her feet. "The tribe welcomes you, sister Elling."

Roeseph sprung upright, shifting awkwardly from foot to foot. "I suppose I'll join too."

Sova coughed into his fist, muttering the word, *'whipped,'* beneath his breath.

"Ah, brother Roeseph," Feran cheered and took him by the hand. "The tribe welcomes you."

"You're all ridiculous," Kyce scoffed through a rising smirk.

"That's fine, Kyce," Roeseph shrugged. "You don't have to join. But you should know that leaves just you and Sova."

Kyce flinched and turned to see Sova smiling brightly at him. "Nope," he grunted as he scrambled away and offered his hand to Feran.

Feran snorted and shook her head, "The tribe welcomes you, brother Kyce."

Sova held up his hands in offense, "Are you kidding me?"

"The council has spoken, Sova," Feran replied in a deep voice.

"Well, fine. If I can't be in your tribe, then I'll make my own. Just me, Whisp, and Saber."

Saber growled in objection.

"Just me and Whisp," Sova corrected himself. The exiles laughed, their hysteria traveling like thunder over the valley. Sova shook his head and stifled the smirk in his lips. "Quiet down," he scolded. "You'll wake up all of Era, you heathens."

"He's just jealous he's not in the tribe," Elling taunted as she and her tribal members settled around the flames.

"There's no tribe," Sova said. "You all are just a bunch of children playing pretend."

Kyce smiled mischievously, his elbow resting on his knee. "So, who should we appoint as chief?"

The smug look on Sova's face vanished in an instant, replaced with the look of a sad pup.

"I nominate, Roeseph," Feran cried.

"Oh," Elling rose her hand in agreement, "I vote Roeseph too."

Kyce did the same.

"Thank you, my brother and sisters," Roeseph bowed. "I am forever grateful to be chosen as your chief."

Sova let out a squeak, sounding like a dog just run over by a carriage. "My title..." he whimpered.

"To the tribe," Feran said as she raised an Eradusk peach to the sky, the others following her lead.

"*To the tribe,*" they cheered with peaches in hand.

Roeseph laughed to himself, his voice rising above all the rest, "To the only tribe fit to destroy the Dire of Vaska. May we hunt him like a pack of wolves."

"To the *Dire Wolves,*" Elling praised.

Feran's grin and heart sunk as she looked around at the smiling faces.

"*To the Dire Wolves,*" the others cried.

SMOKE ROSE FROM THE dead fire like a grey spirit, covering the stars Sova watched as he rested against Whisp. While his comrades basked in blissful slumber, he found himself wide eyed and restless. Every so often, the ruins would crumble, or the forest would chirp, feeding the furnace of the Royal Traitor's ravenous anxiety.

Yep, he thought to himself. *This place is definitely haunted. We're going to die out here. If the ghosts don't get me, Saber will. Of course, Saber would kill me. He hates me. I'm not even a part of the tribe... Stupid tribe. I should've been the chief. I'd make a good chief. Stupid Roe. I would make a much better chief than Roe.*

A presence stirred in the gazebo making Sova jump and cling to Roeseph sleeping next to him.

"Roe, something's trying to eat me," Sova whispered.

Roeseph groaned and lurched his elbow into Sova's ribs. "Go to sleep, Sova."

Sova rolled away, "Tyrant."

The shifting sound came again. Sova peered through the darkness to find Feran maneuver out of the gazebo and to the cliff's edge where she settled and stared at the mist covered valley. Sova arched his brow curiously and followed.

Stopping beside her, he gasped. "Could it be true?"

Feran jumped and spun around.

"Are you going to jump? Have my prayers been answered?"

Feran sighed. "I thought everyone was asleep."

"*Asleep?*" Sova repeated. "Not a chance. I must remain vigilant and keep watch over my comrades."

Feran smirked, "So, what's really got you up?"

"I heard a bunny in the woods over an hour ago, and I haven't been able to close my eyes since."

Feran snorted and shook her head. "Sit here," she patted the grass next to her. "I'll make sure the bunny doesn't get you."

"How do I know you won't push me?"

"If I wanted you dead you'd already be it by now."

"Fair enough," Sova said and settled beside his childhood foe. He breathed deeply, his lungs cleansed by the sharp, pine-scented wind. Lykos laid quietly beneath their feet, under the Falls of Era's twinkling arch of mist.

"Wow," Sova thought aloud. "You can see everything from up here."

"Sure can," Feran nodded.

"I find the view much more enjoyable when I'm not clinging to the back of a massive flying dog that's trying to bite my head off."

Feran chuckled. "Sorry about him."

"It's alright," Sova shrugged. "Everyone learns to love me eventually."

"Is that so?"

"Yup. You'll see."

"Sova, I don't think you and I will ever be able to bear each other."

"Challenge accepted."

"Oh, Lykos—what have I done?"

"Received a blessing."

"More like a curse."

Sova chuckled as the soft wind blew, chilling their skin. "So," he continued, "I know what's keeping me up. What about you?"

Feran drew a deep breath and looked at Sova with eyes void of their usual spite, "Would you believe me if I said it was the bunny?"

"Not a chance."

Feran sighed and fidgeted with her medallion. "If the Eradawns help you...." She stared into the mist-covered Lykos. "...Is Saulder going to get hurt?"

Sova exhaled, already exhausted. "Feran—"

"I know he probably deserves what he gets," Feran interrupted, clasping her medallion tightly. "And that he's wronged so many of you. I mean... he imprisoned Roeseph's father. Kyce's people were torn apart because of his family's legacy. You were cast out from your own home. And Elling—I can't imagine what she's going through. To be stuck in your own worst enemy, that's just..." she paused to swallow the lump in her throat. "I know Saulder's responsible for all this, but I...."

"You still love him," Sova answered. Feran's eyes widened and she looked up to meet her foe's striking silver gaze. "To you, he's still your best friend, the boy you were betrothed to—the boy you were supposed to marry. Honestly, I envy you for that. You remember him at his best so vividly. For me, I—" his jaw clenched, and he looked away.

"Sova?" Feran whispered.

"I'm fine," Sova eased. "... I can barely remember Saulder for what he used to be. A kind, good, promising young man. He was going to outshine all the dires before him. And then my mother went and destroyed it all. She's the reason why my father's sick, and why I lost my brother... But it doesn't matter. Saulder hates me now. Why should I bother torturing myself with the past?"

"*Hates you*?" Feran snickered. "Are you serious?"

Sova eyes narrowing, he tapped the gauze over his shoulder. "He shot me with an arrow, Feran."

"That doesn't mean he hates you."

"Shot. Me. With. An arrow."

Feran shook her head as a soft laugh trickled from her lips, warming Sova's heart.

The Dire's Damsel looked back at him. "Sova, do you know why I hated you so much when we were kids?"

"Because God created you to punish me for some atrocious sin I have yet to commit?"

Feran rolled her eyes and sighed. "Look, Saulder was my best friend and was eventually going to be my husband. We spent every day together. In that time, while I didn't understand it until now, I began to love him. I wanted him all to myself. And then there you were. This little snot-nosed, annoying, obnoxious, intolerable, suspiciously foul-smelling—"

"Is there a point to this?" Sova growled. "You seem to forget you have inconveniently sat yourself on the edge of a cliff."

"What I mean is, you followed us everywhere. I couldn't shake you. Even when I threatened you with hypnotism, you always kept coming right back. You never left your brother's side. And to make matters worse, Saulder loved it. He'd talk all about you and how you were going to be such an amazing warrior. He'd brag on you until I'd beg him to stop. And I'll admit, I was... jealous. That's why I hated you, Sova. I have never been more jealous of another person in my life. And Saulder cared for me a great deal, so that's saying a lot. That's how I know the dire could never truly hate you. Love like that doesn't just go away."

Blinking widely, Sova peered at Feran.

"Don't let that go to your head, Sova," she warned. "I mean it."

"You... were *jealous* of me?"

Feran frowned. "You're letting it go to your head, aren't you?"

"You," Sova repeated with a massive smile, "were jealous of me? Do you have any idea of the massive mistake you've made in telling me this?"

"I am just now starting to realize."

"Ah, Feran," Sova laced his arm around her shoulders. "Who knew that a powerful mind melder such as yourself could be threatened by the likes of a little *snot-nosed, annoying, obnoxious, intolerable, suspiciously foul-smelling* lad like myself. Is your ego so big?"

"Don't touch me, Sova," Feran said as she grabbed his wrist and bent his arm off her shoulders.

"Jokes aside, you had nothing to be jealous of," Sova said, nudging her. "Saulder loved you more than anyone in Lykos ever loved another soul. You were never threatened by the likes of me."

"Maybe," Feran sighed.

"...Did I really have a *'suspiciously foul smell*?'"

"Sometimes, but that was mostly my fault. I *did* hypnotize you to wet yourself every time a rooster crowed."

"Little witch."

Feran snorted. "I'm sorry."

"Meh, I'll get over it... Eventually."

Feran and Sova stared into the still picture of Lykos, listening to the thundering falls as content quiet filled the mountains.

"Sova," Feran began, her voice softer and frailer than before.

The Royal Traitor looked up. "Hmm?"

"Can you do me a favor?"

"Depends. Will you let me into the Dire Wolves?"

"Sova—"

"I get that it's all pretend, but If I'm being honest, the fact that you made Roe chief over me is really bothering—"

"Sova," Feran interrupted and looked up to reveal tears hiding behind black lashes. Sova held his breath, his heart sinking at the sight..

Feran drew a deep, ragged breath. "When you face Saulder again, could you tell him I'm alive? And that I miss him. M—Maybe if he knows..." she swallowed before her voice could break. "Maybe if he knows—"

"I'll tell him, Feran," Sova promised.

"And if he wants," Feran continued, "he can come find me. And—And Lore wouldn't have to know, so no one would get hurt."

"I'll tell him," Sova said again as he wrapped his arms around her.

Feran laid against the gauze of his shoulder, quivering. "I don't want him to get hurt, Sova. It's my fault he became like this. He shouldn't be hurt because of me—"

Sova hushed her. "I'll tell him, Feran. I promise I'll tell him."

As Sova held the mind melder in his arms, a dormant, mythical feeling awoke within—a sort of aching peace—the same he felt back in the cave in Lykos. For a moment, he understood what Saulder saw in the Dire's Damsel, and why her absence destroyed him.

Nestled against his shoulder, Feran cleared her throat. "So, just to be clear, you're not going to tell the guys about any of this? Right?"

"I'll tell them, Feran," Sova repeated. "I'll tell them."

Chapter Twenty-Two: The Vaskan Plague

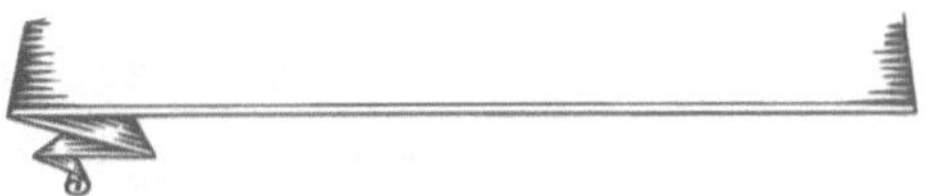

The Eradusk Tribe...

Just as morning clawed out from the eastern cliffs, the dire and his troops struck the mountainside civilization of Eradusk, leaving a landslide of scarlet in their wake. A mother laid breathless in the street, her sobbing child laying over her. A soldier trembled in an alleyway, staring at a bloodied stump in place of his leg. A soaring wolf laid on a slanted roof, arrows riding from its side as it whined for its master.

Kometis ran onto the royal balcony to see the dire marching toward the palace, his black armor gleaming in the red sunlight.

Clutching his medallion, Kometis rushed back into the palace. "Release the soaring wolves!" he shouted. "Release the soaring wolves!"

An armada of Eradusk warriors and their soaring wolves rose like a storm cloud from the heart of the Eradusk palace, led by Kometis on his black steed. The dire and his army were halfway up the mountain when the flying beasts began their descent. The dire looked up, unphased by the airborne ambush.

"Arrows at the ready," a Vaskan soldier shouted as the troops raised their crossbows to the sky. "Aim. Fire!"

The arrows shot through the sky and sliced into the wings, eyes, and hearts of the soaring wolves. The beasts fell to earth, roaring in agony before the ground claimed their life. Kometis laid in the sloped streets of his homeland, an arrow plunged through the bulge of his throat. The dire walked over him, his violet cape dragging the dead Eradusk general's blood like a brush against a canvas as he and his troops ascended the mountain.

JERAH AND WILLOWREED harbored in the throne room, tortured by the cries of their people. Willowreed sat on her throne behind the yellow veil, a tear rolling down her stone-like face.

Teeth gritted, Jerah drew his medallion, "They'll be here any moment now. I need to stop them before they reach—"

"No," Willowreed said calmly. "Eradusk has already fallen. Fighting will do no good. If you wish to help your people, help them escape. I'll stay here and distract the monster."

"Willowreed," Jerah kneeled before his sister's throne, "you can't be serious. If I leave you alone, then the dire will—"

"Do no less damage than he's already done. I won't have you fight on my behalf, Jerah. Just because the chief survives doesn't mean Eradusk will."

"Willow—"

The chief touched her brother's shoulder, smiling a gentle but sad smile. "My big brother, always trying to protect me... You can't save me this time. But you can still save Eradusk. Kometis has not survived the battle—"

"You don't know that."

"I know," Willowreed gulped as another tear caressed her cheek. She clutched her medallion. "You trained him to be like you. He'd sooner die than walk away from a fight... Which is why I have to do this."

The chief drew her medallion and wove it before her brother. Jerah's eyes softened and he sunk slightly, enslaved to her trance.

"*Jerah,*" Willowreed gulped. "*You are relieved of your duty. Leave your chief here to fight her own battles. Find your brothers and sisters and those injured, take them into the forests of Era, and wait there until the dire's plague has passed. Keep yourself alive, and procure the royal bloodline of Eradusk... Go, and don't step foot in Eradusk until the evil is gone.*"

Jerah blinked away his daze and rushed out of the throne room to collect Eradusk's survivors.

"Goodbye, brother," Willowreed swallowed. "I'm sorry."

Not long after Jerah's departure, the Vaskan troops invaded the throne room to find Willowreed waiting patiently behind the golden veil. Surrounding her, they pointed their crossbows at the Eradusk chief. The sound of heavy, iron boots clanked into the throne room as the dire approached the gold veil, his blood-soaked cape painting a long red sash across the floor.

Willowreed raised her chin, unintimidated. "Dire Saulder. This is a surprise. What brings you to Era? Must be important for you to have made such a long journey." The dire drew his sword and slashed the veil down the middle. Willowreed arched her eyebrow. "That was older than the Eradite chief, Illo, you know."

The dire growled, his voice masked by the harsh ring of the metal grate over his lips. "The Rogue Eradite, where is she?"

"The Rogue Eradite?" Willowreed questioned. "Oh, *her*. Yes, she was here earlier with the Royal Traitor, the Last Soldier, an Eradite Exile, and a Hyde Howler. Weren't very appealing company. They left yesterday. Not before robbing my garden, of course."

"Where are they heading?"

"I'm not sure," Willowreed replied. "I turned them away once I realized they were all criminals. Eradusk doesn't associate with sinners of Lykos."

"I have come a long way," the dire seethed. "I won't leave empty-handed."

"I am truly sorry, Dire Saulder," Willowreed apologized. "There is nothing I can do."

"I don't believe that, Chief of Eradusk. I am aware your brother is gathering the last of your people to take to the mountains, and I am willing to turn a blind eye to their *disrespect*."

"Disrespect?" Willowreed spat, her nails digging into the arms of her throne. "You'd consider my people's survival disrespect?"

"I consider anything that defies my authority as disrespect. If I intend for them to die, then they should die. But no matter. As I said, all can be forgiven if you tell me where they are heading. It'll save me a lot of time."

Willowreed's brave façade faltered, and she started to tremble.

"So, where are they?" The dire challenged. "Did they try their luck in Eradawn, or did they cut their losses and head back to Lykos?"

Willowreed gulped, her silence, her answer.

"Very well," the dire growled and turned to one of his soldiers. "Take your regiment into the village and slaughter all you see. You will spare *no one*—"

Willowreed sprung from her throne. "Wait!"

The dire turned to face the noble chief, the mocking tone in his voice revealing the hidden smile beneath his helmet. "Do you have something to say?"

Willowreed gritted her teeth, defeated. "They took the cliffside passage to the east in pursuit of Eradawn. They should reach the tribe by sundown today. I don't know how long they plan to stay. Now, please, leave my people be."

"You would be so quick to give up those exiles?" the dire mocked. "Perhaps the Eradusk people aren't as righteous as they claim to be."

Willowreed slumped back into her throne, her dark brown hair curtaining her face.

"Kill her off quickly," the dire ordered. "If we don't leave now, then the Royal Traitor might slip by again—"

A soft chuckle oozed from the throne, making the dire stiffen and turn to face the Eradusk chief. Her shoulders flinched and sunk with each jarring laugh as she lifted her head to reveal shining eyes.

"It's ironic, Dire," she sighed and rested her cheek on her knuckles. "That mind melder you mentioned, she said something very similar to me about being unrighteous. I must say, I have never seen such eyes in a young person before. I've grown up around mind melders, your Blesser included. And I have to say, I can tell without even seeing her abilities, she will become the most powerful mind melder ever born from the blood of Era. If she isn't already, I mean."

The dire's fists clenched at his side. "Is there a point to you telling me this?"

Willowreed chuckled. "You said I was '*quick to give up*' those exiles. That I was unleashing you on them. But in fact—" she clicked her tongue. "It's them whom I'm unleashing on you. You won't stand a chance against her."

"Enough," the dire snarled as he lunged through the torn veil to stand before the chief.

Willowreed arched her brow. "Have I said something to upset you, dire?"

"*I* am the Dire of Vaska," he growled. "It is she who won't stand a chance against me."

"I seriously doubt that," Willowreed chuckled. "In fact, I think once his sire, the dreaded Dire Saulder, lays eyes on the mind melder. He will fall to his knees and *beg* for her mercy."

The dire drew his sword and pressed the cold blade to the chief's throat, making her flinch.

"I'll have your tongue, you wench," he seethed.

"Do it," Willowreed smiled. "I've protected my tribe. My time is done."

"You believe you've received such a noble death?" the dire shook his head, his burning through his helmet. "No. No, I'm sorry to tell you, Chief of Eradusk. You will not have a silent and respected death. No. You will scream. You will suffer."

Willowreed's smirk faded, and her once impenetrable eyes glowed with fear. Chuckling, the dire snapped her medallion from her neck. "You have the Blesser Casavore, to thank for the monster he's created. It is he who has brought you this fate."

RIDING HIS GREY SOARING wolf, Jerah led the survivors into the mountains beyond their tribe. As the people and soaring wolves scaled the sheer snow lain mount, a shrill cry like a banshee in peril rose over the pine trees.

Jerah looked back, the pain-filled screams of his sister haunting his ears.

"Willowreed..." he whispered and grabbed his medallion as the wind devoured her cry.

One of the survivors, a young girl with her head wrapped in bloodied gauze, ran up to meet Jerah's soaring wolf.

"That was the chief," she panted. "She—She's in trouble. We must go back for her."

Yes. Jerah thought. *We must go back.* "No," he said. "We must press on."

"But she's in trouble. We need to—"

"No one is to set foot in Eradusk until the evil is gone. That's an... order," Jerah gulped, hating his own command. Had he been free of his sister's trance, he would've driven himself back into the thick of battle. But his mind betrayed him, for he could not forsake Willowreed's hypnosis.

"Press on," Jerah ordered. "We'll return once the dire's abandoned Eradusk."

"Why is he here?" the young girl asked. "What does the dire want?"

THE EASTERN CLIFFS of Era...

"Me!" Sova shouted with glee. "She's jealous of me."

Feran exhaled in annoyance as she drove Saber east. Roeseph and Elling rode passenger with her, while Sova rode with Kyce on Whisp.

Kyce smirked at Feran, "You actually told him that? What is wrong with you?"

"It was a lapse in judgment," Feran growled.

Kyce laughed and shook his head. "You do realize he's never going to stop talking about this, right?"

"Yes, he will."

Sova scoffed. "Oh, no, I will not."

"Yes, you will, and all it'll take is one word."

"Oh yeah," Sova challenged, "what?"

Feran grabbed the charred medallion hanging from her neck. "*Rooster,*" she answered.

"Ah yes," Sova nodded. "That'll do the trick."

Elling giggled at the pair, her glee making Roeseph smile.

Feran looked back, catching him in his smitten trance. "What's with the face, Chief?"

Elling looked back at Roeseph, making him straighten and look away.

"Yeah, what's with the face, Roe?" Sova asked, joining in the mockery. "You're turning red. Maybe you're coming down with something. Elling, quick, give him a kiss and make it better."

"Feran," Roeseph called.

"I'm on it," Feran grabbed her medallion, making Sova flail and fall off Whisp. Kyce looked back as the Royal Traitor met the ground, laughter thundering in his gut like a drum. Feran, Roeseph, and Elling joined in his laughter.

"Oh ha, ha," Sova growled as he stood and wiped the snow from his shoulders. "Laugh it up."

"Aww, we're sorry, Sova," Elling apologized.

Feran scoffed, still smiling, "I'm not. Not in the slightest."

"But that's what you deserve for teasing Roeseph like that," Elling continued. "You're making him uncomfortable."

Roeseph blushed and he scooted from Elling.

"Yeah," Sova said sarcastically, his eyes narrowing. "I'm the one who's making him uncomfortable."

Roeseph glared at Sova. Sova winked. As the Royal Traitor teased his love-struck comrade, Kyce looked to the topaz sky.

Feran followed his gaze to what looked like massive buzzards circling overhead. *Soaring wolves*, she thought and grabbed her medallion. "It's the Eradawns."

"Arm yourselves," Roeseph ordered and slid off Saber. Elling clinging to his arm, he and Kyce drew their swords, while Sova looked at the ground, turning in frantic circles as if he were looking for something..

"Sova," Kyce hissed. "What are you doing? Get your sword."

"I can't find it," Sova said. "I think I dropped it when I fell."

"Hurry up, man."

"I don't know where it is."

Elling looked to Sova. "Did you have it with you before you fell?"

"Yes!" Sova said confidently. "...Maybe."

"You don't know, do you?" Elling challenged.

"There's a chance I left it back at the Falls of Era."

Roeseph lashed around and shouted, "Sova!"

"I didn't mean to!" Sova whined.

"How could you forget your sword?"

"Because I felt like using my words today. For Lykos' sake, I didn't mean to leave it!"

"Alright!" Feran yelled. "If you're done arguing, *children*. We've got company."

The soaring wolves overhead descended the path, blocking the exiles' way. The beasts snarled at Whisp and Saber, their silver and grey fur rippling in the early morning sun. Saber and Whisp growled back, their pearly white jaws bared and shining like ivory daggers. Two Eradawn warriors in scarlet garments rode the wolves, their eyes narrowed with spite.

Feran gritted her teeth at the sight of the Eradawns—the very blood of the tribe who kidnapped her father and sold him into slavery. As she reached for her charred medallion, Sova's hand clasped her arm.

"Calm down," he whispered, his eyes filled with worry. "Let's avoid a fight if we can."

Kyce glared at Sova. "Says you," he seethed. "We remembered *our* swords."

Roeseph marched to the Eradawn warriors, leaving his comrades armed in his shadow.

"We mean you no harm," he said. "I am Roeseph, son of Oland. My comrades and I have come to seek council with your chief. It's urgent."

The male warrior scoffed at Roeseph, his eyes flickering with malice. "No one sees the chief. Especially not the likes of you Lykos scum."

Roeseph drew a deep breath. "We have traveled far. And if you'd just let us pass—"

The female warrior laid her hand on her spear. "Did you not hear him?" she challenged. "You aren't welcome here."

Feran smirked, her jaw cocking to the side.

"Look," she interrupted, "you can either take us to your chief, or—" she pulled out her medallion, "I can make you."

The Eradawns looked nervously at each other, then back to the invaders.

"That's an Eradusk medallion," the woman stated. "How'd you get that, you Lykos wench?"

"Funny you ask. My father made it for me," Feran leaned forward on Saber's neck. "Perhaps you've met him?"

"Easy, Feran," Roeseph warned then turned to their foes. "Look, we didn't come here to cause trouble. It's important that we talk to your chief."

"And we told you," the male warrior growled, his hand falling to his holstered spear, "no one of Lykos sees the chief."

Elling stepped away from Sova and stood beside Roeseph. "Please," she begged, "I need to speak to your leader. He's my only hope—"

"Don't make us tell you again," the female warrior snapped and drew her spear. "We will never allow Lykos filth like yourself to taint the sanctity of Eradawn."

Roeseph glared at the Eradawns and clicked his jaw. "Very well," he walked with Elling past the Dire's Damsel. "Feran, do the thing."

"With pleasure," Feran growled and drew her medallion, the sunlight casting off its face as it swung.

Chapter Twenty-Three: Dawn

Under Feran's trance, the Eradawn warriors led the exiles along the mountainside path to a village similar to Eradusk, composed of milky, marble brick carved at the foot of a mountain. Beyond a high wall, Red-clothed villagers tended to their chores.

A father washed his clothes in an ivory fountain while his toddler pulled at his soaring wolf's tail. Two boys played war with blade-less spears in the middle of a limestone road. And a pair of elderly women, sewing old garments, watched the exiles with weary eyes as they passed.

Carved in the side of the mountain, stood a rectangular palace with marble sequoia-like pillars holding up a tall ceiling. Leaving Whisp and Saber at the entrance, the outcasts were led up the marble steps while the unkind eyes of Eradawn followed.

Kyce looked away from the crowd out of fear of being recognized. But Feran returned the glares of the people; the ones who kidnapped and beat her father half to death, only to sell him into slavery to the dire. Seven guards met the exiles at the top of the stairs, spears drawn at their sides.

"What is the meaning of this?" the eldest guard growled. "Why have you brought these outsiders into our village?"

The entranced warriors looked at one another, unsure themselves.

"Because I asked nicely," Feran smirked.

The lead guard stepped toward her, only for Roeseph to block his way.

"Sir," he began, "my name is Roeseph. I'm the son of Oland, leader of the Blind Seers. My comrades and I have come to speak with your chief."

"No one sees the chief," the guard said.

Sova exhaled. "So we've been told."

"Please, sir," Roeseph continued. "We've come a long way, and we just want—"

"I know what you want," the guard growled. "I know your names. You are Roeseph, the Last Soldier. He is Sova, the Royal Traitor. And she is the rogue mind melder who attacked the dire."

Sova smirked, his jaw cocking to the side. "Believe me, pal. She's a whole lot more than that."

"Who wants to break it to him?" Kyce said.

"Nah, don't tell him anything," Feran grinned. "Let's let him figure it out himself."

"I told you that the chief isn't seeing anyone," the guard spat, "and until she tells me otherwise, I demand that you leave this village—"

Kyce's eyes widened. "Wait. *She*? Your chief is a 'she?' What happened to Chief Lanton?"

"That is none of your concern."

"Maybe not," Kyce arched an eyebrow. "But it should be *your* concern."

"What are you getting at, boy?"

"All I'm saying if you don't let us in, your chief is going to have your head."

The guard leaned in an inch from Kyce's face. "Oh yeah? And why's that?"

"Let us in and you'll see."

THE GUARDS ACCOMPANIED the five exiles through two large doors and into a massive space much like the Eradusk throne room. Thick, spiraling pillars held up a tall ceiling, leading to a platform where the throne stood behind a waving scarlet veil. Beyond the veil, a beautiful woman in a flowing red dress with her cherry-red hair pinned in a bun on top of her head sat in a magnificent wooden throne. Unlike the other Eradite royals they came across, she bore no medallion, as she was not a mind melder, meaning, she wasn't of the previous chief's immediate family.

She glared at the Lykos travelers, her yellow eyes burning into their souls like a branding iron.

"Who have you brought me, general?" she said coolly. "A hoard of Lykos spies?"

Roeseph gulped and bowed his head. "No, ma'am," he cleared his throat. "My name is Roeseph. I have come to ask Eradawn to aid our army in the fight against the dire so both our lands might be free—"

Before Roeseph could finish, Kyce stepped forward, gawking at the chief as she glared at him through the veil.

"What are you staring at, boy?"

Trembling, Kyce gulped and took another brave step toward the veil. As the chief stared at him, her eyes sparkled with shock, and she stood from her throne.

"Guards," she ordered. "Leave us."

The guards fled the throne room. The Eradawn chief descended the platform, parted the veil, and walked up to Kyce. He froze, his usual ferocious, fighting eyes doused of flame.

"Have we met before?" the chief muttered.

Kyce gulped and nodded. "Yes, ma'am. But it's been a long time."

"How long exactly?"

"Eight years, ma'am."

The chief stepped closer to find a face much like her own in the exile; only he bore the skin, eyes, and hair of another. A tear racing realization, she gasped, and hesitantly touched the sides of his face.

"Are you..."

Kyce laid his hands over hers, his amber eyes glistening. "Yes, ma'am."

"J—Jerah told me you were banished to Lykos," the chief whispered as tears streamed down her face like two waterfalls. "Uncle Lanton wouldn't let me come look for you. I thought—I thought you were..."

"I'm not," Kyce assured. "I'm here."

"Kyce," the chief gasped and threw her arms around his neck. "My baby. I thought I lost you."

Kyce embraced his mother, his weeping eyes hidden in the fiery locks of her hair.

"That's nice," Sova sighed. "One of Kyce's parents actually likes him."

Feran slapped him on the arm.

The Eradawn chief pulled away, her golden eyes shining with mist. "I've prayed so long for this," she sniffled and wiped a tear from Kyce's cheek. "God finally answered me."

Kyce looked back at his comrades. "Ma," he began and walked her to the four other exiles. "These are the people who helped me into Era—Roeseph. Elling. Sova. And Feran. Everyone, this is my mother. Chief Vohwe."

Chief Vohwe shook each of their hands, ending on Feran.

"Thank you, miss," she bowed. "Is there anything I can do to repay you?"

Feran glared at the Eradawn chief, her hand burning in her grip.

"No," she said, failing to hide the hostility in her voice and pulled away. "I don't think you can."

Roeseph took a step forward. "Actually, Chief Vohwe," he said. "We need your help. We seek to overthrow the dire and were hoping to receive aid from the Eradite tribes. Unfortunately, the Eradusks have already declined—"

"The Eradusks?" Vohwe gasped and looked to her son. "Kyce, you went to see your father?"

Kyce's jaw clenched and he nodded, "Yes. But in all honesty, it wasn't worth the trip."

"What did he say?"

"Nothing," Kyce replied before drawing a shallow breath. "Neither of us said anything."

"Oh, Kyce," Vohwe whispered and reached to console him.

Kyce stepped back. "Look," he said, "these people came a long way. I'd appreciate it if you could give them an answer."

"I—" Vohwe looked back at the exiles. "That's not my decision to make."

Feran's brow furrowed and she stepped forward, "You're the chief, aren't you? Your people sent the dire his Blesser. Shouldn't you be the one to get Lykos out of this mess?"

Sova elbowed Feran in the side.

"I am only the chief temporarily until my uncle recovers," Vohwe declared, making Kyce stiffen at the horrid realization.

"So Chief Lanton still lives...." He uttered.

"*Chief Lanton?*" Sova repeated. "Isn't that the guy who tried to kill—" before he could finish, Elling, Roeseph, and Feran silenced him with their warning glares. "... I'll shut up now."

"Ah," Feran grumbled and looked to the heavens, "a miracle."

Roeseph stepped toward the chief. "Chief Vohwe," he started, "if we may, we'd like to speak with Chief Lanton."

Vohwe nodded, "As you wish."

VOHWE LED THE EXILES out of the throne room and through a series of hallways. As Feran walked, she eyed the medallions of past chiefs lining the walls—past chiefs of the tribe who enslaved her father. It was then she realized she was about to meet the man who reigned over Eradawn when they attacked Casavore. She clutched her medallion, her hatred intensifying with each step as thoughts of violent justice tempted her spirit. A hand fell on her shoulder, and she looked up to see Sova, his silver eyes focused forward.

"Take a breath," he eased without looking down. "Hurting him won't solve anything."

Feran exhaled and released her medallion, as well as her plots of vengeance. Coming to the end of the hall, Vohwe stopped before a lonesome door and looked back at the exiles.

"Before we go in," she began with a warning tone, "I must ask you not to get too close, nor speak to him unless you're spoken to. Don't forget, he is still the chief and has power over my authority."

Elling clung to Roeseph, her emerald eyes glistening as she trembled.

"Hey," Roeseph said softly and rubbed her hand clutching his arm, "everything's going to be ok. He'll be able to help you."

Elling nodded and gave him a meek smile. Feran hoped he was right. For all they knew, Elling could be a Hyde Howler forever.

Vohwe opened the door and led the five into the chamber where an old man with thin white hair, greyish speckled skin, and folded wrinkles laid in bed. Around his neck hung a golden medallion—the mark of a mind melder. Eyes closed, he rolled his head back and forth across the pond in the middle of his pillow, lost in perilous sleep.

Feran glared at the living corpse, her hands coiling at her side. As she stewed in her hate, she looked to see Sova had turned white as a ghost, his silver eyes changing to the color of terror.

Forgetting her hatred, she touched his shoulder. "Sova?" she whispered, making him look down. "Are you ok?"

"I'm fine," Sova gulped. "It's just..." he paused to stare at the strange mind melder laying sick in bed. "The man reminds me of my father. I just..."

Feran squeezed his hand, so his worry oozed out of him like water from a sponge. "Awe, Feran," Sova teased through his distress. "If I didn't know any better, I'd say you'd gone soft."

"Don't read too much into it," Feran warned and squeezed his hand, making his bones crackle.

Twisting painfully in Feran's grip, Sova winced through a soft laugh. "Noted."

As Vohwe walked toward the chief's bed, Kyce's eyes narrowed, the look of hatred in his eyes as apparent as smoke rising from a volcano—a warning of the annihilation underway.

Roeseph nudged his arm. "Are you going to be able to do this?" he asked worriedly.

Kyce drew a deep breath, his jaw clenching as he raised his head. "I couldn't say what I needed to tell Jerah. But *he* will face what he's done."

Sitting on the edge of the bed, Vohwe touched the chief's pale, blue-veined hand.

"Uncle?" she whispered. The Eradawn chief's eyes opened, the color of his iris buried under silver scales.

"Vohwe?" he croaked, his voice like a fading echo in the back of his throat. "Is that you, my child?"

"Yes, Uncle," she nodded. "It's me."

"I dreamt of your father," the man chuckled into a cough. "We were children playing on the cliffs... Mother yelled at us for being so reckless."

Vohwe swallowed, her chin wobbling slightly before she spoke, "Uncle, there's—"

"I thought I was finally dead," the chief lamented. "I thought I was in Heaven. But God still refuses to take me... What more can I do that He needs me here?... I wish He'd let me come home."

"Uncle," Vohwe gulped, her voice starting to shake. "There are some people here to see you."

"Who?" Chief Lanton coughed. "Who has come?"

"Some travelers from Lykos seeking an alliance."

Chief Lanton chuckled. "It's ironic, isn't it? God would sooner allow the blood of Lykos into Era rather than let me into His kingdom."

"Uncle—"

"Who are they. Who have you allowed into my chamber? I can't see their faces. Who are they?"

Vohwe looked at the five exiles and beckoned for a volunteer. Kyce scowled at the dying man on the bed and prepared to step forward, only Roeseph beat him to his prize.

Roeseph knelt before the chief's bed, his head bowed in respect. "Chief Lanton," he said, "my name is Roeseph. Son of Oland, the commander of the Blind Seers. My comrades and I have traveled many miles to speak with you. Lykos is in danger, for Dire Saulder's wrath exceeds all his forefathers. The Blind Seer forces have dwindled in our efforts to free the valley and all its nations. So, we've come seeking your help to liberate our people and yours. I ask you to join our fight so both our lands might be free, and so not another Blesser may be taken from Era."

Chief Lanton coughed, his body arching for breath over the mattress before he collapsed. "You are the son of the Blind Hound, you say?" he rasped.

"Y—Yes, sir," Roeseph nodded. "Oland."

"He is one of the men the Blesser Casavore cursed?"

"Yes. He's a Hyde Howler."

"Poor soul. The Blesser has harmed many with his evil. No true Eradite or follower of Christ would ever act so cruelly."

Eyes blazing, Feran gripped her medallion and started forward, only for Sova to draw her back by the hand.

"And yet myself and my people have acted no differently," Chief Lanton coughed. Feran's eyes widened, and her hand fell from her medallion. "In Era, our people feed off the notion that we are more righteous than men because we read the scriptures and believe ourselves obedient to the word. But in truth, we reject them. We have failed beyond all doubt. *I* have failed beyond doubt."

Kyce's lips parted, and a shallow breath left his lips. "*What is he saying?*" he whispered.

His scaled eyes infected with tears, Chief Lanton sniveled, "I have left Lykos to rot because of its sin, thinking I was protecting my tribe from their sickness. But in truth, the plague has been upon us all along. I have killed many Eradusks in the name of justice for what they've done to my people. For what they did to my sister-in-law. And nothing good has come of it. All I have done is allow the wound to fester. I have wronged so many men. Perhaps that is why God doesn't let me die. He knows earthly agony doesn't hold a candle to Hell."

Vohwe clutched her uncle's hand tighter, speaking through a gulp, "Uncle...."

"I am sorry, son," Chief Lanton looked to Roeseph. "I have seen many men die by my people's hand. I can't allow it any longer. I won't send my troops into battle."

Roeseph sprung from the floor, his eyes big with terror, "Sir, if you don't help us, even more people will die."

"Is Christ still in Lykos?"

"Y—Yes, sir, but—"

"Then death is optional," Lanton sighed. "This dire you have asked my people to destroy, he will never see Heaven. I cringe at the thought of even a man like him being stuck in eternal darkness. No, I won't damn myself further from God's grace. I am sorry."

Fists coiling at his side, Roeseph's head bowed in defeat.

Kyce's hand fell to his shoulder. "Let's go, Roeseph," he said sadly. "There's no hope for you here."

As he and Roeseph turned to join the others, Chief Lanton grabbed Kyce by the hem of his shirt.

"Who are you, son?" he asked weakly. Kyce looked from the chief's frail, grey hand to his white-plated eyes.

"An exile," he stated bitterly. "Like my comrades."

"Your name?" Lanton shivered, his voice forlorn and hopeful. Kyce paused and looked from his mother to the chief. "Kyce," he replied reluctantly.

The moment his name left his lips, the chief crumbled like ancient ruins and a silver tear fell from his blind eyes. "Son of Jerah," he whimpered. "Child of Eradawn and Eradusk... I am so sorry."

Kyce took a step stumbling back, his chest rising and falling in shallow but shocked breaths.

"You were but a child when I sentenced you to that horrible place," Chief Lanton continued. "I did it out of my own pride. I couldn't fathom that my sweet niece would bond herself to a son of Eradusk, so I sought to have my tribe cleansed. But my quarrel wasn't with you. It wasn't with your mother or father either. No. It was with my own prejudice. I thought my virtue qualified me to judge righteously, but in truth, I acted against God's every command. I haven't realized until now how wrong I was to cast you out. I am so sorry, boy."

Kyce's knuckles cracked at his sides as boiling tears rose in his flaming eyes. "And you expect me to forgive you?" he growled, his shoulders shaking with anger. "I was alone in Lykos for eight years. I knew nothing of the valley. You forbid me to return home. Why should I forgive you?"

"You shouldn't," Lanton wheezed. "Boy, I wouldn't forgive myself either. But I ask you to forgive me not for my sake but for your own."

Kyce scoffed, his jaw cocking to the side. "*My own?*"

"Hate is a sweet sedative. It is an armor that protects us from life and all its evil... as well as its sweetness. One can't love Christ and harbor Satan's spell. And so I am sorry that you must go against the primal curse of humanity. I ask you to forgive your enemies along with myself. Not a million years of hate on earth are worth an eternity in Hell. Let yourself be free, boy."

Kyce trembled, his face wrenching in a scowl.

"Free?" he seethed. "I'm not free. I never will be. I'm betrayed by my own blood. I am the spawn of two enemies—a curse upon Era. I can't escape being born in blaspheme. I can never be free."

"These are the lies of Heaven's Exile. While your people call you a curse, God calls you a blessing. No child on earth is anything but. This was the first blasphemy I spoke against God when I told you your only value to Eradawn was your death. I was wrong about you, just as you are wrong about yourself. You are loved and favored. I am sorry that anyone made you think otherwise."

Kyce gritted his teeth and turned to hide among his fellow exiles. Elling stepped out from the group to stand beside Roeseph, her eyes falling to the Eradawn chief.

"Sir," she said softly.

Chief Lanton's silver-plated gaze lifting at the angelic voice of the shepherd girl. "Yes, child?"

"My name is Elling. I am a friend of Roeseph's," she fiddled with her hands, her voice falling out in broken fragments. "I—I was wondering, is there's anyone in Eradawn who can lift his father's curse?"

"His *father's* curse, you say?" Lanton repeated. Even blind the old chief could read Elling like a scroll.

Elling swallowed and dipped her head. "Yes, sir."

"Hmmm," Lanton nodded, allowing what felt like eons of unbearable silence to pass. Shaking his head, the bed-ridden chief let out a sigh, "I am sorry, child. I can't help you."

"That's complete bull dung!" Roeseph stomped in front of Elling, his voice bright with anger. "You won't help her, you won't help me—why? You say you wish to make amends for your eternity's sake, but then you turn away every one of our pleas."

"I mean, I *can't* help," Lanton insisted. "Mind melders have a peculiar gift. We can manipulate emotions like anger, pride, sorrow, fear, or pain—but only to an extent. We can't get rid of them altogether. I can place in you fake love or hate or fear and have complete control over those emotions because I made them—anything genuine I cannot. Trances can be lifted using the medallion that cursed you, the way only one key can unlock certain doors."

"So Casavore's medallion can lift the curse," Roeseph said hopefully and looked at the Blesser's medallion hanging from Sova's neck. "We can remove the Hyde Howler curse ourselves."

"I wish it were that simple," Lanton said. "But in terms of the Hyde Howler, the Blesser has not sired his victim to himself, but the dire. Only Dire Saulder can permanently release his subjects by citing a chant only known by him. In turn, the Blesser's power is useless. As is his medallion."

"How is that possible?" Roeseph snapped. "You just said the medallion that cursed her is the only thing capable of releasing her. We have a mind melder in our midst. She can undo the hypnosis with the Blesser's medallion."

"The Hyde Howler curse is not the same as every other hypnosis. The Blesser has surrendered the Hyde Howler's trance to whoever wears the dire's armor. Until your friend hears from his lips that she is released, then she won't ever be free. In her case, the Blesser's medallion is useless."

Elling cupped her hand over her mouth as scorching rain poured from her lashes.

Roeseph looked down at Elling, the rage in his visage breaking into sorrow. "Elling—" as he reached to console her, she fled from the chief's chamber and out the door. Roeseph chased her, followed by Feran and Kyce. Sova remained.

"So that's it?" he whispered, clutching the Blesser's medallion. "We can't help her?"

"You are the one they call Sova?" Lanton replied. "Your brother is the dire?"

"Yes. He is."

"I am sorry. But until Dire Saulder tells her himself that she is released, no one—not even someone as powerful as the Blesser can free her."

ELLING RAN DOWN THE marble hallway, passing by an array of gold medallions on the wall.

Useless, she wept. *They're all useless!*

"Elling, stop!" Roeseph shouted as he and the others advanced their comrade.

Coming to the end of the hall, Elling dropped to the floor. Not a second later, Roeseph had her in his arms, her ear pressed to his thundering heart as the others circled.

"It's ok," Roeseph assured, his voice shaking. "I'm going to fix this."

"No," Elling sobbed into his chest. "You can't. You heard the chief. I'm not sired to the Blesser. This curse isn't his to lift."

"We—We can try," Roeseph trembled and looked up. "Sova, give Feran Casavore's medallion."

Sova handed Feran her father's medallion and she knelt before Elling. Swinging the gold trinket back and forth, she began her trance. *"Hyde Howler sworn to evil, I demand you release your vessel. Forget your oath to the dire, be good once more. You will never be the Hyde—"*

Intense, unfathomable pain suddenly struck Elling's skull, making her arch forward as her screams marred the echo-prone halls. Feran fell back and dropped her father's medallion, her eyes wide with fear.

"What did you do!" Roeseph shouted as he trapped Elling's writhing body against his chest.

"I—I don't know!" Feran cried.

Elling dug her nails into her scalp, blood trickling down her forearm. "Make it stop!" she wailed, tortured by the piercing sensation of a stake being driven into the side of her temples. "Make it stop!"

"Help her!" Roeseph ordered.

Feran scrambled to pick up her father's medallion and wove it before Elling again. "Uh—um—*forget my trance, forget my meddling. Lay to rest until the dire calls. The Hyde Howler remains, dormant until summoned. Here is my surrender. There is nothing to be done. A Hyde Howler one day you'll always become....*"

The pain subsided, and Elling fell silent in Roeseph's arms, sobbing softly. The group looked down at her, mortified by what had unfolded before them.

"What was that?" Kyce breathed.

Feran gulped and shook her head. "There's some sort of protection trance on her. A second hypnosis that would keep my father from healing the Hyde Howlers the dire forced him to make."

"The Chief was right," Sova whispered. "The Hyde Howler curse isn't sired to Casavore's medallion like most trances. She's been surrendered to the dire. Only he can fix her."

Elling cried into Roeseph's shirt, her warm tears soaking the cloth.

Rocking her gently, Roeseph hushed, "We'll figure this out. We'll figure this out, Elling, I promise."

"No," Elling shook her head against his chest. "I'm done. I can't be fixed. I'm always going to be a monster..."

Chapter Twenty-Four: The Celebration

The blazing sunset shone through the balcony, painting the melancholic faces of those residing in the chamber a somber orange. Whisp slid back and forth across the polished floor, touching her nose from wall to wall. Feran leaned against Saber, staring at the ceiling as she fiddled with her charred medallion. Across from her, Kyce stood with his back to the wall. Elling sat on the bed, her damp eyes resting on her knees she pulled to her chest. Roeseph sat next to her with his arm wrapped around her shoulders and his cheek resting against her head. Sova sat on the rim of the marble balcony, watching the sunset wave goodbye. He drew a deep breath, overcome by a sense of defeat.

Kyce sprung from where he sat. "We should try again," he said and looked to Elling.

Feran stopped playing with her medallion. "It won't work, Kyce."

"And why not? Just because the chief said so?" Kyce challenged. "He doesn't know everything."

"He knows a lot more than I did. And he's right."

"You're more talented than any mind melder to come out of Era. You're the daughter of the Blesser for Lykos sake. Surely you can do something!"

"This hypnosis is different than most, Kyce. Yes, I can withdraw the hypnosis my father placed on someone, but only by using his medallion. I think the chief referred to it as keys and doors."

"Well, then pick the lock!"

"It's not exactly like a key, idiot. Even if it was, it's as if the dire built a brick wall over the door. The Blesser transferred the hypnosis from his medallion to the dire. It's completely out of his hands. Of anyone's hands."

"Well," Kyce looked sadly at Elling, "why don't we at least try again?"

Roeseph snapped, "No. I'm not putting her through that again."

"Oh, come on," Kyce rolled his eyes. "So her head hurt a little. Maybe if she can push through—"

"There's no pushing through," Feran interrupted. "That reaction is her body protecting the Hyde Howler hypnosis. If we were to make her endure any more, she could end up hurting herself. Or worse, the Hyde Howler might awaken."

Kyce shrugged, his jaw cocking to the side, "So that's it? We just give up?"

Elling looked up to reveal red-tinted eyes. "Yes," she whispered dryly. Silence swept the chamber. "I'm done," she croaked. "I'm done hoping. All it does is hurt."

Roeseph pulled Elling tighter to his chest and rubbed her back while Kyce stared sadly at his comrade.

"You know," Kyce said, "you once told me you'd tried the '*whole hopeless thing*.' You told me there were '*better things to believe in*.' Come on, Elling, you know better than to give in to hopelessness."

"I'm not hopeless," Elling gulped. "I'm just done."

Holding her tight, Roeseph shook his head, "Why would the Blesser give up his claim to his own hypnosis? By doing so he's given up any leverage he had over the dire."

Sova scoffed, his silver eyes still locked on the dusk, "Because my father's a genius."

The Royal Traitor swung himself off the balcony and leaned against the archway, the light of burning dusk blazing over his shoulder.

Feran glared at him. "What are you talking about, Sova?"

"I'm talking about Dire Zastar," he replied coldly. "I mean, most dires ruled their Blessers with fear. But to manipulate the Blesser under the false pretense of friendship—" he shook his head, "—genius."

Feran stood with Saber, her hickory eyes blazing. "My father wasn't manipulated into anything."

"Oh, he wasn't?" Sova chuckled. "Your father turned hundreds of innocents into Hyde Howlers. All because he loved Zastar. No doubt, Casavore is the most loyal Blesser Vaska has ever seen. And the most foolish."

"My father isn't a fool," Feran sneered and clasped her medallion. Saber snarled and pressed his shoulder close to hers, his wings coiling tightly to his sides.

"My father is more dead than alive, Feran," Sova hissed. "And yet, Casavore remains loyal to my brother—the most cynical dire ever to curse Vaska. All because he cares for Zastar too much to end his eldest son."

"SO what does that make you?" Feran snapped just an inch from his face. "You tolerated Saulder's wrath. You saw how many people he killed."

"Then I came to my senses. I challenged the dire. And I have this," he slammed his fist against his gauze-wrapped shoulder, "to show for it."

A mad chuckle rolled from Feran's throat, and she shook her head.

Sova looked her up and down, "What are you laughing at?"

"I get it now," Feran laughed. "I get what finally tipped Saulder over the edge. It wasn't me leaving." her eyes became dark, like the moon eclipsing the sun. "It was being stuck with you."

"Watch yourself, Feran," Sova challenged.

"No. You talk about how you attacked the dire out of mercy for Lykos, but let's be honest. It was because you needed to kill the tyrant you made. Imagine—" Feran stopped to laugh, "Imagine being so *awful* to be around that you literally turn the kindest, most harmless soul in all of Lykos into a monster!"

Sova took an aggressive step toward Feran, making her clutch her medallion and Saber snarl. Kyce threw himself between the two before things could escalate, and shoved Sova away.

Roeseph snapped from Elling's side, his eyes blistering with rage. "That's enough! What will fighting do for any of you?"

"Might put us all out of our misery," Feran growled. "I could do without his irritating company."

"Oh, is that so?" Sova shouted and pushed forward. Kyce held him back, fighting to keep the Royal Traitor away as he ranted. "Because if you want to put the blame on someone, let's put it on you! You were the one that left Saulder. You were the one that got us chased by the Vaskan Guards. You're the one who gave us false promises that the Eradites might be able to help Elling. You want to know who I blame, Feran? I blame *you*. For everything!

I might not have been able to fix Saulder, but you're the one who broke him! You're the reason we're all living in Hell!"

"Sova!" Roeseph yelled as Kyce shoved Sova into the wall

Sova huffed, his rage subsiding, and looked to Feran as her face wrenched in a scowl—a mask to hide her pain. His heart fell to his feet, immediately regretting all he said.

"Feran..." he began. The door opened and Vohwe stepped into the room. She stopped, struck by the intense atmosphere brewing between the five exiles.

"Sorry if I'm interrupting anything," she dipped her head. "I wanted to tell you our village will be throwing a feast once the sun goes down. You're welcome to join us—"

"Is there booze?" Feran asked stoically.

"Um," Vohwe paused, "well yes."

"Perfect." Feran shoved past Vohwe and into the hall, Saber at her heels. "I'll meet you guys there."

She slammed the door, causing the chamber to shake.

Vohwe looked to the exiles with concern. "Is everything ok?"

A GRAND CELEBRATION unfolded within the heart of the Eradawn village beneath the night sky. Candlelit tables surrounded the ivory fountain, abound with juicy fruits, sizzling roasted meat, and dry red wine. The villagers, dressed in magnificent red colors, strung hymns from their lyres and sonnets from their drums. While the people ate and danced, their soaring wolves invaded the sky in a game of chase, looking like a stampede of silver comets.

The five exiles sat at a lonesome table at the edge of the celebration, watching the gleeful Eradawn people. Saber and Whisp sat behind their master's chairs, silent as stones. Whisp flapped her stump-like wings as she watched her brethren play in the stars. When she didn't take flight, she whimpered sadly and laid her head on her paws.

The exiles sat in silence, picking at their food but not eating a morsel. Elling pushed her plate away.

"You should eat something," Roeseph urged.

Elling shook her head, "I'm not hungry."

Roeseph opened his mouth to argue. When words didn't come, he looked back to his untouched plate. Further down the table, Sova stared at Feran as she watched the celebration with a bitter gaze.

Swallowing his pride, he reached to console her, "Look, um... Feran."

"Not now, Sova," Feran sighed. "I don't want to give or receive an apology right now."

"I know, but I want you to know that—"

"There's nothing to say," she interrupted. "You and I, we're not friends. We weren't friends back then, we're not friends now. Why should it matter if we get along?"

Sova's head cocked, the tiniest crack in his heart beginning to form. "Feran, I—"

"I need wine," Feran stood from the table and walked into the celebration in search of drink, Saber, as always, at her side.

Sova swallowed hard and looked to the Blesser's medallion hanging from his neck.

"Casavore is no fool," he admitted, guilt piercing his heart like a blade. "I—I'm the fool."

"Can't disagree with that," Kyce said as he chomped down on a stick of celery.

Sova glared at the Eradite Exile, his lips piercing in a thin line, "Thanks, *Mutt*."

"Don't mention it."

Vohwe emerged from the crowd, a soft smile on her face. "There you all are," she said. "I was looking for you. Enjoying the celebration?"

"Oh yes," Sova grumbled and took an aggressive bite of a turkey leg. "We're just *jubilant*."

"Don't mind him," Roeseph eased. "We're very grateful for all you've done for us, Chief Vohwe."

Kyce nodded in agreement, "Yeah. Sova's just bitter cause he got in a fight with his girlfriend."

"She's not my girlfriend!" Sova shouted.

"Want to hear something even sicker?" Kyce snickered. "She's betrothed to his brother."

"Ky!"

Vohwe's eyes widened, and she gasped beneath her breath. "She—She's the dire's betrothed? Is she the Dire's Damsel from the legend? The daughter of Blesser Casavore?"

"That's the one," Kyce nodded.

"Oh, poor girl," Vohwe said sadly. "Where did she go?"

"To hide from Sova. I'm not far behind her."

Roeseph cleared his throat. "Thank you for having us, Chief Vohwe," he said.

"No need to thank me, son," Vohwe nodded. "And please, call me Vohwe. I am merely the temporary chief until Uncle Lanton gets better."

Kyce scoffed and shook his head. "Yeah. *Temporarily.*" His mother wasn't fooling anyone. They'd all seen Chief Lanton. There was no way the old man would survive his sickness. "What are we celebrating anyway, Ma?" Kyce asked.

"Why, your return to Eradawn, of course."

Kyce's eyes widened, as did everyone else's at the table.

"My—My what?"

"Your return to Eradawn," Vohwe repeated. "Uncle Lanton has lifted your banishment. You can come home, now."

Kyce froze, unable to speak, move, or comprehend what his mother said.

Sova perked in his seat, his silver eyes bright. "If Kyce is leaving us for Eradawn, does that mean I can take his place in the Dire Wolf tribe?" Elling and Roeseph glared at him. "I'll uh," Sova muttered as he shrunk into his seat, "I'll let you guys think it over."

Vohwe gazed at her son, her brow furrowed with confusion. "Are you not pleased, Kyce?"

"No—I am," Kyce replied, his voice twinged with panic. "It's just... I didn't think that was ever an option."

"Well, take some time to think it over. You can give me your answer before your friends leave for Lykos," she planted a kiss on top of his head. "Please," she looked to the other exiles, "try to enjoy yourselves."

As Vohwe disappeared into the crowd of dancing Eradawns, Kyce slumped in his chair, his amber eyes wide with shock.

"Congratulations," Roeseph praised and slapped his shoulder. "You get to go home."

"Yeah," Kyce nodded, dumbstruck. "Yeah, I uh... I didn't think that could ever happen."

"Well, it did," Roeseph smiled and shook him lightly. "I'm happy for you, man."

"Yeah. Thanks."

As Kyce stewed in his disbelief, Feran's voice whipped from the crowd. "I found the wine," she cried as she strolled up to the gloomy table with Saber trotting close behind. She held up a bronzed vase dripping with the blood of the vine, smiling victoriously. "I had to fight this big-ole Eradawn for it, but we came to an agreement."

Roeseph eyed her, his brow high with suspicion. "What kind of agreement?"

"Do you want to know?" Feran smirked

"Not really."

"Well, let's just say that he's unwillingly confessing his love to his childhood sweetheart and has forgotten all about the wine he and I were arguing over."

"You hypnotized an Eradawn warrior for wine?"

"Hey," Feran shrugged, "we've had a bad day. Besides, these people owe me a little wine after what they did to my father."

She slammed the vase on the table.

"I have no complaints," Kyce smirked and offered his cup, "fill 'er up."

One by one, Feran filled her comrades' cups, leaving hers empty. She intended to drink straight from the vase. Slumped in her chair, she tipped the vase over her head and devoured the bitter nectar.

"Wow, that's dry," she rasped.

"Heathen," Sova insulted.

Elling moved from her cup, her emerald eyes still dull with heartbreak. "I—I don't drink," she dismissed.

"Tonight, Elling," Feran winked, "you do."

Elling hesitated for but a moment before giving into peer pressure and tipped the cup to her lips. Like a scarlet geyser, she spewed the wretched liquor over the table. Her comrades laughed.

"That's awful," she coughed as she dared smile.

"Just don't think about it," Feran advised and downed the red poison. "If you think about it, it makes it worse."

Elling laughed dryly and drew the horrible poison to her lips.

KYCE, ROESEPH, FERAN, Elling, and Sova found themselves dancing around the white geyser, hypnotized by the happy lyre, and hanging from one another's shoulders in a drunken chain.

Sova raised his cup to the stars. "I *suppose* a toast."

"Propose," Roeseph corrected.

"I propose a toast. To Kyce. The only one of us misfits that actually got what he wanted tonight."

"Here—Here," Elling exclaimed as she and the exiles clinked their drinks together.

Feran arched her brow, confused. "Wait, what did Kyce do? What did he get?"

Sova laid his hand on Kyce's shoulder. "I'm glad you asked, my dear psychotic mind melder. My friend Ky here has been pardoned. His banishment is up. He's been asked to return to Eradawn."

"Well by Lykos," Feran smiled. "Congratulations, Kyce."

Kyce grimaced at the taste of his wine and tossed the empty cup over his shoulder. "You guys want to know something?" he burped. "I'm not sure I want to come back."

Sova giggled and shook his head. "By the dreaded dire's of Vaska, you're drunk."

"I'm serious," Kyce grumbled. "For eight years, I've wondered around Lykos waiting for the day I'd come back and tell off the people who cast me out. And now I... I'm at a loss for words."

Swaying slightly, Feran gave a shrug. "Personally, I think the Eradawns are a bunch of self-righteous hypocrites."

"So you've said," Kyce nodded.

"But we'd be happy for you if you stayed. You'd finally be home," she nudged his shoulder.

"Home," Kyce said to himself. When he thought of home, he thought of the Falls of Era, where he grew up in secret. The place his mother would cast stones with him in the river. The place he and Whisp would discover the sky. The place he and his father would count the stars. Neither Eradusk nor Eradawn was his home, so how could he possibly be asked to return to a place he was a stranger to?

"Hey," Sova grunted and raised his arm. "Just curious, show of hands, how many of us have mother or father issues?"

"Excuse me?" Roeseph arched an eyebrow. "What brought this up?"

"Just curious," Sova shrugged.

The exiles paused and looked nervously to another. Kyce raised his hand first, joining Sova. Then came Feran, and then Roeseph.

"Elling," Sova began in a scolding tone.

"What? I don't count," Elling grumbled. "My parents loved me. *Suckers.*"

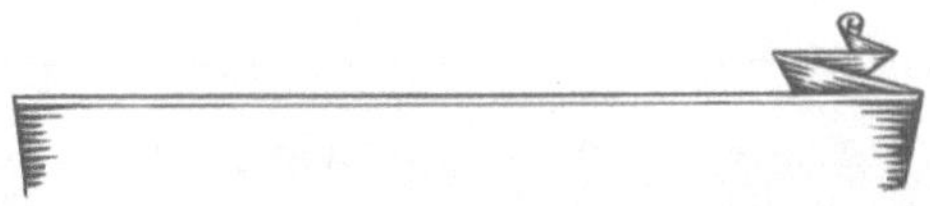

Chapter Twenty-Five: Flight

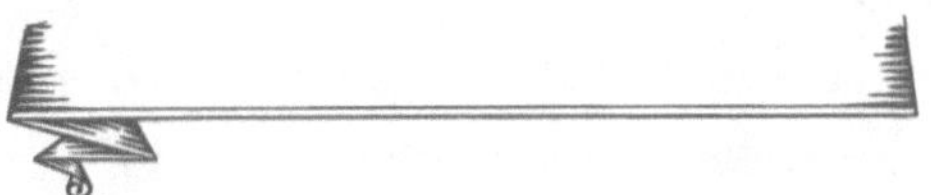

The festivities, as well as the torches, doused to ash as all returned to their chambers. Accompanied by their soaring wolves, the exiles stumbled through the palace, laughing as they walked into walls and tripped over their feet.

Sova laid atop Whisp, conquered by liquor. Sitting up, he prodded the wingless soaring wolf in the side.

"Fly puppy," he chanted drunkenly. "Fly!"

"Stop that, Sova," Kyce slurred as he slid his shoulder against the wall. "She can't—She can't—Doesn't fly."

"Yes, she can," Sova insisted. "*She just a little fly*."

Whisp snorted in optimistic agreement.

After a perilous journey through the maze-like palace, the five drunk exiles came to their chamber. Elling collapsed on the cot, followed by Roeseph, who laid at the far end of the bed. Kyce settled against Whisp on the floor while Sova dozed on her back. And Feran reclined against Saber, lost to the white softness of his fur. Like a wind dousing a candle's flame, sleep vanquished the five exiles.

SOVA GASPED AT THE coldness surrounding him and opened his eyes to find himself standing in a familiar void.

No, he gasped, recognizing the place of his nightmares. *No, please. Not right now. Please, just let me sleep!*

"Who are you?" came the demonic voice of the dire. Sova turned to find the dire's armor standing across the darkness, his hand on a gleaming black sword.

"No," Sova shook his head. "No—No, I'm not doing this again."

Like a fawn fleeing a wolf, Sova sprinted away into the void.

"Who are you?" the dire screamed as he drew his sword.

"Leave me alone!"

"Who are you!"

Sova looked over his shoulder, horrified to find his enemy had disappeared. When he looked forward, the dreaded Dire of Vaska stood dead ahead, sword shimmering in hand. Sova ran straight into the dire's blade.

"*Sova!*"

"SOVA!" FERAN HISSED as she shook Sova.

He woke upright and gasping for breath. He grasped his shoulder where the dire had stabbed him, and looked around the room. Everyone slept soundly except for he and Feran. All was still; frightfully still. He laid on the floor next to Kyce and Whisp. He must've fallen off the soaring wolf's back.

"Where—Where is he?" Sova gulped. Though his nightmare had ceased, he couldn't help but feel the dire's presence. "Where is he?"

"Where's who?" Feran knelt before him, her eyes round like saucers.

"The dire," Sova shivered. "The dire, he was here."

"He's not here, Sova. You were having a nightmare."

"I don't know what he wants from me," Sova put his head down and folded his hands over his neck. "I don't know what he wants from me."

"Hey," Feran whispered, and sat next to him. "Hey, it's ok."

"No. It's not," Sova whimpered, his voice cracking. "He'll never leave me alone."

Feran went silent and hesitantly laid her hand on his back, hushing him as he trembled. "Look, the nightmare's over. You can go back to sleep now."

"No," Sova shook his head. "I'm not falling asleep again. I can't deal with him tonight."

Feran puzzled for a moment then looked to Saber dozing peacefully on the other side of the room, his paw thrashing against the stone floor.

"Well," she stood, "I'm already awake, might as well make use of my time." She offered her hand to Sova. "Come with me."

Not asking questions, Sova took Feran by the hand and started toward the giant, flying beast.

"Maybe we shouldn't disturb him while he sleeps," he cautioned. "Lest I get my head bitten off."

"Nah, he's fine," Feran dismissed and prodded her heel into Saber's side. The massive wolf snarled and sprung upright, his wings outstretched across the ceiling. Sova cowered to the floor while Feran remained standing. When Saber's eyes fell to his master, his snarl faded, and he folded his wings, growling grumpily like an offended toddler.

"Oh, don't be such a baby," Feran teased and ruffled the fur behind his ears. "Feel like a midnight flight, bud?" Saber snorted, his tail swishing from side to side. "Attaboy."

Feran led Saber onto the balcony while Sova followed a safe distance away, watching from the archway as Saber spread his white wings in the light of the moon.

Feran pulled herself onto Saber, sitting just below his shoulders, and stroked the fur along his neck. "Well?" she said, beckoning for Sova. "Are you coming?"

Sova's eyes went wide at Feran's proposal, and he sized the soaring wolf up and down. Head falling back, gut bursting laughter launched up his throat.

"Yeah," he sighed at the end of a chuckle. "Not a chance."

"Oh, come on, Sova," Feran taunted. "The midnight air will do you some good."

"I'd sooner go back to sleep. Besides, you've been drinking. That's got to be frowned upon in the," Sova paused, unable to think of the word. "*Wolf... flying... community...*"

"That's not a thing, Sova."

"It could be a thing."

Feran rolled her eyes. "Even if it was, riding a soaring wolf drunk isn't the same as driving a wagon. Saber won't put us in danger."

Sova glared at Feran, his arms crossing in defiance. "This is how you kill me, isn't it?"

"Get on the wolf, Sova."

Sova exhaled, his heels dragging over the marble floor as he pulled himself onto the soaring wolf. Saber growled as he mounted, his yellow eyes flashing.

"Honestly, what did I ever do to you?" Sova glared at the wolf.

Saber snorted in defiance and turned his gaze to the stars. Feran looked back, an adventurous grin beseeching her face, "Are you holding on?"

"For dear life," Sova answered.

Shaking her head and chuckling, Feran leaned forward. "That'll have to do."

Saber sprung from the balcony and into the wind like a comet going home. Sova screamed as they ascended, his pleas for life devoured by the cold, bladed air. Kyce awoke at the cry and snapped upright.

"Sova?" he grumbled, eyes still closed. "Did you say something?" When Sova didn't answer, Kyce gave a shallow shrug and fell back against Whisp, asleep in an instant.

SOVA CLUNG TO FERAN as Saber dashed through the sky, burying his face between her shoulder blades as they climbed the wind into nothingness.

"This is worse!" he cried through the chestnut hair lashing in his face. "This is so much worse than the nightmares!"

Feran laughed as Saber leveled his flight and soared over the earth. She drew a deep breath, her lungs caressed by the clean, untouched winter atmosphere, stinging like mint.

Feran sighed, enthralled by the beauty, and looked back at Sova clinging to her with eyes unopened.

"Sova?" she giggled. "Sova, you can open your eyes now."

"Nope," he shook his head. "If it's ok with you, I'd rather keep my eyes closed for the rest of my life."

Feran frowned. "Open your eyes, or I throw you off the wolf."

"Opening eyes now," Sova exclaimed. His jaw hung. The starlit heavens loomed overhead, just within reach, while massive clouds floated by in the distance like white islands on a starry sea. Below, the Eradawn village shrunk to the size of a pebble, and the mountains shriveled to grey ant hills. The

Valley of Lykos looked like a bowl, and the mist covered forests, like fluffy white porridge.

"Woah," Sova whispered.

Feran laughed. "See? Not all that scary, is it?"

"Oh, no, it's still terrifying," Sova admitted, making her frown. "But still beautiful."

Feran's grimace faded into a grin. She and Sova flew the border between earth and God's kingdom, outflying the wind and challenging gravity while spinning in loops.

Feran and Sova laughed as they speared the clouds, their lungs moistened by the damp hearts they skewered. Saber panted in the wind, his tongue drying in the airstream. Feran glanced down to see he was growing tired.

"Let's land for a while," she called over her shoulder.

"What?" Sova shouted over the wailing wind.

"I said, let's land for a while."

"I can't hear you."

"I said let's—" Feran shrugged, "you know what. You'll find out."

Saber turned at a ninety-degree angle and dropped toward the snowcapped mountains, causing Sova to scream into the black atmosphere as they fell. They glided toward a cliff overlooking the vine covered ruins of the old Eradite tribe and the Falls of Era.

Saber flapped his wings at the ground, ascending ever so slightly, before he placed his paws on the snowy grass. Feran elegantly dismounted her wolf while Sova half jumped half fell. He popped back up, his eyes wide as he shook with adrenaline.

"Wow!" he cheered, spinning in circles before falling flat on his back. "What a rush!"

Feran laughed and sat next to him, "So I take it you enjoyed yourself?"

"Oh yeah," Sova exhaled, his chest rising and falling rapidly. "I'd take that over nightmares any day."

Feran's grin faded with concern, while Saber couldn't have cared less. The soaring wolf yawned and curled into a ball, welcoming sleep.

Sova stared at the vast armada of stars, lost in a fit of wonder he hadn't experienced since childhood.

"Sova," Feran began gently.

"Mhmm?" Sova mumbled, his eyes latched on the glassy sky.

"How long have you had the nightmares?"

Sova chuckled and shook his head, "You don't want to hear about that, Feran."

"Yes. I do."

"No, you don't," he looked at Feran with blameless eyes. "We're not friends, remember? You said so yourself."

Feran paused, her eyes gleaming with regret. "Well, we're not," she grumbled. "But we're allies, right? Allies have to stick together."

"*Allies?*" Sova tested, his brow arching.

"Yes," Feran nodded. "Allies."

"Fair enough."

Feran reclined on the cliff next to Sova and stared at the crystal constellations. They laid there in silence listening to the crickets' gossip and the low moan of the winter wind.

"So," she began hesitantly, "The nightmares...."

Sova sighed. "A couple months ago I let the Blind Seers into the Vaskan palace with hopes of freeing my kingdom and all of Lykos from Saulder's tyranny. Saulder and I went head-to-head, and I guess I, uh... well I got hurt. Funny thing is, I can't recall half the fight. When I came to, Casavore was standing over me. He looked so scared. He told me Saulder had intentions to kill me. That he, and I quote, '*Wanted to watch the Royal Traitor bleed.*'"

Sova paused to swallow an especially large lump. Feran turned on her side, a sorrowful expression masking her beautiful face.

"Then what happened?" she asked, her voice barely detectable in the wind.

Sova drew a long breath. "Well, then Casavore told me to leave and gave me his medallion." He picked up the Blesser's pendant hanging from his neck and held it before his eyes. "Then I found Roeseph. We've been on the run ever since."

"And the nightmares?"

"They're always the same," Sova dropped the medallion to his chest. "I'm standing in this cold darkness, and Saulder starts shouting at me. 'Who are you?' He does it three times, getting angrier every time he asks, and then he... well, I guess he kills me. Then I wake up."

"This happens every night?"

"No," Sova shook his head. "Just about every other."

"Why does he ask who you are?"

"I haven't the slightest clue. I think maybe it's my brain trying to make sense of what Saulder did to me, but—" Sova pierced his lips, "I don't know. None of it makes sense to me."

"Care if I take a crack at it?" Feran asked rather eagerly.

"Be my guest."

"Ok," she smiled and plopped against the snow-melted grass. "I think maybe it's your consciousness trying to recreate the conflict between you and Saulder so you can come to terms with what he did."

"That is an awful guess."

"I thought it was pretty wise," Feran shrugged.

"Well, you're wrong. I've come to terms with what Saulder did to me. What he's done to everyone. I've dealt with it."

"Obviously, you haven't, or else you wouldn't be dreaming of your brother attacking you every other night."

"Oh, what do you know?" Sova smirked as Feran laughed softly at the sky. His smug grin faded, and sorrow melted into him. "Why do I have to keep reliving it, though? I mean, I can't even look at the scar he left. I always have to have Roeseph re-do the gauze for me because I'm so afraid to see what Saulder did to me. Why can't I just forget?"

Feran drew a heavy breath, her hickory eyes reflecting the diamonds overhead.

"I guess..." she began, her words lingering on her tongue for a moment, "sometimes we'd rather remain in darkness than accept the wrongs of those we love."

Sova's stomach dropped at her words. There was truth to them, though he couldn't decipher the full meaning. "Yeah," he agreed half-heartedly. "Yeah, I guess so."

"Hey," Feran said. "Can I ask you something?"

"Might as well, since you're being so nosy." Feran swatted Sova on the chest, making him chuckle. "I'm kidding. Ask away."

"Do you miss Saulder? I mean, at all?"

Sova smiled at the sky. "I miss the *real* Saulder," he admitted. "The one before you were taken. Before Lore got in his head. Before he was the dire. I miss *that* Saulder. In truth, the dire isn't even my brother anymore. He's gone."

"I wouldn't be so sure about that, Sova."

"Think what you want. I know the truth. Saulder's a monster."

"You don't think he can change?"

"I know he can't."

"You're wrong, Sova."

Sova exhaled irritably and sat on his side. "Oh yeah? And what makes you so sure?"

Feran turned on her side to face him. "When I was little, my mother and father would read Bible stories to me every night. I remember my favorite one was—"

"Saul of Tarsus," Sova finished.

Feran paused as reminiscent grin spread her lips. "The Apostle Paul," she corrected. "That was my favorite story. It was all about this horrible man who went around killing Christians and thinking he was doing so for the betterment of the world. But he was wrong. On his way to Damascus, a blinding light shone down on him, and he heard the voice of Christ. The light was so bright Saul lost his sight. He was healed three days later by a man named Ananias and baptized. *Paul* became one of the most influential voices for Christ and helped save many souls. And in the end, he paid for it. He was beheaded in Rome. But even in prison, he wrote letters telling of Jesus Christ." Feran paused and drew a deep breath. "God turned a murderer into a saint. I don't have a doubt in my mind He can do the same for Saulder."

"Saul of Tarsus lived a long time ago, Feran," Sova reminded. "How do you know God still works miracles like that."

"Well, He brought all of us together," Feran said. "I'd say that's miracle enough. The fact we haven't killed each other yet is a true testament to His power."

Sova chuckled.

"But, man," Feran shook her head. "That Paul... he was a guy. I think if I had a say in it, I'd like to go out like him."

"How?" Sova joked. "Beheaded in Rome?"

"No," Feran said tenderly as she grinned at the star-spangled sky. "Fighting a good fight."

Sova's smirk faded as he stared at the Dire's Damsel. Laying there in the grass, she was not vindictive, nor spite driven, nor cruel like he'd remembered her to be in their childhood. Instead, she looked rather content. Peaceful. Beautiful.

Is this what you saw, Saulder? He wondered. *Is this why she made you lose your mind?* Unaware he was doing so, he reached for her hand.

"Feran, I—"

Before he could finish, Saber's eyes burst open, and he looked to the horizon. Snout drawn in a blood-lusting snarl he rose to his paws.

Sova held his hands up in surrender, "I didn't touch her, I swear."

Feran lurched from the ground, her eyes wide, and threw her arms around Saber's neck. "Saber," she hushed as she stroked his fur. "Saber, what's wrong?"

The white soaring wolf grew more restless, his claws scraping the dirt as his glowing yellow eyes burned through the darkness.

Sova puzzled at Saber, his gut twisting like a rag. *What could've riled him up so much?*

The light flicker of torchlight shone in the distance beneath the cliff, making Sova turn on his side and crawl to the edge. He peered into the ruins of the past Eradite tribe, his eyes widening into two silver moons.

"Feran," he spat beneath his breath. "Feran, get down."

Feran looked away from Saber. "What?"

"I said get down!" Sova hissed so Feran fell to the frigid earth and crawled next to him, her shoulder brushing his.

She gasped. "No..."

Beneath the cliff, as many as five thousand soldiers dressed in glimmering Vaskan armor marched toward the Eradite ruins. Their heavy metal boots clamored like distant thunder, and the embers from their torches rose into the sky like red sashes. They halted before the rabid river. Sova had never seen so many Vaskans in one place in his life; and that was a lot coming from the Prince of Vaska.

Saber growled as he paced the cliff, the hairs along his neck sticking up like tiny white needles.

"Those are Vaskan soldiers," Feran whispered.

"What are they doing here?" Sova sneered.

"They must have tracked us up the cliffs."

"Really? We're worth sending an entire army into the Cliffs of Era?"

"I know. You're *definitely* not worth it."

"Hey—" Sova paused, his gut tightening with fear. Feran had been joking, but in truth, she was right. Sova and Roeseph weren't worth sending an army into Era. Neither were Elling or Kyce. No. They were there for Feran. Feran looked to the horizon, her lips parting to allow a shocked breath.

"Sova," she whispered. "They came from the west. They came from Eradusk."

"Which means they're heading to Eradawn next," Sova growled. "We need to warn Chief Lanton."

Sova crawled back from the edge and snapped to his feet. Quickly, he pulled himself onto Saber, who for once didn't complain at his closeness. Feran hesitantly withdrew from the ledge, her gaze locked on the Vaskan camp.

Sova glanced at Feran, who had yet to board. "Feran," he hissed, making her jump. "We need to go. Now."

"I—I know," she stammered, looking frantically between the Royal Traitor and the Vaskan camp. "But what if Saulder's down there?"

"Feran, are you kidding me?" Sova hissed; his heart burned with hate.

"Just give me a second," Feran whispered as she desperately scanned the camp. "What if he's down there?"

"It's not worth the risk, Feran."

"But what if—"

"If he isn't, then you'd be marching into an entire army of Vaskan soldiers. It won't matter who you say you are. Their orders are to kill you."

"B—But, Sova," Feran shook and turned back to the camp.

Growing impatient, Sova jumped from Saber and grabbed her by the shoulders. "Feran!" he snapped, whipping her around to face him. "I know you want to see him, but Eradawn is in danger. Elling. Roeseph. Kyce. They're all in danger."

Feran trembled, the look of desperation in her eyes striking Sova to his core. "We need to go, Feran," he cupped her cheek. "Please."

The Dire's Damsel looked at the camp then back to Sova. "Ok," she conceded.

Sova watched with a heavy heart as she mounted the soaring wolf. Glaring back at the Vaskan camp, he climbed onto Saber and sat behind Feran. The White Angel launched from the cliff and into the stars, looking like a slow-moving comet against the black sky.

A Vaskan soldier, who had been hammering a tent spoke, looked up to see them dash across the atmosphere.

"There!" he shouted. His comrades looked up. "There it is! It's the White Angel!"

As the Vaskan Soldiers gathered before the rushing river to watch, the dark armored dire peeled out of his tent and approached the crowd. The men stepped out of his way like water before Moses. Standing at the river's edge, the dire caught a glimpse of the soaring wolf pest as it faded over the east horizon.

"There you are..." he said in a smiling voice.

One of the bolder soldiers cleared his throat and approached. "S—Sir. It's the White Angel. Should we press east?"

Staring at the sky, the dire replied, "No. Let our men sleep. I'll take what's mine come morning."

Chapter Twenty-Six: The Good Oath

S*aber hurtled toward* the sleeping village of Eradawn.

"Brace yourself!" Feran called, her voice snatched in the fleeting wind, as Saber soared through the balcony and into the palace chamber where their comrades slept. With the grace of a fawn on ice, he slid across the room, yelping, before slamming into the wall. Feran and Sova fell from his back and onto the floor.

"What in Lykos is going on?" Kyce hissed, his hair disheveled and matted. "Does sleep mean nothing to you?"

Elling yawned through a stretch. "What's going on? Why are you making so much noise?"

Sova snapped from the floor, his silver eyes shimmering with terror.

"The—The Vaskans," he gasped between breaths. "They're here."

THE ROYALS AND HIGH-ranking religious leaders of Eradawn gathered in the throne room before Vohwe's scarlet veil, bleating like frightened sheep. On the outer rim of the crowd, the exiles stood with their soaring wolves, anxiously awaiting the Eradawn chief's announcement.

Vohwe drew a tremendous breath then said with a booming voice, "Leaders of Eradawn. It is with great distress I tell you the Vaskans have scaled Era's cliffs and are now in our midst."

Muted murmurs of fear and distress clamored through the throne room.

"How is this possible?" a priest of Eradawn shouted. "The dire hasn't been in our lands since the days of Chief Illos! Why are they here?"

Roars of panic joined their brother.

"It's because of them!" a general shouted, and pointed at Feran and the outcasts. "The dire has come for them!"

The five exiles huddled together as the mob of angry Eradawn royals enclosed around them. Saber and Whisp snarled, their ivory jaws snapping at whoever dared draw near. Kyce and Roeseph laid their hands on their holstered swords and Feran clutched her medallion.

Vohwe slammed her fist on her throne, sending a thundering echo through the palace. "Enough!" she shouted and snapped from her seat. The mob silenced. "These people of Lykos are guests in my palace and under the protection of Chief Lanton. Those who dare lay a hand on them will face the worst punishment Era has to offer."

Like meek gazelle subdued by the roar of a lion, the Eradawn leaders withdrew from the exiles. When the threat dissipated, Roeseph, Kyce, Sova, and Feran released their weapons.

Vohwe huffed out an exasperated breath, a single hair falling over her rage filled eyes. "Now, if you're done acting like fools," she lowered to her throne, "can we try to figure out a way to deal with this threat?"

Roeseph stepped forward and knelt before the scarlet veil. "If I may, Chief Vohwe. I grew up fighting Vaskan soldiers, and know their battle strategies. If you'd allow me, I'd like to offer what I know."

"Go on, Captain Roeseph," Vohwe dipped her head.

Roeseph stood and turned to face the hostile crowd. He drew a deep breath, his noble eyes unfaltering.

"My father and I have fought Vaskan soldiers all our lives," he said. "From my experience, the Vaskans have no moral code. They'll invade Eradawn and kill everyone in it. Women and children alike."

"Then how can we stop them?" Vohwe asked.

Roeseph gulped and shook his head. "We can't."

Rippling murmurs of panic carried through the throne room. Vohwe closed her eyes and drew a deep breath. "Then what would you have us do, Roeseph?"

"If the Vaskans make it to Eradawn, your people won't stand a chance. But there's a way you can avoid a massacre. The Vaskans have made camp in the ancient Eradite ruins. Walking, they should reach the tribe by the next sundown. Before then, you need to evacuate the tribe to the mountains and send a regiment to keep them away. Hopefully, the civilians can gain enough distance until...."

"Until the Vaskans destroy our troops," Vohwe finished.

Roeseph pierced his lips in a line and nodded, "Yes, ma'am."

An elderly Eradawn warrior sprung from the crowd, his face gnarled with rage. "You would have us listen to the son of a Hyde Howler?" he snarled and pointed at Roeseph, his wrinkled skin dripping off his arm. "This *boy* was raised by a beast—a monster with no soul. He hasn't the slightest idea what is best for us."

Kyce took an aggressive step toward the old warrior, only for Roeseph to lift his arm in his way.

Feran looked up, her eyes cold and emotionless. "You're wrong," she declared. "Roeseph is honestly the most capable soldier among you. He's battled more Vaskans than you've probably drawn breath. If he says Eradawn only stands a chance in retreating, then you should think on behalf of your people instead of your pride."

"*You*," the elder sneered. "Who are you to speak on behalf of Eradawn? We know who your father is. The Blesser Casavore, born from Eradusk. That makes you no less our enemy than Vaska."

Feran paused, her jaw clenching as she turned to address Vohwe. "Roeseph is right in evacuating the village. It's best your people be safe in the mountains should the Vaskans reach Eradawn. But I agree with *Father Time* here," she glanced at the disgruntled old warrior. "Eradawn should not have to be stripped of their home like my father was. I propose I surrender to Vaska so Eradawn might survive."

Sova grabbed Feran by the shoulders and snapped her around to face him. "Are you insane?" he growled, his silver eyes blazing.

Feran looked up. "I am why the Vaskan troops are here. You and the others aren't Saulder's priority. You and all of Eradawn can avoid his wrath."

"Feran, we didn't see Saulder at the ruins. If he's not there, the troops will kill you."

"I'm not expecting Saulder to be there," Feran gulped. The fire in Sova's eyes doused as Feran's words washed over him. She didn't intend to survive the battle.

"Feran," he began in a gentler but urgent voice, "these people aren't worth saving. You know that. I know that. Everyone knows that. What have we been saying the entire time we've been here? Huh? They're self-righteous, hypocritical, conniving wannabe prophets that are too self-centered to administer the word. For Lykos' sake, Feran, these are the people who handed Casavore to Dire Zastar. These people are the reason Saulder got so powerful in the first place."

Feran clutched her medallion, her eyes glistening. "I'm aware of who they are and what they've done. But if I don't help them, then I'm everything I resent them for."

Sova gulped down a ragged breath. "Feran, you can't do this," he pled as his hands slipped from her shoulders to her arms. "You're my ally, remember?"

Feran smirked at her childhood, looking at him with eyes of someone sentenced to death.

"I've got to fight the good fight," she recited and touched his shoulder. "Remember?"

Sova shook his head, "That's not the kind of fight Paul was talking about, and you know it."

Feran smiled and slapped him on the arm. "I know. Still a pretty good fight though."

Before Sova could bargain for her life, Kyce stepped out from behind.

"Then I'll fight that fight with you," he promised. Feran looked to him, her eyes wide with awe.

Roeseph appeared next, his fist crossed over his chest, and dipped his head, "And I as well."

Elling took Feran's hand. "And I as well."

Shaking her head, Feran backed away. "No. This isn't your fight."

"It isn't yours either," Kyce said. "The Eradawns have wronged your family, and still, you chose to stand by my mother's people. The least I can do is stand by you."

Elling smiled at Feran, tears stringing her lashes. "We're a tribe, remember? The Dire Wolves need to stay together."

Sova grabbed Feran's shoulder. "If you go, we all go."

Feran shook her head, "I didn't ask for your help."

"*Mmm,* we don't care."

Feran scoffed as she struggled to suppress a heartfelt smirk. "After all these years, you still can't help but frustrate me, huh?"

"Oh, I live for it."

Roeseph turned to face the scarlet veil and the chief behind it. "If it pleases the chief, my comrades and I will accompany the Blesser's daughter to the Eradite ruins to negotiate peace with the Vaskan army."

Vohwe straightened in her throne and looked to her son.

"And you, Kyce?" she asked. "Do you intend to escort the Dire's Damsel as well?"

Kyce nodded. "Yes, chief. For the good of my tribe."

Vohwe drew a deep breath. "Very well. Eradawn thanks you for your service."

"I wasn't talking about Eradawn."

Vohwe raised her chin slightly. Earlier that night she'd asked her son if he'd stay with her in Eradawn. He'd given his answer.

"Very well then," she said. "I will send a messenger to the Vaskan troops offering the surrender of the *Rogue Eradite*. When we hear word from their army's commander, I'll send you on your way—but not unaccompanied. Should the deal go south, I'll have Eradawn troops standing by."

Chapter Twenty-Seven: The Negotiation

The Falls of Era...

In the crumbling ruins of the ancient Eradite tribe, the Vaskan army stood in silver lines beyond the river. The dire stood at the head in his black armor, his blood-lusting eyes burning the forest in the east. The previous night, an Eradawn messenger had come to their camp saying they'd give up the Rogue Eradite as long as the Vaskans left their village unharmed. The dire had agreed to Eradawn's conditions, and now awaited his prize. Still, the Rogue Eradite had yet to arrive.

Teeth grinding beneath his helmet, the dire growled, "Where are they?..."

THE FIVE EXILES AND their winged steeds hid within the forest shadows, concealed from the Vaskan troop.

Saber and Whisp growled, disgusted by the malevolent scent of the dire beyond the river. Kyce drummed his fingers along the handle of his sheathed blade, pleading for a fight, while Elling clung to Roeseph's arm. It was her first time seeing the dire since he'd attacked her village and summoned the Hyde Howler. Sova glared at the dark figure and rubbed his gauze wrapped shoulder, remembering the tale Casavore told him of how his brother scarred him with his arrow. He hated the dire. They all did.

Feran, however, showed no such loathing. She stared ahead, jaw trembling as she gave a shaken breath. There, just beyond the river, stood the Dire of Vaska. The man she was pledged to marry.

"Saulder..." she whispered with longing.

"I don't like this," Sova growled, his fists clenching at his sides. "This is a bad idea."

Feran turned, her brow drawn in an arch. "Isn't this what you wanted me to do in the first place? Go back to Dire Saulder so his tyranny would come to an end?"

"I changed my mind. Nothing's going to change Saulder. Not even you. This whole thing is just a very, *very,* bad idea.

Feran stared at Sova, taking notice of the fear and rage in his silver eyes, and took his hand. Sova flinched at her touch. He wasn't used to his childhood foe being so gentle.

"Everything's going to be ok, Sova," Feran said. "Once I've cleared everything up with Saulder, he'll leave Era. Maybe I can even talk him into pardoning you and the others."

"And how do you know he'll listen?" Sova challenged as his gaze panned to the dire.

"Because he was my friend, Sova—"

"And how do you know he won't just take you and burn Eradawn to the ground anyway?"

"Because he wouldn't do that."

"Oh, yes, he would," Sova sneered, his jaw cocking to the side. "Childhood friend—future spouse or not, Saulder is a monster. He'll never be anything else."

Feran swallowed and threw her arms around him. Sova froze, unsure what to do as he stood with the Dire's Damsel hanging from his neck. His discomfort fading, he took her into greedy arms.

"I'll be ok, Sova," Feran whispered. "Everything's going to be ok."

Sova croaked, his grip tightening, "How do you know?"

The dire's voice rose above the morning mist, masked by the metal ring of his ghastly helmet. "Mind melder! I know you're out there! Reveal yourself or Eradawn burns!"

All but Feran flinched at his wrath. Feran looked to the Vaskan army, the lump the size of a boulder burrowing in her throat.

"I—I got to go," she stammered and tried to pull away.

"Wait," Sova grabbed her and slid something into her hand. "If he doesn't stick to our agreement and tries to hurt Era..." he folded her fingers around the unseen treasure, "Use it."

Feran looked down, her eyes widening at what she saw. "Sova, I—"

"Just take it. Please. It never belonged to me anyway."

Feran nodded and tucked the unknown object in the safety of her pocket.

Roeseph stepped forward. "We're right behind you if you need us."

Feran turned to each of them, disturbed by the worry in their eyes. "Everything's going to be fine. You'll see. Try not to look so glum," she looked to Sova once more. "You're not nearly as annoying as you used to be," she grimaced, regretting her choice of words. "I'm trying to compliment you."

"You did your best," Sova smirked. "Hey, if he listens, tell Saulder I want a re-match."

Feran grinned and shook her head. "You were more than an ally to me," she said. "You know that, don't you?"

Sova's smirk faded, and he dipped his head. "I know."

Feran looked to her comrades, the walls of her pride crumbling to allow a glimpse of what hid within. "You all were."

Kyce looked away, refusing to look her in the eye lest he shed tears.

"Softie," Sova muttered under his breath. Kyce's elbow found his ribs not a second later. "Ouch."

"Be safe, Feran," Elling whispered.

Feran nodded, and taking one last glance at Sova, walked toward the wall of light beyond the shade. Saber whined and took a frantic step after her, only for Sova to block his path. "Woah there, boy. She'll be ok. She needs to do this alone."

Snarling, Saber snapped at Sova.

"By Lykos, I'm just trying to help," Sova hissed. "Is nothing I do or say good enough for you?" Saber huffed out a hot breath of resentment in Sova's face. "*Harpy-dog*," he insulted.

"Will she be alright?" Elling whimpered as she watched Feran grow further away.

Roeseph nodded. "Vohwe's troops are scattered all around the Vaskans. If the dire tries to go back on our agreement, we'll have them on standby."

"Are there enough?" Elling gulped. Roeseph kept his silence. Truth be told, the Vaskans outnumbered them five to one. An inevitable loss.

"Feran's the dire's one weakness," Sova added. "If there's anyone who can reason with him, she's our best bet."

"And if he won't listen to her?" Kyce asked, turning to face the Royal Traitor.

Sova drew a deep breath. "Then we bring down hellfire and get Feran as far away from him as possible. If Saulder's not willing to change, he'll never see her again."

"MIND MELDER!" THE DIRE bellowed, his iron-altered voice violating the morning's gentle song. "Show yourself! Or Else!"

A shadow formed in the shade of the mountain wood, tracing the silhouette of a young woman. Hood hiding her face, she stepped past the border between darkness and light. The Vaskan soldiers raised their crossbows, only for the dire to hold up his hand to halt their fire.

"Wait," he growled. "She's mine to kill."

Sova drew a deep breath, Elling clung to Roeseph's arm, and Kyce gripped his sword as Feran stopped short of the river, the boarder between she and the Vaskan tyrant.

"Dire Saulder," she said. "You wished to see me?"

The dire chuckled, his voice dark and chilling. "You are the Eradite that caused my kingdom so much trouble? You're barely grown."

"If it pleases the Dire, I had hoped to speak with his majesty before drastic measures are taken."

"And why would I do that? Do you think me so foolish to trust the likes of you?"

Feran withdrew her charred medallion, shining like a second sun in the center of her hands, and clasped it tightly. "I do not take you to be a fool, Dire Saulder," she said and tossed her father's gift to the dire.

He examined the gold weapon, in awe of the power he held but would never wield. "Perhaps *you* are the fool, Eradite," he looked up. "It is not wise for a soldier to surrender their sword."

"That may be," Feran nodded. "But I am no soldier... I'm your betrothed."

The dire froze, paralyzed. Tucking the charred medallion into his belt, he stomped across the river, his metal boots chiming against the current.

Saber growled within the darkness as Sova grabbed hold of his fur in an attempt to keep him steady.

"She's ok, boy," he hushed. "She's going to be ok."

He wasn't so sure himself.

Feran took a step back as the dire ascended the frosty current, towering over her like a mountain.

"What are you getting at, mind melder?" he growled.

Feran withdrew her hood, allowing the golden light of early morning to caress her delicate features and illuminate her dark eyes. The dire's breath halted and he took a jolting step back.

The dead maiden Fala, slain by the Venom Tongue gangsters of Seavale, stood before him—alive.

"Fala," the dire quivered, convinced he stared into the eyes of a ghost. "This can't be."

"I am not Fala," Feran said. "I am her daughter. And the daughter of your Blesser, Casavore. I am Feran."

The world stilled. Not even a blade of grass dared flicker, nor a bird sing.

The four exiles watched anxiously from the shadows, distressed by the silence.

"What's going on?" Elling whispered. "Did she tell him?"

Sova gulped. "She told him," he said beneath his breath. "She told him."

"Well, what's he doing?" Kyce seethed through gritted teeth. "What are they saying?"

Roeseph turned to Kyce, his dusk-blue eyes blazing. "Be quiet."

The dire gawked at Feran, the shapes of his eyes wide though the holes of his helmet. "This is impossible," he uttered. "You're dead."

"No," Feran shook her head. "The Venom Tongues kidnapped me, but I was able to get away." She reached for the dire, making him step back. When he settled, Feran laid her hand on the sides of his helmet and stared into his hidden eyes.

"Saulder," she whispered, catching the faintest glimpse of an iris in the dark. "I never wanted to leave you. But it was dangerous for me to return to the palace, for you have a traitor in your midst. Lore let the Venom Tongues into the palace to assassinate Dire Zastar, you, and Sova. She would've killed me had I come back."

The dire straightened and let out a slow, shaken breath, "Who else knows of this?"

"Just me, Sova, and the others," Feran replied. "We can help you. We can help bring Lore to justice and save Vaska."

"Yes," the dire nodded. "Vaska must be protected."

Feran swallowed, her heart tendering to the point of pain. She had finally found him. Her Saulder. The man Sova was so sure was extinct. Her beloved. Her betrothed.

Sova watched, his jaw hanging, as the dire laid his gloved hand on Feran's cheek and gazed into her eyes. Sova took an anxious step forward, his dead hopes resurrecting.

Has she reasoned with him? He asked himself. *Could Saulder really come back?*

Feran nuzzled into the dire's hand, comforted by the cold touch of his metal glove.

"Vaska must be protected," the dire repeated, and clasped her throat. Feran gasped, her eyes wide as his grip tightened.

"Feran!" Sova shouted as he, his comrades, and the two soaring wolves raced out of the forest.

The dire looked up. "Stay back!" he yelled as he twisted Feran around and forced her to her knees. She gasped, the butterflies in her stomach burning alive as a cold blade pressed to her throat.

The four exiles came skidding to a halt, their soaring wolves with them.

"Let her go!" Roeseph ordered as he drew his sword. "This wasn't the deal."

The dire laughed and pressed the blade deeper to Feran's throat, making her flinch as a teardrop of blood ran along the edge. "Oh, I believe it is you who has forsaken our deal," he challenged. "You see, you were to deliver the Rogue Eradite to me and then be on your way. But here you are, defying our agreement."

"Are you mad, Saulder?" Sova roared. "She's Feran—your best friend. Your betrothed!"

Feran gasped, her red-tinted eyes straining to look at the dire as she wheezed, "Why are you doing this, Saulder?"

"Because, *my love*," the dire lowered the grate of his helmet to her ear, the feeling his breath against her lobe making her spine coil. "You are a threat. To me and my kingdom."

"I have done nothing to you," Feran croaked. "I didn't do anything."

"Such a liar. Have you forgotten? You sicked that flying dog of yours on your beloved dire not several months ago."

Saber snarled and scraped his claws over the grass, his jaws yearning for the dire's flesh.

"Those people were in danger, Saulder," Feran gulped. "I—I didn't know you were there when I sent Saber. I would never deliberately hurt you—"

"Silence," the dire spat and pressed the blade harder to Feran's throat. "Your groveling irritates me. And you," he looked to Sova. "Why would you ally yourself to the enemies of Vaska?"

Sova glared at the dire, his fists coiling at his side. "Because you're a monster, Saulder. One who needs to be killed. And since Casavore wasn't man enough to end you, I will."

The dire stopped, confused by something the Royal Traitor had said.

"By Lykos," he exhaled, his eyes wide behind his helmet. Head falling back, he laughed from the depths of his gut, scaring the birds from the trees. "I don't believe it. *He's* really outdone himself this time."

"Release her, Saulder," Sova ordered, ignoring his brother's sudden burst of madness. "Now!"

"I'm afraid I can't do that, *Little Brother*," the dire scanned Sova up and down. "She's a danger to Vaska."

"*You're* a danger to Vaska, Saulder!" Sova bellowed. "You're a tyrant! A tyrant to our kingdom and a tyrant to our family. Feran is the one person left in Lykos that actually cares for you, and you have her at knifepoint. I was so sure if there was a chance anyone could save you, it was her!"

The dire snickered and shook his head, his grip tightening on his captive. Feran cringed and made a small yelp-like noise, making Sova's sneer faulter and heart shatter.

"You were wrong, Brother," the dire mocked.

Sova's heart stooped to the earth and his eyes went wide.

He's going to kill her, he whispered to himself.

"Go on, Brother," the dire challenged and pushed Feran forward, hovering her over the grass. "Say goodbye to the *Dire's Damsel*."

Feran looked up at Sova, her chestnut hair falling over her tear glistening face. "You were right," she coughed. "By Lykos, you were right. I'm so sorry. I'm so sorry I didn't listen to you."

"It's ok, Feran," Sova eased, the blade of her pleas twisting in his heart. "This is my fault." Gritting his teeth, he fought to speak over the crack in his throat. "I told you in that cave you were the only one able to save Saulder from himself. I was wrong to place such a burden on you when I couldn't even save him. I am so sorry for doing this to you... I want you to know, that despite everything we went through as kids, I can see now that knowing you has been a true *blessing*."

Feran froze, the fear in her eyes subsiding for just a moment at something Sova had said. He gave her a subtle nod, confirming what she thought.

"How touching," the dire growled as he raised the blade up Feran's neck to make her look him in the eye. "So sorry to see you go, Feran. I can see why Zastar wanted you to marry into the crown so badly. You would've made a devastatingly beautiful queen."

Feran gritted her teeth. "That's not why Zastar promised me to you," she said as she snuck her hand into her pocket. "This is—"

She lashed the Blesser's medallion out of hiding, the one Sova had secretly handed to her. Fearful of the medallion's golden rays, the dire shouted and fell back into the river with a splash.

Freed from his blade, Feran fled toward the exiles and into Sova awaiting arms, where he trapped her against his chest.

"Are you ok?" he asked as he pulled away to examine her face. Feran trembled as a single bead of blood trailed from the small slit in her neck and collected in the dip of her collarbones. Voice cracking, she nodded, "Uh huh."

The dire pulled himself from the river's current, water droplets cascading down his black armor as he raised his finger to Feran and the other exiles. "Kill them," he ordered. "Kill them all."

Chapter Twenty-Eight: The Red Falls

"*Get down!*" Roeseph screamed and threw himself on top of Elling as the Vaskan's raised their crossbows.

The dire gave his command, "Fire!" To his and the exiles' surprise, not a single arrow broke the wind. The dire spun around. "What are you doing? Kill them!"

The Vaskan soldiers took a nervous step back, their armor trembling like wind chimes as they gazed at the sky. The dire followed their eyes to the horizon to see something emerge from the iridescent dawn.

Kyce looked up from his cowering. "Look!" he cheered and pointed to what looked like a hoard of geese flying in the distance.

The roar of a thousand Eradawn warriors filled the air as their soaring wolves fled toward the Ruins of Era, looking like Heaven's armies come to purge the earth. Vohwe led the sky attack on a slender burnt-red soaring wolf, spear at her side.

Sova smiled at the sky, his silver eyes shining. "*The Eradawns are coming,*" he chanted in a patriotic jingle. "*The Eradawns are coming.*"

Like shooting stars, the Eradawns hurtled into the fight.

Drawing his sword, the dire cried, "Attack!"

Like two tsunamis, the Eradawns and the Vaskans rammed into each other head-on. The songs of gnashing fangs and striking swords stained the air as blood splurged between enemies.

Roeseph drew his blade, his dusk-blue eyes blazing. "For Lykos!"

Kyce riding Whisp, he and Roeseph rushed into the fight. Sova turned to Elling, who had no fighting knowledge outside the Hyde Howler curse, and handed her a blade.

"Go hide in the forest," he ordered sternly. "If any Vaskan tries to make a break for Eradawn, take them down."

"T—Take them down?" Elling stammered. "But I—"

"Go!" Sova shouted and Elling rushed into the woods. He turned to Feran next, her face ashen and eyes clouded.

"Feran," he said urgently and grabbed her by the arms. "Are you going to be able to do this?"

Feran gulped and blinked away her daze. "Y—Yeah. Yeah, I can do this."

Climbing atop Saber, she launched into the sky. Sova drew his sword and stared into the battle, yearning for the dire's dying breath.

I won't lose this time.

Blood poured from the battle and into the river, turning the Falls of Era a gruesome rosy color for all the Valley of Lykos to see. Feran descended into the heat of the fight, clutching her father's medallion as Saber stood at her side, snapping at those who dared come near.

She grabbed hold of a passing Vaskan and forced his eyes to her medallion. "*Vaskan intruder,*" she charmed, "*crude and cruel. Flee from this battle, forget your duty, Lay down your right to this duel.*"

The Vaskan soldier blinked and scampered out of the battle and into the mountains.

Kyce hurtled through the fight atop Whisp, laughing maliciously as he swung his sword. "*Now* this feels like home!"

Hypnotizing another Vaskan, Feran looked to her comrade, "I am very concerned for you, Kyce."

Roeseph joined them not a moment later, his sword coated in Vaskan blood.

"How are we doing?" he called as he pressed his back to Feran and scanned the battle.

Kyce kicked a charging Vaskan in the head and jumped off Whisp to the red-spotted snow.

"Not great," he growled and pressed his shoulder blades against Feran and Roeseph's.

Feran's gut churned, her eyes lashing from side to side as Eradawns and soaring wolves alike fell around them, their blood-muffled cries staining the air.

"There's too many of them," she shouted. "We can't win."

"We don't need to win!" Roeseph grunted as he caught the blade of a Vaskan soldier against his and shoved him right into Saber's passing jaws. "We just need to hold them off until Eradawn is evacuated. Where's Elling?"

"She's in the woods," Feran shouted as she trapped a Vaskan soldier in a headlock and forced him to meet the Blesser's medallion. "*Run. Run Vaskan soldier. Leave this place, obey this trance I have spun—*" the soldier fleeing, she turned back to Roeseph. "She's going to stop the Vaskans should they push through."

Kyce laughed, the edge of his sword catching a Vaskan's eye. "What's she going to do?" he taunted. "Herd them like sheep?"

"At least she's trying!" Feran shouted. "What are you doing, Kyce?"

"My most favorite thing in the entire world," he laughed as he grabbed a passing Vaskan by the throat and rammed his forehead into his. The soldier fell, knocked out cold as Kyce howled over him.

Feran cringed, disturbed. "This is the last battle I fight with Kyce."

"Agreed," Roeseph nodded.

SOVA MANEUVERED THROUGH the battle, careful to avoid tripping over the dead. He stopped, his sword drawn and breath thrashing as he searched for the wolf amongst sheep. His gaze fell to the dire standing across the way, cutting down Eradawn warriors like a woodsman with an ax.

"Saulder!" he roared, spittle raining from his jaws as he raced toward his foe.

The dire turned at the Royal Traitor's voice, his violet cape lashing in the wind. "Come to finish the job, *Brother*?"

Sova roared and threw his sword on the dire's blade. The dire pushed him back, making Sova stumble.

"I see you've been busy, *Royal Traitor*," the dire taunted as he circled. "Allying yourself with the Blind Hound's spawn—our nation's greatest enemy—and gallivanting with my betrothed? Your cruelty knows no limits, Brother."

"You're not my brother," Sova snarled and rushed forward.

Elling guarded the woods beyond the battle, her back pressed to cold bark as she clutched Sova's blade. She panted, terrified by the battle's roar, and peeked out from behind her tree. Five Vaskan soldiers rushing the forest, bloodied swords in hand. She ducked back into hiding.

"You can do this," she whispered to herself, gripping the blade. "You can do this—I can't do this. I'm doing it anyway."

Lunging from her hiding place, she grabbed one of the passing soldiers around the neck. Before she could bring the blade to his throat, he grabbed her arm and threw her into the unforgiving embrace of a sturdy tree. Lungs flattened, she pressed her back to the bark as the soldiers surrounded.

"Well—well—well," one of the soldiers chuckled, his eyes sparkling with devious delight. "What have we here."

"A Mosharick girl, it seems," another replied.

"I know this woman. She was the one from the night the White Angel attacked. She's a Hyde Howler."

"How interesting." With a pleased grin, the first soldier drew a bugle from his belt—just like the one the dire used to turn Elling into a monster. "I knew this would be of use."

Elling's eyes widened as the dormant Hyde Howler stirred within her like a caged dog taunted with a bone. "No—No, please," she begged. "Please don't."

"Sorry, m'lady," The soldier chuckled as he brought the bugle to his lips. "All is fair in love and war."

A dark figure crept behind the soldiers, a gold medallion shining from his neck. "Indeed," the figure agreed.

The Vaskans lashed around just as jagged spears pierced through their centers and they dropped to the grass. When the Vaskans fell still, four shadows surrounded Elling, among them, her medallion wielding savior.

"You," she whispered. "What are you doing here?"

BACKS PRESSED TO ONE another as they fought, Feran, Roeseph, and Kyce watched perilously as Vaskan blades struck down winged wolves, and brave warriors converted into corpses.

Kyce thrust his sword at a Vaskan, only for the soldier to dodge him effortlessly. Fe fell to his knee to catch his breath. Whisp stopped circling with Saber and fled to her master's side, wedging her nose under his arm, and helping him to stand.

"We're outnumbered!" Kyce panted.

Saber roared in the face of a Vaskan soldier, making him scream and run away.

"What do we do, Roeseph?" Feran cried as she swung the Blesser's medallion around her wrist.

Roeseph panted, his sweat-stinging gaze lashing around the battle. The Eradawn forces had dwindled greatly. For every Eradawn standing, so stood another ten Vaskans.

"Roeseph!" Feran shouted again.

Roeseph gulped, unsure what to say in the face of hopelessness. "Stand your ground."

SOVA AND THE DIRE STARED into the other's blood lusting eyes, separated by their silver blades. Teeth gritting, Sova shoved the tyrant back.

"I have to say, Brother," the tyrant chuckled, "your skill surprises me."

"Stop calling me your brother," Sova snarled. "I'm not your brother."

The dire laughed and shook his head. "You're right. I'm not... No *Royal Traitor* is fit for the dire's blood."

"And yet I'll have it," Sova threatened, and lashed his sword at the dire's neck. The dire evaded the blade, only to slip in blood-stained snow and fall to the ground. Taking the opportunity, Sova pointed his sword under the dire's chin.

"Well, isn't this exciting," the dire jeered under Sova's merciless silver gaze. "I am quite proud of you, Traitor. I bet you've dreamt of nothing but this moment for months."

"Something like that..." Sova growled, his mind falling back to his nightmares. "Any last words, *Dire Saulder*?"

"As a matter of fact, I do have one..." the dire said as he looked to the side. "*Feran*."

His brow furrowing, Sova followed the dire's gaze to Feran, Roeseph, and Kyce surrounded by a multitude of soldiers. Saber and Whisp warded away the incoming enemies, but their efforts were pointless. There were far too many.

"No," Sova whispered, his heart dropping to the bloodied snow and grass.

"It seems she'll die with me should she and your friends remain un-helped," the dire taunted. "So, what will it be, Brother? Your friends, or my life?"

Sova glared at his victim and pressed the blade deeper to his throat. "You're not in the position to mock me, Saulder."

"Well... I have been told I can't help but taunt."

Sova gritted his teeth, his sword trembling, as he looked from the dire to his comrades. Giving a frustrated roar, he withdrew from the tyrant and sprinted toward his friends.

The dire rose and rubbed his throat, glaring after the Royal Traitor as he fled. The vanquished wails of dying Vaskans rose into the wind. He lashed around to see the Eradawn chief, Vohwe, taking on three of his soldiers at once—and winning. One by one, the Vaskans fell, blood splurging from their throats and guts like water out a geyser. The dire's eyes burning with malice, he stalked toward his prey.

KYCE, ROESEPH, AND Feran stood back-to-back while Saber and Whisp circled them. Despite the beasts' attempts to defend their masters, Vaskans continued to break through their barriers.

"Roeseph," Feran gasped, her lungs throttled with exhaustion, "what do we do now?"

"Hold your ground!" Roeseph ordered.

"We don't have any ground to hold!" Feran argued back.

Kyce gritted his teeth in determination as two soldiers pressed against his blade, his arms trembling beneath their weight. Sova darted from the chaos and drilled his shoulder into the ribs of the two soldiers, forcing them to the ground.

"Sova!" Kyce shouted with relief.

Sova jumped into their defense circle. "Hey, Ky," he smiled. "Did you miss me?"

"Where in Lykos have you been?"

"Family reunion," Sova answered as he lashed his sword at an oncoming soldier. "Didn't go well."

As the exiles fought, the Dire of Vaska stalked out from the crowd, dragging an Eradawn woman by her scarlet locks. Kyce looked ahead, his fiery amber eyes freezing over with terror.

"Ma, no!" he shouted and lunged toward the dire and his mother. A Vaskan soldier lashed his sword at him, the jagged edge of the blade skimming his chest and making him fall back into Roeseph's arms. Roaring, Whisp leaped to defend her master's mother.

"Whisp no!" Kyce ordered, and she stopped.

The dire chuckled and forced Vohwe to kneel. "Is this your chief?" he mocked.

Feran cringed at the sight of the wicked man—her once beloved betrothed. *Sova was right,* she thought. *He is a monster.*

"Let her go," Kyce roared. Whisp growled in agreement, her tongue rolling over her icepick fangs.

"I'll let her go," the dire said and tilted his head. "But only if I am given what I was promised."

Sova stepped in front of Feran, his face wrenched in a snarl. "Not a chance."

"You can save her, Feran," the tyrant said. "It's what your God would want you to do, right? After all *'greater love has no one than this: to lay down one's life for one's friends.'"*

Feran gulped and looked to Kyce as he glared at the dire, his snarl matching that of Whisp's. She thought of her mother, and how the Venom Tongues killed her before her very eyes. *No one should have to go through that.* If she could spare Kyce such suffering, she would.

"Don't listen to him, Feran!" Vohwe shouted. The dire pulled her hair, making her cringe. "You owe me nothing. This is the price I must pay."

"Chief Vohwe," Roeseph called, "we're going to get you out of there."

"No," she trembled. "The reason the dire is so powerful is because the Eradites have been ruled by fear. That's the truth, really. We're a fearful people. That's why we betray our brothers and sisters and give them to Vaska to serve as the Blesser with each turn of the century. That's why the great Tribe of Era fell apart in the first place. Fear... It's my people's fault Casavore was made the Blesser. You owe me nothing, Feran... Let me pay the price."

Feran swallowed, heart wounded by the chief's final plea. Since she was a little girl, she hated the Eradites; the Eradawns most of all. It was only fitting for one of their own to die in place of herself. After all, they made her father the dire's puppet. They should be the ones to pay. And yet, Feran shed a tear.

"Ma, stop talking," Kyce yelled.

Vohwe sobbed, her yellow eyes misting like the sun in the dusk. "I'm so sorry, Kyce. Please... Please just stay away."

"I've stayed away for eight years!" he bellowed. "I'm not losing you again!"

Unable to look her son in the eye, Vohwe turned to Roeseph.

"Watch him," she pled. "Protect him. Protect them all."

"Enough of this!" Kyce shouted and roared forward. Sova and Roeseph grabbed him by the arms, dragging him away as he kicked and screamed for his mother like a terrified child. "Ma! Ma, no!"

The dire exhaled, his head rolling on his shoulders. "Is that all?" he asked and drew his sword. "Very well. Then let this be the day that the dawn never rises again."

"No!" Kyce screamed.

An arrow sliced the air and nicked the dire's wrist, making him scream and drop his sword. Vohwe scrambled away and into her son's embrace.

"What in the name of Lykos!" the dire snarled and lashed around. "Who dares to—" he went quiet.

Across the river stood the entire Eradusk army atop their soaring wolves with spears in hand. Jerah, the sole survivor of the Eradusk royals, led them on a dark grey soaring wolf, Elling sitting behind him.

Sova, overcome with a surge of excitement, bellowed into the war plagued air, "Yes! Yes! Thank you! Thank you, God!"

"It can't be," Kyce whispered. "Why would he come?"

Before he could answer, Jerah pointed his spear to the battle. "Defend Era!" he cried, his amber eyes burning. "Defend your brethren!"

The roar of Eradusk nearly sent the Ruins of Era crashing down as they charged the Vaskans. The dire stumbled back and disappeared into the cloak of war. Sova laughed as he fled, amused by his cowardice.

"This is it, my friends!" he shouted and looked to Roeseph. "What do you say, *Chief*? You ready to lead this tribe of *Dire Wolves*?"

Roeseph raised his chin, his dusk-blue eyes swelling with hope. "Let this be the day the dire fears our names," he shouted and raised his sword with Sova. "Let this be the day Vaska falls from Era!"

Blades and medallion raised, Feran, Kyce, and Sova pledged their battle craved roars to their leader.

"Yeah!" Sova shouted as they sprung into battle. "Send them running for the hills! Or—mountains."

The Eradusk army hit the battle like a tidal wave and trampled the Vaskans like foam over-sand as blood lusting snarls and clashing spears stained the air. As the four exiles fought side by side, Jerah rode up to them, Elling clinging to his back.

Roeseph looked up. "Elling!" he cried.

Elling slipped from Jerah's wolf and hurtled into Roeseph's arms, her eyes bright with tears.

"Are you ok?" Roeseph said. Elling nodded. He hugged her closer. "Oh, thank Lykos."

"Hey, love birds!" Sova mocked as he sparred with an especially ambitious Vaskan. "Think that can wait, maybe?"

Jerah rode up to Feran and Kyce, sending the Vaskans they fought running scared. Feran looked up, her father's medallion clasped tightly in hand.

"Jerah," she greeted through ragged lungs. "Long time no see."

Kyce glared at his father, his jaw clenched tightly. "What are you doing here?"

Sova looked up from rolling with a Vaskan soldier. "Don't ask him that!" he cried as he fought and tumbled. "We are very grateful to have you here, sir!"

Feran kicked the soldier in the head, knocking him unconscious as Sova scrambled to his feet. "Nice shot."

"I was aiming for you," Feran said.

Jerah looked to his son. "I'm here to defend Era," he answered. "To defend Era, I must defend Eradawn. Now, keep your head up and your sword close. We aren't done here yet."

Before Kyce could open his mouth, Jerah rode off into battle.

"I think that went well," Sova said as he looped his arm around Kyce's shoulders. "I think there was some definite healing there."

Kyce's glare slowly turned to the Royal Traitor, his amber eyes blazing.

"What?" Sova shrugged.

Chapter Twenty-Nine: The Lost One

As *the battle waged on*, the exiles' advantage began to wither. Even with the Eradusk forces, they were severely outnumbered.

"We're taking too much damage!" Elling cried.

"Thank you, Elling," Sova shouted as he lashed his sword at an oncoming Vaskan, "thanks for pointing that out. Super helpful!"

Feran fought between Sova and Kyce, her medallion swinging in hand. "Elling's right," she huffed. "We need to do something. We've been fighting too long with too little success."

"Awe," Sova hissed. "Are you tired playing with that *heavy* necklace of yours? How about you try carrying a Lykos forsaken sword?"

"*Shut up, Sova!*" all shouted in unison.

Kyce roared, frightening an incoming Vaskan into the woods. He looked up to see the dire across the battle, striking down every Eradawn and Eradusk who came his way.

"We need to end this," Kyce growled and stepped away. "We need to end this now."

"Kyce," Roeseph snapped, "stay with the group!"

Kyce leaped onto Whisp and charged toward the dire, trampling every Vaskan in his path.

"He's going to get himself killed!" Elling shouted.

Kyce and Whisp thundered toward the dire. "*You are mine,*" he vowed, and gave a mighty cry,

The dire lashed around to see the wingless soaring wolf lunge, her jaws open and gleaming. Giving a nightmarish cry, the dire swung his sword low and plunged upward. Whisp yelped and tripped over her paws, throwing Kyce from her back, and collapsing over his legs like a fallen tree. Kyce cried out in agony, his knee crackling beneath the weight of his wingless soaring wolf.

"Kyce!" Roeseph shouted, his cry attracting the attention of Jerah and Vohwe.

They looked up from the battle to see their son pinned beneath his motionless soaring wolf.

"No!" Jerah shouted.

Kyce struggled beneath Whisp, his teeth gritting as panicked breath tore down his throat..

"Whisp?" he huffed, frightened by the stillness of his beloved companion. "Whisp, are you ok?"

She gave a low whimper. Blood gushed out a hole in her chest, drenching her brown fur and surrounding Kyce like a warm scarlet shadow.

"Whisp, no!" he cried and shook her vigorously. "Whisp, get up!"

Whisp whined, her eyes craning to the sky. Unlike the battle, the crisp blue atmosphere was so quiet—so still. Giving her stump-like wings a little flap, she lifted her nose toward the blue, trying her hardest to skate the wind like she used to.

"Whisp, get up!" Kyce pleaded, unaware of the dire stalking toward his prey. "You're fine! You're fine, Whisp. Get up!"

The dire loomed over Kyce, his dark shadow containing the coldness of winter. "How cruel," he said, making Kyce look up. "It's so inhumane to keep a creature so pathetic alive."

"You," Kyce snarled. "You'll pay for this!"

"Don't be sad, warrior," the dire taunted. "At least now she'll finally be able to fly."

Whisp growled at the dire, too weak to move as Vohwe and Jerah rushed from one side of the battle, and the exiles from the other. The dire drew his sword, stopping them dead in their tracks.

"Quite the popular one, aren't you?" he chuckled.

Jerah drew his spear, Vohwe following his lead. "Leave my son alone," he threatened.

"Or what?" the dire challenged. "Look around you, Eradite. Even with your miserable tribes united, Vaska thrives."

Feran clung to Saber's side and scanned the battlefield to find their forces were dropping rapidly. The dire was right. They were losing. She needed to do something, and she needed to do it fast. Leaping on top of Saber, she rode away from the dire.

"Feran!" Sova called, though she was long gone.

The dire chuckled. "Look how your saving grace runs. Is this your victor, people of Era? Your champion who runs away in the face of danger. Who abandons her friends in their time of need?"

Sova turned to the tyrant, his teeth gritting in a snarl.

"Dear Sova," the dire pouted. "What did you expect? This is the girl who ran away from Vaska when the Venom Tongues threatened her. The girl that made your life a living Hell. The same girl that left you and Casavore. She's no hero. She's a coward. At most, she is a legend. *My* legend. *The Dire's Damsel.*"

Was he right? Sova wondered. *Did she really just leave us?*

The dire looked back at Kyce as he struggled beneath Whisp's weight. "No matter. I'll go after her once I've killed all of you." He raised his sword, the shadow of the blade dividing Kyce's face. "Let's begin with you, *Mutt.*"

"*No!*" cried those who loved Kyce.

Before the blade could fall, a dark shadow eclipsed the sun, and the battle paused. All looked to the sky. Looking like a warrior of Heaven, Saber hovered over the Ruins of Era, the Dire's Damsel clinging to his back.

"Feran..." Sova whispered, his heart daring to rise from the depths of hopelessness.

Feran sat up straight, her eyes burning with spite. "He's not the one you want, Saulder!" she shouted and opened her arms against the sun. "I am!"

The dire chuckled and abandoned Kyce. The Vaskans surrounded their master, gazing at the famed White Angel in awe, while Vohwe, Jerah, and the exiles hurried to Kyce's aid.

"All together, we lift on three," Jerah directed. "One. Two. Three—"

Gritting their teeth, they lifted the injured soaring wolf. Kyce's knee crackled from the relieved pressure, and he wailed. Roeseph hung Kyce's arm over his shoulder and helped him to stand.

"Are you ok?" Roeseph asked.

"I'm fine," Kyce grunted, and looked to Feran. "What in Lykos is she doing?"

Sova peered at his childhood enemy, his stomach twisting. "I don't know."

The dire cackled at Feran, his hands on his hips. "Quite the entrance there, m'lady. I never knew you to be the dramatic type. That was more Sova's specialty. Though, I suppose a lot can change when one lives as a hermit for ten years."

Feran glared at her ex-betrothed, the thunder of Saber's wings blaring through the ruins.

"I was never your enemy, Saulder," she shouted from the sky. "I stayed away from Vaska because I was a scared little girl who had just lost her mother. I heard rumors of your cruelty and refused to believe them. Now I see you're more of a monster than that witch mother of yours!"

"Sticks and stones, *m'lady*," the dire taunted. "No one likes a sore loser, Feran. You've lost. I have conquered Era. And now Vaska's greatest threat is about to paint my blade."

"Stop calling me that!" Feran roared, Saber growling with her. "I'm not your lady!"

"But of course you are, m'lady. You're the Dire's Damsel, are you not?"

Feran's scowl faded, and her rage filled eyes glimmered with regret. She once favored the name *The Dire's Damsel*. In fact, she doted over it; romanticized it. For even in death, the people recognized her as Saulder's betrothed—his one true love. Now the name sickened her.

The sun blazing over her shoulder, Feran glared at the dire. "I wasn't a threat to you before, Saulder," she cried. "But now I say to you, as long as I draw breath, I will make it my life's mission to tear down everything you've ever built. To humiliate you. To make you the laughingstock of Lykos and Era alike. I will make you fear every breath you take and every dawn, dusk, and night that plagues Vaska. You will fear me, not as the Dire's Damsel, but as your *curse*. May the Heavens hear my oath, I will destroy you, you tyrant of Vaska!"

The dire's amusement fled him like a fleeting shadow, and rage came to mask the fear in his eyes. "Soldiers!" he shouted. "Ready—"

The Vaskan army fell to one knee and pointed their crossbows to the sun.

"That's right, Dire!" Feran taunted, her arms opening wide. "I'm right here! Take your best shot!"

"Aim!"

The four exiles watched, horrified as Feran taunted death.

"Feran, no!" Sova shouted and started toward her, only for Elling to take him by the arm. "Feran!"

Hearts stopping mid-beat, the exiles watched as the dire gave the final order. "Fire—"

Feran lashed out the Blesser's gold medallion, the sun reflecting across the battlefield. Realizing what she was doing, the dire dropped and hid his face against the grass. The exiles and Eradites looked away, for they also knew the great power of a mind melder's medallion. The Vaskans, however, were not so wise. Entranced by the golden hue, every soldier of Vaska froze.

Feran drew a deep breath and closed her eyes as she muttered, "God, please let this work." When they opened, her iris blazed with violent fire. "*Soldiers of Vaska, hear my cry*," she bellowed as she wove the medallion from side to side. "*You have overstayed your welcome and have made yourselves my enemy. You have drawn blood outside your borders and have demanded submission in place of a massacre. Well, this I command of you... Each of you is to return to Vaska. None is to eat, drink, nor sleep until each boot has graced your homeland. And when you return, this trance will cease. But this you will carry with you. As long as you draw breath, you will never—ever—step foot on Era as long as you live. And if your dire ever forces you, you will throw yourselves and your comrades from these cliffs. Hear my words, Vaska, and hear my words o-dreaded dire. You have lost.*"

As Feran's voice faded, the Vaskans rose in perfect unison and marched west from which they came. The dire sat up from his cowering and watched as his army fled. Fearful of the mind melder's wrath, he hurried after them. Stopping short of the forest, he looked back. Feran glared at him, her gold medallion still swinging as she and Saber's shadow eclipsed the battleground. He gawked at her, amazed by the young mind melder's power.

Smirking darkly, he faded into the shadows.

When Feran was sure the Vaskans were gone, she lowered her father's medallion and collapsed against Saber. He whined and looked back at his master, worried.

"I'm ok, boy," Feran panted. "I'm ok."

Sova and the others watched from the ground, in awe, for the Dire's Damsel had just hypnotized an entire army with a single medallion.

"There is no doubt," Vohwe whispered. "She is the most powerful mind melder Era, or Lykos will ever know."

Sova looked back to the sky, marveling at Feran as she and Saber descended the heavens. "Yeah," he muttered. "She really is."

A quiet whine oozed into the air, making the exiles turn to Whisp.

"Whisp," Kyce gasped as he fled from Roeseph's shoulder, and collapsed at her side. He pulled her head into his lap, stroking her fur as he hushed. "It's ok, Whisp. You're ok. You're going to be ok."

His comrades surrounded him, their hearts heavy with sorrow.

"You can't leave me, Whisp," Kyce sniveled as he hugged her tight. "Everyone leaves me. You're all I have left. You were the only one who... Please, Whisp, you can't leave me too."

Saber descended the ruins, his heavy paws making the earth quiver. Feran leaped off his back and sprinted toward her comrades. Sova looked back, his eyes wide with relief.

"Feran," he gasped and opened his arms. "Thank goodness you're—"

She blew right past him and stopped short of Kyce and his wingless soaring wolf. She gasped, her eyes bright with tears. "No," she whispered.

"Whisp, please," Kyce sniffled. "I'm so sorry. This is all my fault. I made you fight. I'm the reason you got hurt. I'm why they took your wings. I'm so sorry, Whisp. Please be alright."

Whisp craned her head and lapped at Kyce's tears. Saber walked to Feran's side, his nostrils flexing at the wretched scent of blood. He whined. Whisp jolted and looked up, her tail shifting ever so slightly, pleading for a game of play.

Saber edged closer and pressed his nose to Whisp's, making her stump-like wings flicker giddily. He spread and flapped his mighty wings. A great wind showered on his frail friend, creating the illusion she was in the sky. Whisp yelped at the familiar sensation. Eyes craning to the blue overhead, she embellished in the might of Saber's wind and flapped her little stumps. She could feel it. She was flying. After all those years, she was finally flying. Her stumpy wings stopped, and her head went limp in Kyce's lap. Thanks to Saber, she died how she wished to live—flying.

"Whisp?" Kyce croaked. She didn't answer. "Whisp?" he said again, more urgently than before.

Saber stopped flapping his wings and whined, his head dipping at the stench of death. Feran looked away. Only Kyce's stifled sobs filled the silent battlefield.

"She died in battle," Jerah said sadly. "It's the duty of Era to send their fallen brave to the sky so they may never go a day without the gift of flight. Come nightfall she'll be set free."

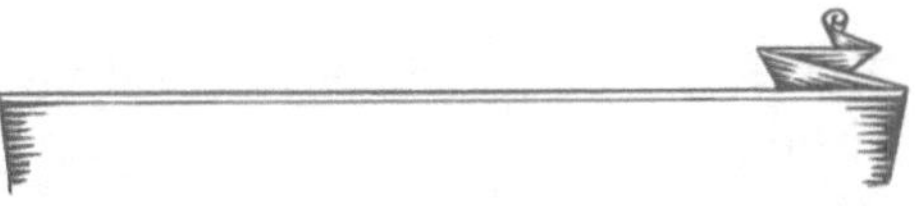

Chapter Thirty: The Pyre Promise

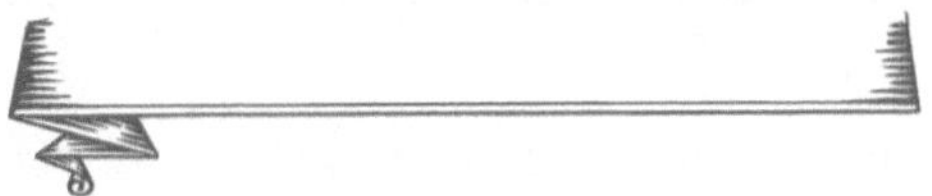

The moon shined on the ruins of the once great Eradite tribe. Hundreds of low platformed pyres stood along the cliffs, laid with bodies wrapped in silk, while those who survived the battle stood before the corpses, torches in hand.

Roeseph, Feran, Kyce, Sova, Elling, and Saber gathered before a huge funeral pyre where a wingless soaring wolf laid lifelessly under a silk veil. Kyce shuddered, his heart wounded by her stillness. Whisp was always so lively—incapable of tranquility. But now, her stumpy little wings didn't so much as flicker. Throat tied in a knot, he walked to Whisp's pyre with torch in hand.

"I'm sorry, girl," he whispered beneath his shaken breath and laid the torch in the hay beneath the platform. He stalked back to his comrades and watched as the fire consumed his best friend. Flames enveloped every pyre, and the dead fluttered into the sky in a cyclone of sparks, rising like the wings of a phoenix.

Behind the exiles stood Jerah and Vohwe, the presiding royals of their villages. The Eradawn chief looked to Jerah as he watched the ember filled night.

"Thank you, Jerah," she whispered, making the Eradusk chief straighten at her voice.

"Sorry?" he replied, shocked she was even talking to him.

"Thank you for coming to our aid," she repeated. "I know fighting along the likes of Eradawns couldn't have been easy for your people. So, thank you."

Jerah swallowed and looked forward. "You have no need to thank me," he assured. "The dire would've laid waste to the rest of Era had he not been stopped... And I owed it to our son to look out for him. God knows I've done a horrible job as his father."

"The blame is to be shared then."

Jerah looked back at Vohwe, his heart wounded by the way her scarlet locks whisked in front of her tear misted eyes. Even in grief, she was beautiful.

"You said you came because you feared the dire would lay waste to the *rest* of Era," Vohwe said. "Was this not your first confrontation with Dire Saulder?"

Jerah sighed. "No. The dire laid siege on Eradusk a couple nights back looking for our son and his allies. Everything's destroyed... Including the royal bloodline of Eradusk."

Vohwe's eyes widened. "Is Chief Willowreed—"

"Dead," Jerah said in a deep voice riddled with sorrow. "And her son, Kometis as well. The only reason I'm alive is because she made me run. When the survivors returned to our village, everything was ridden to ash and gravel. There's nothing left."

"Nothing..." Vohwe whispered.

Jerah chuckled softly and shook his head, "Don't pretend to be sad, Vohwe. Eradusk is gone. Eradawn mourns tonight, but they'll rejoice in the morning."

"I would never be happy about this, Jerah."

"Why not? They're not your people, Vohwe."

"No, but you were—" Vohwe bit her tongue and looked away before she could say something she'd regret. Jerah stared at her, once again, taken aback by her beauty. Vohwe drew a deep breath and looked back to her son's father. "You and your people are the reason we draw breath this day. So I ask you, Chief Jerah, if you'll allow me to repay your kindness. I would be honored if you and your people would stay in Eradawn until the ruins of Eradusk can be rebuilt."

Jerah scoffed, unable to hide the smirk on his lips. "With all due respect, Vohwe, the Eradusks would sooner make their beds in Lykos than accept the help of Eradawn."

"Then order them to," she said in a cool but demanding voice. "You are their reigning chief. Order them to accept our help. They are allowed to complain all they want, but they will do so on soft mattresses, underneath strong roofs, with full bellies."

"You would have an Eradusk in your home?"

"My home is Era. And you saved it today. So yes. I would tolerate an Eradusk in my home."

Jerah nodded. "Very well, Chief Vohwe. My people will accept your kindness."

While Jerah and Vohwe negotiated, Kyce, Roeseph, Sova, Elling, and Feran watched as Whisp's embers floated into the sky. Saber laid his head on Feran's shoulder and gave a low whimper. Feran stroked his face, her eyes glistening in the orange sparks.

"He did this..." she whispered. "He did all of this."

Sova looked down, his heart pained with sorrow.

"I was so sure you were all wrong," Feran continued. "You all kept telling me what a monster he was, and I didn't listen. Saulder killed all these people and would've killed—"

She bit her tongue to stop her voice from breaking. Sova laid his arm over her shoulder and pulled her close, his chin resting atop her head.

"It's not your fault, Feran," he whispered.

"It is. I'm so stupid. I hate him. I hate him, Sova..."

"You don't hate him."

"I do," Feran gulped. "All these people are dead because I was too blind to realize the boy from my childhood grew up to be a monster. He's not like Paul. There's no redemption story, or Damascus Road, or grace of God for him... I'm going to fix this. I swear by it. I'll be the reason the dire bleeds. I'll be the reason he falls."

Sova hugged her close as she shivered. "We can talk about this later, Feran."

"What's he going to do to my father?" she whispered. "I was so sure he wouldn't hurt me, but I was wrong. What does that mean for my father? What's going to happen—"

Sova squeezed her tight. "We'll get him, Feran. We'll get Casavore out of there," he promised. "But there's nothing we can do right now. For now, just be here for those we lost and those we didn't."

Feran gulped and looked to Kyce, his gaze sworn to the stars.

"I was alone in Lykos for eight years," he said quietly. "I was sixteen when they cast me and Whisp out. They even cut her wings so I could never return to Era... She didn't deserve that."

"Neither did you, Kyce," Elling said.

"She was all I had," Kyce shook his head. "I was alone for eight years in Seavale. But she was with me. She was always with me. And now she's gone... And I'm completely alone."

A hand fell on Kyce's shoulder, making him look back to see Roeseph.

"You're not alone," Roeseph corrected. "And you'll never be alone again."

Kyce swallowed, his gaze falling to the pyre where a pile of ash laid in place of Whisp. "She's gone," he whispered.

"Come on," Roeseph slung his arm over his shoulder. "It's time to go."

Kyce under his arm, Roeseph led the outcasts toward Eradawn. Feran looked back at the funeral gathering, her soul bitter by betrayal. She clutched her father's medallion, not used to the smooth touch. Her medallion was charred, rough, and now in the possession of the dire—her enemy.

Know this Saulder, she vowed. *You have known the last of my mercy. There will be no Damascus Road for you...*

Chapter Thirty-One: The Sun Truce

The Eradawn village...

The third sunrise since the tragic victory rose on Eradawn, dressing the marble palace in golden light. Kyce stood alone on the tallest balcony, gripping the railing as he stared at the peach-tinted morning. He drank in a deep breath, trying to sooth the grief building in his chest.

"Your mother said you'd be here," came a deep, refined voice.

Kyce looked over his shoulder to see Chief Jerah make his way toward him, his gold medallion shining in the sunlight. Kyce looked away, his jaw clenching with disdain. Jerah stood beside his son, listening to the cold wind as they stood in agonizing silence.

"I have to say," Jerah scoffed as he peered into the Eradawn tribe. "I'm surprised our tribes are behaving so well together. I was sure we'd have a dispute by now, but everything seems to be running smoothly." Kyce didn't so much as pry his gaze from the horizon. Jerah sighed. "You know I've been here for three days now, and you haven't said a word to me."

"What would you have me say?" Kyce said, refusing to look away from the dawn.

"Anything," Jerah pleaded. "For eight years, I've been worried sick about you."

"Well, I'm sorry my exile was so hard on you."

"That's not what I meant—" Jerah stopped and drew a heavy breath. "Your mother and I have spent a lot of time together since the battle."

"Oh good, is my broken home finally coming together?" Kyce said. "This is every child's dream."

"She says Chief Lanton pardoned you, and that she asked to return to Eradawn. She says you denied her offer."

Kyce shrugged, "What can I say? Lykos grew on me."

"I want you to know that if my being here is the reason you refuse to stay, then I won't be a problem. Once Eradusk is rebuilt, my people and I will return to our village, and I won't burden you any longer."

"I'm not leaving to punish you," Kyce looked at his father. "I'm leaving because..."

"Because of those Lykos exiles?" Jerah asked.

"Of course not," Kyce lashed around. "It's because Dire Saulder took Whisp from me. He'll pay for what he's done. That miserable band of misfits are just my ride."

"Mhmm," Jerah eyed his son up and down. "Well, they seem like noble people, for Lykos folk. I hope you can actually learn to enjoy yourself around them."

"Not a chance."

"Well, you should probably head back. The *band of misfits* are preparing to depart. You don't want to miss them."

Kyce started into the palace, leaving Chief Jerah to stare at the sun.

"Kyce," Jerah called, making his son stop and slump around. Kyce paused, taken aback by the sorrowful look in his father's once strong eyes.. "I need you to know not a day goes by I don't regret standing up for you. Your bloodline should've never warranted your exile. You were innocent, and you were my son. I'm sorry..."

Kyce clenched his jaw and looked away, irritated by his lack of satisfaction with his father's groveling.

"Well, there's nothing that can be done now," he grumbled. "The past is the past."

"Still. I'm sorry, Kyce. And," Jerah stopped and swallowed. "I love you."

Kyce jaw cocked to the side, a vortex of anger swirling within. "You love me? Huh... You know what, Jerah. If you love me, then you'll prove it. Stay here with my mother. In fact, keep all of Eradusk here, or move all of Eradawn to Eradusk. Make the tribes one again. Make the tribe I would've been able to grow up in. And don't leave my mother alone when I leave."

Jerah raised his chin. "Return to us one day, and you'll find it will be so."

In the gardens behind the Eradawn palace, a glassy river fled from the mountains, running through a lush orchard of pear trees. Saber yawned in the shade, his large white paws dragging against the grass as he stretched. Feran, Roeseph, and Elling tied sacks of fruit and grain to his back while Sova occupied himself in other matters.

"Sova," Roeseph scolded. "Why don't you help us pack?"

"I am helping," Sova argued.

Elling stood from her work, brow drawn in an arch. "No, you're not. You're just picking pears."

"For the journey," Sova said as he lingered in the emerald shade of a pear tree.

"We already have enough fruit," Elling said.

"This is for me! Get your own, you selfish—"

Roeseph straightened and glared at Sova, scaring the Royal Traitor silent.

"These ten should do," Sova said and trotted toward Saber and the others.

Feran snapped her fingers, making Saber stand and stretch his massive white wings. He let out a yawn, his ivory jaws flashing in the light of day.

"Awe," Sova pouted at the White Angel. "Were you tired laying around all morning while we were working, big fella?"

"*We*?" Elling snapped.

"Yes, we," Sova argued. "I got the pears."

"We already had—" Elling stopped and turned from Sova. "You know what, it's fine. We got pears. That's all that matters."

"*I* got the pears. You, El, did nothing."

Elling's eye twitched. Roeseph chuckled. As the group laughed lightly amongst themselves, Kyce emerged from the palace and into the garden.

"Ky!" Sova exclaimed. "Come to see us off?"

Kyce smirked and walked toward the group. "Actually," he crossed his arms. "I was wondering if Saber has enough room to carry one more."

Sova dropped his pears at his feet while he group froze to gawk at Kyce.

"You're not staying?" Roeseph asked.

"No," Kyce shook his head. "No, there's nothing for me here."

Sova gawked at him. "Are you insane?" he cried. "Why would you want to leave this place? You—You," he picked up one of the pears and shoved it in Kyce's face. "You guys have mountain fruit! We don't have mountain fruit in Lykos. Only valley fruit. It's not as good as the mountain fruit. *Mountain fruit*, Kyce!"

"Get the pear out of my face, Sova," Kyce growled. Sova doubled back, shielding the pear against his chest.

"What the idiot means to say," Feran interrupted, "is that we're curious as to why you'd want to leave. You're safe up here. The dire can't reach you in Era."

"That's exactly why I can't stay," Kyce answered. "Dire Saulder took Whisp from me. The least I can do is pay him back tenfold."

The Dire Wolves looked curiously to each other, both admiring and fearing Kyce's tenacity for blood.

"I'm sure we can make room for you," Roeseph said and offered his hand. Kyce stared at Roeseph, and then, bearing a smirk, shook his hand.

Sova threw his arms around their shoulders. "Well what do you know. Looks like the *Dire Wolves* live to see another day," he smiled. "Kyce the *Eradite Exile*. Roeseph the *Last Soldier*. Elling the *Feral Shepherd*—"

"I don't like being called that Sova," Elling grumbled.

"You get what you get, El," Sova spat. "Me, Sova, the Royal Traitor. And Feran, the Dire's Damsel."

Feran looked up from her work, her eyes colder than winter itself. "No," she said.

"No what?" Sova asked.

"No, that's not what I want to be called."

"Well, what would you want to be called?"

"Not the *Dire's Damsel*. I won't be known by that name anymore."

"Then make yourself a new name," Sova challenged. "Be the exact opposite of the Dire's Damsel."

Saber walked up to stand beside his master and nuzzled her shoulder. "His curse," Feran answered. "The Dire's Curse."

Roeseph laid his hand on Feran's shoulder. "Then his curse you'll be. Alright, *Dire Wolves*, let's get going. I want to reach Lykos by sundown."

"I call the front seat!" Sova shouted.

Elling watched as they loaded onto Saber, her jaw hanging. "Hold on. Why does Feran get a name change, and I don't?"

"If you can think of a name better than the *Feral Shepherd,* then you can change it," Sova argued as he pulled her onto Saber's back.

"Well, can't I just be *Elling*?"

"No," Sova snapped, almost offended. "No new name for you."

SABER AND THE DIRE Wolves made their way to the cliff's edge overlooking the Great Valley of Lykos. The Eradawns and Eradusks gathered around, eager to see off the Lykos legends. Chief Jerah and Chief Vohwe parted from the crowd and walked up to meet their allies.

"You've done us a great service," Vohwe dipped her head. "We are forever in your debt. When the time comes for you to take back Vaska, Eradawn will stand by you."

"As will Eradusk," Jerah agreed and bowed with his fist over his chest. "Our forces are yours to command."

Roeseph nodded gratefully to the chiefs. Perhaps there was hope in freeing his father and winning the war after all. Vohwe looked to Kyce, her eyes starting to mist.

"Kyce," she said with a watered-down voice. "You be careful. That's an order from your chief."

"I will, ma'am," Kyce promised as Saber spread his wings.

Elling peeked past Roeseph's shoulder, her Mosharick-green eyes shining bright. "So. What's the plan, Captain?"

A subtle red tint in his cheeks, Roeseph puffed out his chest and raised his chin. "We build our army," he said. "Find allies, find friends. And after we've returned to Era to collect our forces, we'll storm Vaska and dethrone the dire... And we'll make him free you and my father from the Hyde Howler curse."

Hopeful tears in her eyes, Elling hugged Roeseph tightly, making his face turn bright red.

Feran knotted her fists in Saber's fur. "Hold on tight," she warned through a determined smirk.

Elling clung to Roeseph.

Sova did the same to Kyce, making him growl. "I'll just fall," Sova muttered and scooted back.

Leaning forward, Feran kicked Saber in his side, and he leaped into the air. The Eradites cried out for joy as they soared, their voices lifting Saber higher as he advanced the fleeing sun. His howl stained the sky, warning the valley of those who were to come.

The new legends of Lykos; The Dire Wolves.

Chapter Thirty-Two: The New Blesser

The Kingdom of Vaska...

A distinct coldness filled the Vaskan throne room as the black-armored dire sat on his throne, holding Feran's charred medallion before his eyes.

Feran, he thought to himself. *How wrong I was about you...*

The doors opened wide, casting golden light across the floor as two guards walked in, dragging the once-mighty Blesser of Vaska toward the platform.

"Casavore," the dire greeted as the guards threw him to the floor. "There you are. I was hoping you would swing by. I'd like to have a word with you."

Casavore coughed, his lungs folding from the fall. "I have nothing to say to you," he sneered. "You have no power over me."

One of the guards kicked him in the side, making him gasp and coil into a ball, "Show some respect, you bloody—"

"That's enough, soldier," the dire dismissed. Casavore lay motionless on the floor, his long, tangled hair falling over his face like willow branches. "Rough night in the dungeon, Casavore?"

Glaring through his hair, the Blesser cursed at the dire.

"What foul words," the dire gasped. "Casavore, I am shocked. I always took you to be a holy man." He looked to his guards. "Leave us."

The guards departed from the throne room. As they closed the doors, the light streaming in panned toward Casavore and then disappeared over his back in a perfect line. The Blesser looked up, his once forgiving and God-fearing eyes now hard with hellish hate.

"Why have you called me here?" he grumbled. "I've told you hundreds of times before. I will never serve you."

"That's perfectly fine, Casavore," the dire said. "I don't desire your loyalty any longer. Nor your talents."

The Blesser looked up, his blue eyes narrowing. "Just like that? A month straight of beatings, just to simply give up?"

"I'm not giving up, Casavore," the dire replied, a sort of dark satisfaction in his voice, as he tossed the charred medallion to the floor. The Blesser picked up the burned trinket, perplexed by the familiar craftsmanship. He'd seen it before.

"This is a mind melder's medallion?" he growled. "Where did you get this?"

"I'm surprised you don't recognize it, Casavore. You made it after all."

"What are you talking about?"

"That is the medallion you made for your precious daughter. Feran."

Casavore's eyes widened, and his heart burst with hope and adrenaline.

"Feran?" he quivered as he clutched the charred medallion. "She—She's alive?"

"Indeed. She's allied herself to the Royal Traitor and his band of refugees. She's the one who controls the White Angel."

"How is that possible? I never taught her how to tame a soaring wolf."

"Your daughter is an extremely gifted mind melder, Casavore. You should be proud that she should exceed your title."

Casavore's blood turned frigid, and he looked up, his quivering hand clutching the gold medallion so tightly it cut his palm. "What are you talking about?"

"Your daughter is perhaps the most powerful mind melder ever to be born in the history of Era. Three sunrises ago, she was able to capture the minds of over a thousand men in one trance. That power I once feared and sought to destroy," the dire shook his head, chuckling. "But now I see I was blind to her potential. With her power, Vaska could vanquish all of Lykos, Era, and whatever lays beyond the mountains."

"No—"

"Congratulations, Casavore. Your daughter is to become the new Blesser of Vaska."

"No!" Casavore lunged, holding out his daughter's medallion to entrance the dire. The black-armored tyrant lashed out his sword and cut the Blesser's palm, making Casavore shout and drop his weapon.

The doors to the throne room swung open and two guards rushed in. Before Casavore could grab his daughter's medallion, they pushed him to the cold floor, twisting his arms behind his back as he shouted in painful frustration.

"Don't test me, Casavore," the dire snapped as he settled back on his throne. "I won't let you fool me again."

"She'll never serve you!" Casavore cried. "Zastar's son will never let you near her!"

The dire chuckled. "Oh. You are mistaken. The Royal Traitor and Feran may not concede to my rule willingly, but I have my ways of making them submit."

"How?"

The dire stepped down from his throne and picked up the charred medallion Casavore had dropped.

"You, Zastar's beloved Blesser, will deliver her to me."

What comes next?...
The Blesser
And the Curse of Damascus

More of The Blesser...

1. *The Blesser... And the Charred Medallion*
2. *The Blesser... And the Curse of Damascus*
3. *The Blesser... And the Prodigal Prince*

More to come...